THE CROWN OF NIGHT

LOU WILHAM

Midnight Tide
PUBLISHING

PRAISE FOR THE HEIR TO MOONDUST SERIES

"Lou has done it again! The adventures in this book are even more high stakes and they kept me turning pages. Lou wove everything together beautifully and kept things mysterious enough to leave you hanging and begging for more."

- **Whitney L. Spradling**, Author of *The Obsidian Sword*

"The Heir to Moondust Series pulls you deep into a magical land filled with shifters and curses. Book Two, The Prince of Daybreak, raises the stakes with a journey that will have you questioning every alliance and prejudice, and eager to find out what Wilham has planned for the series next."

- **H. R. Truelove**, Author of the *Alter Series*

THE CROWN OF NIGHT

THE HEIR TO MOONDUST: BOOK THREE

LOU WILHAM

PROLOGUE

Time, like stories, has a way of taking on a life of its own.
And also like stories, it can be a fickle creature.

It is a living, breathing thing that will not be held down, or manipulated by anyone. And even when used wisely, it still manages to slip through one's fingers like so much sand. The harder one tries to be careful with it—to hold onto it—the more it seems to slip away. Lost. Never to be returned.

And this, my dear reader, is very much a story about time. About how it ebbs and flows.

How once, two princes were separated by it for years, powerless in time's grasp.

How it was not kind.

How the goddess Selene herself could do nothing.

THE YOUNG PRINCE OF HELIO, prince Takayoshi, knew all too well the fickleness of time. For he had watched as his time with the prince of Lunette, *his* prince, flew by, while the time away from Cricket plodded along, sticky and slow like honey in winter. Only not near as sweet.

What he had not considered, at all, was how time moved differently in magical places. One would have thought that someone who had experienced that difference as Takayoshi had, up close and personal, would realize such a thing. He had not.

Still, with war on the horizon, and Cricket in danger, Takayoshi endeavored to keep Cricket safe. So, he pulled from the archive the array he had once used to curse himself, and prepared to make a deal with a goddess. For it had worked once before, why would it not work now?

"And she'll answer?" Leo asked, his dark eyes fixed on the circle etched into the grass of the clearing.

"She has in the past." Takayoshi turned quickly, making sure that he had the characters right. He had the sisters write them down for him, but he still needed to be sure. He could not afford to make a mistake, not now, not with this.

"I don't see why you're bothering. It can't take us that long to build a boat." Leo leaned hard on his crutch, the leg of it tilting dangerously under his weight. If he fell, he would no doubt ruin whatever progress he had made in healing. But Takayoshi was not going to tell him off for it. He was a grown man after all, he could do what he liked.

"What will you bargain with?" Claudia asked, ignoring the disgruntled look Leo shot her.

"I have not thought about it. I hoped perhaps she would not ask for something in trade this time." That was a lie. He *had* thought about it. He had gone back and forth for three nights straight about what he would give to have Selene look after his prince. Anything, had been the answer. He would give *anything*. But in the end, he decided he would offer up his ability to make music, whatever that meant. It was something he held dear, something he loved, and he thought it would be payment enough for her to save Cricket from himself, and Sunil.

"Maybe." Claudia tilted her head, scratching at her cheek. She did not look convinced, but that was all right. She was not the one he needed to convince.

He did not wait for any further discussion, there would be no need for it. Instead, he pulled the dagger from his belt, and cut into his arm just under a patch of feathers. The blood cooled in the chill night air, dripping sluggish and slow down his skin, until it fell onto the array.

The characters flared to life, charged by the magic singing in his blood, and the wind picked up around them. But where once there had been the lilting voice of the Lady Selene, now was only silence. The air hummed with emptiness.

"Did it work?" Claudia whispered.

Takayoshi shook his head, he was not sure. But he felt that maybe Selene was listening, even if she had not said as much. So he took a breath, and prepared himself. "Goddess Selene, I ask only this, that you protect Cricket until I am able to. From both himself, and his uncle. I worry it will take me too long to reach him, and by that time the damage will be done. Please. . . do all you can to look after him in my stead."

She did not answer, and the array continued to glow steadily. It turned Takayoshi's stomach to see it, and he shifted on his feet, uncertainty raking along his nerves.

"If there is a price to pay, I give my ability to make music. Make me amusical, for all that I care. Just— Just protect *Cricket*." The last word broke coming from his lips.

The array faded without any response, but the wind picked up, pulling leaves from the surrounding trees to flutter in a lazy circle. And then Takayoshi saw it, a white rabbit peeking just around a tree trunk, its fur glowing in the moonlight. He let out a breath, his shoulders relaxing.

"Well?" Leo asked.

"I think it worked." Takayoshi felt himself smile, if just around the eyes.

What he did not know was that while Selene could protect Cricket, her magic drifting to him on the currents of the air like those leaves had, she could not change the flow of time. And what felt like no more than a few months on that tiny island off the coast of Lunette—not even quite a year to Takayoshi and his friends—would be far longer to his prince.

For across the small space of the sea of Selene, in the capital of Lunette, years passed...

Much can happen in three years, and in the ones that stretched between our prince and his hero, much did. Two springs (arguably the best season if you asked Cricket) came and went. And our prince grew into a fine young man, a capable future king.

He fought battles, kept his people safe, and saw to his ailing father. He had not been happy, perhaps, but he had been content in his duties, and his life. His uncle's forces kept at bay by Lunette's love of her king, and some bit of magic that no one seemed able to explain. He grew more scales, and the antlers which sat atop his head lengthened enough that they might very well interfere with his crown. But he maintained control, and that was enough.

And all through it, Selene watched over him, just as she'd been asked. Just as she'd promised herself she would, all those years ago.

In early spring of the third year, King Jaxith, weakened by the attempted poisoning from his once dear brother, succumbed to an illness which for many others would have been not but a seasonal cold.

"I don't think I can do this without you," Cricket said, holding his father's hand tightly. The king had not opened his eyes in many days. And Cricket knew that he would soon pass on, likely that very night. But he could not let his father go without trying at least once more to coax him back. "I'm not ready to be king."

His father let out a breath like a sigh, his lids fluttering, and for a moment Cricket thought perhaps he'd wake. Perhaps he would come back to Cricket, and all would be well. But in the next moment the king's fingers went entirely limp and his form, already bedridden, seemed to slump against the soft mattress.

A breeze drifted in through the open windows, letting in the warm air of the early spring night. A few cherry blossom petals from the trees outside, the ones the king planted for his late wife, came with it, and drifted around the king's head.

He will be well taken care of. A voice soft, and comforting, appeared in Cricket's mind.

"Who said that?"

Someone who you can trust.

"I can't– I can't do this alone," Cricket protested, his eyes still focused on his father whose mouth had gone slack.

You are not alone. You will have help.

"I'm not ready to be king." Cricket's breath came in hitching sobs, but he sucked back the tears.

You are.

Then the petals settled onto the king's chest, and the young prince let himself cry. For in the morning, he would need to begin planning his coronation.

BOOK I
CORONATON

CHAPTER 1

The little fishing town along the shore named Coinín was smaller in Takayoshi's memories. Not as small as the village where they lost their horses, and his would-be daughter, no. Certainly not as large as the city with the silkworms, whose name he had forgotten while trying to absorb as much of the knowledge as the archive could provide him with in just three months. But now Coinín sprawled along the coast. There were docks, and piers, and even a sun-washed boardwalk along the beach. It had gone from mere fishing town to. . . whatever this was.

"A vacation spot," Claudia supplied for him when she saw him looking perplexed. "You know? Where people go on holiday? Hasn't the royal family of Helio ever gone on holiday?"

"What is a holiday?" Takayoshi turned to her, his eyes a little wider than usual. He had learned so much over the last few months, and yet he found himself consistently learning more. Claudia and Leo themselves were a well of knowledge, battle tactics and history, weapons mastery and magic.

"Forget that. Look at this." Leo ripped a paper from one of the passing newsboys.

"Hey!" the child protested, reaching for it, but Leo held out a few coins, not meeting the boy's eyes.

"We knew about the coronation," Claudia said, leaning into Leo's shoulder to get a better look at the paper.

"No. Not that. Look at the date." Leo tapped at it with one scarred finger, and Takayoshi's stomach dropped out through his feet. An unfamiliar sensation he decided on the spot he did not care much for at all.

"It can't have been three years." Claudia's tone was a whisper of disbelief, a tremor of fear, and something else, something lower. Like maybe she thought if she did not say it loud enough then it would not be true. "We were only on the island nine months."

"I have to— I have to call home." The words shook in Takayoshi's throat. What would Uncle Reiji think? What would Atsuko? What would *Cricket*? Would they think that he abandoned them? That he had died in his quest? And what of Claudia's family? Leo had no one left, he knew that, but Claudia had sisters, parents. They would be confused. They would be upset. This was all his fault. He had dragged them after him, and did not once think of the consequences.

"Breathe, Yoshi," Claudia said, her voice sounding like it was underwater.

And oh.

Oh.

He was not breathing. He had forgotten how to under the weight of three years away from home. He could feel it pressing down on his lungs, pushing the air from them, and keeping him from filling them back up. Like someone had dropped a boulder on top of him.

"He's panicking." Leo's hands were on his shoulders, steering him through the crowd, Takayoshi thought, but the pressure was distant.

"I can *see* that he's panicking, Leo!" Claudia snapped, her hands gripping Takayoshi's forearms a little harder than perhaps they ought to, nails digging into the skin through his long sleeves. "Let's just get him sitting down."

The noise of the street became muffled, then there was the sound of something shutting, a door perhaps, and Takayoshi was pressed by his shoulders down onto a hard bench. He thought it was a bench. It might have been a chair or the floor or a table. He was not sure, and he did not think it really mattered. At least not in the grand scheme of things. For he had been gone for *three* years. No, not he, *they*. They had been gone for three years, and he was very sure that his sister had held a funeral, buried an empty coffin in the place of the brother she thought was never coming back. How could he have abandoned her? How could he have abandoned Helio? And Cricket. . . How could he have abandoned *Cricket?*

For what?

For what?

For what?

He was no closer to saving Cricket from becoming a dragon than he had been before he left. And what if he had lost Cricket in the interim? What if his prince had already succumbed to his nature?

No.

They would not be holding a coronation for Cricket if he had lost himself to the dragon. Even so, that did not mean there was much time. Cricket was clever. He could be hiding how badly off he was. The only ones who would know would be his inner circle, and even then, it might only be Ignacia who knew the true depths of the trouble he was in.

"Breathe. Just breathe, Yoshi," someone was still saying. Claudia, maybe. As a glass was pressed in between his fingers and he was encouraged to drink one small, careful sip.

The water slid down his throat, taking with it some of the

cotton that muffled his senses. And he was finally, *finally*, able to breathe, to think.

"Oh, thank Selene," Claudia's shoulders slumped a little. "You really had me worried there for a minute. You were practically turning blue."

"I am fine." It was technically a lie; he was not fine. He did not feel even remotely fine. But he also did not want his friends to continue to worry. Not when there was so much to do. "First, we will contact our families. They must be worried, and we should let them know that we are all right."

"Good idea." Claudia settled onto the bench beside him. Leo was still hovering over them, his hands fidgeting at his sides as if he wanted to help but was not sure how.

"And then what?" Leo asked, pressing his hands behind his back to hide their fidgeting. If Takayoshi had not spent the last two years—five, he supposed—with Leo, he would not have seen it for what it was. He would not have seen the nervousness, and the worry that etched Leo's movements. But Takayoshi had grown to know these two, these friends of his. Still, there was not much he could do to assuage Leo's worries.

"Then we will head for the capital. We must speak to the prince. Preferably before his coronation." Giving orders left Takayoshi with a sense of accomplishment—of control—that he would not have otherwise.

"Right." Leo nodded, letting out a breath that relaxed his rigid shoulders. A soldier trusting his commander. "What do you want me to do?"

"Read through the paper. See what information you can gather for us. After we have spoken to our families, I will see about hiring some horses. I do not want to waste time making the journey on foot." Perhaps Takayoshi should be standing to give these orders, but he had grown so comfortable and used to his friends that, despite them standing above him, he did not feel inferior.

"We'll make it before the coronation," Leo said with all the certainty of a man who could make things happen. Takayoshi was lucky to have friends like them. Lucky to have met two people who seemed to understand him in all his strange intensity, and inability to fully express himself sometimes. "We'll save your prince."

"Thank you." His tone was soft, his words sincere, and if Takayoshi were the type to smile, he may have in that moment.

Leo did not say, '*of course.*' Leo did not say, '*that is what friends are for.*' He did not even say, '*you are welcome.*' He did not need to. He just gave Takayoshi a shallow bow, a little smile, and turned on his heel to find a private table and order himself a pot of tea as he settled in to read through the paper.

"You ruined your mirror when we were trying to create a communication array, did you not?" Takayoshi asked as he and Claudia made their way up the steps to the rooms they had rented for the evening.

"I did." Claudia nudged the door open with her hip, her hands still occupied with hovering over Takayoshi as if he may faint at any moment. It was endearing but unnecessary. "But you should go first. My sisters, and dads will just wind up keeping me on forever. Better you go first so we don't waste time."

"If you are sure."

"I'm sure. Besides, this isn't the first time I've disappeared for a while. Although. . . not usually for *years* at a time. But—" She shrugged, seeming unbothered. "I'll go down and see about getting us some lunch. Give you some privacy."

"I promise I will not be long."

"Nonsense. Yoshi, you take all the time you need."

Claudia gave his shoulder an affectionate squeeze, then she headed out the door again. Leaving Takayoshi sat on one of the thick cushions at the low table in the middle of their rooms.

He pulled the mirror from his traveling pouch, and set it on the table in front of him with a gentle *thunk*. The weight was still there. The weight of years. But he could breathe through it now. Because he was not alone in this. Because they had a plan. Because the responsibility of accounting for those three years did not sit on his shoulders alone.

Takayoshi pressed his finger to the surface of the mirror, murmuring, "Atsuko" as the glass rippled like water.

It took a moment, longer than he would have liked, during which he hardly breathed. But when the ripples melted away, Atsuko stared back at him, her eyes wide with shock. The fringe she cut into her hair just before he left had gotten longer, now down past her chin, and hanging dangerously close to blocking her vision. There were lines at the corners of her eyes, and she looked a little thinner. But she was. . .

Well, she was still Atsuko.

"Shishi?" she asked as if she was not really sure what she was seeing.

"Yes." Takayoshi felt the corner of his own lip twitch up into a small smile. "It is good to see you Koko."

"Yes. Yes, it is." A smile split her face, so big that it crinkled her eyes. And suddenly, no time had passed at all. For that was the magic of a bond like theirs. Time could not touch it. Not really. "Did you find it? The archive?"

"I did." Takayoshi let out a relieved breath, his own posture relaxing as he leaned forward to get a better look at her. She looked well enough. She looked *happy*. She did not look like she had been mourning him. "I hope I did not worry you. I have just been made aware that I was gone for quite some time."

"I knew you'd be back," Atsuko said with such certainty that there was no room left for doubt, even within Takayoshi. "Uncle Reiji thought perhaps you had— But I knew it wasn't true. I knew you would be back. You are— You are coming back. Aren't you?"

"I will be soon. I must see Prince Cricket before I do. Then I will be on my way home, if you can wait but a few more months."

"Ah yes, of course, the coronation. I was invited but given everything that's going on between him and Sunil, I decided not to attend. I mean with all the—"

"What is going on between him and Sunil?" Anxiety crawled along his nerves again.

Atsuko stopped, blinking for a moment, then frowned. "Shishi, have you not heard? Sunil has officially declared war against Prince Cricket. He has vowed he won't stop until he rips the imposter from his throne. He's— He's gaining quite a following. People who've felt slighted or wronged by Jaxith. And with the rumors of Cricket's. . . condition. I just. . . it didn't seem safe for all the monarchs to be in one place.

"Cricket understood, of course, when I sent my regrets. Your beloved is a kind and benevolent sort. You really *did* choose someone worthy of—"

But Takayoshi was not listening anymore. For he had heard enough. Enough to make his heart pound like a drum against his ribs. Enough to have the pressure on his lungs return, making it hard to breathe. And then Claudia burst in.

"There are mercenaries in the tavern!" Claudia's glasses were askew, her chest rising in harsh pants. "And a camp out on the edge of town. They're planning to attack the coronation."

"Where is Leo?" Takayoshi sat up straighter, his attention

turned entirely from his reunion with his sister to the safety of his friends, and his prince.

"He's getting the horses ready. He said to come get you. We have to go. We have to warn them." Claudia rushed across the room, grabbing the bag she set down earlier and throwing it over her shoulder as she did a quick spin to check that they were leaving nothing behind. They had not been there long enough for that, but she liked to check, Takayoshi knew this.

"Could you not simply call?" Atsuko asked, but her eyes had gone wide with worry. Her face was pale in the glass.

"An open call to a mirror in the palace is dangerous, there are chances that it would be intercepted if Sunil has men on the inside. We cannot risk it. I will speak with you soon, Koko." Takayoshi was on his feet, already, gathering what few possessions he had, and stuffing them into his travel pouch.

"Be safe." Atsuko bit at her lower lip, her brow wrinkled in the middle.

"We will look after each other. Do not worry, Koko." Takayoshi offered her a shallow bow, the corners of his mouth turned up just the slightest. "We always do."

That eased something in Atsuko's face, and she let out a breath. "Very well. Get in touch when you have seen the prince, and are on your way home. Yes?"

"Of course. Be well, sister."

"Be safe, Shishi."

Then she was gone, and Claudia was standing at his side, her satchel slung over her shoulder.

"How long do we have?" Takayoshi asked, already heading for the door.

"A little less than a week. They plan to have the ceremony on the prince's twenty-third name day. But we don't know when Sunil will attack." Her words were hushed as they made their way to the back door of the inn.

"Then we must be quick." Takayoshi nodded, and sent up a silent prayer to Selene that it would rain, and make travel for a group of that size difficult. If only to slow them down. If only to buy him and his friends time.

The wind picked up in answer, but he did not pay it any mind as they found Leo, mounted their horses, and were off.

CHAPTER 2

Cricket always thought that the coronation would be the easy part. He knew he'd never be ready to be king, even if Father lived until Cricket himself was fifty, he'd never be ready. But for some reason he always thought the ceremony bit, the crowning, and the pageantry, *that* would be easy. Because what was it but just a big party?

The rub was Cricket always assumed he wouldn't be planning it alone. He always thought, rather naively he was realizing now, that Father would be there, and Marwa, and Anstice. That he'd have his family to support him. But. . . but they were all gone now. Anstice was in Helio, and Father and Marwa were. . .

Well. They weren't there to help, anyway.

"I miss them too," Ignacia said, her voice soft but carrying in the quiet of the meeting hall. It was that way now. Had been that way for four years. Quiet seemed to seep out of every crevice of the palace. Even in the noisiest rooms.

"His Highness could name a new—" one of the young guards started to suggest. He was new. And obviously an idiot. *Read the room Phillipe!*

"His Highness will be doing no such thing." Cricket's voice was hard, cut from steel, and twice as cold. "His Highness will not be naming a new advisor. His Highness will keep the council of his head of the guard, and his staff. That is all."

"But an—"

"You are dismissed," Ignacia said, the order clear in her tone.

"Dismissed?"

"Yes. Head back to your quarters, and get some rest. We have a long week ahead of us." Ignacia's gaze narrowed on the young man, as if begging him to give her an excuse to dismiss him entirely from the guard. Not like attempting to argue with the prince wasn't enough. It would be, if Cricket wasn't doing exactly as he said, keeping the council of the people around him. Letting guards, and servants, tell him what they thought at any turn. It wasn't a terribly efficient way to gather information, but he'd learned a great deal from them over the years.

The door shut softly behind Phillipe, and the three other young guards in the room straightened as if they were under inspection. They were not. Not by Cricket, anyway.

"It *has* been four years," Ignacia hedged, not meeting his eyes. She fixed her gaze on the map of the grounds they'd sprawled in the middle of the table. Probably for the best, Cricket didn't want anyone to see the look of hurt and vulnerability that flashed across his face before he could tuck it away again, as he did all his weaknesses these days.

"I will not be bringing on a new advisor. Not yet." He sat up straighter, adjusting his tunic, and ignoring the way it rubbed at the scales beneath uncomfortably.

"She's not coming back, Cricket."

She wasn't. Cricket knew she wasn't. Anstice had made a new home for herself in Helio. She'd even captured the eye of the queen. Cricket always said she had the makings of a princess, and now it would seem she was well on her way to becoming one. Even if Cricket had kept Anstice's hand in things from being exposed, he couldn't ask her to leave that behind.

"I've made my decision, Ignacia."

"Then at least hire one of the party planners Youta found," Ignacia pleaded.

"You're just trying to get out of having to choose the draperies for the receiving hall." Not that he could blame her. He didn't quite understand why they *needed* new draperies for the receiving hall. The guests would only be there for all of five minutes as they paid their respects to the young king-to-be, then they'd be shuffled off to their quarters to rest from their journeys. Why couldn't they just leave the receiving hall as it was?

"Cricky," Ignacia all but whined. "I've looked at so many fabric swatches recently that I don't think I can even tell the difference between a satin and a silk anymore. Much less the quality of the silkworms."

There was a pout in the words, a pout that Cricket planned to ignore. But maybe a party planner would make things a little easier. And he *could* use some time for himself. The ability to step away, and know it was in good hands would be a relief. Especially when there was the security of the palace to think of. He was spreading himself entirely too thin. He knew that.

"Have they all been properly vetted?"

"As vetted as they can get." Ignacia shrugged. Which didn't sound terribly promising, but Cricket knew that Ignacia had been thorough, even if she found most people insufferable, not the least of which party planners.

"All right, have Youta pick her favorite, and I'll meet with them after supper. Now, can we please get back to the guard rotation for the day of?"

"Stars, *yes*." Ignacia sighed, her shoulders deflating a little to hunch over the map again.

YOUTA WAS WAITING for Cricket when he returned to Father's—his—study. He had to remember, everything that had been Father's was his now. She had set out tea for them on one of the low tables in between two overstuffed wingback chairs. Much like himself, and Ignacia, there were dark circles under her eyes.

"It's not good news, is it?" he asked before the door closed. Hated that wan look on her face. He hated it on all of them. But once the coronation was over things would settle down a little. There would still be the threat of Uncle to consider, but at least the party planning would be over.

"I'm afraid not, Your Highness. Shall we?" She gestured to the chairs and the tea, and he nodded even as he strode across the room to slump into one of them.

"This isn't the night time tea, is it?"

"No. But I still think you need to try that. You aren't sleeping, Your Highness, and you have people who are depending on you. We can't have you exhausted." Youta poured them each a cup, and settled into the other chair, her cup already lifted to her lips.

"I can't afford to be incapacitated the following day if it carries over."

"It wouldn't."

"Youta."

"All right, I'll stop." She set her cup down on the saucer with a soft clatter of ceramic.

"Thank you." Cricket let out a breath, reaching for his

own cup to take a grateful sip. It wasn't the concoction Youta made to help people sleep, but it was relaxing. The warmth crawling down his throat and spreading through his body, chasing off the cold the dragon often left lingering under his skin.

Youta shifted in her seat, which to anyone else might have seemed like it was nervousness, but Cricket saw it for what it was. She was gearing herself up to tell him something that she knew would make him uncomfortable. So he kindly averted his eyes and focused on sipping from the teacup while she prepared herself.

"That bad, is it?" he asked when the silence stretched on for far too long.

"It's not good." Youta sighed, picking up her cup again, and holding it carefully between her fingers. Her nails tapped against the ceramic in a gesture that he'd grown used to in these last few years.

"Well, best to rip off the bandage, I think." Cricket tilted his head, offering her a dimpled smile. It was forced, they both knew it. So many of his smiles were these days, even when he was with the people he loved. There had been a gaping hole in his chest since Anstice left that grew larger when Yoshi followed her, and again when Father died. Now he wondered if he lost another person would it swallow him whole?

"Yes, I suppose it is." Youta shifted again, sitting up straighter, and cleared her throat. "Sunil has men in the palace."

"We knew that." Cricket was kind. He wasn't naive. He knew that even after he exiled Uncle, and punished his men, there would be those that lingered. There was no way to completely purge them. Not when Uncle spent his entire life building his network. "But that's not all, is it?"

"No. That's not all. Some of Anstice's sources have

noticed a lot of. . . travelers headed this way in the outlying towns."

"Travelers?"

"I hesitate to say mercenaries, but Your Highness, they do not look like your typical coronation guests. And I know they weren't on the invite list."

"How trustworthy are Anstice's sources?" Cricket rubbed at the bridge of his nose where a headache had begun to form.

Youta shot him a look, and he sighed.

"Right." He didn't even know why he was bothering to ask. He knew the answer. For all Anstice had done, she was still his sister, she was still his family. If she trusted these people, then he should too. She would not steer him wrong. Cricket tilted his head back in the chair, careful that his antlers didn't catch on the fabric. They had a nasty habit of tearing things. "What are we going to do about it?"

"I'll tell Ignacia what I've found. She'll need to know to look for uninvited guests."

"Not that she wasn't already expecting them." That was the whole point of all the meetings they had lately about guard rotations, and positioning.

"Right. But. . . I suppose there isn't much we can do, is there?" Youta hummed, her fingers holding the teacup so hard it almost shook with a rage she seemed willing to swallow down instead of release. "We can't bar guests from the ceremony. We can't call it off entirely. Both would be seen as a weakness."

"They would. And Uncle would use it against me. To prove to the people that I can't keep my promises." Cricket had thought that years later his stomach would stop churning every time he thought about Uncle Sunil's betrayal. But it hadn't. It still made him sick to think that one of the people he loved, one of the people who helped raise him, had turned on him so thoroughly. He must have done something terrible in a previous life to deserve this.

"Exactly." Youta refilled their cups, seeming to need something to do with her hands. Cricket took a grateful sip from his refreshed cup for the same reasons.

"When do you think they'll attack?"

"No one has been able to get a timeline for me." Youta looked back to the circular window. The one Father stood before all those years ago when this first began. When Uncle sent a man to spread curses and discord through the land hoping to lure away the army. Hoping to make his brother and adopted nephew weak. Hoping to kill both and take the throne for himself. Styx, it had been so long. And Cricket felt so old.

"Of course not." Cricket tugged at the end of his braid, smoothing the hairs down for a long moment to soothe himself. It did nothing. That motion had long since stopped working, but he couldn't seem to break the habit. "Nothing for it, I suppose. We'll just have everyone on high alert."

"I'll make sure the staff we can trust knows."

"Be sure they're armed, too. I know Ignacia has been training some of them." He hadn't liked the idea of training the staff. It wasn't their job to protect their lives and the lives of the royal family. But he couldn't risk it, if only for their own safety.

"She has."

"Then we'll see that they have weapons. Something easily hidden on their person. If I know Uncle, he'll strike at the most dramatic time possible. And he'll want an audience."

"So, after everyone has arrived."

"I'd think so. Then he'll be sure all of his pieces are in place." Styx, his head was already starting to pound. Cricket was no Go player; he never had been. Not like Uncle. Not like Anstice. Father taught him to play, but he never had the skill for sacrifice and manipulation that it required to beat opponents like Anstice and Uncle. "The day of the official crowning ceremony, I think. Likely during it, when everyone has their guard down."

"I'll make sure my people know." Youta finished her tea, and set the cup down again, her hands moving to settle into her lap. "Now, if you don't mind my saying so, Your Highness, you should get some sleep."

"The party planner?"

"My daughter. She's a little young still, not quite twenty, but she has an eye for these things, and we can trust her." Thank the gods for Youta. She'd looked after Cricket since he was a child, and it seemed she was still willing to look after him. Then cutting the crusts off his sandwiches, now acting as his head of staff. "She's already been working with Ignacia to disguise some of the soldiers. It won't look like we have quite so much to be afraid of."

"Right. We can't appear weak in the face of my guests." Cricket wanted to snort, and roll his eyes at that, but it was the truth. Uncle Sunil was not the only threat he faced should Lunette appear weak to the other kingdoms.

"We can't." Youta smiled; the expression worn around the edges. "Your Highness, it is time for bed."

"Yes, yes. I just need to finish looking over the itinerary for the guests, then I'll be headed to my rooms. I promise."

Youta pursed her lips, her expression not quite convinced, but Selene bless her, she didn't say as much. She gathered the tea things and made her way to the door. "You need to rest, Your Highness. If Sunil does attack, we'll need you at top form so you can fend him off."

"Ah, but Youta, that's what the dragon is for. Isn't it?"

Youta clicked her tongue, disapproving, and shook her head.

"Fine. Fine. I'll head up to bed in an hour. You have my word."

"I'll hold you to that. If I find out you've broken your promise. . ."

"I know. You'll start drugging my tea." It was said like a joke, but he wouldn't put it past Youta. She was the type to do that sort of thing, for a person's own good. "Good night Youta."

"Good Night, Your Highness." She bowed her head deeply, then left him to it with only a vaguely threatening backward glance.

CHAPTER 3

"So, what's the plan here?" Leo asked, as he pressed his heels into the flanks of his horse to push the animal faster. The rain had begun in earnest, but Takayoshi would not let that slow him down. Not when he did not know how many other groups of mercenaries awaited the signal from Sunil. Maybe even some already in the capital. "We're just going to barge in and demand an audience with the prince?"

Takayoshi did not turn his head to fix Leo with the annoyed narrowing of his eyes, but he wanted to, oh how he wanted to. He knew Leo was trying to help, in his own snarky way, but sometimes Takayoshi just wished his best friend would be silent.

"I was invited," Takayoshi reminded, keeping his tone as calm as he could with his heart pounding in his ears, and cool rain sizzling where it touched his bare skin. He thought he had the phoenix under control, but it would seem he did not. At least not if Cricket was in danger.

"Your *sister* was invited." Leo shook his head, shaggy hair falling into his eyes, and plastering to his forehead.

Takayoshi did not growl at Leo, but he did finally turn his head to cut a dangerous glare at him. Leo looked completely unbothered by it, likely used to it after four years of receiving such a look any time he was being vaguely annoying.

"You haven't spoken to Cricket in four years," Claudia reminded, but she sounded like she was trying to do so gently. Like breaking the news to a very stubborn, very small, child.

It still stung, because she was right. Even before he left on his quest to help Cricket, Takayoshi had not spoken to his prince in a year. He had pushed it off, telling himself that he would reach out only when he had answers. Only when he could provide something. One week turned into a month and a month turned into six, then he was loading up Lily in search of an ancient archive that may not have even existed. And now. . . now it was four years later, and he had never so much as written. He wondered for a moment if Cricket sent him any letters. If Cricket tried to bridge the gap. Would Atsuko have told him? Had there even been time?

"He probably thinks you hate him now," Leo said, breaking Takayoshi from his spiral. Takayoshi's head whipped to the side so hard, he nearly jerked the reins of his horse and sent the poor creature down into the mud. Leo blinked innocently at him. "What?"

"He does not think I hate him. He cannot." Of that, he was certain. Takayoshi had made himself perfectly clear, even before he left. They were friends. Cricket was his *first* friend. He left his earring with Cricket, a promise to return. A promise that he was not truly gone. Only. . . only that had been *five* years ago.

"No. Not hate," Claudia agreed, and Takayoshi felt relief roll through him like a wave. "He may think you haven't forgiven him though."

"Forgiven him?" Takayoshi turned his eyes back to the

road ahead of them. They had been traveling for hours, and still the capital seemed so far away. Another day's travel, even at this pace. "There was never anything to forgive."

There was not. Not in Takayoshi's eyes. Cricket did nothing wrong. He told Takayoshi to go home, yes, but he had every right to do so. Cricket had been stressed, and there had been a lot going on at the time. Takayoshi understood that. And really, he always meant to return. He just. . . he just had not.

"Yoshi," Claudia said, her voice soft enough that it was almost lost in the *drip-drip-drip* of rain around them, and the wind through the trees. The storm was picking up. They would need to find some place to ride out the evening soon. But even now he felt the tug of his connection with Cricket like a string around his heart, pulling him onward.

"We will have to stop soon," Takayoshi said, hoping to waylay whatever conversation Claudia thought they needed to have. He would prefer not to discuss this any further. Not if he could help it. It was already going to be a messy thing, seeing Cricket again after all these years, he did not need his own feelings wound up in it. Not with the danger ahead.

"Yoshi." Claudia tried again, her voice louder. The tone of a friend, a sister, who wanted nothing but the best for him.

"He's right, Claud. Let it go for now." Leo glanced worriedly at Takayoshi from under his wet hair, but he did not say as much. He would not say as much. He seemed to understand what Takayoshi was going through. Perhaps more intimately than even Takayoshi himself.

"We still have a day, a day and a half, till we reach the capital," Claudia said, clearing her throat, and looking at the path before them.

"We should ride until we cannot possibly continue any longer." Takayoshi hated to ask this of them. His friends had already given him so much. Four years of their lives. Blood, sweat, and tears. And with Leo, his mobility. His leg would never be the same. He would never be the warrior he once was. "Please let me know if that is too much."

"Of course, it's not." Leo snorted. And that was the end of that. They would hear no further protests; they would court no other options. They were in this, with him, and Takayoshi was content knowing he need not even have asked, not really.

IT WAS STILL RAINING a day later when the capital came into view. The lights of the city were a beacon in the gloom. Warm and inviting. Takayoshi would expect no less from Cricket's home. From the place that raised the bright-eyed, beautiful young man who spoke pixie, and laughed off his pain.

"We should get a room at one of the inns," Leo said as they slowed their pace to trot through the empty street. "Give you a chance to freshen up. Get your head on straight."

It was not a bad proposition, and in another circumstance, perhaps Takayoshi would have heeded Leo's advice. But he felt the danger of the situation chasing them, making the hair on the back of his neck stand on end. There was not time enough for him to freshen up and make himself presentable. Not time enough for him to settle his racing heart and get his thoughts in order.

"No. Claudia and I will head straight for the castle." Takayoshi shook his head, taking in a deep breath. It did little to help.

"You're going to go see your prince. . . like that?" Leo

asked, a teasing glint lighting his eye as he gave Takayoshi a once over.

Takayoshi glared, but Leo had a point. He had gone months with a proper haircut and shave. His clothes were the same ones he had worn while they fought silkworms, and man-eating plants. Nothing about his appearance said Prince of Helio. Still.

"Fine. Fine. What do you want me to do? I can't go up there. Someone might recognize me."

Takayoshi doubted that highly. It had been many years since Leo was amongst the society of royalty, since Lionel the Valiant, and he had changed drastically. But Takayoshi could see the words for what they were, an excuse. Leo was no longer comfortable in that world, and Takayoshi could not blame him for it when that world once tried to kill him.

"Find a place to stay in town while Claudia and I head to the castle," Takayoshi instructed. "See what you can learn about any possible forces close by, and if any more arrive. Whatever you find, report it to us, immediately. We need to assess this threat thoroughly." It was not a lie, they did need to assess the threat, but it was also not quite the truth. For he was already there, he was already about to seek an audience with the prince. But he knew the relief on Leo's face almost as much as he knew the loosening of his own shoulders.

Leo did not say *thank you*, or *yes, Your Highness*, both would be a superfluous waste of words. He just bowed his head in understanding and veered his horse down one of the side roads, separating from the group.

"How will he report to us?" Claudia nudged her horse into motion again, guiding it through the streets toward the wall of the palace.

"You are both very clever, I am sure you will sort something out." Takayoshi focused on the gates which had come into view. He did not remember them being quite so tall. Everything seemed smaller in his memories. "Perhaps you might try smoke signals."

Claudia barked a laugh, her eyes narrowing with a smile behind her rain dotted spectacles. It was a nice sound, the chortling, noise of a friend finding amusement in something he said. It made Takayoshi breathe a little easier as the walls loomed over them.

The gates opened, and they dismounted. Takayoshi pulled his chin up, his posture straightening.

"State your business," one guard said, her voice gruff, but her face so, *so* young Takayoshi had a hard time really taking her seriously. She could not have been much older than Cricket was when they first met. Too young to be protecting something so precious. Too young to be so serious.

"I am Prince Takayoshi of Helio. I am here to speak with the crown prince. Please relay the message and ask him to grant us an audience." Takayoshi resisted the urge to bow his head in respect to the young woman. It had been too long since was been in this type of setting. His court manners were rusty, but he knew enough to know they would expect Takayoshi the prince. Not the travel worn warrior.

The girl looked him up and down, likely noting the threadbare tunic, the stubble on his face, and his unkempt hair. Then she raised her brows. "Prince of Helio?"

Takayoshi let out a breath, and did not roll his eyes, although it was a near thing. He reached into his travel pouch and pulled from it the Helion seal. "Do you need further proof?"

"Ah! No. Your Highness." The young woman bowed deeply. "Just– Just wait here. I'll go– I'll see if we can– I'll be right back."

"Thank you." Takayoshi tucked the seal into his bag, and watched the guard skitter away, leaving them under the slight overhang of the guard post by the gate. The other guards turned back to watching the entrance, their eyes narrowed through the gloom.

"You're nervous," Claudia whispered, pressing her shoulder into his. A solid warmth at his side that Takayoshi would be forever grateful for.

"Mm." He supposed that was what the racing of his heart and the sweating of his palms meant.

"You have nothing to be nervous about."

That was not quite true, and they both knew it, but he did not think arguing with her in front of the guards was wise. They needed to present a united front, and the guards were unlikely to take him seriously if he were seen arguing with his companions. "What if he has not forgiven me?"

"I'm sure that he has." She pressed her shoulder in harder. Takayoshi did not lean back into her, but he relaxed against her warmth.

"What if he does not recognize me?"

"Thinking you should have taken Leo up on that offer of a haircut last week?" Claudia teased, her eyes bright behind her spectacles, her mouth twitching up at the edges.

"Perhaps."

One of the guards around them cleared their throat, and Takayoshi felt himself scowl. He had forgotten that there was no privacy in court. That it was no longer just he and his friends traveling together. Things would be expected of him here. And the easy camaraderie he had with Claudia and Leo would not be fully understood. Not by anyone who had not been there and seen all they had.

Claudia straightened up, hands smoothing over her trousers to try to press out some of the wrinkles. "You'll be fine," she muttered out of the corner of her mouth just as the first guard returned.

The poor young woman looked harried, her eyes wild, and

her face pale. "The umm– The head of the guard– She'll umm– She's coming to umm–" She coughed, her eyes flicking down to her boots. "She'll escort you in."

"So, it *is* you," a familiar voice said from behind the young woman.

Takayoshi lifted his gaze to meet that of Ignacia. She had gotten taller in the years that spanned between them. Her hair now pulled back into a single, severe braid, and her eyes seemed harder, if that were at all possible. She had gone from bodyguard, handmaiden, sister, best friend to head of the guard, and he saw it in every line of her face.

"It is." Takayoshi bowed his head just slightly in deference to her position. He knew well enough who she was to the prince. Knew that one wrong word from Ignacia would send him home before Cricket ever agreed to meet with him.

Claudia, for her part, made a sound like air slowly leaving a slightly uncorked bottle beside him.

"This is my friend, Claudia Durante." Takayoshi gave Claudia a gentle nudge with his elbow, and Claudia bowed her head. "Claudia, this is Ignacia Firenze."

"A pleasure. I'm sure." Ignacia's eyes swept over Claudia once then went immediately back to Takayoshi, before narrowing. "What is it you need to see him about? We're a little busy, in case you haven't noticed."

"I apologize for the timing." Takayoshi let out a little breath that was almost a sigh. There was water trickling down the back of his tunic, and his toes were beginning to go numb in his boots. He was sure that Claudia was faring far worse as she did not have phoenix fire singing through her veins to fend off the chill. "I would be happy to explain more thoroughly what this pertains to, but first, could we please get out of the rain? Claudia and I have been traveling for two days through it."

Ignacia's gaze had yet to relax, her posture rigid. She

looked like she wanted to take the sword from her belt and run him through with it. Not that he could blame her. He had not left on the best of terms after all. Then she rolled her eyes and turned on her heel. "Come on then. We had rooms prepared for your sister, but she decided not to come. I think Youta left them open."

"That is very much appreciated." Takayoshi followed behind her, and only glanced back once to look worriedly at Claudia when she stumbled to catch up.

"You didn't tell me she was pretty," Claudia hissed under her breath, her eyes fixed on Ignacia's retreating form as they headed up the path toward the palace doors.

Takayoshi huffed something that might have been a laugh. The corner of his lips twitched in an almost-smile. "I did not think that was relevant to the conversation."

"Wasn't relevant to the conversation, he says. Like he doesn't have eyes in his head, he says. Really, Yoshi, I wonder about you sometimes." Claudia muttered to herself, and after a moment the quiet words devolved into quiet curses that Takayoshi was grateful he could not quite make out.

Ignacia led them through the corridors to the guest wing where there were, conveniently, two rooms made up side by side. "I will speak to His Highness and see if he can make time for you in his schedule. But our other guests begin arriving shortly, and he will need to give them the attention they deserve." She did not exactly sound sorry about it. Takayoshi supposed that was fair.

"I understand." And Takayoshi did. He knew exactly what Ignacia was saying to him, even if she did not speak the words. That he had no right to Cricket's time, not now. Any time Cricket gave him would be a gift. She did not approve of him coming here. Yes, he understood perfectly. "Whatever time he can spare me would be greatly appreciated."

"Right. Of course." Ignacia snorted, rolling her eyes. "I'll have some fresh clothes brought up for you both, and baths drawn. If you need anything, let one of the servants know, they'll see to your needs. You are still emissaries from Helio, of course."

"Of course." Takayoshi waited until Ignacia turned the corner to look back at Claudia. She still had that dumbstruck look on her face, and if he could see color, he was sure he would find pinkened cheeks, giving her away. "You are drooling."

"I am not!" Claudia squawked, swatting at him. But she rubbed at her mouth with the back of her wrist just in case. "So, we're just going to what? Wait for him to have time to spare for us?"

"No." Takayoshi frowned, his eyes flicking to follow a couple of maids who were working to prepare the rooms across the hall from his and Claudia's.

"Then what?"

"Well. . ." Takayoshi pressed his lips together, inhaling through his nose. "He must be around here somewhere. Ignacia cannot confine us to the guest quarters, though I am sure she might like to."

"So, we're going to wander around and hope to run into him?"

"It sounds foolish when you say it that way." Heat licked up the back of his neck and into his ears, and he thanked Selene that his hair had gotten long enough to hide it. Otherwise, he was sure Claudia would make fun of him for it.

"What way? Like the truth?" Claudia smirked at him; her eyes alight with amusement. Styx, and he thought he left the most troublesome of his friends at an inn.

"Do you have a better plan?"

"Of course, I do." Claudia's eyes swiveled away from him to the pretty young maid now leaving the room across the hall with a cart full of old linens.

"Watch and learn, Your Highness," Claudia whispered, then she walked up to the maid, leaned on the cart, and smiled at her in that way Claudia had of smiling at people.

He wondered if she could teach him that, but then he realized even if she could, she probably would not.

CHAPTER 4

"You can't avoid him forever," Youta said, her eyes fixed on the mending she'd been working on when the guard reported that Prince Takayoshi was at the gate. They'd been having a nice, quiet conversation about where to stick the less savory of their incoming guests (preferably as far away from Cricket's wing as possible), and he was just beginning to relax after a long day of planning when the young guard burst in, eyes wide, wild, and hair floating around her face, loose from her braid.

They weren't expecting guests for at least another two days. Poor kid.

"I'm not avoiding him," Cricket rushed to reply, and the response sounded rehearsed even to his own ears. *Styx.*

Youta just hummed and didn't bother to lift her eyes from the little tunic in her lap. But there was a crinkle around her eyes, a note of mischief in her voice. *Blast.*

"I'm not!"

"Then it doesn't matter that I've told Ignacia to settle them in the East wing, just down the hall from you, does it?"

"No. Of course, it *doesn't.*" Cricket's voice broke on the

last word, but he cleared his throat to cover it and looked back out the window.

"That was where you meant for the emissaries from Helio and Hermes to go," she continued, brutal in her efficiency to flay him alive and leave him open in the middle of his study. Gods, when had he become so obvious?

"It was." Likely when he'd told Youta to put the Helio guests as close to his own quarters as possible. That's probably what gave him away. But there had been some not-so-secret hope that Yoshi would join them, and Cricket could talk to him finally, in person. In retrospect, it had been a foolish hope, and he'd definitely done this to himself. "Where are we putting Craven and his lot?"

Youta raised her brows, her focus still on the needle swishing in and out of the little tunic in her lap, but she didn't look up, and she very graciously allowed the subject change. "As far away from you as possible. Per your request."

"Good." Cricket heaved a sigh, his shoulders relaxing a little. "At least one thing has gone right so far."

IT WASN'T that Cricket was hiding from Yoshi. But it wasn't. . . *not* that either. He just didn't have the energy for a confrontation, and he knew that if he ran into the stoic prince Yoshi would insist on them having a *Conversation*. So he decided to forgo some of his usual wandering around the castle and stick to his own small corner of it.

"Idiot," Cricket muttered to himself as his eyes settled on the straight-backed posture of Yoshi. He had gotten taller, broader, his white, blond hair longer. Almost unkempt where it hung past his shoulders. He looked. . . Selene, he looked so handsome. More than those fuzzy memories ever seemed to portray. Cricket supposed that's what trauma did to a person. It made the memories hazy and indistinct. And none of his prepared him for the man walking toward him with long, purposeful steps. Cricket swallowed, his throat clicking a little with how dry it suddenly was.

"My Prince," Yoshi said, and it sounded like he was struggling to get the words out past a lump in his throat. His eyes were a little wider than usual, like he was surprised to see Cricket there, in his *own* castle, near his *own* quarters.

"Uh. . . hi." Cricket laughed, giving a wave. Which was a completely normal thing to do, right? Right.

"Hello." Yoshi's eyes scrunched up a little at the corners, not quite a smile, but one was well on its way. Or maybe he was laughing at Cricket. Cricket was honestly out of practice reading the subtle shifts in Yoshi's expressions, and he probably would remain out of practice. Because when this coronation was over Yoshi would return to Helio.

"It's– It's been a while."

"Papa! Papa! Papa!" A little voice cut Yoshi off just as he opened his mouth to respond. The shout accompanied by the slapping of bare feet on the cold granite of the palace were the only warnings Cricket got before Becka's little body collided with his legs, nearly sending him sprawling to the floor.

"Papa?" Yoshi asked, his voice doing something. . . *strange* as he stared down at the dark-haired child clinging to Cricket's leg. A blush crawled up the back of Cricket's neck, hot and stifling under his hair.

"Papa, who's that man?" Becka looked up at Yoshi, her little nose curled in curiosity.

"This, little sunflower," Cricket said, scooping her up to rest on his hip in one well-practiced motion. She was almost too big for it now, but Cricket was loath to give it up. Especially after those first six months when Becka had been terri-fied of everyone including him. "Is Prince Takayoshi. He's the prince of Helio, the queen's little brother. You remember the queen?"

She nodded, little hands clutching at Cricket's tunic. Nervous, but still not looking away from Yoshi, not hiding. And Selene, Cricket loved her so much, his brave little girl.

"I think you ought to introduce yourself to him properly, just as Mistress Luna taught you. It'd be good practice, don't you think?"

"Right!" Becka nodded once, firmly, then set her face in a very serious expression, her cheeks puffing out just a little. "Good morning, Prince Taka. . . Taka. . ."

"Takayoshi," Cricket whispered to her.

"Prince Takayoshi. I am Princess Yue Becka." She bowed pointedly, and Cricket only just managed to keep her from toppling out of his arms.

"And we are," Cricket prompted, having to bite his tongue to swallow down the laughter that threatened to spill out of him. Yoshi watched Becka with wide eyes, his jaw almost relaxed enough to fall open. If he weren't so stern, he'd probably be gaping like a fish.

"Oh! And I am very happy to meet you!" Becka gave another little bow. Her long hair fell haphazardly into her face, where it'd slipped through the braid Cricket somehow wrangled it into that morning. He'd have to try and get her to sit still during lunch long enough for him to tie it back again.

"It is a pleasure to meet you as well, Princess Becka," Yoshi replied with an awkward bow of his own.

Becka let out a delighted little *meep*, clutching tighter onto Cricket's clothes, and snagging some of his hair in the process.

Yoshi turned questioning eyes to Cricket. He didn't have to say it, Cricket knew what he was asking. *Papa?*

"Ah." Cricket sighed, hitching Becka up higher on his hip to keep her from slipping to the floor. "Becka's family lived in Candra. It's one of the towns un–" He cleared his throat, reminding himself firmly that he was no longer calling Uncle that. At least not out loud. "Sunil attacked near the border. Early on. And. Well. . ." Cricket shrugged, swallowing hard around the grief that threatened to claw its way up his throat at the memory of Candra. The smell of burning wood, and. . . and a tiny little girl, bundled up under a white cloak that managed to protect her from the falling embers. "Her family didn't– And when I went to Candra to help with relief, she was there. I don't know it felt kind of like I was meant to– Like Father had with me."

"Selene helped Papa find me," Becka declared, pride glimmering in her eyes. "So I could be a princess. And live with him, and Grandfather, and Aunt Iggy, and–"

"Princess Becka! Your lessons weren't through yet, little miss," Mistress Luna shouted from down the hall, and Cricket could almost hear her bracing her hands on her hips.

"Uh oh." Becka looked up at Cricket with wide eyes. "Papa, put me down."

"Yes ma'am." Cricket set her gently on her feet and bit down on the inside of his cheek to keep himself from cackling like a maniac as she disappeared around the corner opposite where Mistress Luna's voice was coming from. Cricket held his finger to his lips to signal to Yoshi not to tell anyone that he'd seen Becka.

"Where *is* that girl?" Mistress Luna hustled down the corridor, her skirts pulled up around her ankles to make it easier to chase down the runaway princess. "Oh. Your Highness."

"Mistress Luna." Cricket smiled, offering her a little bow. "Can I help you with something?"

"Yes. Yes, you can. Have you seen that child of yours?"

Mistress Luna's hair had fallen mostly out of its tight bun, and her clothes were looking more than a little rumpled. Cricket supposed that's what happened when you spent much of your day chasing a mischievous six-year-old.

"I haven't, I'm sorry. Was there something important?"

"Well, I'd say so! She's missing her etiquette lessons. We can't have her acting like a. . ." Mistress Luna drifted off, seeming to realize what she was about to say could be considered offensive, and pursed her lips.

"If I see her, I'll make sure she knows where she's supposed to be." Cricket had the audacity to give her a wink, which only made Mistress Luna huff.

"Honestly. When my father said you were the most troublesome student he ever had, I didn't believe him. But your child is–"

"An absolute delight?" Cricket supplied for her, a wide, almost threatening grin spreading across his face, one pointed tooth snagging on his lower lip. He would not tolerate anyone disparaging Becka, and Luna knew that well enough.

Luna narrowed her gaze on him, then rolled her eyes. "An absolute delight. But a mischief maker nonetheless."

"Of course. Now, I suggest you check the bunny pen in the yard. That's where I always find her."

"Yes. Thank you, Your Highness." She bowed, and turned back the way she'd come, her skirts sweeping out behind her in her rush. From somewhere down the other side, Cricket heard Becka let out a soft snicker.

"You, little miss, better be back in your classroom before Professor Qiren gets there for your Magics lessons," Cricket called, not even bothering to look for her. "I don't care if you miss etiquette, but you better not miss the useful stuff."

"Yes, papa!" Becka yelled back, and he heard her feet slapping against the floor again, headed back toward the library and the classroom. When the sound faded away, he turned back to Yoshi who was staring at him with an expression he'd never seen on his face before. It was something. . . *complicated.*

"Right. As I was saying. . . What was I saying?"

"Her family?" Yoshi asked, his hands tucked behind his back where Cricket couldn't see them.

"There was no one left. There was. . . there were very few people left in Candra at all, even before Sunil attacked it. Which reminds me," Cricket said, his own hands flying up to pull his braid over his shoulder and tug at the ends. "I found a horse that looked oddly like Lily there. Did your girl perhaps have a twin? She's out in the stables if you'd like to have a look."

"You did?" Yoshi's face did something else strange, his mouth falling open in what could only have been delight.

"Yes. If you want to go and see her, just let the stable girl know I sent you. She'll show you to her stall. And if you want to take her home with you, feel free. I'm sure Lily would be happy to have her around. She's very sweet." Cricket couldn't help the way his chest warmed at the knowledge that *he* had done something to bring that expression to Yoshi's face. *That was me.*

"I will. Thank you."

"Of course." Cricket shrugged off the thanks, ignoring how it made his toes curl in discomfort in his boots. Such open sincerity from Yoshi felt. . . weird. "Anyway, I've got a meeting with Iggy I need to get to. And I'm probably already late." He looked down at the watch hanging from a chain on his waist to avoid Yoshi's steady stare. Selene, he was in trouble if Yoshi decided to stick around. "But we should catch up. I'm sure you have lots to tell me about your. . . about where you've. . . Well. I'm sure we have lots to catch up on. How about we meet for supper this evening? You can introduce me to Claudia, and I'll bring Iggy, and we'll make a family dinner of it. Okay?"

"Yes. I would like that."

"Perfect. I'll have one of the servants come by and let you know what time. I hope you're getting settled well. But really, I have to go. Feel free to ask for anything you need." Cricket turned on his heel, refusing to look at Yoshi any longer, because he couldn't. He just *couldn't*. And all but fled down the corridor toward the war room. He needed. . .

He needed some distance. To breathe. To think. To remind himself that Yoshi wasn't really there for *him*.

CHAPTER 5

"No," Claudia said, her arms crossed over her chest.

"No?" Takayoshi did not think Claudia had ever told him no before. At least not when it came to a dinner invitation. She always seemed happy to share a meal with him, or at least happy to get free food out of the bargain, he never figured out which it was.

"No. I'm not going to be your third wheel with Prince Cricket. And I have it on good authority that no one else will be there either. You two need to talk, and I'm not putting myself in the middle of that. You'll just have to go it alone this time, Yoshi." She reached up to grab at his shoulders, steering him back toward the door to their quarters. Claudia could be unrelenting when she wanted to be, it was likely why they got along so well.

"On whose authority?" Takayoshi did not dig his heels in. He was not a toddler. He was a grown man for Selene's sake. But he did look over his shoulder to get a glimpse of Claudia's amused smirk. He decided long ago, he did not like that expression. It usually meant trouble for him.

"Stop being stubborn for once—"

"Not stubborn."

"—and just go. I've got things to handle here, I don't have time to play sidekick this evening," she continued without bothering to acknowledge that he had spoken.

Then she gave him one more shove, and shut the door behind him, leaving him standing in the corridor outside their rooms feeling rather silly. He supposed he could knock, and tell her to let him back in. He could order her to come with him. But Takayoshi had never been the type to swing his title around that way, and he certainly was not about to start with one of the few people he called friend.

So, instead of demanding she let him back in, and hiding himself away, he took a breath, straightened his clothing, and made his way to the dining room.

Cricket was there waiting for him, sitting at the head of the table, with his cheek smashed against one fist where he leaned on his elbow. His free hand twirled his fork in between his fingers lazily. And Takayoshi's breath left him for the second time that day.

Awestruck. That was what that feeling was. It left him speechless, almost dizzy with it, the first time he saw Cricket in that hallway. He was. . . He had changed. The antlers on either side of his forehead—which to some may have been a deterrent—just made him look more beautiful. Ethereal. Not of this world. His copper skin had grown warmer somehow, likely from all the time he had to spend outside to combat Sunil. And where once he was lanky, all swinging limbs, and careless grace, now Cricket was something else entirely. Strong, tightly controlled. A dragon in human skin. It. . .

Takayoshi shook himself, reminded himself to breathe. Lovestruck fool that he was. A reminder that only helped for all of a few seconds before Cricket looked up, those blue eyes sparkling with a laugh when they met Takayoshi's, and he forgot how to exhale.

"Well. . ." Cricket said, rising from his seat so he could pull a chair out for Takayoshi. A gesture which was frankly ridiculous, and Takayoshi would have said so if his tongue could remember how to form words. It could not. It was laying limp in his mouth like a dead fish. Stars, he was hopeless. "It seems we've been set up."

"Set up?" That is not what he meant to say, but Cricket had brushed a hand accidentally against his shoulder as he pushed Takayoshi's chair in for him, and Takayoshi's focus narrowed down to that singular point of contact.

"Yes." Cricket laughed, the sound too high, forced, and settled into his own chair again. It was all the way across the long table, too far away. Takayoshi knew that being sat at the head as he was, was an honor. It was a sign of respect from one heir to another. But at the same time he could not help but note how very far away it was. So far away that he could not even make out the color of Cricket's eyes any longer, and the thought made him want to grumble, pick up his place setting, and move. He did not, because it went against every rule of decorum he had ever learned. "Not even Becka had time tonight for her dear old papa."

Takayoshi took a sip from his water glass. *I should tell him.* All about a 'two and a bit' year old Becka sipping tea next to him in an inn. About the promise he made to her and her grandmother that he would come back for her. About how he had broken that promise. About the grief he felt when he thought he lost a child before ever really having one. About the joy that shimmered through him at seeing that child again. . . in Cricket's arms. Happy, and whole. He should tell him. He should *thank* him. He did none of those things.

"It would seem so," is what he said instead, and it felt like a lie by omission. A half-truth, even when the comment itself was noncommittal. Because it had not been what he wanted to say at all. Takayoshi's hand gripped the glass tighter, the heat under his skin making it fog up. He put it down, hoping Cricket had not noticed. When he looked up to check Cricket was staring down at his own hands, watching the way the light played on a patch of scales on the back of his right wrist.

"Why are you here, Takayoshi?" Cricket sounded tired. More tired than Takayoshi had ever heard him. Even back in Nishi when he went days without sleep. Their dinner had not even been delivered yet, and Takayoshi could feel the fight brewing in the air between them. He did not want it. But it would be inevitable. It was best to get it over with.

"To warn My Prince." Takayoshi bowed his head in deference to Cricket's position, and authority, maybe. Or maybe it was just so he did not have to see the furious look Cricket would send his way. "There are rumors—"

"*Rumors?*" Cricket laughed. Sharp. Hollow. Humorless. "You came to my coronation not to—" He shook his head, abandoning whatever he had been about to say, letting out a loud breath through his nose that curled with steam in the air. He was angry. Oh Selene, he was so angry. "But to throw around vague speculation? Rumors? *Hearsay?*"

Takayoshi cringed inwardly, his toes curling in his boots.

"I know you're mad at me. I'm sorry I didn't write to apologize. But Takayoshi. . . you just. . . you just *left*! Off to fight dragons halfway across the continent! Without a word!" Cricket's hand was balled into a fist on top of the tablecloth. It was doing nothing to hide the way his eyes glowed, the scales on his skin moved, grew. Furious. He was furious. And Takayoshi could not blame him.

"There were no dragons." The words left him before Takayoshi even had time to properly think about them, and once they were out he realized how stupid they sounded. How foolish he looked in front of Cricket. He should have written. He should have reached out. He should have. . . he should not have left in the first place. But what was done, was done.

"That is not the point!"

"You were upset with me." Weak. He was weak. He was so weak. Why had Takayoshi not seen it before? Why had it taken four years to realize what a child he had been when he met Cricket? What a child he still felt like when faced with Cricket. Even at near thirty.

"We argued. People argue, Yoshi. You didn't even give us a chance to talk it out. You just— You just disappeared for five *years*."

How did he tell Cricket that it had not been five years for Takayoshi? How did he explain that it had only been two, if that? He could not. And it would not matter. Because Cricket was right. Takayoshi had hidden for a full year before he left Helio on his quest. A full year when he did not reached out. Followed by a year of journeying to find the archive, and three more stuck on the island. Five total.

"You never wrote. You could have written," Takayoshi said, and the sound was foreign to his own ears. He was making excuses, but he could not stop himself. He could not control the torrent of words bypassing any type of filter and flowing straight from his mouth. "I thought you had not forgiven me."

"I could have. . . I could have *written?*" Fury flared sharp in Cricket's features, and Takayoshi wondered how much of this was legitimately Cricket and how much of it was the dragon. How much of it was the stress of the situation. How much of it was the wild magic running through his veins unchecked, with no pearl to help him harness it. "What about you? I wasn't traveling. I didn't go anywhere. I was here the whole time. *You* could have written."

"You are right. I am sorry." Takayoshi bowed his head again, closing his eyes so he did not have to see the way the heat of his hands burned holes into his borrowed tunic. It would need mending. But that was a problem for later.

"So that's all you came for then?" Cricket asked, and it sounded like he was giving up. Like a surrender. Stars, Takayoshi hated it, but he could not will his tongue to say anything to the contrary. "To warn me? About Sunil's attack?"

"You know about it."

"Of course, I know about it! I'm not a fool, Takayoshi, whatever you might think. I've known for months. I've been planning for *months*. Which you would have known had you bothered to reach out."

Takayoshi nodded, lifting his chin to meet Cricket's eyes once he had swallowed back the burning in his veins. It was too much to hope that they could repair the damage. He would just have to continue on without Cricket's forgiveness. "I also came to inform you that I have researched your condition–"

"My *condition*?" Cricket practically spat and rose from his chair so abruptly that the legs scraped loudly against the stone floor. "My condition is none of your concern. I am fine."

Takayoshi wanted to tell him that he was not fine, he was not all right. That he could see the way the dragon was eating away at Cricket, making him wild with it. But he bit the inside of his cheek hard enough to draw blood, lest he say something else he would regret. He was *already* regretting the entire conversation; he did not need to add to it. He could sense the sleepless night, lying awake as he replayed this conversation over and over and over.

"I think you should leave," Cricket said. His tone was steel, cutting into the soft fleshy bits of Takayoshi's torso.

But the coronation, he thought to argue, but Takayoshi knew better. Cricket had made up his mind, and he would not be swayed. He would need time. Not too much, but enough.

And Takayoshi could not help him, not if he stayed in the palace. Not if he was there when Sunil attacked. He needed to go. No matter how much he did not wish to. He needed to go, and prepare an army. He needed to bring them back to Lunette to protect Cricket. He could not do that here.

"I will be in touch." Takayoshi stood from his chair, giving Cricket a deep bow. "If you should need anything, please, do not hesitate to ask for it. Helio will provide any aid you might require."

Then he turned, and left, without another word. Without looking back.

Claudia was still in their rooms, pouring over some book she found in the library when he stormed in. She did a double take when she saw him reaching to gather his things.

"What– What are you doing?" She rose from her seat.

Takayoshi did not answer, he simply continued packing his bag, grateful he had not come with much, and they had not been there long enough for him to acquire anything new.

"You can't just leave him! They're coming!" Claudia sounded half hysterical. When Takayoshi looked up, he saw that she was clutching the back of her chair so hard her fingers were turning pale.

Takayoshi took a breath and stood from where he was stuffing an extra blanket into his bag. "If I am going to save My Prince from his uncle and his own foolish pride, I will need an army. I do not have one of those here."

Claudia took a moment, but then she nodded, her hand dropping away from the chair. "I'll gather my things."

"No."

She stopped, her head tilting in question.

"I need you, and Leo to stay here. I need you both to watch over Cricket in my absence. I will be flying. We do not have time to waste."

"Flying?" Claudia frowned. "But your feathers."

Takayoshi did not shrug, but he turned back to packing, dismissing Claudia's concern. "It will be all right. Please. . . if something happens, I need to be the first to know. Am I clear?"

"Yes. I'll reach out to Leo and let him know what's going on. We'll protect him while you're gone."

Takayoshi nodded, once, and fled the room. He would have to ride out to the edge of the capital, to where no one could see him, before taking flight.

CHAPTER 6

"You sent him away." Ignacia was glaring at Cricket, and he wasn't entirely sure why. She'd been the one, after all, to say that Yoshi shouldn't be there. She'd been the one to tell him that the prince of Helio would be in the way. Why was she acting so surprised that he'd done just as she thought he ought?

"Yes. I did. You were right, he would only be a distraction, and I've got too many other things to focus on right now. The guests begin arriving tomorrow, and there's still much to do." Cricket ducked his head back to the document on his desk. He'd left the dining room without bothering to eat and holed himself up in his study. It wouldn't be long before Youta came by with a plate of food and a disapproving frown, but Cricket hoped to be deep in his work by then.

Ignacia was silent for far too long. So long, in fact, that Cricket had to look up to make sure that she was even still there. And what he saw on her face when he did, made him frown. Instead of the delighted half-smirk half-smile she usually wore when he conceded that she was right, she was scowling, a sad look drawing her brows down. If he didn't know any better, which he did, he'd say she was regretting having ever said such a thing.

"What? Changed your mind?" He teased, but it didn't make her look any less upset, and that was worse. He sighed, leaning back in his chair, and stretched his legs out in front of him. "Ignacia, I don't have time for. . . whatever Takayoshi and I are. I have a daughter. I have a kingdom. I have a coronation to plan. And I have an uncle who is plotting a civil war. Whatever. . . *that* is. . . that crush? It doesn't have a place in my life anymore."

"I see." Ignacia straightened, her chin tilting back just a little. She didn't approve. Which was annoying, but Cricket wasn't going to get into a fight with her too. He didn't think he'd survive it.

"I'd ask you what that means, but I have a seating chart to go over, and not long at all to do it. We can't have a war breaking out because I sat the wrong duke next to the wrong lord." It was a joke, but even to Cricket, it sounded grotesque. In poor taste. Wrong.

"You know you're going to have to face your feelings for him one day." Ignacia's voice had gone soft around the edges. The big sister, not the hardened head of the guard.

Cricket swallowed around some unknown ache in his chest and forced himself not to look at her. It wouldn't do either of them any good to get soft, not now. Not with Uncle Sunil beating down their door.

"Yeah, if I live that long," he muttered.

Ignacia didn't say anything else. She turned, and stormed out of his study, slamming the door behind her. Cricket winced at the sound echoing in the empty room, his shoulders hunching further over the desk. She was right, of course. He would have to face up to those feelings one day, but at the rate he was going, that day may never come. And until then. .

. well there were other things to worry about. Like keeping his people, and his daughter safe.

THE HALL WAS full of people. The noise deafening as Cricket watched them mill about. Sipping from glasses and chatting amongst themselves. The general hum of contentment and celebration should have felt like a victory. It should have felt like he'd made it. Fulfilled his promise to Father.

It didn't.

He tipped the golden circlet further up so he could scratch beneath it where the metal was irritating a patch of scales on his forehead. The hollowness in his chest as he looked out over everyone was harder to ignore now that the rush of everything was done. Now that he'd been crowned, and they were meant to be celebrating the new king of Lunette. Because the truth was, the only thing Cricket had ever wanted was to make his father, his family, and his people proud. And as he looked out over the room of lords, ladies, dukes, duchesses, princes, princesses, and everyone in between, he saw surprisingly little of the people who he cared the most for.

Not even Ignacia was amongst them as she had stationed herself at the main gate. He tried to convince her he wanted her at his side that night. He'd told her she needed to keep her king safe, but Ignacia just rolled her eyes and gone and done what she wanted to, as always. Which, Cricket supposed, might be for the best, as he wasn't the only one in danger if Uncle attacked. There was Becka to think of too.

Becka who had been so good through this whole thing. Who sat beside her papa and smiled winningly as they greeted most of their guests. Becka who was now tucked away in her bed, where she belonged after a long day that only seemed to drag longer. Where Cricket wished he could be, as he swallowed back a yawn that made his eyes water.

He wondered if he could sneak away and maybe–

The doors to the main hall crashed open, slamming against the walls beside them. Ignacia stumbled in, holding a wound at her side, blood dripping loudly in the suddenly silent hall.

"He's coming. He– He has Becka," she rasped once she was close enough.

Cricket's heart plummeted, every inch of his body breaking out into a cold sweat as fear settled into every cell of his being.

He has Becka. He has my little girl. He has her. He's going to hurt her. She must be so scared. I need to get to her. I need to protect her. That's my job. I'm her father. I promised her she'd never have to be scared again. And he has her. He has her. And he's going to hurt her. And she must be so scared. And I– I–

Uncle Sunil strolled into the hall like he owned the place, a group of mercenaries at his back. A murmur went through the crowd. Cricket stood from his throne, straight-backed— hoping Uncle Sunil wouldn't see how all of the color had washed from his face—and made his way stiffly down the dais to meet Uncle at the bottom of the stairs.

"Uncle. While it's sweet that you wanted to be here for my coronation, I believe the conditions of your exile were that should you set foot on Lunette soil again, your life would be forfeit." Cricket smiled tightly, forcing it onto his face as one might a mask. The dimples cut into his cheeks like the point of a knife. Uncle Sunil had to know that he couldn't show his true power here. He had to know that without the dragon, Cricket was vulnerable. He had done his research. This was calculated. But then Cricket had never actually expected any less from Uncle. He only wished that Anstice were there to help him launch a similarly conniving defense.

"I am here under the authority of King Craven—"

Ah, so that's why that weaselly bastard isn't here, Cricket thought and as he scanned Uncle's envoy, he saw Prin Estia among them. Zir posture slouching, ducking behind one of the bigger mercenaries.

"—to arrest you under suspicion of murder," Uncle announced to the hall, smirking. A cat just before it jumped on someone and clawed at their face. Cricket resisted the urge to shiver.

"Murder?" Cricket couldn't help but laugh. "And who, may I ask, have I murdered?"

"My brother, king Jaxith." The words seemed to echo. Not just through the painfully silent hall but also through Cricket himself. Like his insides were hollow and all there was was that accusation. That he killed Father. That he deprived Becka of more time with her grandfather.

"Fa— Father," Cricket choked on the word, his focus narrowing down to a pin. Uncle thought he had killed *Father*? All of these men? They thought that too? How could anyone think that he could. . . that he could *possibly*. "No. I'd. . . I didn't." But even to his own ears the protests sounded weak. Like he wasn't really sure he hadn't. Like maybe he had, but it had been an accident.

"Well, we'll just see about that won't we?"

Then there were the whispers. The hushed voices. The low murmur of gossip. Uncle couldn't have picked a better time. To come at Cricket newly crowned, in all of his glory, in front of any and every royal who would have ruled beside him. This was the best time to accuse him of such a thing.

"Yes, we will." Cricket lifted his chin, forcing breath into his lungs. "I have nothing at all to hide. I invite my peers to investigate to the best of their ability. Please, see if you can find proof that I was responsible for my father's untimely death. Or maybe you will find that—"

"You misunderstand, *nephew*," Uncle said the last word like it tasted bitter on his tongue. "This will not be an open investigation. This is a Lunette matter, and as a Lunette matter, it will be handled amongst. . . *family*." His smile slashed, a wound across his face, sharp, and bleeding with insincerity.

Cricket's hands clutched into fists at his sides. For all the people knew of what Uncle had done, he could not be openly combative in front of those in this room. These people who would judge him, who would decide his fate should he need aid in the future. Aid. Oh how he wished in that moment that he had listened to Yoshi. That he had accepted the help that was offered to him. Now, it would seem that it was too late.

"Of course, Uncle. Let us handle this matter quietly." Publicly would be better for him. So much better. But it would invite scrutiny. It would invite those around him to take sides. And it may very well provide him with more enemies in the end than he started with. It might splinter his country into more pieces. He couldn't. . . he couldn't chance that.

"In the meantime, I hope your guests will excuse us. As this is family business, I think it best that they all head home. Don't you?" It was not a question. Uncle was not giving him an option. Cricket could send these people home, or he could stand and watch as Uncle stole the last people Cricket called family from him. It was clear from the thirsty look in Uncle's eyes, almost begging Cricket to make that choice, that he would relish either outcome

"Yes, I think that would be best," Cricket said, somehow managing to not clench his teeth around the words. Thank Selene for small miracles. "I beg you will to excuse us, and make your own arrangements to get home safely? When we next see each other hopefully there will be much more to celebrate. In the meantime, Uncle, perhaps you'd be so kind as to follow me to the study?"

A discontented murmur went through the gathered dignitaries, but Cricket paid them no mind as he turned on his heel and headed through the back doors down the corridor toward his study. He heard Uncle Sunil and a few of his men behind him, but he didn't turn back. Uncle had made the effort to make all of this very public, he wouldn't kill Cricket. Not yet, at least. He needed to wait. To make it look like Cricket had done something wrong. To sway the opinions of those in that room even further. Cricket and his family were safe, for now.

"That bastard," Ignacia growled at his side. Her steps were stuttered, and uneven, but someone had bandaged her up sometime during the mess, and while she was still pale, she didn't look like she was bleeding out anymore. "He jumped us."

"Was anyone seriously injured?" Cricket did not look away from where he was headed, and he kept his voice low, not wanting to draw the attention of Uncle or any of his men.

"No. Everyone's all right." Ignacia shook her head.

"And the library?" he asked, his voice soft so only she could hear it. Not the library, not really. The dormitory. The place where Becka stayed when her lessons ran long, or when Cricket had things he needed to attend to, so that her tutors could look after her. The safest place in the palace, very likely, considering the strength of her tutors and the extra guards Cricket had set up there.

"Yes."

He didn't ask the question, but he didn't think he had to. Ignacia knew what he was getting at.

"From what I've seen, she's unharmed. Scared. But

unharmed."

Relief washed through Cricket at that. His daughter was safe, for the time being. How long that would last, he did not know. But he prayed to Selene that it would be long enough for him to get her out of there. For him to send her away with Youta, and Ignacia, and all the others. Leave him to deal with Uncle Sunil on his own.

"How many?" he murmured out of the side of his mouth. They had prepared for this, but the fact remained that a large part of their forces was out helping with relief aid of the towns and villages Uncle Sunil had already attacked, leaving the castle with a small contingent of knights. Enough, Cricket had thought. And maybe they would have been, had Uncle Sunil not gone for Becka first.

Ignacia shook her head.

Cricket stepped into the study, and shuffled over to sit at his desk, his fingers steepling in front of his lips as he leaned back in his chair. A posture that was so falsely relaxed he was surprised Uncle didn't laugh out loud. Still, he did not want to put Uncle on high alert, and the best way to do that was to lean into what Uncle thought of him. Lean into the arrogant princeling.

"Well? I believe you have something to say, Uncle?" Cricket asked, one dark brow raised as Uncle's steps brought him to the other side of the desk. He stayed standing, not even sparing a glance to the chairs on the other side, and leaned over the desk, his presence looming threateningly.

The door shut behind the small group of men he'd brought with a soft sound that echoed in the silence of the room.

"You will give me this kingdom," Uncle said, his eyes bright with some vicious understanding that left Cricket cold. This– This was not a game Cricket could win. Not yet. Not now. Not with Becka's safety in Uncle Sunil's hands.

"And if I do not?"

"I will make them suffer." Uncle's lips twisted up into that same rictus of a smile as it had in the banquet hall. Sure, and calm, and powerful. "All of them. Your people. Ignacia. That prince you're so fond of. Anstice. . . Even your daughter."

Cricket kept his gaze firmly on Uncle's face, looking for any hint that he was lying, any hint that he might be bluffing. There was none. Just the surety of a man who had stacked the deck in his favor. "So you want me to what? Just. . . hand over the crown? Give you the throne and walk away?"

"No."

"No?" Cricket's eyes narrowed.

"No. Your people would never allow that. All the good you've done fighting at your borders, solving curses, and adopting orphans? No. They'd never allow it."

Cricket couldn't help but smile at that, the grin slipped easily onto his features at the praise, even for all Uncle didn't mean it as such. "You're correct. They wouldn't ever allow it. Kind of ruins your plans, doesn't it, Uncle?"

"Not at all." Uncle settled into a chair, finally, his expression all smug satisfaction. "That's why you and I are going to make up. You're going to pardon me of all crimes, say you made a mistake. And then you'll go about ruling Lunette, just as you'd planned."

Cricket's brows raised. "That's all you want? A pardon?"

Uncle Sunil snorted, rolling his eyes. "No. Of course not. Idiot child. No. I plan to stay here, and make myself quite at home. If I can't take the crown from you, I'll just have to make you use it how I want to."

"Excuse me?"

"I'm going to make you my puppet, *nephew*, and you're going to let me. Or your little girl will be orphaned for the second time in her life."

CHAPTER 7

The ability to fly was something all elven children dreamed of from the moment they realized that some of their fae cousins had been gifted it from birth. Takayoshi, too, experienced that jealousy upon realizing that pixies in particular could flit around at will without any thought to what it meant to be able to do so. He had dreams of soaring through the air, Helio spread out beneath him like a map on a page.

The reality of such an ability was very different. Takayoshi realized the first time he had done it, he could live a thousand years and never grow accustomed to the swoop of his belly at takeoff, and the way his head spun when he landed. Nor would he ever become used to the way his muscles would bunch and ache for days after. Being a phoenix was not at all what he dreamed of as a child.

Even still, it was the most efficient way to travel from one place to another when he was alone. And he did not have the time, nor the patience, to move at the speed of a horse when Cricket's very life may hang in the balance. A thought that made Takayoshi's stomach drop far more than watching the landscape of Lunette shift and change beneath him. His breath came in steamed puffs the higher he went up the mountain toward the capital of Helio.

He realized—belatedly because he had been in such a hurry and his mind had been so preoccupied during the flight —that he had not thought of a safe way to land in Helio without attracting attention.

Foolish.

Still, needs must, he was not about to waste time circling while he thought up a good alternative. So, he took a breath, and leaned into a dive that would bring him to settle onto his taloned feet right in the main courtyard of the castle.

There was a shout, a general panic from the guards in the towers, and around the gates. The rushed sound of feet crunching in frosted grass. And Takayoshi let the phoenix fall away as one might a cloak. Shedding the feathers to the ground where they burned into ash almost as soon as they touched the snow. When they were gone, he felt a new patch of feathers lingering uncomfortably under his hair, pressed down, and shifted at an odd angle against the back of his neck. He would have to do something about that, but now was not the time.

"Where is my sister?" Takayoshi asked the first stunned guard he saw. The young person seemed to be choking on their own tongue, their eyes wide enough in their face that it looked like they may pop out of the sockets. Poor child. "My sister, the queen, where is she?"

They lifted one shaking arm to point to the north wing of the castle on the far side of the courtyard, where the queen's personal study was. *Good. We will need the privacy.*

"Thank you." Takayoshi bowed his head in respect, and started off in that direction, stride unhurried, but not sluggish. One did not run in the courtyard once they had become an adult, Uncle always said. But Takayoshi was not going to walk sedately either. There would be time for decency and decorum later. For now, he was just thankful that his appearance left the guards so shocked they had not tried to stop him.

He did not knock on Atsuko's door when he reached it, as he normally would have. Another slight against polite society, that Takayoshi thrilled in. Maybe that was why Uncle Reiji so often went against his own rules when he was frustrated. It was very satisfying.

Atsuko looked up from her desk, her mouth already open to politely scold whoever was interrupting her, but the words seemed to die on her tongue. Instead, she sat there, her mouth hanging open until Takayoshi shut the door behind himself, and made his way to her desk. His hands folded neatly behind his back.

"Your Highness, I am here to request a contingent of soldiers." Takayoshi bowed deeply, and waited until his sister cleared her throat before he rose again.

"What for?" Atsuko asked.

Takayoshi raised a brow, but he did not say anything about his sister's slip in professionalism. What did professionalism matter in the face of all that was happening around him? It did not. And Takayoshi did not have time to bother with it, not really.

"I wish to return to Lunette and aid King Cricket in his fight against Yue Sunil." Takayoshi watched as his sister's face shifted through an assortment of emotions, and settled on fond exasperation. An expression he personally found taxing. It usually meant that Atsuko was going to be softly condescending.

"Takayoshi, there is no war between King Cricket and his uncle."

"You are mistaken."

"I'm not," Atsuko said, her voice soft as if trying not to

frighten a small animal. "I just received word this morning that all has been settled between them. Sunil has received a royal pardon, and accepted the position of advisor to the king. It seems they have made amends."

"Made amends?" The words sounded foreign to his ears, and something in Takayoshi's stomach turned sour. Likely the meager food he managed to choke down in the days that passed since leaving Lunette. How long had he been gone before Sunil attacked? How long would he have had to stay to protect Cricket from him? A day? Two? It had only been four since he walked out of the dining room and taken flight.

"Yes. It seems this feud between them was all some misunderstanding. Just some–"

"No. There was no misunderstanding." Takayoshi took a deep inhale and forced his hands not to shake where they clasped one another behind his back. Still, the rage simmered under his skin, a flame that would not be blown out. What had Sunil done to Cricket to make him agree to that? Had he. . . had he threatened Becka?

"That's what it looks like, Shishi. I mean. . . it's been years. Maybe some new proof came to light that Sunil wasn't really behind the curses and Jaxith's illness after all. Maybe it was all just a misunder–"

"I was *there*, Atsuko. Sunil used me and Ignacia as leverage against Cricket to control him. He had a man hold a sword to my neck, and threaten to kill me to bring his nephew to heel. There was no *misunderstanding*. Sunil means to be king, and he will feel no remorse hurting Cricket or his daughter to do it." Takayoshi's words were quiet, but cold. He knew the truth of what happened, and he would not be swayed by whatever lie Sunil forced Cricket into telling.

"Shishi. . ." Atsuko let out a soft sigh, her shoulders hunching forward a little. She had aged since they last saw each other face to face. Running Helio alone had been hard on her. He knew he should feel something about that, guilt, maybe, but there was no room in him for it, not with all the anger still humming away in his veins. "Cricket himself pardoned Sunil. Whatever we know happened, I cannot wage war on the royal advisor, and uncle, of another kingdom's king."

Takayoshi wanted to ask *why not?* But he knew that question would go over about as well as this conversation had. Instead, he nodded once, then bowed curtly before turning to head back to the door.

"Wait. Where are you going?" Atsuko rose from her chair, the legs scraping against the wood floors, and made to follow him. "Shishi?"

"I am going to find someone who will help me, since you cannot." He did not mean for it to sound as cold as it did, but he knew the words landed like a slap across his sister's face. He heard her gasp behind him. Takayoshi knew he should apologize. He should turn back around and try to explain to his sister what was going on. But there would be time for emotions, and hurt feelings later. "Where might I find Anstice?"

"Annie?" Atsuko asked with a familiarity that made Takayoshi's jaw clench. It had been a long time, had it not?

"Yes."

"In the library. But Shishi, I don't think that she can—"

"She was there. She saw everything Sunil did while Cricket was away. She is Cricket's sister. She will know how to help him." Takayoshi did not look back, he gave another little bow of his head, then fled from the room to head toward the library. His footsteps were too loud in his ears, his blood rushing, and heart pounding in time with them. It almost drowned out the sound of the mirror alerting him to a communication in his pouch.

He ducked into an empty study room near the library and

pulled out the hand mirror. With one quick tap, Claudia and Leo's faces appeared in the glass. Their shoulders pressed so tightly that it looked like it might hurt.

"Finally." Claudia breathed. "We've been trying to get through to you off and on for days." There were dark circles under her eyes, and her glasses had been discarded somewhere.

"I have only just arrived in Helio. Tell me what has happened." Takayoshi stood in the middle of the darkened room; his eyes fixed on the faces of his two friends. The two people he left in charge of protecting Cricket. He did not blame them for their failure. How could they have done what Cricket's own army had been unable to? And he did not regret leaving them behind. They would be able to provide information, if nothing else.

"Not even an hour after your boy was crowned, Sunil barged in and said he was there to arrest Cricket under suspicion of murdering King Jaxith." Leo's tone was even, neutral, but Takayoshi could tell his jaw was clenched, his hands tightened into fists somewhere out of sight. "Estia was with him."

Ah. That was why.

"Of course the claims are ridiculous. Everyone knows Jaxith's health never really recovered from the poison Sunil gave him." Claudia scoffed, rolling her eyes. Takayoshi loved his best friend for her inability to suffer fools gladly. And for the trust she placed in Takayoshi's word above all others. Where someone else might have questioned the story he told, may have believed Sunil's lies, at least in part, Claudia saw what he said as truth.

"What is going on inside of the palace?" Takayoshi asked, ignoring the way his hands began to sweat, the mirror threatening to skid from his tight grasp. "Do you have any news on if anyone was hurt?"

"We don't." Leo shook his head, frowning.

"It seems to me that Sunil took Becka hostage. And he's likely using Cricket's people as leverage to get what he wants. We think his plan is to–"

"To rule through Cricket for a time before slowly poisoning him as he did Jaxith," a voice said from behind him. Takayoshi turned, and saw Anstice in the doorway, her figure silhouetted by the lights of the hall.

"Yeah. That's what it looks like." Claudia narrowed her eyes as if she could see who had joined them.

"Lady Dresden." Takayoshi bowed his head in respect, perhaps not as low as he would others, but Anstice did not seem to care one way or the other as she flounced in, and perched herself beside him to look at the mirror.

"Please, call me Annie. We're almost family after all," Anstice said, her voice light, and her eyes sparkling with mischief. Takayoshi tightened his jaw, and hoped when she said that she meant because he was going to marry Cricket, and not because she was going to marry his sister. Although he had a sinking suspicion it was the latter. "I heard you were looking for me. Hello everyone!"

"Who is this?" Leo's tone had turned gruff, and suspicious.

"I'm Cricket's little sister, and the daughter of Jaxith's late advisor, Marwa Dresden. My friends call me Annie." She winked, and Leo rolled his eyes. "Now, where were we?"

Claudia, Selene bless her, did not even blink, she just delved right into explaining everything she had just told Takayoshi all over again before asking, "Do you know what poison he used on Jaxith? If we know then we can sneak in an antidote maybe? It won't be much, but it should buy us time."

"I do, but he won't reuse ir." Anstice shook her head. "It wouldn't work on someone like Cricket. Especially not now that he's. . . Well. . . you know."

"A dragon?" Leo prompted, his tone flat.

"Yes. That."

"Then what would he do?" Claudia shifted in the frame, likely to grab a pen and paper so she could begin thinking of ways to combat Sunil's attack.

"He would curse Cricket. Something lingering. Something that seems innocuous, but isn't. Something tied to his magic." Anstice hummed in thought, tapping her lips with a neatly manicured fingernail. "I couldn't tell you what curse he'd choose. He had access to all of Lunette's knowledge growing up but. . ."

"But he won't pick something that Cricket could easily recognize. He'll look for something obscure. Probably something older. Something that no one would be able to break before it was too late." Claudia finished the thought for Anstice, she looked like she was doing her level best not to get too excited by the prospect of a new puzzle to solve, but it was not quite working. "I'll have my sisters pull some books, and we'll see what we can find."

"If we knew where he was hiding all this time." Leo scratched at his stubbled jaw, his brows pinched together.

"I heard," Anstice said, leaning forward and lowering her voice as if it were some great secret. Takayoshi let out an annoyed huff at the theatrics. They did not have *time* for it. But they also did not have time for him to fight with Anstice either, and whether he liked it or not, she was an ally. She still loved her brother, and he did not doubt that she would do anything in her power to keep him safe. "That he showed up with Prin Estia at his side, and a declaration that any claims he made were backed by King Craven."

"We knew that," Leo said, then grumbled something under his breath that sounded like a string of curses ending in a promise to end Craven the moment he saw him again.

Claudia deflated, her shoulders hunching a little.

Something lodged itself in Takayoshi's throat. That was

why, then. A backing from a monarch would lend credence to Sunil's claims. It would leave Cricket very little room to escape before the noose tightened around his neck.

"So," Takayoshi started, his mouth dry, tongue scraping against his teeth, "his options were execution by order of King Craven, or do whatever Sunil said."

"Yes, that is what it sounds like." All of Anstice's dramatics had fallen to the wayside, her own face contorting into something more. . . *anguished* than Takayoshi had ever seen it before. He should not have been surprised to know this hurt her as much as it did him, but he was.

"We need to get him out of there," Claudia said.

"He cannot leave his daughter behind. We will have to form a plan to help both of them escape." Takayoshi gripped the mirror more tightly, the edges cutting into his palm.

"We'll need decoys." Anstice dropped into one of the chairs, and grabbed a bit of paper from the center of it along with a pencil. "We can't have Sunil finding out about this until Cricket and his daughter are well and truly safe. Maybe not even then."

"Why? Do you think he'll–? He wouldn't hurt the people in the palace." Leo's voice was faint, like he could not believe what he was hearing. Like the idea that someone who wanted to rule would harm the very people he was trying to reign over in petty revenge against his own family was not possible. Leo had never met Sunil. Although he had met *Craven*, so Takayoshi did not know why this surprised him.

"He would. So we will have to be careful." Takayoshi settled into a chair beside Anstice. "You know the palace well."

"I do. I can get your people in, and get Cricket out." Anstice's hand flew over the page, neat and precise handwriting flowing out behind it to form a list before she paused, frowning. "But. . ."

"But we will still need someone to reach out to those on the inside. To make sure they are ready with a decoy." Takayoshi opened and closed the fist of his free hand for a moment. "Leo, see what you can do? You are the best we have at infiltration."

"Right." Leo straightened his posture.

"Claudia, we will need a spell of some kind to create a decoy."

"I hate to say this, Yoshi," Claudia said, biting at her bottom lip, "but we'll neeed people pretending to be them inside of the palace if we're going to trick Sunil for any length of time."

"A glamor then." Anstice's lips crept up into an expression that Takayoshi supposed some might consider a smile, but he did not. It was. . . sharper than that. More manipulative. "Leo, see if you can get in touch with Youta. She's the head of staff."

"What about Ignacia?" Takayoshi ran down the list of people he met while in the palace, and settled on the image of Youta standing before their cell with sandwiches cut into neat triangles, the crusts removed. She had just been a kitchen maid then, but she seemed very capable. And trustworthy.

"She's the head of the guard now. Sunil will be watching her too closely. But he never did have enough respect for the servants to realize the danger they posed him. That's how I got him the first time." Anstice's smile crept further up her face, growing a little manic around the edges. Takayoshi forced himself to look away from it. He would not want to be on the receiving end of Anstice's fury.

"You two begin on that. Anstice and I will work on the map in the meantime. We will reconvene in forty-eight hours."

"Right," Claudia and Leo said as one, then the connection

was closed, and the mirror reflected only Takayoshi and Anstice.

"I know you don't trust me," Anstice murmured into the stillness left behind. "I know you're still angry with me for what I did to him back then but. . . But I want to make up for it. I want to be. . . I'd like it if we were friends, Takayoshi."

"I will consider your apology when I have My Prince and his daughter safe with me." Takayoshi knew it was petty, but it was the best he could give her at the moment.

"A niece." Anstice let out a long breath that turned into a soft whistle, seeming to decide to ignore the fact she had not yet been forgiven. "I have a niece. What's she like?"

"Lively." The corners of Takayoshi's lips turned up into a small, soft smile. He had only seen Becka for a few minutes, but he had seen enough of her and Cricket to know the kind of relationship they had, and that she was well cared for. Cricket had done for Becka what he was unable to. He would never stop being grateful for that. "Very much like her father."

"Good. I'm glad. We need more people like him in the world."

Takayoshi could not help but agree.

CHAPTER 8

"We have to get you out of here," Ignacia said the moment the door to his quarters shut behind them. It was the only place they had any illusion of privacy in the palace now. The only place where Uncle or one of his guards was not a constant shadow. And all that did was make the space seem small. Claustrophobic.

"I can't leave." Cricket shook his head, dropping onto the end of his bed in a slump. Stars, but he was tired. *So* tired. It had only been a couple of weeks since Uncle Sunil had taken over, and it seemed like Cricket hadn't gotten any rest in that time. Uncle was forever dragging him through the streets of the capital to show the people that they had made up, or making him meet with some dignitary or another to discuss trade negotiations, or simply harassing him into rerouting tax funds however he wanted. Cricket wasn't sure how it all fit together, not yet, but he was going to find out.

"Can't or won't?" Ignacia asked, and Cricket looked up at her with a frown. They both knew that question was deeply unfair. They both knew it wasn't even really a question.

"If I go, I take what little protection I can provide you,

and the others in the palace, and my people, with me. I *can't*." The word caught like a hook in his chest, making it hard to breathe. He couldn't leave. He knew he couldn't. The moment he did, Uncle would take it out on those around him. The people of the castle who had taken care of Cricket all of his life, who were there when Father died, they would all suffer. He couldn't leave them to that. What kind of king would he be if he did? "At least not until our knights can return from the front. And I won't sacrifice the relief effort because of my discomfort."

"He's hurting you." Ignacia's words left her a little strangled, like she was trying to hold back a sob. Cricket looked down at his hands so he couldn't see the glassy sheen to her eyes.

"I'm all right." He was. Uncle had done nothing to hurt him physically, not yet at least. It was just his pride that was wounded, nothing more. At least, that's what he told himself.

"You haven't been eating."

"I'm fine, Iggy. I promise." Cricket shrugged off her concern, and lifted his chin to meet her gaze, hoping the eye contact would convince her. It likely wouldn't, he knew about the dark circles that ringed his eyes. He knew how his face sagged with exhaustion. "Besides, we need to know what his plan is. We can't leave here without knowing what he intends to do with his new position of power."

"I think that's fairly obvious, he means to rule Lunette." Ignacia snorted, moving to settle next to him on the end of the bed which dipped under her weight and nearly sent him knocking into her. "Once he's gotten you out of the way."

"It's too early for that yet." Cricket sighed, running his fingers through his unbrushed hair till they caught in the knots left behind. He hadn't had time to braid it today, and it would no doubt take hours to untangle now. "There's something else. Something he's gearing up for."

"Too early for what?"

"For him to get me out of the way. He still needs me as the face of everything, for the time being. We have time." They did, he told himself. They had months, perhaps, before he finally outlived his usefulness to Uncle, maybe more. Although the words sat like acid on his tongue. The thought of only being seen as a tool by his own family, one of the people who helped raise him, it made him want to throw up. How wrong he'd been about Uncle. How little he'd seen even when it was right in front of his own eyes. How he'd loved–

No. No, he wouldn't think of that. He wouldn't think of the happy memories.

Ignacia leaned into him, her shoulder a warm press against his own. A comforting weight at his side. It was almost enough to lull him into relaxing, *almost*. If there was another weight at his other side. Another shoulder pressed into his, as there had been all of his life, it might have been. His heart ached with the memory of he, Ignacia, and Anstice sitting just like this after a particularly hard day. Of them providing comfort in the only way Cricket knew how to accept it, through silence and the solid press of their shoulders against his. A gentle reminder that he was not alone in this. That they would help him shoulder the weight of the world. But Anstice was gone now.

"We have time," he repeated, mostly to convince himself.

"How much time?" Ignacia's voice was quiet, like she hadn't meant for the words to slip free from her lips. But they were out there now, floating around the space between them, and making it hard for Cricket to breathe again.

"Plenty, I'm sure." Cricket wasn't sure. He wasn't sure how long Uncle would be content to rule from the shadows. He wasn't sure how long before Uncle took matters into his own hands and killed Cricket in his sleep. But he needed to be reassuring in this situation. He needed to convince Ignacia, even if he couldn't convince himself, that he was all right.

"What about Becka?"

"Becka's fine, for now. Uncle won't even go near her. He's afraid she'll latch on like a barnacle. And the men he has stationed around her just watch." Cricket chuckled on a long exhale, and scrubbed at his face with his hands, wincing when calloused fingers caught the scar on the side of his face. It didn't hurt. But it was a reminder. A symbol of what he'd already given up for his people. What he'd continue to give up for them. "He's not going to hurt her. Not if he wants to live to see the next full moon."

Ignacia didn't say anything, she didn't even nod. She just pressed her shoulder more firmly into his arm, hard enough that the bone dug into his muscle, leaving behind a warm ache.

"If you can, get a message to Youta. I want her to send someone trustworthy into the town, see if they can get a message out to our allies in Hermes. I need to know where we stand as far as things go after the coronation."

"What about Helio? If Yoshi knew—"

"He'd blaze in here with a sword, and a glare, and Uncle would slice down half of the castle's residents in retaliation." They were outnumbered, at least for the time being. Cricket had to bide his time. "I don't want to start a war, I just want information. I want to know how the other nobles from the coronation see me after what happened. Their opinion will give us some kind of gauge as to how long before Uncle makes his move." Cricket didn't say, *how long I have to live.* But the words hung there between them in the air, unsaid, and no less suffocating for it.

"You should get a message to him." Ignacia sounded almost disappointed in him. "He'd be able to help."

"I don't *want* his help. This is a family matter, and we'll handle it on our own!" Cricket snapped, his head whipping around so he could fix Ignacia with a hard look.

She sat up, and let out a little sigh. "All right. I'll speak to Youta, and see what we can find out."

"Thank you. Now, I'm going to bed. I'll see you in the morning." He didn't wait for Ignacia to respond. He rose from his bed and headed to the bathroom to get changed into his pajamas. By the time he returned, she was gone, and he let himself sink down under the covers, even though he knew sleep would likely never come.

THEY DIDN'T HAVE AS much time as Cricket thought.

And he realized far too late, as Uncle's words sank into his mind a few days later. "I'm sorry. *What?*"

"There are some outliers along the coast. I want the dragon to go and put the fear of Selene in them again." Uncle shrugged. He was sitting behind Father's desk, Cricket's desk —the *king's* desk—in the study. His feet kicked up on the edge, looking entirely relaxed with what he was asking Cricket to do. Which was, in Cricket's mind, an act of war on his own people.

"No," Cricket said, his voice barely above a whisper. He wouldn't. He *couldn't* do something like that. Not to those who had put their faith in him.

"I think you're misunderstanding me, *nephew*," Uncle said, dropping his feet and leaning forward. Cricket hated the way he said "nephew" now. It made something in his chest hurt. "This is not a request. You will do this, or I will have you executed."

"Perhaps that would be best." Cricket felt his shoulders

threaten to hunch inwards. He didn't want to die. But if his choices were die or use his powers against his people, then he'd take whatever death Uncle Sunil planned to give him. He forced his posture straighter, lifting his chin.

"You'd leave your daughter an orphan?"

"She won't be an orphan. She'll have her aunt." Cricket was positive of that. Ignacia wasn't great with children, but she liked Becka. And she'd try, if it were Cricket's child. She'd do her best. And maybe. . . No. He wouldn't think of Yoshi now. It wasn't the time.

Uncle frowned. It would seem Cricket had called his bluff. Not that Cricket meant to, really. "If you don't do this, it'll be your staff that suffers for it. We'll start with that head of the maids. . . what's her name?"

"Youta," one of the guards supplied helpfully.

"Yes. Thank you. We'll start with Youta. She has children of her own, doesn't she? And how well do you think she'd be able to perform her duties if she were, say. . . missing a hand or two?"

"You wouldn't." Cricket narrowed his eyes on Uncle. But he knew better. He knew better than anyone that Uncle had no qualms about hurting people who he deemed as less than. Anyone not born of royal blood was fair game.

Uncle raised his brows, leaning back in his chair again, his hands folded over his stomach. Entirely relaxed, even as he threatened the very people who depended upon him for their livelihoods. Even as he forced his own family into doing something against their will. It made Cricket sick. It made him sick, and violent. It took everything he had within himself to swallow down on the urge to let the dragon free, and slice through Uncle like an over ripe tomato. He needed to bide his time. He needed to understand Uncle Sunil's plans. He needed to wait until their army returned from the relief effort. He needed to know that Becka was safe.

"Very well." Cricket clenched his hands at his sides, feeling the way the talons cut into skin, blood trickling down his knuckles to patter against the floor. "When do we leave, Uncle?"

"Uncle?" Uncle tilted his head in question.

"Your Highness," Cricket corrected, but the words tasted like dirt on his tongue as he ground them out through his teeth. "When do we leave, Your Highness?"

"Better." Uncle's smug expression was almost enough to make Cricket see red. Almost enough to draw the dragon forth. But then there was the reminder of the damage Uncle's men would do to his people should he try. Even if he should succeed in killing Uncle, Cricket had little doubt that Uncle chose men who would be happy enough to paint the palace in blood without their leader controlling them. Or, and this was worse, show the people how their dragon king lost control of himself in a rage, and killed his uncle. Not that what Uncle was asking him to do wouldn't vilify him, but no one would die. "We leave in a week's time. I suggest you get some rest between then and now."

"Yes, Your Highness." Cricket dipped into a bow that was just low enough to keep Uncle Sunil from flying off into a rage, but shallow enough to show Uncle there was no respect behind the gesture. It was funny what someone could display through a mere bow. Yoshi taught him that.

Ignacia was waiting for him in the hall, and he could tell from the pinch of her brows that they would be *Discussing* this. That they needed a plan. A better one than simply running away.

The door to his quarters shut behind them, and Cricket tilted his head to lead Ignacia to the bathroom where he turned the water on in the tub, hoping to hide the sounds of their voices.

"If I leave, he'll kill everyone here." Cricket sat on the

edge of the tub, his shoulders hunched forward as all of the fight left him boneless. "And if I stay, he'll use me as a weapon against my own people."

"How long do we have?" Ignacia paced, her hands brushing through her loose auburn hair. She'd taken to wearing it down, likely to hide her sour expressions every time she was within Uncle's line of sight.

"A week."

"Right." Ignacia stopped, her hands lowered to her sides where they clenched at the loose trousers on her hips. "I'll speak to Youta. We haven't sent anyone into the city yet, but we should have some answers for you by tomorrow afternoon."

Cricket nodded. "If I go, Becka has to go with me. I can't leave her behind."

"Of course." Ignacia scoffed, rolling her eyes. "I'll speak to Qiren about preparing her things."

"What about you? What about the others? If I'm gone. . ." Cricket had already said what would happen if he was gone. He knew Uncle wouldn't hesitate.

"We'll think of something. But our first priority is getting you and Becka to safety. Everyone else. . . they'll understand, Cricket. They know what you are. They know what would happen if he used you that way. You have to– They'll understand."

"I hope you're right. But we have no way of knowing for sure. There are some who seem . . . *happy* he's back." Cricket leaned forward, hunching over his knees, and letting out a long breath.

Ignacia shot him a baleful glance.

Cricket chuckled softly, and said again, "I hope you're right."

CHAPTER 9

"I've heard that he's a changeling. Put in place by a demon to overthrow Selene's kingdom and bring us all to ruin," Uncle Reiji said, his hand tightened into a fist around his teacup. Takayoshi was unsure how they had gotten onto this topic, but he wished that Uncle Reiji would be quiet. Especially as Uncle Reji seemed grossly misinformed.

Takayoshi's gaze cut to Anstice who was scowling behind a wide-open fan, careful to keep the expression from Uncle's view. But there was murder in her eyes. The likes of which Takayoshi was glad would likely never be directed his way.

"Superstitious nonsense," Takayoshi said, forcing his voice to remain steady. It was a struggle. Especially when Uncle Reiji snorted into his cup of tea, but Takayoshi managed it. "Dragons are not demons."

"Shishi's right. In the legends, dragons were sent down by the gods to protect us from the wild magic of the world. They were never seen as evil." Atsuko smiled serenely, reaching over to fill Uncle Reiji's teacup.

"The history books have them as great protectors."

Anstice nodded, lowering her fan long enough to take a sip from her tea. She was smiling again, the expression almost fond as she turned it on Atsuko. Takayoshi wished he had not noticed.

"Either way, dragons are long gone," Uncle continued, not listening to his children scold him for his ignorance and small mindedness. "And what do we really know of this child? Of his lineage? He's not of royal blood."

Anstice's grip on her fan tightened enough that it shook. She lowered it into her lap, her head ducking to follow it so that she could hide behind her long curly hair.

"We know that he was raised to be Jaxith's successor," Atsuko said, her voice kind, but ultimately non-confrontational. She did not want a fight with Uncle Reiji. A sentiment that Takayoshi could not say he shared.

"We know that he was a good prince." Takayoshi set aside his full cup. It had gone cold, and though he could likely heat it with just a touch, he did not want to. He wanted to end the conversation before it really got going, and slip away where he could make contact with Claudia and Leo again. He wanted to go out into the courtyard and practice his sword forms until his arms were numb. He wanted to disappear into the library where he could research any and every curse Sunil might use on Cricket. But no, it was family tea, and he was stuck with Uncle Reiji in the too stuffy receiving room of his quarters, until Uncle had enough of Takayoshi and sent him away.

"We know that when someone attacked his people with curses, he risked his own life to go out and save them. We know that in the past few years, while Jaxith's health has declined, he has acted in his stead. We know that during that time Cricket proved himself a fair and just ruler. And that when it came to it, he could not kill his own uncle who meant him harm." Takayoshi let his words wash from him slow, and even, as if he were disinterested in the topic when he was anything but.

"That's hearsay!" Uncle pointed at Takayoshi, his finger shaking just the slightest. "I know Sunil. We grew up together. He isn't capable of—"

"Regardless of what Yue Sunil may have been capable of as a teenager, the fact stands, he poisoned his brother, and tried to kill his nephew." Takayoshi's gaze narrowed on his uncle, challenging him to argue further.

"Hearsay! Rumor! Speculation!"

"Which is exactly what you were just citing when saying that Cricket is a demon spawned to bring ruin to the great kingdoms." It was a struggle but somehow, Takayoshi kept himself from yelling. He was *not* able to keep his touch from burning a hole in the linen napkin across his knee, but that was all right.

"You're just being contrary." Uncle Reiji rolled his eyes.

"No. I am being honest. You ought to check your biases, Uncle." Takayoshi rose from his seat and bowed deeply to Anstice and Atsuko, then he turned on his heel without bothering to bow to his uncle.

"Rude boy!" Uncle Reiji shouted after him, but Takayoshi was already in the hall, and did not care to listen any longer.

His steps were hurried as he made his way to his own quarters, and it was something of a relief to slam his back against the door, holding it shut lest his uncle's words follow him there. The sound of the door slamming echoed in the quiet of his rooms, but it felt easier to breathe there than it had all afternoon with Uncle Reiji in front of him. Taking a moment to settle his nerves, Takayoshi headed for his desk, and pulled the mirror from his travel pouch where it had found a permanent home.

His fingers drummed against the map Anstice had drawn for them as he waited for someone to pick up on the other side. It felt like forever before Claudia's face rippled into view.

"Sunil's smear campaign has spread to Helio," Takayoshi said, the words rushing out of him.

"Styx, it's moving faster than we expected." Claudia's brows met in the middle, a wrinkle forming between them. She was right, it was moving far too fast. Someone must be helping it along. Craven perhaps. Or Estia and zir network of contacts. "If it's gotten that far, I don't know who can be relied upon to provide him with sanctuary."

"I will speak to Atsuko. There must be others who see what Sunil is doing as we do." Of that, he was not sure. Takayoshi wanted to have faith in his fellow royalty, but there was a reason he stepped down from being king. Because politics, and that life had not suited him. He would never have been able to smile to the faces of his enemies as Atsuko did. "If not, then he will find sanctuary here."

Claudia nodded almost absently, her eyes not looking at him in the mirror, but at something off to the side. Likely her notes. "I've had no luck on the curse so far, but I figure that's a bridge we can cross when we come to it. From what Annie said, whatever Sunil uses will be slow acting. It'll give us time to counteract it."

"What information have you had from inside the castle?"

Everything about Claudia went still, even her breath it seemed.

"Claudia. What is it?"

"Sunil means to use Cricket as a weapon against his own people. Likely to further his claims that Cricket's dangerous."

"He means to make his own people afraid of him?" Takayoshi's hand tightened into a fist in his lap, but he forced his fingers to unclench. He did not need to burn through another pair of trousers. The royal seamstress was already quite tired of seeing him.

"I'm sure he realizes the only way to really have Lunette as his own is to kill Cricket and all that he stands for." Claudia's words were almost absent, like she was not paying attention to them as they left her lips. She winced when she seemed to realize what she said. "I'm sorry, Yoshi. I didn't mean—"

"No. You are correct in your assessment. It would take an army to fell a dragon. And he will not be able to raise an army, a real one, against Cricket so long as his people think he is good. He needs to make Cricket into a monster."

"Exactly."

"He is being so obvious about all of this, I cannot believe that people would—"

"If Cricket burned down a village or two, people would believe it," Claudia said, making the breath stutter in Takayoshi's chest. *Yes. That would do it.* "Maybe not the towns that he visited, maybe not the people who have met him. But Lunette is large, and even when he was traveling. . ." She let the words hang there, her shoulders slumping forward. "He'll need protection when he leaves here. Leo and I can—"

"No. I need you to stay there. I need you to watch over his people." Takayoshi frowned, resisting the urge to run his fingers through his hair in a vain attempt to alleviate the weight that had settled onto his shoulders. "If they are lost because of Cricket there will be no coming back for him. Even if we do find his pearl. He will— He will—" The words choked him. Lodging somewhere in his throat.

"All right. All right." Claudia lifted a hand as if she maybe wanted to pat his shoulder, but could not. And although the touch had not happened, Takayoshi felt the comfort of it just the same. "Besides, they'll need all the help they can get to maintain the ruse for as long as possible."

"If you are found out—"

"You let us worry about that, Yoshi." Claudia's lips tilted

up into a smirk, and she winked at him. "Leo and I may not be a phoenix, or a dragon for that matter, but we're not incapable of protecting ourselves. We'll be fine."

"Good." Takayoshi let his muscles relax. It was a relief to think that Leo and Claudia would be all right even without him there to protect them. "Cricket will have to travel here on his own. A man and his child traveling with an armed guard would be more conspicuous than a refugee traveling alone."

"He'll need to disguise himself to escape."

"Yes. I believe Anstice has found a potion that can do just that."

"She has. We'll have it brewed within the day. In the meantime, you do what you can to make sure your prince has a soft place to land." Claudia smiled at him with an ease that Takayoshi was not sure was appropriate for the situation. But it was nice to know that even in the face of this she still could.

"I will." Takayoshi's lips twitched, threatening to turn up as well, but he swallowed down the urge. "I will check in with you later about the potion. Atsuko should be done having tea with Uncle now, and I can find her in her study."

"Good luck." Claudia gave him a little wave, and the mirror rippled. His own face stared back at him, eyes narrowed, lips pressed into a firm line. Takayoshi took a breath, forcing himself to count an inhale and an exhale before he tucked the mirror away and rose. His sister would not deny him this, he was sure.

ATSUKO FIDDLED with the ends of her hair, her face set into an expression of sadness as she watched her older brother stand before her, stone-faced, and serious. "What if he doesn't seek refuge here, Shishi?"

"Then we must ensure that the other rulers will provide him with sanctuary." Takayoshi was not above flying off to every castle, and banging the door down until the other kings and queens saw him. If that was what it would take to ensure that Cricket and Becka were safe, then that was what he would do. "I am sure you could convince them of such a thing."

Atsuko sighed, her mouth slipping into a tired line. "I'm sure I could, given enough time. But you've said I have a week. You understand it takes longer than that to send a letter to even our closest allies."

"Then you can contact them via mirror."

"And what would you have me say, Takayoshi?" Atsuko's shoulders sagged a little, head leaning back against her chair.

"I would have you tell them the truth."

"I can't tell them that Sunil is lying about everything and they should take in the man who many are saying murdered his father."

"But it is the truth." Takayoshi frowned, his chin tilting back, teeth grinding in frustration. "That is what is happening."

"It is. But you know as well as I do that it's all about perception. And the perception right now is. . . It's not good for Cricket. It would be best if you made sure he came here."

"He may not want to." The words tasted like burnt tea on his tongue, but Takayoshi said them anyway. Because it was the truth. "We fought the last time we saw one another. I do not think he would seek me out for help."

"Oh, Shishi." Atsuko sighed, shaking her head. "Well, I

hope your friends can convince him otherwise. I don't think it will be safe for him to go anywhere else."

"I will have them relay the message." Takayoshi nodded, ignoring the way his chest clenched at that news. Cricket loved life, he loved people, and Sunil had turned anyone he could against Cricket. It soured what little food Takayoshi had eaten in his stomach. "We will offer sanctuary if he comes here?"

"We will." Atsuko nodded.

"Thank you, sister."

"Of course."

CHAPTER 10

Sleep did not come easily to Cricket in the days leading up to their assault on the village. The knowledge of what he would have to do weighed on him, making him heavy, sluggish, and tired. But when he laid in bed at night, sleep was illusive. His mind raced with anything and everything that could go wrong. Scenes of blood, and screaming, played out behind his eyelids over and over again until eventually it was hard to breathe lying down and he had to sit up in bed.

Many mornings, Ignacia would find him like that, curled up against his headboard, his knees tucked to his chin. Half asleep. Not enough to really rest, but enough to keep him going, he supposed. Then the day would start again. The planning would start again.

He was no closer to understanding what Uncle was up to than he'd been days ago. But he thought he was starting to see the shape of it coming together. If he had more time, maybe he could figure it out, but he was rapidly running out of days.

"I won't let him force you to do this," Ignacia said like she had any power to make it stop. She didn't. They both knew that. Their only option was for him to escape, just as they'd planned, but then what?

"I don't have a choice." Cricket clutched at the legs of his trousers so hard he could feel the seams creak under his grip.

"You could run." Youta's tone was calm, but Cricket could see how the last few weeks had aged her. Her posture sagged where before it had been upright at all times. He knew he didn't look much better.

"We've had this talk. I can't, not yet." Cricket shook his head, leaning back in his chair, his head hanging over the back of it to stare up at the ceiling. It hurt his neck, but that ache was better than the numbness which slowly seemed to be taking over the rest of him. The army wasn't coming, they'd received word days ago. He didn't know how his uncle had managed it, but they'd been attacked while helping with the relief aid, leaving too many of them wounded to be of any real help if they did manage to make it to the capital in time. What little hope Cricket had was dwindling down to nothing. He needed to get Becka out of Lunette, before something terrible happened. "After this first attack, we'll have a little bit before he wants me to do it again. We can use that."

"Otherwise, he'll realize the person you've left in your place isn't you. Yes, we know." Ignacia rubbed at the bridge of her nose, pinching it between two fingers.

"It'll put you all in immediate danger. We need time to evacuate as many from the palace as we can. Where are we with that, Youta?"

"The magistrate of Luna has been very helpful. Between them and the other villages you've helped we should be able to house the refugees from the palace easily. Although I don't think Sunil will be looking for them." Youta shook her head. She was likely right, when Uncle Sunil realized Cricket was gone, it wouldn't be his palace staff Uncle would be looking for, it would be Cricket himself. There would be a manhunt. Uncle Sunil would turn him into a criminal, and turn the kingdom upside down in his search.

"I think he means to make it look like you've gone insane." Ignacia's voice shook with barely contained fury. "Then no one will fight for you when he takes the crown."

"If you do this, the damage to your reputation will be done, Your Highness." Youta bowed her head, hiding her expression in her hair, but her shoulders shook with a choked off sob.

"It doesn't matter."

"It does!" Youta looked up, her eyes blazing through the tears. "Your people will hate you. You and Jaxith should have exposed him fully when all of this came to light then there would be no question–"

"Father didn't want to completely ruin his brother's reputation, I couldn't go against him, even if I'd wanted to." Which he didn't, went unsaid. "And there have been many hated kings in history." Cricket didn't bother to sit up from where his head was still tilted back. His neck was really starting to hurt, but it didn't matter. None of it mattered. There was a strange. . . distance between himself and the events around him. A hopelessness that he couldn't identify the source of. Maybe the dragon was driving him insane. "I'll reign for a couple of decades, do the best that I can, and when Becka is old enough she'll take over. She'll be the ruler I can't be."

"So you've given up." Cricket could hear Ignacia's voice trembling again, the fury burning through her body only just contained. He imagined she wanted to grab him and shake him until his teeth rattled. It wouldn't be the first time. And he couldn't blame her for the desire. But this was the hand he had been dealt, and he was playing it the only way he knew how.

"I don't see where I have much other choice, Iggy. I can't let him hurt all of you. And what will he do if I don't do this? How would *he* punish this village? At least this way I have some control over what happens, I can ensure no one gets hurt."

Ignacia groaned loudly, throwing her hands up.

"I'm not letting you go down without a fight," Youta said, her voice hard. "People talk, and I'll make sure they're saying the right things."

"Feel free to try." Cricket sat up, rubbing at the back of his neck to ease the ache. It did little to help. But he likely deserved the impending headache for the betrayed and hurt looks two of the four most important women in his life were giving him. "You two should get to bed. We leave in a few short hours. And once we're back, we'll need to set things in motion quickly here."

"I already have the first few servants ready to leave."

"Won't Sunil notice if he's suddenly short staffed?" Ignacia frowned.

"No. I'm staying behind, so are some of the other older staff members. We'll ensure things stay running as smoothly as possible." Youta's lips were pressed into a thin, determined line. "You leave that to me. Just worry about getting His Highness and the princess to safety."

THE FOLLOWING day dawned too bright, and too early. A headache had formed at some point behind Cricket's eyes, likely during the third round of discussing the plan with Youta and Ignacia. He didn't want to know where his people were headed, or when they were leaving, but he did need to know they would be safe. Otherwise, all of his efforts would be wasted. He trusted Youta and Ignacia to ensure that wouldn't happen.

Still, there was the issue of Youta and Ignacia, and the small team of staff who had agreed to stay on to keep the palace running smoothly. He didn't like it. The thought of leaving them behind sat like lead in his stomach. But he knew there was little other choice. He had to at least get Becka to safety. Then he could return for the rest of them. They understood that.

Cricket yawned into his elbow, forcing his posture into something that was insolent, and nonchalant. Not at all what he felt. Not at all giving away the tension that hummed under his skin like a live vein of magic.

The village of Artemis loomed atop a cliff face overlooking the sea of Selene. It was a small place, the population hardly more than a hundred or so. And Cricket couldn't see how this village in particular could pose a threat to Uncle Sunil's plans. But he supposed it didn't really matter. Not in the long run. He'd send money to help them rebuild when all of this was finished. He only wished he could have evacuated before he and Uncle showed up. But that would have looked too suspicious.

"What did the people of Artemis do?" Cricket asked, his feet flexing in his boots on the dry road. He had to ask. He needed to know. If he could. Not that it would stop what was to come, but maybe it would give him a better understanding of what his uncle meant to do.

"They have information I want." Uncle Sunil shrugged, as if that were slight enough to bring devastation to someone's home. It was not, in Cricket's mind.

"Then why not ask nicely?"

"You really are just a child, aren't you?" The words made Cricket bristle. He was anything but, hadn't been since he left home all of those years ago to save his people from their own king's brother. Teeth gnashed at his cheek to keep from saying as much.

"What information is it you want?" Cricket turned his head to fix his uncle with a pleading look. He didn't honestly think he could sway Uncle. But he could try. Maybe buy the people of Artemis time. "Perhaps it's something I found while on my travels. I could–"

"Shut up!" Uncle Sunil spat, his arm swinging out to back-hand Cricket with a blow so hard it made Cricket stumble, and left a stinging pain in its wake, his teeth rattling against each other.

Cricket took a breath, squeezing his eyes shut for a moment to force away any pain that might linger on his face, and opened his eyes again.

"You can't make me do this," he said in a voice full of more certainty than he felt. His jaw tight around the words.

"No. But if you don't, you know what will happen."

"There is no one with us for you to threaten, Uncle. You left them all at home." Cricket smiled, showing pointed teeth as his pupils narrowed to slits. He wouldn't use the dragon against Uncle Sunil or his men, but Uncle didn't know that.

Uncle jerked his head, and several men surrounded Cricket suddenly. One clamped an iron cuff round his neck, and the others held him in place. The iron forced the dragon back down, under his skin, where it roared in frustration. Then one of the men swung a fist at Cricket's jaw, and he didn't have time to duck, or think before the group of them took turns punching and kicking him. Each blow landed heavier than the last. And all Cricket could do was curl in on himself to protect the softest parts of his body.

It lasted. . . it lasted for what seemed like forever. Cricket lost count of how many blows they landed before his uncle finally called them off with a murmured, "Enough. Sit him up."

Cricket was forced onto his knees again. His head yanked back by his hair so Uncle could stare down into his face. The iron around his neck burned into the tender skin at the base of his scalp, but he didn't so much as wince.

"Continue being a petulant child, and I'll let them do that to that pretty little girl of yours. She wasn't built for fighting like you were. I wonder how many blows she'd be able to take before she lost consciousness."

"I hate you." Cricket spat, venom sharpening every word to a point. But they didn't cut, because Uncle Sunil didn't care if the only family he had left thought him despicable.

"Good. Then we're finally getting somewhere." Uncle patted Cricket's cheek, making the bruise along his jaw sting. "Cut his hair."

"What?" Cricket jerked away from his uncle's touch.

"If you're going to act like a beast," Uncle Sunil said, tone almost affectionate. "I'm going to treat you like one. It's in the way of the collar."

"We wouldn't want that." Forced bravado, that's what that was. It tasted like bile on his tongue, but Cricket wouldn't give Uncle Sunil the satisfaction of seeing how frightened he was of being cut off from the dragon. Of how he'd grown used to feeling the creature under his skin, always waiting.

"No. We wouldn't." Uncle stepped back, and Cricket barely had a moment to register the feeling of a blade pressing lightly against the back of his skull before his long hair began to fall to the ground in thick clumps. It took too long, long enough for Uncle Sunil to grow impatient and stalk off to do something else, but eventually Cricket was surrounded by a nest of midnight blue hair. He hadn't even noticed the first few tears as they burned tracks down his face, but they cooled then against his skin, making themselves known.

"Make sure to gather up as much of it as you can. We wouldn't want it falling into the wrong hands." Uncle twisted a long strand of hair around his fingers idly upon his return. There was a gleam in Uncle Sunil's eyes that made dread squeeze like a fist around Cricket's lungs, making it hard to breathe.

"Now, nephew, we're going to remove the collar, and you're going to go scare the living daylights out of the people of Artemis. You don't have to hurt anyone," Uncle said, condescension dripping from every word. "But maybe burn down a couple of buildings. Give them a real fright. Do you think you can do that?"

Cricket nodded weakly.

IF HE'D THOUGHT the dragon would spare him having to witness his own actions, Cricket had been wrong. It allowed him to remain awake, conscious, even for all he was no longer in control of his very limbs. The screaming echoed through his mind, ringing in his ears. One would think he might go numb from the pain of it, that eventually he'd be able to tune it out, one would be wrong.

Another building collapsed in on itself, an inn, or a home, he couldn't tell which, and the family ran screaming from inside. A woman clutching a babe in her arms, took one look at him, her eyes wide, and fell to her knees. She begged, although he couldn't make out the words, he understood the sentiment. But he couldn't stop. Not until Uncle Sunil had gotten what he wanted. Not until the dragon was finished.

The dragon's rage had simmered for weeks, waiting to be unleashed, and now that it was, there was nothing to do but bear witness to the destruction of Cricket's legacy.

THE SCREAMS WERE WORSE than the smell of the village burning, Cricket realized. The screams were what would haunt him for the rest of his life. The image of people running, with full abandon, their eyes jerking up to him in the sky in terror. It felt like a nightmare, but the ache from his still healing wounds was a reminder that it wasn't. It was real. All of it. And he was the monster they were afraid of. The one they would blame for this. The one those children would see in their nightmares.

When it was done, Uncle Sunil went into the village and spoke to the people. Cricket couldn't hear what he was saying over the echoing of the screams in his ears. He couldn't tell if Uncle was apologizing for his nephew's behavior. Or if he was demanding they provide him with whatever he had asked for before, lest he sick the dragon on them again. It didn't matter. Like Youta said, the damage was done.

The ride back to the capital was a blur. And Cricket didn't really come back to himself until he was sitting in the floor of Becka's room with her bundled up in his lap, sobbing into his chest.

"It's okay little sunflower. Papa's okay," he soothed, rocking her gently, his hand rubbing slow circles into her back. "Everything will be okay now."

"It will be," Ignacia agreed, suddenly at his shoulder. Or maybe she had been there the whole time and he just hadn't noticed. "Because we're getting you and your papa out of here. Tonight."

"Tonight? But Professor Qiren hasn't even—"

"Professor Qiren didn't have to," another voice called, and when Cricket looked over Ignacia's shoulder he found a brown-skinned woman with smiling eyes behind spectacles, and short cropped hair. "I made up a potion that'll allow us to impersonate you and your daughter. Ignacia will have to take it, she's the one who knows you best."

Ignacia nodded. "And Leo will take my place amongst the guards."

"He will."

"Us. . . who?" Cricket blinked, his eyes jerking from the woman to Ignacia and then back. He recognized her, but there had been so many people coming and going from the palace lately he couldn't place her.

"Apologies, Your Highness. I'm Claudia Durante. I'm your. . . Well, I'm Yoshi's best friend." Claudia smiled, her head tilting to the side. "Well, one of them. But we don't have a lot of time for introductions. Yoshi can explain everything to you when you see him again. Until then, perhaps we should retire to your rooms?"

"I uh. . ." Cricket looked back to Ignacia, but she showed no visible sign that Claudia was a threat. In fact, she seemed to be studiously avoiding looking at Claudia altogether. Strange. "Yes, I think that would be best. I'll need to pack."

"Professor Qiren has already packed a bag for Becka, it's under your bed." Ignacia reached to take the little girl from his arms, but he clung to her, pressing his face into her hair.

"I've got her."

"All right." Ignacia took him by the elbows, and helped him to his feet, balancing Becka carefully on one hip. "Maybe you should walk Becka?"

"No!" Becka's hands tightened on Cricket's torn and stained tunic.

"I've got her." Cricket repeated, narrowing his gaze on Ignacia, and she backed away, hands in the air.

"Let's go then," Claudia chirped, bouncing on her toes as she held the door for them. "Youta and Leo have cleared a path for us back to your quarters, but I don't know how long it'll last."

Cricket dipped his head in thanks, and followed her out into the hall, Ignacia close behind them.

CHAPTER 11

"After what he did, if he doesn't come here, I can't guarantee protection for him. Shishi, I'm sorry." And she genuinely did sound sorry. Atsuko never said things she did not mean, at least in part, and she had never been anything but sincere with her elder brother. But that did not make Takayoshi feel any better about the outcome of this conversation.

"He was forced." There had never ever been a doubt in Takayoshi's mind that Cricket would do something like attack a village without coercion. Even if the wild magic was corrupting him, he still was not capable of such a thing. Thus, the reasoning that Sunil forced his hand. He had known that even before Claudia and Leo said as much in their last communication. "He would not do that of his own volition."

"I'm well aware you believe that," Atsuko said in that tone that meant she was being diplomatic. It made Takayoshi's gums ache to snarl at her. He did not want her to be diplomatic. He wanted her to see the good in Cricket just as he did. But then he supposed, she did not know Cricket the way he did. "But the other nobles aren't likely to agree. Especially after all the rumors that have been floating around."

"The rumors Yue Sunil has spread," Takayoshi corrected.

"Be that as it may." Atsuko sighed heavily, her shoulders sagging a little. "Should he seek asylum in another kingdom they're unlikely to grant him the protection we will."

Takayoshi nodded, his hand lifting to rub at the bridge of his nose. Stars, he was developing a headache with this whole mess. If Cricket had just *listened* to him in the first place, then this would never have happened. Yue Sunil would have been executed for treason, and there would be no way he could return to wage a war against Cricket.

"You'll have to be the one to reason with Uncle," Atsuko said, drawing Takayoshi out of his thoughts.

Takayoshi pressed his lips together hard enough to hold back the words, '*Are I not always?*' Because it would be rude, and Atsuko did not deserve his ire. Yes, he was annoyed with her, but she was just being honest with him. She was just trying to tell him what he would have to do to protect Cricket.

"And, of course, you'll have to convince Cricket to come here, somehow. I know you two didn't end things very well, but I hope he'll see reason." Atsuko stood from where she was seated at her desk, and moved around it slowly. She telegraphed her movements, making it clear she intended to reach out to Takayoshi lest he decide he did not want the physical contact. Then she pressed her hand onto his shoulder and gave a firm squeeze. "Do you think you can do that?"

"I do not know," Takayoshi said honestly. The words stung his ears, even if they were from his own lips. He hated the not knowing. Perhaps if he had spoken to Cricket more clearly, things would have been different. *I should have stayed,* he thought not for the first time. *I should have stayed, and tried again. I should not have run away from the difficulty that communicating presented.* It was cowardice, and he was ashamed to say he was facing the consequences for his actions.

Atsuko sighed, her hand squeezing more tightly around his shoulder until Takayoshi looked up at her. "You need to tell him how you feel, Shishi."

"I do not think that will help." After all, what would he say to Cricket if he were to tell him how he felt? Would Takayoshi simply bare his soul, and tell Cricket he loved him. Had loved him almost since the moment he saw him. No. That was foolishness. All it would do was scare Cricket.

"Okay, maybe don't tell him that he's your soulmate." Atsuko teased, her eyes crinkling a little with the joke. "But you should tell him you're worried about him, and that all you want is to make sure he and his daughter are safe. I'm sure he wouldn't begrudge you that."

"There is not time for us to speak." That was not technically true. He was sure if he wanted to, he could make time. He could have Claudia sneak into the palace with the mirror and he could have a full heart to heart conversation with Cricket if Cricket would allow it. But ultimately, he was a coward, at least in this. "And it is something best explained through actions, I think."

"Yes. Because that's worked out so well for you thus far." Atsuko did not roll her eyes, but Takayoshi could tell from her tone she very much wanted to. "Maybe have Claudia and Leo deliver a letter for you. You were always much better at expressing yourself on paper."

Takayoshi took a deep breath, made the conscious effort to unclench his jaw, and nodded. "I will consider it. For now, I must meet with Anstice to discuss our final preparations. If Cricket and Becka are coming to Helio they will need supplies to get up the mountain."

Atsuko let her hand fall away from his shoulder, a serious

expression back on her face. It made the lines around her eyes seem more pronounced, and Takayoshi was reminded once again how many years passed while he was gone. "I will reach out to our contacts in the villages along the path up the mountain. They'll need places to stop where they know they're safe. You said Becka is how old?"

"Six. She will not be able to do long treks at a time. It may take many weeks for Cricket to reach us."

"Then I'll do my best to ensure they're safe along the road."

"Thank you, Koko." Takayoshi reached out, taking her hand in a tight grip, and giving it a squeeze. "You do not know how much this means to me."

"Nonsense. Just get him here, then you can thank me." She returned the squeeze, her smile wide enough to crinkle her eyes.

Takayoshi swallowed around the well of affection he felt in his throat for his sister, gave her a curt little bow, and headed out of her study without another word. He had too much to do to wallow in that soft fuzzy feeling of sibling love.

"I think a letter is a good idea," Anstice said, pushing off from the wall she had been leaning against outside of the study. Takayoshi would scold her for eavesdropping, but there was little point in it. She would continue to do as she pleased, and she would continue to get away with it as Atsuko smiled indulgently. It was annoying, but Takayoshi saw no real harm in it. Not when he saw Anstice give Atsuko the same look in return. It was easy for everyone, except perhaps Uncle Reiji, to see how close the two had gotten over the years.

"And what would you have me say in it?" Takayoshi asked, not breaking stride as he headed to the study room they had taken over to be their war room. On the big table Anstice had sprawled a blueprint of the palace. Takayoshi was not sure if she drewit herself or if she had it stored somewhere, but he knew they had no such thing in the Helio library. Either way, it was a useful tool to plot the entrance and escape of the people they trusted.

"Maybe start with an apology." Anstice shrugged, her oversized tunic, which may have been one of Atsuko's, shifted so it slipped off one shoulder. She reached over to pull it back up without taking her keen eyes off of Takayoshi.

"I will take it under consideration."

"Sure. Like you're taking Atsuko's suggestion under consideration." Anstice shook her head, pressing the door open to their study room with a shoulder.

Takayoshi looked at her out of the corner of his eyes, and she held up her hands.

"Right. Right. Sorry. Well, let's get this meeting over with, and then you can go talk to your uncle."

Takayoshi's shoulders sank, maybe not enough for anyone else to notice, but to him it felt like he was slouching. "I thought I might cross that bridge when I came to it. We are not sure Cricket will come here."

Anstice's brow rose, a knowing smile tugging up one corner of her mouth. "If you don't speak with your uncle, you have to write the letter or I'm telling on you."

"You are aware that I am the elder sibling, are you not?" Takayoshi leaned over the table to get a better look at the blueprints. They would need to plan a route that did not require Cricket and Becka to go over the palace wall.

"Oh. I'm aware." Anstice leaned back in her chair, her posture relaxed, insolent. "But that doesn't really change anything, does it?"

"Fine." Takayoshi looked up to meet her gaze, his eyes narrowed. "I will write Cricket a letter. I do not think it will help to convince him that we are his best option. Nor will it likely mend the fences–"

"Bridges. Fences are to keep people out."

"–between us," Takayoshi continued as if Anstice had not spoken. "But I suppose it would not hurt to make it clear we cannot guarantee any of the other monarchs will be willing to go against Sunil."

"That's all I'm asking." Anstice tilted her head to the side for a moment, then sat up straighter. That was not all she was asking, they both knew it, but it was likely better if they not get into a deep discussion about Takayoshi's feelings when there was so much else to see to. "Now. Where were we?"

THAT EVENING as he lay in bed thinking of all of the things that could, and likely would go wrong before Cricket could reach Helio, Takayoshi let himself think on what he wanted to say to Cricket. There was no way to explain away everything he had done, not in a letter. But Atsuko was right, he had always been able to make people understand him better via the written word. And perhaps it would show Cricket how serious he was about this whole thing.

There would be no way to send it in time, of course. Claudia would have to– No. Actually. Leo had better rewrite it for him and present it to Cricket. Claudia's handwriting was abysmal. All he need do was tell Cricket that he could guarantee him and his daughter safety when no other could. That they had reached out to their contacts far and wide, and cleared a path for him that would ensure they both reached Helio unscathed.

Takayoshi sat up, pushing the blankets from his legs, and made his way over to the desk. It took a moment to find an empty scrap of paper amidst the plans sprawled all over the surface, but when he did, and was seated, the words seemed to come easily enough.

My Prince,

I am aware that when we last met, I did not express myself clearly, and for that I must apologize. I am merely concerned for the situation you find yourself in, and my concern grows steadily the longer your uncle holds you hostage.

I understand if you do not wish to see me again, and if you cannot forgive me for the ignorant way in which I have presented myself to you. But Sister and I have been in contact with the other kingdoms. It would seem that your uncle's smear campaign has made it so many of them will not provide you asylum should you seek it. That being the case, I feel your only option is Helio.

Sister and Anstice have worked tirelessly for the last week to clear a trail for you, so to speak. Claudia and Leo have a map of it they can provide you. Every town along the path will have at least one home willing to keep you hidden should Sunil choose to hunt for you.

It is not much. I wish that I could meet you and bring you here myself, but I fear that would draw too much attention to your and Becka's escape.

Wherever you choose to travel once you are free of the tyranny of Sunil, I hope you know that should you need assistance the kingdom of Helio will always provide.

Please be safe.

He did not bother to sign the letter. It would have to be read to Leo and rewritten anyway, but it felt good to get his thoughts onto paper. It felt good to tell Cricket how he felt, even if it were in the vaguest, most formal way possible. Now all he could do was hope that Cricket would heed his warning.

And perhaps—just maybe—he would be able to better express himself in person. Should Cricket choose to come to Helio. Takayoshi could only hope.

CHAPTER 12

It was amazing how little a person actually needed to survive, Cricket thought as he stuffed a thick cloak into his bag. There wasn't room for much else once he filled the bag with clothes, and that was likely for the best since he'd be carrying Becka's bag as well. They wouldn't even be able to use horses for the first leg of the journey, it would draw too much attention.

"I think that's all we need," Cricket said, pulling the drawstring on the bag before throwing it over his shoulder. He hadn't even been able to pack any books. He'd have to continue Becka's lessons on his own without them. It would put her behind, but he was sure under the diligence of Professor Qiren—when this was all over—she'd get caught up quickly enough.

"Papa, what about the bunnies?" Becka asked, from her perch on his bed where she'd been watching him pack her lip wobbling a little.

"Oh, sweet girl, we can't take them with us. There's no space in our bags, and besides, they'd miss their home, wouldn't they?"

"I'll miss our home." Her voice sounded distinctly quivery, her big dark eyes looking up at him so wide and shiny with unshed tears it nearly broke Cricket. If it were up to him, they'd stay. They'd stay and fight this. But he knew that was not a possibility. It would put Becka in too much danger. No. If he was going to fight Uncle Sunil, he'd have to do it after everyone else was safe. Especially Becka.

"I will too, little sunflower." Cricket moved to squat before her, heedless of the injuries that pulled a wince from his lips. He took her little hands in his, and gave them a gentle squeeze. "But we'll be back here one day, I promise."

"What about Auntie Iggy? And Professor Qiren? And. . . And. . . And. . ." Her breath stuttered out of her lungs, threatening a full-on sob.

"We can't take them with us either. But they'll be safe. Auntie Youta and Auntie Iggy are going to look after everyone for us, aren't you?" He turned to Ignacia who had remained silent through the entire exchange. She looked like she was on the verge of tears herself, and was having more of a struggle holding them back than Becka.

"We will. I swear." Ignacia held up her hand, fingers pressed together in an oath. "Will you be a good girl for your papa? Will you look after him while you're away?"

"Mm." Becka nodded, scrubbing the heels of her hands across her eyes. "We'll take care of each other, and we'll come back safe. Promise." She held up her little hand in an imitation of Ignacia's, her fingers pressed together tightly.

"That's my girl." Ignacia's smile trembled, but she gave Becka a little bow in respect.

The door opened and Claudia, and a man who Cricket could only assume was Leo joined them.

"Youta's headed down to the servant's quarters to get the first group ready. We plan to smuggle you out while they're leaving. We'll disguise you so you'll blend in with them." Leo's voice was curt, to the point. Almost like Takayoshi's, but not nearly as gentle. "That should provide you enough protection to at least get out of the city."

"What has she told Uncle about them?" Cricket stood, straightening his rough-hewn trousers.

"Just that they're staff that she's found lacking. She suggested he have a hand in replacing them. It's a gamble. It'll give him a better foothold in the palace, but it'll also allow us to maybe get the others out too without too much of a fuss." Claudia leaned over to dig through her messenger bag for three bottles of subtly glowing orange liquid. The disguise potion. "We'll need a bit of your hair."

"I had one of the soldiers from the trip to Artemis collect some." Ignacia pulled a thick pouch from her belt. "There's more of it hidden away in my room for later. But this should be enough to get us started." Her eyes didn't drift to Cricket, but he could see the guilt written in her expression. One of their own had to go along with the assault in Artemis. One of their own had *beaten* Cricket.

He shook his head, and hoped she caught the motion from the corner of her eye. That she read it for what it was, a dismissal of that person's and her own guilt. He couldn't hold grudges, not now. Not when they were all just doing what they must to survive.

"Have you decided where you'll go?" Leo asked, already dropping a few hairs into one of the bottles and shaking it hard. The liquid bubbled, and changed from orange to yellow to blue in the span of a few seconds.

"I have allies in Hermes." Cricket tugged on his tunic, wishing he still had his braid to brush with his fingers. But it was gone, and the reminder still made his chest ache.

"No. You don't." Claudia frowned as she dug in her messenger bag again to retrieve a folded-up piece of paper. "Yoshi wanted me to deliver this to you. He—" She pursed her lips, taking a deep inhale. "He's been trying to find you someplace safe. We think you should go to Helio."

"No." Cricket narrowed his eyes, not bothering to reach for the letter. "I have no desire to endure his condescension any further."

"Cricky," Ignacia said, her hand on his shoulder, giving it a squeeze, then traveling down his arm till she found his hand which he hadn't noticed was clutching tightly into a fist right where his sword should have been. Styx, he missed his sword. She took his hand, peeling his fingers back one by one before she could wrap her hand around them and give it a firm squeeze. "Prince Takayoshi won't let anything happen to you or Becka. I know you're worried about your–"

"Don't you *dare* say pride. This has nothing at all to do with my *pride*. I won't be some– I'm not a charity case. I won't take his pity. And I certainly won't allow him to experiment on me as he tries to *cure* me." The words were cold and steel in his mouth. So cutting he thought he might taste blood on his tongue.

"Can you give us a moment?" Ignacia didn't look away from him, but Claudia and Leo nodded anyway, excusing themselves to the adjoining sitting room, and shutting the door behind them.

"This isn't about that," Cricket said, but he could feel the lie like a weight on his shoulders. It *was* about that. It *was* about his pride. It *was* about chasing Yoshi away, and telling him never to come back, only to go begging on his knees for asylum. It *was* about admitting that Yoshi had been right about Uncle Sunil all those years ago. It was about. . . *everything.*

"Of course not." Ignacia's tone was placating, but Cricket knew he hadn't fooled her. She was likely the one person in his life who he couldn't fool. At one point there were two, Anstice, and Ignacia. His sisters. His best friends. Now there was just Ignacia. And she'd taken her role as big sister more seriously than ever. "But think of Becka."

Becka who had grabbed the book from Cricket's nightstand and was flipping through the pages looking for pictures. She wouldn't find any, but he was grateful she'd chosen to entertain herself during this conversation.

"Just read the letter, then decide. Maybe it'll change your mind." Ignacia turned his hand over in her own, and set the piece of paper in his spread fingers. He wasn't sure when Claudia passed it off to her, but this whole thing had obviously been orchestrated by the two women. He didn't know whether he should be annoyed or impressed.

He decided after a moments' thought. Annoyed.

With a huff, Cricket flopped down beside Becka, and opened the letter. The words on the page were not written in Yoshi's hand, but the tone of them was his. The soft, firm, sincerity. The stilted fashion of not using contractions. The awkwardly formal way he tended to word things. So much so that Cricket could hear them in Yoshi's voice in his head.

It took Ignacia clearing her throat for Cricket to realize that he'd been smiling the entire time he read. He folded the letter back up, pressing his lips into a straight line, and nodded.

"Papa, are we going to meet Auntie Annie finally?" Becka asked, her eyes bright. He didn't think she'd read most of the letter, she had likely homed in on Anstice's name. And he supposed it was that question more so than the letter itself that sealed his fate.

"Yeah, little sunflower, I think we are. You'd like that wouldn't you?"

"Mhm!" Becka nodded eagerly, her face lighting with a bright smile, all thoughts of everyone they'd leave behind forgotten. "I want to show her my best dress."

"Well, I doubt Professor Qiren packed that for you, but

I'm sure Aunt Annie will be happy to help you find one just as nice. What do you think, Aunt Iggy?"

"Oh definitely." Ignacia was grinning at them, a relief had settled onto her shoulders, letting them fall away from her ears. "And maybe this time your papa will give Prince Takayoshi a minute to say what he needs to say, instead of talking over him. Huh?"

"Yes!" Becka agreed, and both ignored the glare Cricket shot their way as he tucked the letter into the pocket of his cloak.

He went to open the door and nod Claudia and Leo back into the room. "Yoshi says there is a map with stops on the way to Helio that will keep us safe?"

"Right!" Claudia grinned, digging around in her bag again to produce another piece of folded up paper. "We don't have any guarantees of towns in Lunette."

"We won't be able to stay anywhere in my kingdom." Cricket shook his head looking over the route Takayoshi had planned for them. It was a little out of the way, not the one he'd have chosen if he were traveling to Helio for political reasons, or some kind of event. But then if he were going for those reasons he would be traveling with a full retinue of soldiers, and servants, and he wouldn't be trying to hide. "We'll have to stick to camping until we've crossed the border."

"We've packed you enough provisions to last that long. Youta will have them for you down in the kitchens." Leo moved across the room to check the hall. Uncle Sunil hadn't put guards on him while he was still in the palace yet, but it was only a matter of time. "You'll need something to hide that cuff around your neck until Yoshi can get it off."

"Leo will get you as far as the edge of the city, from there you're on your own." Claudia pulled a vial from her bag and portioned off a little of the potion to hand over to Ignacia. "Let's give it a test run before we set off."

"You aren't coming with us?" Becka frowned, her eyes flicking between the new adults in the room. Cricket wasn't even sure she'd caught their names, but that didn't seem to matter.

"No, I'm afraid not." Leo moved to sit beside her on the bed, leaving a gap between them likely so she wouldn't scuttle away and hide behind her father. "Our friend has given us a very important mission."

"What's that?" Becka blinked up at him, dark eyes widened, and mouth hanging open in awe. Leo was quite dashing in his way, Cricket supposed. All roguish and unkempt. The perfect opposite of Yoshi's pressed, clean-shaven, princely good looks. There was a story there of how these two men who were so alike and so different became friends that Cricket ached deep in his bones to hear. But there wasn't time for it.

"He asked us to stay here and look after the rest of your family. To make sure they're safe while you're gone."

"Oh!" Becka perked up, dropping the book onto the bed and launching herself at Leo to hug him tightly. "Thank you!"

Leo patted her back awkwardly, looking to the others for help.

"We should get going," Ignacia said in a voice that was not her own, from a mouth that was not her own.

Cricket frowned at her, or rather at the himself that was her, or maybe the her that was himself? He wasn't sure, this was all very confusing. And *I don't stand like that. Do I?* His nose curled up in disgust as he asked, "Is that what my hair looks like now?"

"Cricky."

"What? I'm just asking!"

"Not the time."

"Oh fine." He rolled his eyes, and scooped up Becka's bag on his free shoulder. "Come on little sunflower, it's time to hit the road."

Becka nodded, and slid from the bed, her hand clasping Leo's tightly. Leo for his part looked entirely lost, but Cricket wasn't about to save him. There wasn't really time for a crying Becka.

The path out of the palace was easy enough that Cricket thought maybe he should be worried about the security of the place when he returned. But then Ignacia was giving him one last hug, and Youta was pressing a small but heavy traveling pouch into his hands, and he had no more time to think about it.

Leo led them down the back alleys of the city once they were out of sight of the guard towers. The darkness hiding them from view.

"How did you meet?" Cricket asked when the silence of the barren streets got to be too much. The capital had been eerily quiet since Uncle Sunil took over. Just as it had been the first time. Like the people of Lunette were afraid to breathe incorrectly in Yue Sunil's presence.

"Meet?" Leo frowned, looking back from where he'd poked his head out of their current hiding spot.

"Yoshi. How did you meet Yoshi? Claudia said you three are best friends." Cricket hoped the hood of his cloak was hiding the way his nose wrinkled at the thought of someone like Yoshi using the term *best friends*. It just didn't fit.

"I met them on the road while they were searching for the map to the archive." Leo motioned for Cricket to follow, as he hitched Becka up higher onto his hip. She'd fallen asleep at some point while they ducked between shadowed alcoves and behind discarded wagons. It was probably for the better, she would need her rest in the days to come. Cricket wouldn't be able to carry her the whole time.

They were silent for a while longer, the edge of the city creeping closer and closer. Cricket was sure there was some strategic logic to Leo's movements and how slowly he was walking, but he couldn't see it. In his mind, they should have just gotten out of the city as quickly as possible. But a man running through the streets with a child on his back would likely have drawn too much attention to them.

"He saw you, you know," Leo said, breaking the silence.

"Saw me where?" Cricket's frown deepened, tugging the hood more tightly around his head.

"On the road. Whenever he was in danger, you were there. You helped him. Guided him. Brought him comfort." Leo refused ot meet Cricket's eyes, and he wasn't sure what that meant. "I think he thought you were a dream, or a hallucination those first few times. Just something to keep him going. . ." Leo drifted off his jaw clenching.

"But?" Cricket prompted when the silence stretched on too long between them.

"But we never figured out what it really was." Leo shrugged, but the words sat heavy in the air, like they weren't quite true. Cricket wasn't sure how to drag honesty from this man he hardly knew, and he didn't exactly have time to try. "You'll have to ask him about it."

"Yes. I will." Cricket added it to the mental list of things he'd confront Yoshi about once they were together again.

"This is as far as I go," Leo said, leaning against the wall of one of the small homes on the outskirts of the capital. There was one more street to go, then they could dart across to the forest and hide there. "You shouldn't stop for the night. I know you're tired, and hurting, but you need to put as much distance between yourself and this place as you can."

Cricket nodded, reached for Becka, and pulled her into his chest where her arms automatically wrapped around his neck.

"Travel at night as much as possible. It'll be safer than traveling during the day," Leo said.

Cricket already knew all of that, but he didn't say as much. Instead, he said, "Thank you" and offered Leo a small, grateful smile.

Leo reached over to pull the hood more securely over the antlers on Cricket's head, and nodded to himself. "He'll be expecting you. But even with that, you might have some trouble getting into the castle."

"Of course. Thank you again, for all you've done. And send along our thanks to Claudia."

"No need. That's what friends do for each other." Then Leo turned and disappeared down another alley, and Cricket was left to travel the rest of the way on his own with Becka breathing deeply against his neck.

He didn't look back once he reached the edge of the city. He didn't look back when he reached the hill that overlooked the capital either. It would be too hard, knowing that he was leaving his city and his kingdom behind, and that if things didn't go his way he may never return to either.

BOOK II
ESCAPE

"He's on his way to you," Claudia said the night Cricket escaped. And the relief that washed over Takayoshi had been like a full body exhale. But that was weeks ago.

A fortnight without a word from Lunette, or Cricket, or Takayoshi's forces embedded in the castle. Two weeks of no news good or bad. It was enough to make him lose his appetite. Enough that when he practiced the sword with Atsuko, she got more than a fair few strikes in past his guard.

"You're distracted." Atsuko lowered her sword, bracing her free hand on her hip.

Takayoshi frowned, gripping his own more firmly. He did not want to discuss this with his sister. She had her own things to think of. She need not concern herself with him or his problems. "It is nothing."

"It's not nothing." Atsuko sheathed her blade, and stepped forward, reaching for him. He allowed her to get close enough that she could grip his shoulder, forcing him to meet her gaze. They were of a height. They had not always been, but since reaching adulthood, their growth spurts ceased, and they settled into being roughly the same height. With the same warm golden eyes, or so he had been told. The same pert nose. The same high cheekbones. Close enough in looks that they could have been twins if not for their differing ages, and the fact that Atsuko had the dark hair of their mother, while Takayoshi inherited the almost white-blond of their father.

"It is." Takayoshi stepped back, out of her grasp, sheathing his own blade and moving to grab a towel to wipe the perspiration from his brow. Even in the chill of the barely heated training rooms, he worked up a sweat. It did not seem to quell the anxiety that had settled into him like a second skin though, and that was concerning. He had hoped exertion would at least quiet the racing of his mind. It did not.

"Shishi," Atsuko said, her voice soft as she moved to pour a cup of water from the pitcher the servants had set aside for them. "He will come."

And it was those soft words—more than anything else Atsuko said that afternoon—that broke the dam. Takayoshi let out a shaking breath, his hand clutching the hilt of his sword hard enough the edges dug into the meat of his palm. "We have not heard anything."

"I know." Atsuko's tone went soft, and placating, and Takayoshi hated that his *little* sister thought she needed to soothe him. That she needed to be the one to bear his burdens for him, when it should have been the other way.

"From any of them," he continued, unable to keep the words in his throat even as he tried to swallow them down.

"I know."

"In over a *fortnight*." He practically choked on the last word. Felt it clog at the back of his throat as he forced it past his tongue.

Atsuko let out a sigh, and moved to take his hands in her

own, giving them a comforting squeeze. "No news, is good news."

"What does that even *mean?*" Takayoshi whispered, a harsh gasp scraped its way out of his chest. "Why do people say that?"

"It means that the fact that we have not heard anything about him means he is still alive, and out of harm's way. It means he's still hidden."

"He could be dead in a ditch and we would not know." Which was a fear Takayoshi had not allowed himself to think of until that very moment, and once he did it was all he *could* think of. His mind filled with the image of Cricket's long midnight hair sprawled around his still body as he lay face down on the side of the road somewhere. Blood staining the earth around him, and not a shuddering breath to be heard.

"Shishi," Atsuko said curtly, her hands on his shoulders again, giving him a little shake. "The fact that we haven't heard anything means he and his daughter are all right. It means Sunil hasn't realized what's going on yet. It means he is still on his way to you. And once he's here, we'll keep him safe. I swear it."

Takayoshi met her gaze again, and saw only honesty there. It eased something in his stomach, something that had grown so tight over the past week he found it hard to eat or sleep or think. He gave his sister a nod of thanks. Then he took a breath, and before he could think better of it, pulled her into a tight hug, hooking his chin over her shoulder, heedless of the way it made his tunic stick to him.

"Oh Shishi," Atsuko breathed, ducking her face into his shoulder as she patted his back awkwardly. After a moment of standing there, she pulled back, and offered him one of those wide smiles of hers. "Now, go get cleaned up. We have supper with Anstice in a couple of hours."

Takayoshi fell into a small bow, then turned to head to his quarters.

It was a while later, after he had finished bathing, gotten dressed, and was sitting down to comb out his damp hair, that the mirror on his desk chimed softly. It took every bit of composure he possessed to not scramble to the desk, nearly knock over the chair, and drop several pens to the ground in his attempt to get the mirror set up in its spot on the desk. He tapped it, fingers shaking, remembering Atsuko's words. No news is good news. This must be bad news.

Claudia's face appeared in the glass, her eyes wild behind her spectacles, her mouth agape as she panted softly. Wherever she was, it was dark, her face only just visible in the gloom.

"He knows," she whispered, like saying the words more quietly would make them less true. Like tucking them into a whisper would make them less heavy. It did neither of those things. The words sunk into Takayoshi's stomach like a stone, dragging the organ down to his feet.

But worse still was the dizziness he felt as she whipped the mirror around to show him a wanted poster tacked to a wall somewhere. He could not tell if it was to an alley, or a tree, and he did not think it mattered. Because there was Cricket's face, smiling as it always did beneath the words WANTED in bold letters. Beneath that, were words Claudia did not give Takayoshi a chance to make out before she spun the mirror back to her face.

Takayoshi wanted to ask how Sunil found out, but he did not think it mattered. Not when there were other, more pressing, issues. "How are Cricket's people?"

"We managed to get most of them out."

"Most?"

"Ignacia and Youta stayed behind. They said they needed to keep up the ruse. Leo's with them, but Sunil hasn't noticed him yet. Leo managed to get himself a place amongst the palace guard. He'll have to be our inside man now. The security is tighter than ever before, and Sunil replaced all of the staff with his own people."

"Where are Youta and Ignacia being kept?"

"In the palace somewhere." Claudia wore on her lip with her teeth. It looked chapped, like she had been biting it a lot in the last few hours. "We don't think he'll hurt them. Not yet."

"Not yet?"

"Not until he knows where Cricket is, and knows how to get a message to him." She fell silent for a moment, her eyes flicking nervously over whatever expression had taken over Takayoshi's face. He was not sure what it was, but he could feel the muscles doing something. Worry maybe. Or upset. Maybe a bit of both. "He'll want to use them to draw Cricket back, I think."

"Very likely." Takayoshi forced his hand to unclench when he felt his nails digging into his palm. She was right, of course, Sunil would use Cricket's love for his people against him. Sunil would wait until he was sure that Cricket would hear about their treatment, then he would publicize it, or send a message to Cricket directly with a threat. It would be the most expedient way to bring his nephew to heel. "Then we will have to ensure he does not know where Cricket is."

"That was Leo's thought." Claudia's lips tugged at one corner, a knowing smirk lighting her face. "It won't keep them safe forever, but it might keep them safe long enough for us to form a plan."

"Mn." Takayoshi smoothed a hand through his damp hair to push some of the pale strands from his face. "Please let me know if anything changes."

"He hasn't arrived there, has he?"

"No. And we have not heard from any of our safe houses

either. He must not have crossed the border into Helio yet. We will know when he does."

"You're worried." It was not an accusation; it was a statement of fact accompanied by the frown of a friend who was also worried.

"I am. But I did know that it would take him time to reach Helio. And as Atsuko has told me, no news is good news." He forced himself to relax with the reassurance. He forced himself to remember that Cricket was strong, and capable, and he would not let any harm come to himself or his daughter. It did precious little to calm Takayoshi's racing heart.

"Don't do anything rash, just because you're worried."

"Has he set a reward for Cricket's return? What are the stipulations?" Takayoshi asked, ignoring her warning. It would do nothing to stop him should he decide to do something reckless, and they both knew it.

"No reward yet. Just good faith." Claudia shook her head. "He's telling people—" She stopped, her eyes flicking past the mirror to something she must have heard beyond in the darkness. She stood as still as she could for a long minute, Takayoshi's heart beat loudly in his chest, then she relaxed. "He's telling people Cricket tried to kill him in his sleep. He's telling them it was because Cricket wanted to ensure his own place as king, and felt threatened by his blood lineage."

"Ridiculous."

"Well *we* know that," Claudia agreed, releasing a soft chuckle but the sound was mirthless and hollow. "But there are some in the capital who seem to believe him. I just— I hope he gets out of Lunette soon."

"I will check with Anstice to see if he has made it to any of our safe houses. If not—" Takayoshi bit his tongue to keep from telling Claudia that if not he would likely go and search for Cricket himself. He knew that was the very definition of *'doing something rash'.* "If not, we will cross that bridge when we come to it."

Claudia eyed him suspiciously, but did not call him out on his near slip. She never did. She was a good friend that way. Instead she nodded. "I'll check back in, same time tomorrow."

"Stay safe."

"Yes, Your Highness." Claudia dipped her head in mock politeness, and her image faded from the mirror. Takayoshi sat back in his chair, breathing deeply for a moment before he rose, tied his damp hair back, and headed for Atsuko's study.

He pushed the door open, not even bothering to knock. Atsuko seemed to be waiting for him, her eyes lined with stress.

"You have heard," Takayoshi concluded without even having to ask. For he knew his sister better than he knew anyone else, and he could see it there, written plainly on her pinched face.

"Sunil has reached out to me and asked that should his nephew arrive in Helio, I return him to Lunette at once to be tried," Atsuko said, her words quiet but firm, not trying to soften the blow. "I have little doubt he has done the same with the other ruling families."

Takayoshi did not even have the patience to hide his snort, or restrain his eye roll at the comment. "Of course he has."

"This will make things difficult with Uncle Reiji." Atsuko's fingers drummed on the smooth surface of her desk, shiny lacquer that Takayoshi had not seen when they weresparring shone at him from her nails. He wondered if Anstice had done it for her, and what color it was. They had been spending much of their time together as of late, and he was not sure how much of it was chaperoned. Not that he could say much to the queen about such a thing. But as her older brother. . .

"Uncle always makes things difficult." Takayoshi settled into the chair across the desk from Atsuko. His hands folded in his lap.

"He was friends with Sunil before the exile." Atsuko looked nervous, her posture somehow too straight, even for her. "I don't know that we'll be able to keep him from reaching out to him and letting him know his nephew is here. Especially with how Sunil is accusing Cricket—"

"Let me deal with Uncle," Takayoshi said with more certainty than he felt. He was unsure how he would do such a thing, but there was little choice in this matter. Atsuko was correct in her assumptions, if Cricket sought refuge in Helio, Uncle Reiji would report it to Sunil, unless he was convinced, or ordered not to. While Atsuko had the power to do such a thing, it would put a strain on their relationship. A strain Takayoshi hoped to prevent if he could. "And in the meantime, write a royal proclamation that everyone in the capital knows Cricket is under our protection. He is not to be harmed, or ousted to Sunil under any circumstances."

"I don't know if that will be enough." *And I can't very well go around arresting everyone who looks like they might spill our secrets to Sunil's men*, went unsaid. She could. But there would be little point in it, and with Helio's citizens spread out so far over the mountain, it would be hard to enforce.

The light glinted off Atsuko's lacquered nails again as she rubbed at her eyes, exhaustion making her movements clumsy and slow. Takayoshi very much wanted to hug her in that moment to thank her for all she was doing simply because she knew he loved Cricket. She was a good sister. And an excellent queen.

"It will have to be. At least in the beginning." Takayoshi forced his shoulders to relax as a thought struck him. A plan.

More reckless behavior, but he was realizing more and more lately that is what Cricket made him. Reckless.

"In the beginning?"

"Mm." Takayoshi looked up from his hands to meet his sister's gaze. He did not say he was certain that Cricket could win them all over. He did not say he was sure that after not more than a month the people of Helio would be as protective of Cricket as he himself was. Or that if it came to it, he would marry Cricket himself, and give him the Caldwell name to wear as armor. Instead, he just offered his sister a small, barely-there smile.

"Very well." Atsuko grinned back, easing some of the worry from her shoulders.

CHAPTER 14

Weeks of hard travel left Cricket tired and worn. He could feel what was left of his strength beginning to fray. But he couldn't stop. He *wouldn't* stop. The border to Helio wasn't far. Another four days. Maybe a week. It would take longer, Cricket knew. They would have to avoid the townships and main roads, at least until they'd crossed over into Helion territory. But still, it was something to cling to. Something to hope for. To keep him going.

Becka wasn't faring much better. She'd never been the nocturnal type, always wanting to wake early with the sun and drag her papa out of bed before he was ready to greet the day—hence little sunflower. But now all of their movements had to be under the cover of night. It was making her antsy. And when she *was* awake the only amusement he could provide her was stories.

By the sixteenth day of their trek, Cricket was losing his voice. A scratchy cough starting somewhere in the back of his throat that made it hard to talk for long periods of time.

And by the eighteenth the cold of the turning season made his lungs ache, and every step became a trial.

"We need to take a break, little sunflower." Cricket rasped softly, pulling Becka to a stop. She looked up at him with wide eyes. It hadn't been long since they started out, just past dusk, but he could feel the way the chill in the night air settled into his chest. He swallowed roughly, forcing down another choking cough. It wouldn't do. He couldn't let Becka see him weak. Not when they were so close.

"But Papa. . . we just started." She blinked up at him, a little frown creasing her nose.

"I know, but we've been making such good time, we could use a break, right? Maybe make a little tea? Do you think you can build a fire like Aunt Iggy taught you?"

"Yeah!" Becka brightened, her hand falling away from his, and she scurried into the surrounding tree line to look for dry twigs.

"Don't go too far." Cricket settled onto the ground, not even bothering to lay out the tarp to ensure the cold and wet didn't seep in through his trousers. What did it matter? He'd managed to get himself sick anyway.

He pulled a water skin from his belt, pouring some into the kettle Youta somehow packed away in with the food. Cricket waited, listening to Becka scuttle about in the woods. The moon was full, watching over them on their journey.

"Please," Cricket whispered into the night, his eyes focused on the watery light of it. "Just let us get there safely. I just need to make sure Becka is safe. I'll. . . I'll do anything. I'll be your most faithful servant." The words rang through the clearing, honest, and aching. It may not have been the best idea to promise *anything* to a goddess, but he didn't think he had much choice in the matter. He laid their fate at her feet.

"Papa, that's you!" Becka called, her little voice ripping him from his thoughts.

He looked over to where she had dropped her sticks to point at a poster tacked to a tree. The paper was curling in the damp air. But even in the dark, he recognized himself. Above it in big bold letters read WANTED. From a distance he couldn't read the small text below his picture, but he decided quickly that was likely for the best. He didn't want to know what it was Uncle was telling everyone he'd done. It would just make the ache in his chest worse.

And then it struck him. . . someone had to *put* that sign up. Someone had to come into the forest, where they were currently hiding, to post it. And there wasn't just one. No. Every tree along the small river they'd stopped next to had a poster tacked to it.

Cricket's heart clenched, and he started coughing around the anxiety in his throat. Something wet, and papery came up with the cough, but he wiped it away, not wanting to see or even think about what it could mean.

"Papa?" Becka asked, her voice small and confused.

"We've got to pick up the pace." Cricket moved to scoop her up into his arms, and turned away from the river. It had been a good guide to follow. All they had to do was head up stream toward Helio. But that was gone now. He'd have to make the rest of the journey based on his wits alone. It might take longer, but he'd do anything to keep Becka safe. *Anything.*

"I thought you needed to rest?" Becka's arms were crushing around his neck as his stride moved quickly into the darkness of the forest. Maybe if they got deep enough inside, he'd be able to keep traveling during the day. He could do with less sleep if it meant they would reach Yoshi and the safety he was promising quicker.

"I'm all right, little sunflower. We just need to get up the mountain before the snow starts. You're excited to see Prince Takayoshi again, right? And to meet Aunt Annie?" The words were hollow in his chest, but he pushed them out with an air of enthusiasm he didn't think he'd actually felt in three years.

"Yeah!" Becka cheered, her little mouth too close to his ear, making him wince away from her bright voice. "But papa, I can walk."

"I know sweetheart, but we've just got to get a little further away from the river then I'll put you down." He thanked the goddess for the full moon, for the warning he'd been given, for his sure footing, and for the weight of Becka in his arms. Because he knew without her warmth against his chest he would have just turned himself in. He'd have gone back to the capital and let Uncle do as he wished. But Becka was important. Becka was the future of Lunette. He had to protect that.

Becka didn't say anything, but he could feel her little heart beating rabbit fast against his chest. She knew the danger they were in. She was afraid. And Cricket hated himself for that. But he didn't have time to worry about it. Not yet. Not now. He would have time, maybe, when they reached the border.

THEY CROSSED the border four days later. There was no marker to say they were in Helio, but Cricket could feel the subtle shift in the magic under his feet. There was also the slight incline of the trail as they began to travel up the mountain. The snow hadn't started yet, but it wouldn't be long, he was sure.

"Papa, I'm tired." Becka whined into his hair at the back

of his head. Her voice muffled by the thick scarf he'd wrapped tight around her neck.

"I know, sweetheart. But we'll be able to stop at an inn soon. Prince Takayoshi and Aunt Annie have found us a place to stay once we're a little further up the mountain. We'll be able to sleep in a nice, warm bed, and have some nice warm food. What do you say, princess? Can you hang on a little longer?" Cricket hopped a little, pushing her further up his back where she'd begun to slide down. "Just another few hours or so, I think."

"Okay!" He could feel her nod eagerly enough that she almost over balanced and fell off his back.

"That's my little sunflower." Cricket laughed softly, and let his pace quicken, more sure-footed in the night after nearly a month of traveling through it.

The forest was dark, and quiet around them, and Cricket let himself believe that in this place they were safe. He let himself sink into the idea that Helio would provide them shelter where Lunette had not. He let himself have faith in Takayoshi and Anstice's efforts.

The sun rose over the horizon warm, and bright, and Cricket stepped out of the forest near the first town Claudia circled for him on the map. Cricket was sure the lightness in his chest meant they would be safe. He was sure this had all not been in vain. He was certain soon he and Becka would be able to curl onto a proper bed.

"Papa," Becka whispered into his ear, her little arm outstretched past his head to point at where someone had slapped wanted posters along the tall wall of the little town. "What does 'wanted' mean?"

Cricket tried not to let his shoulders droop. He was so tired. And the tightness in his chest had only gotten worse in the passing days. So much so that he found himself coughing sometimes for ten minutes at a time after Becka had gone to sleep, tucking the strange feather like bits of whatever was growing in his lungs under leaves and debris where she wouldn't see. "It means we're going to have to keep going, sweetheart."

"But. . . But you said Aunt Annie and Prince Takayoshi would take care of us." Becka's voice wobbled a little. Cricket didn't have it in him to tell her not to cry, because the truth was, he wanted to cry too. He could feel the itching burn of tears pressing at the backs of his eyes.

"I'm sure they tried, sweetheart," he whispered around the feeling of another cough crawling up his throat. Or maybe it was the anguish that squeezed his chest. They were indistinguishable these days. "Maybe some of the towns closer to the capital will be safe. But we can't— We can't take the chance here."

"What does it mean?" Becka's little fingers clutched more tightly at his cloak as he turned to head back into the forest. They'd just have to keep making their way as they were. Hopefully they wouldn't run out of food before they found someplace safe.

"It means that someone told them Papa did something bad, and they want to arrest him." Cricket took in a slow breath, pressing it down into his lungs past the upset roiling in his sternum.

"But can't we just tell them that you didn't?"

"We can, but I'm afraid no one would believe us right now. We have to get to our friends up the mountain, and hope they'll help us prove it. Do you think you can walk for a bit? Papa's getting a little tired."

"Okay Papa." Becka scrambled down off his back, and they started through the woods again. Following the slight incline of the mountain that would lead them to the capital of Helio.

IT WAS A LONG WALK, and another couple of weeks before they reached the looming walls of Helio's capital city. They hadn't managed to find a place that didn't have wanted posters plastered all over it, and in the end, Cricket had taken to sneaking into the towns when the markets were at their thickest, to steal what they needed to make it up the mountain.

The snow had started in earnest about halfway up, and Cricket managed to steal a donkey from one of the farmers, leaving some meager payment behind. It wasn't much, but it was enough to keep them both moving. And all the while the tightness in his chest grew. The cough becoming more of a problem.

By the time they reached the open gate Cricket could no longer feel his toes through boots not built for the deep snows of a Helion winter, and he was coughing into the lining of his cloak every few minutes.

"Papa, you should ride for a bit," Becka said, her voice tired and travel worn.

"No need, sweetheart. We're almost there." Cricket tugged the hood of his cloak up further around his face, ducking into the shadow of it to hide his antlers and midnight hair. The people of the capital bustled around them, all dressed in thick cloaks and coats, far better suited to the cold of Helio than anything Cricket had ever owned. "Remember to be polite, and respectful."

"Of course, Papa."

"And what do we say to Prince Takayoshi when we meet him?"

"Thank you for helping us, Your Highness. Please take good care of me and my Papa."

"Good girl." Cricket nodded and headed up to the gate of the palace. Where the city was walled in to protect against the cold, the castle itself seemed walled in to protect against a possible siege. Guards posted along watch towers every few feet, and he heard the boot steps of patrols along the inside. The gate itself was open, but there were several guards standing in the way of their entrance. Each dressed just as Yoshi was the first day they met. Pale blues, and whites, with the Helion crest emblazoned on their breast.

"Who goes there?" a booming voice called as one of the captains stepped forward. Her lips were pressed into a hard line, jaw ticking, so reminiscent of Yoshi that Cricket wondered if this was just how people in Helio were. If it was the mountain air that froze them over and made them stiff.

"I umm. . ." He started, and swallowed roughly around the cough scratching at the back of his throat. "We're here to see Prince Takayoshi. He's expecting us."

"And who, may I ask, are you?" She narrowed her eyes on Cricket, nose wrinkled in disgust. Which he supposed was fair. It had been a long, hard month of travel. He hadn't the time or resources to shave or bathe adequately. And he spent most of it going lean on his own meals to make sure that Becka was well fed. Add to that the thick iron collar pressed tight to his neck only just covered by a scarf, and he was sure he looked like some kind of escaped criminal. In a sense, he supposed that he was.

"Tell him Prince Cricket is here to see him."

A soft murmur went through the surrounding guards. Expressions varying from wide eyed and surprised to disbelieving. The head of the guard merely narrowed her eyes further. "You don't *look* like Prince Cricket."

Cricket let out a breath, his shoulders sagging a little as he leaned against the donkey. Becka crossed her arms and looked like she wanted to tell off the knight in no uncertain terms, but Cricket shook his head at her. Then he tucked his hand into his pocket and pulled out the dangling amber earring. "Give him this and tell him Cricket is at the gate. He'll come."

The guard snatched the earring, hardly even looking at it as she tightened her fist around it. If she'd bothered to examine it, she'd realize it was Helion amber. She'd see it was the mate to the earring Cricket had seen Takayoshi wearing when he'd come to visit Lunette.

But she didn't. Instead, she said, "Watch them. I'll be back." And turned to enter the castle proper.

CHAPTER 15

A month of waiting and not knowing left something aching and raw inside of Takayoshi that he tried his best not to examine too closely. There had been no word of Cricket staying at any of the safe houses Takayoshi or Anstice found for him. No rumors of him traveling through Takayoshi's kingdom at all. Just the whisper of a prince missing on the wind. But Takayoshi forced himself to find peace in that. Forced himself to acknowledge that so long as Sunil was searching, Cricket and Becka were safe. It was not the most comforting thought, but it was something.

Still none of that could have prepared Takayoshi for the way his heart pounded in his chest when the knight said, "there's a man at the gate who claims to be Prince Cricket."

"Claims?" Takayoshi almost could not hear his own voice over the sound of his blood pumping in his ears.

"He just looks like a homeless beggar to me. Why anyone would pretend to be someone who's wanted by half the nation, I don't know." The guard rolled her eyes, and Takayoshi had to swallow down the harsh reprimand that sprang to his lips. Her tone was far too casual, and cavalier for his liking. But he found more and more of that had happened while he had been gone, and he did not have the time nor the patience to train it out of the fresh crop of knights. There were other things to attend to.

"But," Takayoshi prompted, because she would not be there telling him what was going on if there were not something to signify that maybe the man was actually Cricket. Takayoshi's palms grew slick with sweat against the sides of his trousers, as he fought to stay standing where he was in the corridor and not run off to see for himself. It had to be Cricket, it just had to be. As she said, there was no reason for someone to lie about such a thing.

"He had this with him." She pinched her pointer and thumb together, and released the rest of her fingers till something dangled from her hand. It glinted warm, and golden in the light, and it took Takayoshi a moment to process exactly what he was seeing. The matching earring hung from his ear, the other lobe empty even after he returned home where he could have switched the pair out for a complete set. It had not felt right to do so. It felt better to cling to the earring that matched the one he had given Cricket. To wear it always as a reminder of everything he had given away and left in the care of the prince. "He said you'd–"

Takayoshi did not wait for her to finish that sentence, he snatched the earring from her, and strode back down the corridor toward the nearest exit onto the grounds. He was not running, but it was a near thing. Certainly in such a rush that he garnered plenty of attention.

"Wait! Your Highness!" the guard called from behind him, but he would not be stopped. Not when Cricket was so very *very* close.

The air was cold when it hit his face, but it was not enough to slow Takayoshi down. Not enough to keep him from running toward the main doors and all but skidding when the little group came into view. There was a donkey, a child sitting atop it, and a tall man holding the reins. It took Takayoshi far too long to realize that the child with her dirty face half covered by thick furs was Becka. And that the too-thin man standing beside her, his gaunt cheekbones covered in scruff, was Cricket.

Takayoshi stumbled to a stop in front of them, his palms itching, and muscles twitching to reach out to them. To pull them in to him to stave off the chill in the air. To stop the slight trembling of Cricket's shoulders. The prince was not dressed near as warmly as his daughter, likely having given everything he could find to Becka, including what little food they had. The first order of business would be a warm meal for both of them, Takayoshi decided, and something in that decision settled him.

"The donkey isn't mine," was the first thing Cricket said to him in months. And it sounded so wretched and broken and beautiful that Takayoshi wanted to weep. Wanted to fall to his knees, and press his face into that hopelessly ruined cloak clinging to Cricket's form, if just to confirm that this was real. Not some fever dream. "I can tell you where I got it though, so you can return it to the owner."

Takayoshi's breath stuttered in his chest, his eyes burned. There were words on his tongue, too many and too fast for him to even sort through them all properly enough to express himself. So instead of letting them out into the frigid air, he stood staring at Cricket. His eyes drinking in the softness of Cricket's blue eyes, the way the midnight hair on his cheeks and jaw made him look so much older, and so much more tired.

"Can we– Can we come inside?" Cricket asked, his voice soft, like he was afraid he might be rejected out of hand. Like he doubted how much Takayoshi wanted to sweep him into his arms, and never let him go again. That would not do.

"Your Highness?" one of the guards asked, his voice unsure. "Do you know this man?"

"Papa," Becka whispered, her little body shifting uncomfortably atop the donkey.

And that ripped Takayoshi from his stupor. He swallowed the words of foolish pining down, and lifted his chin. "Send a messenger to my sister, tell her our guests have arrived. I will see to the rest."

Cricket relaxed visibly. His shoulders sagging under the relief of it. "Thank you."

Takayoshi did not acknowledge the words. There was no need for thanks, Cricket told him that once, and he believed it now more than ever. There would never be a need between them. "Come, I will have the kitchens send up some food. You can eat while your rooms are prepared. How do you feel about stew, Princess Becka?"

"Oh. Yes please!" Becka nodded, her arms outstretched toward Cricket as her father swooped in to help her down off of the donkey, although he did not put her on her feet. He held her close, his grip like iron around her waist, even as his arms shook. "What about our friend?"

Takayoshi burned to close the gap between them, and wrap the little family up in his arms. To hold them close, and never let another person so much as look upon them. Instead, he asked, "Your friend?"

"Duncan the Donkey. What about him?"

Takayoshi turned to one of the bewildered knights, and the young woman blinked at him, her mouth hanging open just a touch. A smile twitched at his lips as he said, "See that Duncan the Donkey is well taken care of. There should be room in the stables. We will return him home when the snow breaks."

The woman blinked again, her jaw snapping shut at the

clear order in Takayoshi's tone. "Yes, Your Highness." She bowed deeply, then moved to take the reins from Cricket.

"Will that be all, Princess Becka?" Takayoshi met the little girl's gaze, the magic of Cricket's color bleeding over onto her to reveal warm chestnut eyes, and a light brown face, framed by black hair.

"Mhm!" Becka nodded, the motion almost too much for Cricket's arms.

"What do we say?" Cricket prompted.

"Oh! Thank you!" Becka grinned, showing off a gap where she must have lost a tooth along the journey.

"Come along then." Takayoshi turned on his heel, to hide the way his heart was still pounding loudly against his chest. Hopefully they had not heard it. Hopefully they had been too distracted with the promise of food, and warmth. He took a breath, forcing his hands to remain at his sides even as they itched to reach out for them. There would be time for that later, he was sure.

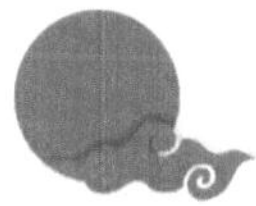

It was a relief to see Cricket cleaned up, properly clothed, the iron collar removed, and glowing from the fullness of his belly. It settled something within Takayoshi which had felt out of place, and wrong-footed for the last month. Cricket was doing better, and Takayoshi had been the one to provide that.

Still, he had hoped that a conversation with his sister could wait at least for a full day. Until Cricket and Becka had some proper rest at the very least. Apparently not.

"Your Highness." Cricket dropped into a low bow, his

short, unevenly cut hair falling into his face. It was jarring to see him without the long braid. That coupled with the hunted look of a man on the run made Takayoshi ache with the need to hide Cricket away from the world, but he would not.

"There's no need for that, Prince Cricket. We're all friends here." Atsuko laughed, waving her hand from where she sat behind her desk. It was cluttered with more paperwork than Takayoshi had ever seen on it, but she did not look as stressed or as tired as she had since before Anstice came to stay with them. Takayoshi decided he would pry into that later, after everything else was settled.

Cricket nodded, and rose from the bow, but Takayoshi could see the way he shifted his weight on his feet. How his hands tucked behind his back to hide his fidgeting. "I'd like to thank you for providing us with all you have so far. Knowing there was someplace safe for my daughter, someone who would protect her, was–" Cricket broke off, clearing his throat around something that seemed to get lodged there. "Well. I'd like to thank you."

"We're happy to provide sanctuary to our friends when they're in need." Atsuko's voice was soft, warm.

But Takayoshi picked up on the words Cricket said, and the ones he did not. A safe place for his daughter. Protection for Becka. Not for himself. Not for–

Takayoshi frowned at the realization.

"What is your plan?" he asked, the first words he had spoken since the three of them sequestered themselves in Atsuko's office. He had thought it best to let Atsuko handle this delicate situation. Clearly, he was mistaken.

"I'm sorry?" Cricket tilted his head as if he were confused, but Takayoshi saw the way his eyes narrowed. "My plan?"

"You do not intend to stay here." The words left Takayoshi cold. He could not imagine why Cricket would go back. How he could think that returning to Lunette would be a good idea. Especially when the skin of his neck was still raw from the bite of the iron collar Sunil forced him into.

"I don't see where that's any of your—"

"You plan to return to your uncle?" Takayoshi did his best to keep his voice even, but he could feel the words shake on the exhale. The urge to grab Cricket by the collar and— No. He had to remain calm. "To turn yourself in so that he can execute you for crimes against a crown that was never his to begin with?"

"Prince Takayoshi—" the tone sounded like a warning, but Takayoshi was not having it. He would not, he could not, let Cricket return there. Not now. Not so long as he looked as if his own daughter could take him in a fight.

"No."

"Excuse me?" Cricket's eyes narrowed further, and Takayoshi could smell his magic on the air. The sharp bite of ozone, and sea water.

"Shishi, I really—" Atsuko tried, but was cut off by a firm look from her older brother.

"You can leave," Takayoshi said, ignoring the way Cricket's eyes widened in shock, "if you can best me in a duel. If not, you will stay here until you have fully recovered."

Cricket released a soft snarl, more beast than man, the low light reflecting off teeth that were too-pointed to be elven. "Very well."

"I will meet you on the training field tomorrow at dawn." If he had to force Cricket to take better care of himself, so be it. Takayoshi was not above such things. Not where Cricket was concerned.

Cricket muttered something under his breath that sounded suspiciously like a curse, and turned on his heel to leave in a huff of irritation.

"Rest well, My Prince." Takayoshi was barely able to repress the way his lips twitched up at the corners. It was good to see some fight in Cricket again. Good to see some of that lingering strength.

"You likely shouldn't have provoked him like that. Not if you want him to, you know— *Like* you." Atsuko sighed, scrubbing her hands over her face.

"Uncle Reiji is still away at the monastery?" Takayoshi asked, cleanly changing the subject.

"He is not meant to return for at least three weeks. But with the weather changing as it is, I wouldn't be surprised if he came home sooner."

Takayoshi nodded, his hands flexing at his sides for his sword, body itching for a fight then and there. But that could wait. There were other, more important things, to be dealt with first.

"You don't think he'll try to turn Cricket in, do you?" Atsuko sounded genuinely worried about it. Takayoshi turned to her, and sighed a little, his rigid posture relaxing. There were times when he forgot he was the elder of the two. Times where the position of Queen seemed to be all that Atsuko was. But when it came to their uncle, she was still so very young. Still a child in many ways, hoping for Uncle Reiji's approval.

"I think he will pose a problem." Takayoshi wished he could trust his uncle to realize that the right thing in this circumstance was not the thing the law seemed to dictate. He wished his uncle would see where the rules had failed Cricket, and would continue to fail him. But the old man had always been very rigid, and Takayoshi did not see him softening any time soon.

"I'll have to forbid it." Atsuko's hands shook a little at the thought.

Takayoshi moved closer to her side, resting a hand on her shoulder and giving it a gentle squeeze. "I will stand behind whatever decision you make when it comes to Uncle. But my hope is that in meeting Cricket and Becka, he will change his mind." It might be in vain, but Takayoshi had more foolish hopes in his life. This was nothing compared to begging a goddess for help.

"Helios willing," Atsuko let the words out on a breath, and Takayoshi did not bother to correct her. He had long since stopped seeking Helios for guidance when Selene was the goddess who always answered his prayers.

CHAPTER 16

"I told you Annie, I'm fine," Cricket said, trying to brush off the way Anstice's fingers fluttered around him. She hadn't stopped moving since she entered his temporary rooms. Circling, and fussing.

"You don't look fine." She grabbed at his tunic, tugging it out to illustrate how large it was on him. "You're too thin."

Cricket thought to remind her that this was a borrowed tunic, something one of the Helion servants brought for him to replace his clothing that was ruined in his journey, but that wouldn't be technically the truth. Because the clothes he'd worn while coming up the mountain had started to sag on him in a way he knew was not from their repeated wear. "Well good thing you're here to fatten me up then."

Which seemed to be the exact right thing to say, because Anstice stopped her movements altogether and looked up at him with wide eyes, made glassy by unshed tears. "Oh Cricky, I've missed you."

"I've missed you too." He slumped forward, gathering her to his chest, and held her as tightly as his arms could manage. Normally, she might have complained he was squeezing too tight, or she couldn't breathe, but Cricket felt the tension leave her body right before she hugged him back just as tightly, and he knew there would be none of that. Not today.

"Come now," Anstice said, scrubbing at her face to hide tears Cricket wasn't going to comment on either way, "you need your rest. I heard you have a duel with Takayoshi in the morning."

Cricket groaned. "Honestly, that man. He's so. . ."

"Handsome? Dashing? Charming? Sweet?"

"I was going to say frustrating." Cricket mumbled, rubbing at his face to hide the heat threatening to take over his cheeks.

"Mhm. Sure." Anstice patted his shoulders, her grin all good-natured teasing. "Either way, get to bed. You have a big day tomorrow, and you look like you haven't slept in–" She pursed her lips, her eyes narrowing. "A long time."

"When you're right," Cricket yawned into the back of his hand, "you're right. You should too, when Becka wakes up she's going to want to have your undivided attention."

"And she'll get it." Anstice laughed, shooing Cricket into his bedroom, and shutting the door without another word.

"I'm not really sure how a duel is going to solve anything." Cricket stretched one arm back over his head, tugging at his elbow to loosen up the muscle in his sword arm. He didn't like the idea of fighting Yoshi. Especially with how tight his chest still felt. It had been a full twenty-four hours of warmth, and good food, and as many hot baths as he wanted. But the steam hadn't made the tightness go away. He thought maybe he should tell Anstice he needed to see a healer, but he didn't want Yoshi to get wind of it and decide to lock Cricket in his room, or something.

"That's just how he communicates sometimes," Queen Atsuko said sagely. She was as different from her elder brother as the sun was the moon. While Yoshi was all stoic silences, and having to guess at what he was feeling from the micro expressions that managed to slip through his calm mask, Atsuko was all smiles. Her eyes shone with a thousand emotions. And she seemed perfectly happy to speak her mind without any of the reserve her brother showed. It was a wonder they were related at all, much less raised by the same people. But then. . . maybe Helio didn't send their daughters to the monks, only their sons? Cricket wasn't sure.

"Still." Cricket huffed, shaking out his shoulders. He really didn't want Yoshi to put him on his ass in the snow. Thankfully, Anstice had taken Becka to talk about ribbons. Becka had taken to her Auntie Annie far quicker than Cricket had ever seen the little girl take to anyone, himself included. He was glad of it, but he hoped it wasn't a sign of underlying trauma from the circumstances they found themselves in.

"He wants to ensure you're healthy," Queen Atsuko said diplomatically, but Cricket could swear he saw a knowing smirk twitch up the corners of her mouth like she found this whole thing very amusing. Which, he supposed he might too, if their positions were reversed.

"Isn't that what a healer is for?" Cricket hoped he didn't sound as petulant as he was feeling, because he was definitely feeling petulant. It just didn't seem right that Yoshi was demanding a duel after Cricket had been traveling for a month, mostly by foot.

"Yes. But a healer can't assess how well you'd fare in a battle. A duel with my brother can." It sounded reasonable when she said it that way, but Cricket also would swear to

Selene herself that he heard Atsuko laughing. Hopefully at her brother, and not at him.

"Still seems a bit much." Cricket grumbled, lifting the sword that he'd been loaned to weigh it in his hand. It had more heft to it than his own blade. It would be cumbersome, and would likely throw his balance off if Yoshi tried to upset his footing. Wonderful. One more thing to stand in Cricket's way of getting this whole thing over with.

"For the record," Queen Atsuko said in a lowered voice. Her honey golden eyes, so, *so* much like her brother's, flicking to the door of the training ground as if to make sure they wouldn't be overheard. Cricket had gone down to the grounds early to get a feel for the terrain, to account for the advantage Yoshi would have of knowing his home field far better than Cricket, and trying to minimize that advantage as much as he could. Cricket turned to watch her, his brows raised toward the shaggy bangs he refused to let Anstice even out for him. "I don't think you should go back either. Sunil will kill you."

Cricket knew she didn't mean for the words to be a chastisement, or to scare him, but they settled like a stone in his stomach all the same. It wasn't like he didn't know they were true, he did. He'd known since the moment Uncle returned to the capital, that it would come to that. Uncle would have him killed one way or another. It was just a matter of waylaying it until Cricket could get everything he needed to, done. Primarily, ensure Becka's safety. And she was—he swallowed around the thought—she was safe now.

Cricket forced his words to leave him in a steady tone. "So, I should do what? Stay here? Wait for Sunil to wage war on your kingdom when he finds out you're protecting me? Watch as more innocent people die just because they got in the way?"

"No. I suppose not." Queen Atsuko let out a sigh, her shoulders sinking. Cricket knew that would be the reaction.

She understood him. She was a ruler too. She felt the weight of the lives they were responsible for on her shoulders as much as he did.

The door banged against the wall beside it, opened much too hard for the calm mask that Yoshi had plastered onto his face. And it was a mask, for Cricket could see the tell-tale twitch of his eyebrow. The way Yoshi was too rigid, too upright. He had very rarely seen Yoshi truly angry, but the signs were carved into his mind, just as every other expression Cricket had been able to catalog from the stoic white knight were. Cricket's foolish heart gave a pang.

"You could always bow out," Atsuko said, her gaze tracking her brother as he trudged across the snow-covered training ground. "Just do as he asks, and stay with us until we can come up with another solution. But," she let out a long breath, sounding very tired all of the sudden, "I suppose there isn't much chance of that. Is there?"

"Not really." Cricket tilted his head from side to side, stretching out his neck. "Like you said, this is how Yoshi communicates. I need to let him get whatever this is off his chest."

Atsuko nodded, giving him a polite bow, and stepping back out of the way as Yoshi came to stand before Cricket. Cricket tightened his grip on his sword, drawing in a breath that ached when the cold air hit his lungs. "Prince Takayoshi."

"My Prince." Yoshi bowed deeply, his white-blond hair falling into his face to hide whatever expression was painted there. When he rose again, his eyes were hardened, resolute. "I want your word, on your honor as a king, that should you lose this duel you will not leave Helio without me."

Cricket bit the inside of his cheek to keep himself from saying the first snide thing that sprang to his tongue. Antagonizing Yoshi wouldn't make this situation any better. "You have my word."

"Thank you," Yoshi seemed relieved, his shoulders drooping just a touch. Cricket bit down on the reminder that he wasn't being given much choice. That the royalty of Helio had all but ganged up on him to keep him there. A thought that should have annoyed him, but actually, strangely, comforted him. Settling into his bones like a warm weight.

"Then, let us begin." Atsuko clapped her hands, looking too delighted by what was about to happen, and the two men fell into defensive stances.

Cricket lunged first, his blade singing out to make a swipe for Yoshi's shoulder, but it was batted away easily with Yoshi's own sword. Cricket tried again, pressing the advantage he had, but found each thrust, and lunge blocked by Yoshi's sword.

A feint, that Yoshi side stepped, his feet hardly making a sound against the crunching, frozen grass.

An attack met with a parry.

Another thrust met with a repast.

And on and on. Each movement met with a purely defensive maneuver, as if the other man were simply playing with him. As if Yoshi were letting Cricket tire himself out.

And indeed, after a quick pivot that had Cricket skidding on the icy ground beneath him, Cricket found himself with a sword point pressed to his neck. His breath heaving in his chest, sending out puffs of steam in the cold air.

"I believe that I have won." Yoshi pressed the point a little further till Cricket felt the bite of the frigid metal against the heat of his neck. Not hard enough to cut, but enough that he knew one wrong move would draw blood.

"Okay," Cricket said, his tone reedy around the shallowness of his breathing. "Okay. I won't leave Helio without you."

Yoshi stared at him for a long time, his golden eyes narrowing, his grip unwavering. "Your word."

"Yes. Yes. You have my word." Cricket lifted his free hand to force Yoshi to lower the blade slowly. Once it was no longer pressing into his neck Cricket gave into the tickle at the back of his throat, and coughed into the elbow of his tunic. "I'm sorry," he wheezed when he felt Yoshi's hand reach for him, brushing warm fingers against Cricket's wrist as if to pull his hand away from his mouth for a better look. But not latching on. "The cold air."

"Get him inside, and settle him before the fire with some tea," Yoshi ordered, already reaching to take the borrowed sword from Cricket's fingers. "You should have told me you were feeling this unwell."

"Then you definitely would have made me stay." Cricket laughed around another cough as he managed to swallow a mouthful of pure white petals. He forced down the urge to vomit, and pushed himself to his feet, to bow deeply before Yoshi. "Thank you for taking care of us, Prince Takayoshi."

Yoshi looked at him, eyes narrowed, lips pursed, as if he were trying to figure something out. Trying to understand. But he did not say anything, he merely nodded. "Please go get warmed up. We will discuss what to do with Yue Sunil later."

Cricket pressed a smile onto his lips, and straightened his posture, hiding any signs of his labored breathing until he was out of sight.

CRICKET HAD CURLED up to nap away the exhaustion of the duel, after he'd shaken the chill from his bones, and quieted his cough. Becka curled tightly to his chest. But sleep was rudely interrupted by the sound of angry footsteps, and angrier voices outside the doors to their rooms.

"The king is looking for them. There's a man hunt, Takayoshi," a voice said sharply. Cricket pulled Becka in closer to him, checking to make sure she was still asleep, before pressing a kiss to her forehead. She needn't hear what was going on. She needn't know that their own family was trying to—

"Yue Sunil is *not* the king of Lunette," Yoshi's voice quivered with rage right outside of the door. Cricket could imagine him turning his back to it, his eyes narrowing to face down the threat of whoever this was. Whoever. . . No, it must be Yoshi's uncle. No one would dare speak that sharply to the prince of Helio. No one who was not family.

"He is the king by bloo—"

"Yue *Cricket* is king. And when he passes, his daughter will be queen." Yoshi's voice was steady, and quiet, but stern. A fired blade ready for a fight. "Yue Sunil has no rightful claim to the throne of Lunette by law. Blood be damned."

"You will bring us to ruin, Takayoshi. You will pit our kingdom against Lunette, and all their allies. There will be a war, and our people will die. All for some. . . some. . . *crush* on a *murdering demon*! Is that what you want?" Yoshi's uncle hissed.

"You forget yourself, Uncle. This has nothing to do with my feelings for Yue Cricket, and everything to do with what is right. Yue Cricket is the rightful king of Lunette. Yue Sunil is an invader. I would suggest, you reconsider your friendship with such a man." Yoshi's voice was soft, deadly. And his shadow remained in place just outside the door, a barrier between his uncle and Cricket and Becka. It was. . . a *relief*.

Yoshi's uncle made a dismissive noise, and Cricket heard him storm back down the corridor. He waited one breath, two, thinking that Yoshi would leave, but when Yoshi didn't

Cricket let out a sigh and rose from the bed. He readjusted Becka's blankets around her and went to open the door. Leaning against the doorframe he could see where Yoshi still had his back turned to their room.

"Your uncle is. . ." Cricket struggled for a moment before settling on, "problematic."

"Hm." Yoshi's shoulders looked stiff beneath his pale clothes, rigid. Cricket wondered if it was lingering anger about what his uncle said, or something else.

"Does he even care about the truth?" Cricket imagined this would not be the last time he was faced with the weight of Uncle Sunil's words. Uncle Sunil had made it his mission over the last few years to sow the seeds of discord against Cricket right underneath their noses. If Cricket hadn't been so concerned with putting out every fire Uncle Sunil set to village after village, maybe he would have seen the signs. But he'd been busy, and missed it. Maybe if Anstice had still been– No. He wouldn't let himself dwell. Not now. Not when he was faced with this.

Yoshi sighed, his brows pinching together to cause a wrinkle that Cricket itched to rub away with the pads of his fingers, and turned to face Cricket finally. "He does. He just does not want to believe that an old friend would do something like this. It is easier to believe that–"

"That an orphan with no idea where he came from would kill his father for a chair."

"A throne." Yoshi's eyes flicked away from Cricket's searching gaze as if in thought. "I did not say it made sense." Then with a tone of sheer determination, "Uncle will see reason."

Cricket had to bite the side of his tongue nearly hard enough to draw blood in his attempts to swallow down his laughter. Now was no time for such silliness. But he couldn't force down the question of, "Are you going to *make* him?"

"If I must." Yoshi didn't shrug, but he looked like he might have thought about it. "You should return to your rest. I know you are not feeling well. I will have dinner brought to your rooms in a few hours."

"Thank you." Cricket bowed his head.

Yoshi frowned at the words, shook his head, then turned to leave. But not before murmuring, "there is no need" over his shoulder.

Cricket wasn't sure how long he stood there smiling like an idiot, but eventually Becka's grumbling in her sleep pulled him out of his reverie.

CHAPTER 17

"Keeping him here isn't really a solution to the problem," Anstice said as she rearranged her skirts to sit next to Takayoshi in the library. He thought he had picked a corner where no one would see him. Where he could hide from the rest of the inhabitants of the castle and just watch Cricket interact with Becka. Watch the color return to their cheeks, and their smiles become more real. But of course, Anstice would find him. She always had a way of sticking her nose in where it did not belong.

"It is a temporary solution to a long-term problem." Takayoshi was man enough to acknowledge that.

"Have you thought of a long-term solution for our long-term problem?" Anstice picked at the ends of the sash on her deep colored gown, her lacquered nails in sharp contrast.

"The long-term solution is the death of Yue Sunil." Takayoshi lowered his voice so no one could overhear him, but the words sounded just as hard as they had the moment he realized what must be done. There was no way around it. Cricket exiled the man, and he had come back. If they imprisoned him, there was a chance of escape. The only solution was to execute him for his treason, and hope that his followers would disband without someone to lead them. "I see no other way."

Anstice nodded, her gaze flicking to where Takayoshi was watching Cricket and Becka. Cricket still looked sick, and drawn. Like there was something eating away at the heart of him. Something that three square meals, and a warm bed had not been able to cure. He still looked too thin, and there seemed to be a tightness to his breathing that was not there before. Takayoshi noticed it that first day in the rain, but then on the training ground it seemed to have gotten worse. Cricket refused to see a healer, even when Atsuko—

"There will be a war," Anstice said, breaking off Takayoshi's thoughts before they could spiral further.

"There will be. Cricket will have Helio's army at his back."

There was a sound from beside him, and he turned to look at the expression on Anstice's face. It was something complicated. Takayoshi was not good at reading people, and Anstice especially seemed to hide things away behind a mask. But her hand tightened on the fan in her lap hard enough to make it shake a little. So there was something going on. Something that they may not be prepared for.

"What is it?" He had a sinking feeling in his stomach that perhaps he did not want the answer to that question, but he needed it. If Takayoshi was going to protect the man he loved, he would need to know all there was about the situation, however difficult it might make the task ahead of them. Selene would be with them. Takayoshi knew that much for certain.

"I have heard that Sunil is dabbling in black magics." The words left Anstice hushed, and a little strangled, as if giving sound to them would make them truer than they were.

"What types of black magics?" Takayoshi turned his head

to look back at Cricket to make sure he would not overhear them. Although, they would have to discuss it with him soon, he did not think Becka needed to hear that her great-uncle was doing something dark and twisted as a means to kill her father.

"Spirits." Anstice's gaze looked around the room to make sure they were not being eavesdropped on, even though that was strictly forbidden in the castle. Takayoshi approved of her weariness. They were unclear on how far Sunil's spies reached, and it would be better if Sunil did not learn how aware they were of his movements. "I don't know much yet, but I know that he's been experimenting with creating hungry spirits. Like the ones you fought while in Cytherea."

"I will discuss this with Cricket this evening, but I want as much information as you can gather on this topic by week's end," Takayoshi said on reflex. He knew Anstice was well aware of what needed to be done now, but that did not change the squirming emotion twisting his stomach into knots. "We need to know what he plans to do with them before the war begins."

"How long do you think we have?"

"I am hoping that he will hold off at least until winter breaks, but if he intends to use spirits to fight his battles, he does not need to consider how the low temperatures would affect the performance of his army." Takayoshi's brows pressed together, a wrinkle forming between them as he thought.

"He'll need someone close by to control them. Someone with a good handle on Lunette's magical theories."

"Not if he simply lets them loose on the people." Bile crawled up Takayoshi's throat, and heat settled beneath his skin. He pulled his palm away from the table just as a small flame lit along the back of his hand. Damn. He thought he had developed better control than that.

"You don't think he'd—"

"Do you not?" Takayoshi turned to Anstice with his brows raised in question.

Anstice swallowed audibly, her eyes widening in fear.

"Gather what information you can. The better informed we are, the more likely we are to win this war."

"Of course, Your Highness." Anstice bowed her head in respect. "I hope you will protect my brother and niece, no matter what Sunil tries."

Takayoshi did not dignify that with an answer, it went without saying that was what he planned to do. He let his eyes find Cricket and Becka again. He knew Cricket would be furious when he found out, as he rightly should. Restless spirits were not uncommon in their land, but to weaponize them. To turn them loose on the living. That was something else entirely. Even if it was something the people of Lunette had invented, had utilized before in a desperate attempt to protect their people, that did not make it right.

"MAYBE I SHOULD JUST GIVE it to him," Cricket said, his voice trembling a little with the strain of the news he just received. It had shaken him far more than Takayoshi thought it should have, but then he supposed his opinion of Yue Sunil was drastically lower than Cricket's as he was not the man's family. "The kingdom, I mean. It would keep anyone else from getting hurt. And I'm. . ." He drifted off lifting his sleeve to show Takayoshi an arm full of glittering deep blue scales.

Takayoshi bit back a horrified gasp. When had Cricket's condition gotten that bad? How long had he been pushing himself to the very limits without once thinking of his own safety? And how much longer did he have to find his pearl before the damage was irreparable?

"I may not be an elf much longer." Cricket laughed, but the sound wobbled, like the joke got lodged somewhere in his throat.

"Do not say that." Takayoshi clenched his hands in his lap, ignoring the way his palms warmed, and sweat gathered.

"Say what?" Cricket looked up at him, eyes too wide, and mouth hanging open a little. Like he was no longer sure what he was seeing. Takayoshi did not understand the look that was suddenly in Cricket's eyes, but he decided now was not the time to discuss it. Not when there was so much else going on around them.

"That you would want to give up your kingdom to that—" He cut himself off, taking a breath to keep the disgust he felt for Sunil simmering in his blood from overflowing. "Just do not."

"Well what choice do I have? Soon enough I won't be elven anymore, Yoshi. We both know it."

"That is what I was trying to tell you before, when I came to your coronation." Takayoshi tried to keep his tone from sounding petulant. How often would they start this conversation for it to end in a fight before it really began? "While I was away, I learned about dragons."

"Of course, you did." Cricket flopped into a chair, letting all of the air out of him in a whoosh that sounded like it ached. Takayoshi wanted nothing more than to reach for him, to make this easier on him, but he could not. Not now. Not yet.

"Will you allow me to tell you?"

"I don't suppose there's any way of stopping you."

Takayoshi lifted a brow, and waited until Cricket waved

his hand for him to continue. "When you became a dragon, you should have grown a dragon pearl."

"Grown?" Cricket blanched.

"I am not sure how it works. But I do know that every dragon has a pearl which allows them to control their magic. And without it they. . ." Takayoshi gestured to Cricket as if to make his point.

"Lose control of the ability to shift back and forth." Cricket hummed, fingers picking at a loose thread on his trousers as if he were disinterested in the conversation. He was not. Takayoshi could see his mind working behind that blue gaze, cleverness shining through in a way that made Takayoshi's heart skitter over a beat. Styx, he was gone on Cricket, wasn't he? "I have never seen a pearl. I don't think I have one, and if I do, I don't know where it is."

"We should search for—"

"We don't have time for that." Cricket jerked his head upward to meet Takayoshi's eyes, his own face gone weary and lined. "Not while Uncle has my kingdom in his clutches."

"But if we—"

"Enough, Yoshi!" A snarl vibrated Cricket's lips, and he bared pointed teeth. "We don't have *time*! Uncle will come for me, and when he does, he will raze anyone and anything that stands in the way. Your kingdom and its people included. We don't have time to go on a quest for something that could be *anywhere*!"

Takayoshi's ears rang in the silence that followed Cricket's shouts. He took a moment to swallow down the words that sprang to his tongue, and tug his sleeves further down his wrists to hide the feathers clinging to his forearms. There was no sense in upsetting Cricket further.

"I think we should discuss the elephant in the room," Anstice said, her voice forced into lightness by a faux smile.

"What elephant?" Cricket scrubbed at his face with the

heels of his hands, heedless of the way his rough palms agitated the scar and scales that clung to his cheeks turning them red.

"The best solution to deal with hungry spirits." Anstice made it sound like whatever she was saying was obvious, and Takayoshi did not like what she was suggesting before she even suggested it.

"Oh yeah? What's that?" Cricket's head thunked back against the chair.

"Historically, when hungry spirits were a much bigger issue because we did not have the funeral rituals we have now, the gods kept them in check with celestial beasts." Anstice's voice was steady, and smooth, like a teacher schooling a room of children.

"Celestial beasts?" Takayoshi frowned.

"That's just a legend, Annie." Cricket sighed, his body sagging further as if all the fight had left him. "There aren't really—"

"What? Dragons? Phoenixes? Kitsune?" Anstice raised her brows, a laugh making her voice sound strange. "Which are you taking issue with, Cricky? Because you're a dragon. And Yoshi is a phoenix."

"A phoenix?" Cricket's eyes narrowed on Takayoshi as if Anstice were lying, and Takayoshi shifted under the searching gaze. Throwing something at Anstice for her words would not help anyone, but that did not make Takayoshi wish to do it any less.

"I only started exhibiting signs of phoenix abilities shortly after I left to discover more about your draconic nature." Takayoshi ignored the urge to itch at his feathers. To bare the marks of his otherness to someone who would perhaps understand better than anyone else. Because the moment he did, Cricket would begin to put the pieces together. He would see how his magic was affecting Takayoshi's. Takayoshi had little doubt it would send Cricket spiraling, and they did not have time for whatever fallout would come from such a revelation.

"No." Cricket rasped, eyes wide.

"It seems that proximity to you activated whatever nature I had that lay dormant." The lie was heavy on Takayoshi's tongue, but it did not matter. What mattered was that Anstice was right, the best way to combat hungry spirits was to fend them off with something stronger. And by nature, elves were not. But dragons? Phoenixes? They could turn the tide of a war that had not even yet begun. And Takayoshi's nature could act as the element of surprise that would save them all. "No one outside of the castle, and my friends who I left in Lunette to look after your people, know."

"So Uncle can't possibly. . ."

"Plan for this? No. He can't." Anstice's smile turned sharp, a knife's edge ready to cut. "We just need to train the both of you so when Sunil does decide to attack, we're ready."

"Train us?"

"I have not used my phoenix abilities extensively, and I am sure that you have not used your own in combat. We will need practice to keep them in check so we can be effective without hurting those around us." Relief flooded Takayoshi. With this secret on the table, and Cricket's seeming acceptance of it, there was one less weight settled onto his shoulders. And now they had a plan.

"How long do we have?" Cricket's gaze had not left Takayoshi, his eyes wide but assessing, as if he were searching for signs of the phoenix on his skin.

"Takayoshi hopes that we will have until the season breaks, but if he is using spirits as the main force of his army. . ." Anstice let the words drift off, the insinuation clear.

"Uncle could attack any day now." Cricket filled in, needlessly.

"We will begin preparations tomorrow." Takayoshi rose from his chair. "I will inform the knights."

"In the afternoon?" Cricket asked, hopefully.

"At dawn."

Cricket groaned loudly, flopping back into his chair again. Takayoshi turned before Cricket could see the smile tucked into the corners of his mouth.

CHAPTER 18

Do not say that, Yoshi said.

Cricket didn't know what about the words had drawn him up short. What about them created an echo in his head. Well. No. That wasn't true. He *did* know. It hadn't been the words themselves, it had been the tone, it had been the expression Yoshi wore as they left his lips. So earnest. It was the most open Cricket had ever seen Yoshi's face before. Like the thought of Cricket giving up had cracked something within him, and let everything he usually held so close to his vest out.

It was like seeing Yoshi, the real Yoshi, for the first time. Seeing down into the depths of him. Cricket always knew that Yoshi felt more deeply than he could express. That there was more to the white knight than a stoic nature, and the whisper of a wrinkle when he frowned. But he hadn't been expecting there to be so. . . so *much*.

And Cricket remembered thinking simply, *Oh*, so loudly that it left him dizzy with it.

It made his chest tighten further. The thing that had settled into his lungs gripping harder.

Cricket coughed around the feeling of that thing crawling up his throat. So similar, and yet so different from the black water that lived in his lungs years ago in Nishi. But no less terrifying. He coughed again, hoping Becka was deep enough asleep she wouldn't be woken by her father choking on whatever had taken hold of his body.

He coughed.

And he coughed.

And he *coughed*.

Till hot tears streamed down his face, leaving burning trails over the scales on his cheeks. Till he could hardly breath past the hacking sounds wracking his body. Till, at last, one long stemmed flower came from his throat, and splattered against the floor. Spittle and phlegm making the pure white petals of the snowdrop shrivel and glisten a little at the edges.

"What, in the name of Styx?" Cricket poked at the flower tentatively as if it would latch onto him again, curl around his arms and reach for his neck to continue to choke him. It didn't move. It just laid there looking beautiful, and deadly all at once.

"Cricky, I got the books you– What is that?" Anstice stopped in the door, her arms full of the books he asked for so he could research celestials on his own time. Her mouth fell open on a soft cry that she didn't even bother to muffle. "Where did that come from?"

"I. . ." Cricket cleared his throat around the hoarse, raw feeling the flower left in its wake. "I coughed it up. I seem to be a little bit sick, of late."

"When did this start?" Anstice set the books down on the desk in the far corner of the little sitting room that accompanied Cricket's quarters. Then knelt beside him on the hard stone floor.

"I don't remember, exactly. I thought it was just– I mean

it *is* just a cold from when we were traveling." He told himself the same thing enough times it didn't even feel like a lie as it left his lips. Still, he continued, rambling as his brain tried to make sense of what he was seeing. "It was logical that I had a tickle in my throat. And then– And then there were petals. And now– Now there's this. I think it's a snowdrop. That's what it is right?"

"I don't see how what kind of flower it is matters!" Anstice's voice went up an octave, like she was choking on the words.

"I suppose not." Cricket leaned back on his heels, gaze flicking over the flower. It was really quite pretty, when it wasn't choking the life out of him. "It seems to be getting worse."

"Obviously." Anstice grabbed a blanket from the back of the sofa to settle around his shoulders before she grabbed him and manhandled him up into the cushions. "I'll have to do some research, but I think I know what this is."

"You–" Cricket swallowed around another tickle in the back of his throat. "You do?"

"Hanahaki. It's a. . ." Anstice licked her lips, her dark eyes drifting back to the flower sitting in the middle of the floor, its white petals catching the light of the still roaring fire. "It's a love curse."

"A love curse." Cricket repeated the words like saying them himself would make them make sense. It didn't. "Where would I have picked up one of those?"

"Probably from your wretched uncle!" She growled, all fury, but then it settled, and her tone turned pensive, thoughtful. "Although why he would choose something like this to– Unless he didn't really know what he was looking at." Anstice hummed, her fingers rubbing soothing circles into Cricket's back. "Maybe he was just looking for something slow acting that would mimic another illness."

"But flowers?" Cricket almost laughed at the question, because it was so. . . so *ridiculous*, wasn't it? To be coughing up flowers.

"Well, yes. The curse is set when you swallow a seed. Then it grows into your lungs. It's. . ." She drifted off, her hand stilling against his back.

"It's fatal, isn't it?"

"No."

"Don't lie to me, Annie. It's fatal unless certain conditions are met, isn't it? There is no work around."

"No. There isn't a work around. At least, not a documented one." Anstice shifted uncomfortably in her seat. "But that doesn't mean we can't find one! I'm sure I could come up with–"

"What are the conditions?" Cricket leaned further into the cushions, exhaustion making him curl in on himself. If Anstice were trying to skirt around the truth then it was something impossible. For all he was ready to give himself over to his uncle, and his machinations, he did not want to die.

"It's a love curse, Cricky. You know what the conditions are."

Ah. That.

"True love's kiss. How delightfully maudlin." Cricket choked out another laugh, and it set him off coughing again until he was leaning forward, clutching at his stomach to try to hold himself together. That went on for a while until he'd coughed up a few more blossoms, and Anstice forced some water into him. "And of course, it'll have to be *romantic* love, because that's how these things are. It can't be broken by the love of my daughter, or my sisters."

"Who is it?" Anstice's words were hardly above a whisper. Like she was afraid of the answer.

"Does it really matter?"

"We could talk to them. We could–"

"No. I'm going to bed." It was sweet that she thought there was a chance. But Cricket knew better. "I've got training in the morning." Cricket rose from the couch, pulling the blanket tighter around his shoulders. "Thank you for the books. Good night, Annie."

"All– All right." Anstice nodded. Her hands twitched, but she didn't reach out to stop him, and Cricket was grateful for that, because all he wanted in the moment was to be alone.

A love curse. How fitting love would be the thing that felled the dragon. He snorted.

CRICKET TIGHTENED the scarf around his neck. The blasted thing had appeared right alongside a new cloak on the rack in his quarters by the following morning. He didn't have to guess to know that Anstice had spent hours digging up something that would keep him warm, and keep his coughing down to a minimum. He would have to thank her for it, later. Now– Now he had to swallow around a biting inhale as the air in Helio turned colder.

"Couldn't we have done this inside?" He leaned his shoulder into the wall, letting it take most of his weight as he watched the soldiers suit up.

"No. We could not." Yoshi looked a little worse for wear himself, although Cricket couldn't point out what about him had given Cricket that impression. There was just an aura of vaguely rumpledness about Yoshi that wasn't usually there.

"It's so damned cold here." Cricket breathed into his hands, rubbing them together to try to force warmth back into his fingertips. It did very little, but it was better than nothing.

Yoshi took Cricket's hands in his, ignoring the startled yelp that came from Cricket. Bare skin glowing gently with warmth that seeped in through Cricket's gloves. Cricket blinked down at their joined hands. *This must be the magic of a Phoenix. How fascinating.*

"You are not all right," Yoshi said, but the words sounded like they meant something else. Something that Cricket couldn't quite grasp. His heart squeezed in response.

"I'm fine. Let's just get this over with so I can go back inside." Cricket grunted, pulling his hands from Yoshi's and heading toward the men at the center of the field. "So, what's the plan?"

"We will train alongside these men in our celestial forms. This will ensure that we know how to use our magic in a battle scenario. Hopefully, we can find some way for our magic to work well alongside their training." Yoshi's boots crunched on the grass as he settled back at Cricket's side, warmth seeping from him and into Cricket's arm making the opposite one seem all the colder for it. "Do you have control over your dragon enough to decide when to shift?"

"Sort of." Cricket scrubbed at his nose, letting out a little bit of a laugh. "I tend to have better access to its magic when I'm, you know, upset."

Yoshi tilted his head, his eyes narrowing in thought. "That will not do."

"Well if you're so smart, you control your–" the words were cut off by the shimmering of the air, like when the summer sun got too hot and it made a person's very vision of the world ripple like water. A moment later a white bird, standing as tall as Cricket, was in front of him, its tail feathers licked by white flames hot enough to melt the frost on the grass and singe the blades. Whatever he was going to say completely dried up. Because if he'd thought Yoshi was a beautiful man, a beautiful elf, that was nothing compared to the form of a phoenix which he had taken. Which was *breathtaking*. "Uh..."

"You were saying?" Yoshi's voice had a proud, smug lilt to it. Although his beak didn't move, it seemed the words just appeared in Cricket's mind, and for some reason they were more expressive than when they filtered through his lips. Was this what he sounded like in his own mind, when he wasn't constantly trying to keep himself in check? Cricket swallowed, throat dry.

"How'd you do that?" he asked, resisting the urge to reach out and see if the down under one of Yoshi's massive wings was as soft as it looked. Would it be inappropriate to curl up there, close to Yoshi's chest, soaking up the warmth of his phoenix form? Probably. Did that make Cricket want it any less? Not really.

Yoshi tilted his head, took a deep breath, and the air shimmered again. A moment later the massive bird was replaced with Yoshi, his eyes crinkled slightly in silent laughter.

"Well?"

Yoshi hummed thoughtfully, then nodded when he seemed to settle on whatever he was going to say. "It is like a call, in the back of your mind. A voice asking to be set free. I simply heed the call."

"I don't— I don't hear anything like that." Cricket frowned. Any time his dragon took over it was involuntary. A moment of stress, or anxiety. The dragon took over because his upset made him weak. It didn't politely ask, or call to him like a friend the way Yoshi made it sound. It was an assault, a hostile takeover, not a conversation.

"You do not have a clear head." Yoshi rapped his knuckles

lightly against Cricket's forehead, an almost fond expression crinkling at the corners of his eyes.

Cricket blinked at him, ignoring the way heat crawled up the back of his neck, and wished that his hair was still there to hide the flush.

"I have had much practice clearing my mind and listening to my inner self."

"So, you're saying I need to try meditation." Cricket grumbled, his shoulders slumping.

"It could not hurt."

"Well, that doesn't help right now, does it?"

"No. I suppose not." The frown-wrinkle made another appearance as Yoshi shifted his weight on his feet, his eyes drifting from Cricket's down to the scorched earth that his tail left behind. Then a thought seemed to strike him, and he looked up at Cricket again. "Perhaps it would be good if you thought of a specific memory. One that triggered an emotional state. At least for the time being. Think of something that upsets you."

Cricket huffed, squeezed his eyes shut, and lifted his hand to rub at the bridge of his nose. It was a reasonable suggestion, but it also sounded painful. Still, if it would save his kingdom. . . "I don't really have much other choice."

"No. For now, you do not. But we will start on meditation practice this evening."

"Ugh. Fine. But I'm not responsible for what happens once I've upset it." Cricket shook a finger at Yoshi.

"I trust you." Yoshi met his gaze meaningfully, and Cricket found himself pinned to the spot. Yoshi trusted him. Why?

Then Yoshi took a step back to leave Cricket room to transform.

It was the memory of the screams. The smell of burning. The image of a tiny body curled up beneath a white cloak, shivering, sobbing, retching. Left behind by everyone she had ever loved.

Cricket felt the way his bones shifted, not painful, just a strange sensation of movement and wrongness. The way the scales left behind spread across his skin, growing, and thickening to be more protective than any armor he'd ever worn.

When he opened his eyes again, the world swam strangely, like everything was underwater and tinged in the colors of fear, and rage.

His breath came in hard pants, chest heaving as his slitted eyes flicked from one dumbstruck soldier to the next. Then one of them tightened their hand around their weapon, and fear became the prevailing emotion. The world tainted in yellow, and grew cold.

The dragon reared back, his long sapphire tail flicking out to knock several soldiers from their feet as he roared loudly. Ice made the air sparkle on his breath, and coated the grass in a thick layer of frost that had the soldiers skidding.

Someone shouted something, a name maybe, or an insect, the dragon was not sure, and he did not care. His head whirled, lips pulling back in a snarl, as he fixed his gaze on the white bird. Its flaming wings spread wide, back to the soldiers. Defensive. Protective. *Foolish.*

"Move," the dragon ordered, words a cold snap in the mind.

"I will not," the bird replied, tone soft and almost soothing.

"Then I will *make* you!" The dragon leapt at the bird, tackling it to the ground, claws digging into downy white feathers.

CHAPTER 19

Takayoshi took in a breath, the air freezing his lungs as the temperature dropped rapidly around them. A storm raged, not just in the dark, slitted eyes of Cricket, but in the air. The sky grew so dark it looked like night had fallen early, and snow began to drift down in soft flakes. Then Takayoshi was closing his third eyelid to brace himself against the wind whipping debris into his face just before Cricket lunged.

One breath, and Cricket was on top of Takayoshi, claws swiping at the delicate ends of his tail feathers. Takayoshi took to the sky, hoping to draw Cricket away from the soldiers, and give them enough time to escape whatever destruction Cricket would inflict on them.

One of the generals gave an order, and the knights ran for cover, which was likely for the best. Elves would be no match for Cricket in this state, only another celestial could get him under control, calm him down, and bring him back to himself. But Takayoshi had to get a handle on Cricket's rage first.

Takayoshi swooped higher into the air, narrowly avoiding Cricket's lashing tail.

"My Prince, that is enough." Takayoshi did not think that Cricket would listen, but he had to try. What other option was there? "You need to calm down."

"I am calm!" Cricket's long serpentine body wound its way around Takayoshi like a snake, giving him little space to move or escape.

"You are not." Takayoshi let himself meet Cricket's gaze again, hoping to see the gentle man in his eyes, but he was not there. That man had all been burned away with whatever memory Cricket used to shift into the dragon, leaving behind only the rage, and desperation of a caged animal.

"Who are you to tell me what I am and am not?" Cricket snarled, pointed teeth dangerously close to Takayoshi's right wing. Takayoshi jerked, flames sizzling along his feathers where Cricket's icy breath got too close. "Who are you to tell me *anything*?"

Takayoshi took a breath, reminded himself that Cricket was not himself, and snapped his beak at Cricket in warning. "I am a friend."

"I do not have *friends*!" Cricket lashed out, one clawed paw swiping at Takayoshi's wing, and catching it, tearing through the feathers and down to the delicate skin surrounding his hollow bones. A caw of pain left Takayoshi, but it did not stop the assault, or the fury in Cricket's gaze.

Something in Takayoshi's chest clenched, turning icy at the broken sound of Cricket's voice in his mind. The way the dragon met his gaze with not a single ounce of recognition. He wanted to tell Cricket he was wrong. To remind him about their journey through Lunette. To say the names of every person who had ever loved Cricket, and hopefully bring him back. But the moment those thoughts flew to his mind, there was a crash from the ground below them.

Takayoshi did not have time to process the knight splayed on the white ground, their shield and weapons flung around them, because when Cricket saw them, he dove.

"Cricket! No!" Takayoshi flung himself through the air after him. He reached Cricket just before the dragon reached the knight, barreling into him, and taking them both tumbling to the icy ground. His wing was crushed beneath them, feathers displaced, and torn away by the hard earth. But when they finished rolling, Takayoshi managed to force Cricket down, his talons sinking in just enough on the dragon's neck to secure him from moving further.

"Let me go!"

"I will not. Not until you have calmed." Takayoshi tightened his talons in Cricket's thick scales until he felt them give beneath him, a pin prick of blood staining the snow. "Yield."

Cricket slumped against the ground, his breath coming in hard pants, as if all of the fight had simply gone out of him. "Fine."

A low sound like the last whimper of a caged animal left Cricket, then the form of the dragon beneath Takayoshi shimmered, and flaked away like dead skin. The dark scales sloughing off to join the now steadily falling snow before all that was left beneath Takayoshi was the shivering body of Cricket.

"You're hurting me," Cricket said, his voice so soft Takayoshi almost missed it.

"Apologies." Takayoshi withdrew, his wings fluttering uselessly as he perched on the ground. He closed his eyes, taking a moment to calm his own racing heart, then let the phoenix retreat back under his skin, white feathers joining Cricket's scales on the ground, freckled with droplets of blood. Cricket's neck was bleeding, but only just, only enough to serve as a reminder for the force Takayoshi had to wield to bring the dragon to heel. But once the feathers finished floating away, Takayoshi found a deep slash through the sleeve of his tunic. Blood spilling out to stain the snow.

"I did that." The words broke, brittle and hard, coming out of Cricket's mouth as he moved to his knees to get a better look at the wound on Takayoshi's arm. His sword-calloused hands were gentle against Takayoshi's skin, seeming afraid to apply too much pressure lest he further injure him. "I'm so sorry. I didn't mean—"

Takayoshi opened his mouth to tell Cricket it was all right. That there was no need for thank yous and I'm sorrys between them, but the words died in his throat when another voice broke the silence of the frozen courtyard.

"Didn't mean *what*?" Uncle Reiji asked, anger making his voice shake. "Didn't mean to scare the living daylights out of our knights? Didn't mean to hurt my nephew? Didn't mean to show yourself for exactly what you *are*?"

"Uncle," Takayoshi said, his tone a warning.

"No! I *told* you this would happen, Takayoshi. I told you that he was not to be trusted. I told you that—"

"That is enough, Uncle!" Takayoshi's eyes narrowed, flames licking his palms as he rose from the ground. He moved, his body shielding Cricket from his uncle's cutting glares. "Cricket and his daughter are under the protection of the crown, and you would do well to remember that."

"You mark my words, Takayoshi, that boy will be the end of us."

"Consider them marked, and disregarded." Cricket gasped softly behind him, but Takayoshi did not turn to see the look of shock on his face. He kept his gaze fixed on his uncle's showing no weakness, and not backing down. "I expect to see you at supper this evening. Atsuko has missed you these last couple of days, and we would hate for the queen to be displeased. Would we not?"

Uncle huffed, his eyes flicking to something over

Takayoshi's shoulder, likely Cricket having risen from his crouch on the ground. "Very well. I shall see you at supper."

"Yes, you shall see *us* then." Takayoshi ducked his head in a barely respectful imitation of a bow, and forced himself to breathe through the laugh that threatened to choke his words when his uncle clicked his tongue and stalked off again.

"He's not wrong." Cricket moved to stand beside him, his head turned to watch Uncle Reiji's retreating back.

"He is." Takayoshi dipped his head to look at his still bleeding arm. It would heal quickly, but it would take time. Takayoshi would need for it to be bandaged and tended to before then. And it might scar, though Takayoshi found comfort in that thought. It could join the litany of other marks left on his skin by everything he had done for Cricket. Another symbol of the love that threatened every day to burn him alive.

Cricket sighed, shaking his head so his knotted blue hair fell into his eyes. "Let me see that." He reached for Takayoshi's arm, and Takayoshi let him take it to get a better look at the jagged cut down the length of his forearm. "I am sorry. I told you I didn't have control over it."

"You will develop control. We will start on meditation in the morning."

"Do you really think that'll help?"

"It is the only way I was able to learn to control my phoenix." Takayoshi winced as Cricket prodded thoughtfully at the wound. "We should move this indoors. The snow does not look like it will stop."

"All right. I'll help you wrap this once we're inside."

Takayoshi hummed in agreement, and led Cricket from the courtyard.

ATSUKO HAD FORGONE SITTING at the head of the table, as was expected of the queen. Instead, she and Anstice sat side by side across from Takayoshi, Cricket, and Becka. Becka sat in between himself and Cricket, her wide eyes gone wider and curious as she stared at Atsuko across the way. Takayoshi watched, bemused, as Anstice plucked choice vegetables from her own plate to settle onto Atsuko's without a word, and Atsuko kept eating and speaking as if this were common practice.

The only one of them who had stuck to tradition, was his uncle, who sat at the other head of the table, his back ramrod straight, and his hands gripping his silverware a little too hard. Uncle Reiji's silence would normally have been a heavy weight during a meal, but it was hard to even notice it over the pleasant hum of chatter that surrounded the table. A strange warmth curled up in Takayoshi's veins—like coming home—as he watched Atsuko regale Becka with yet more details of some ball or another, Takayoshi had quite lost track.

Takayoshi reached for his knife, wincing when the grip of it tugged at his bandaged arm. Cricket reached over, without a word, and took Takayoshi's plate from in front of him. Blinking, Takayoshi watched Cricket cut his food for him into manageable pieces, and slide the plate back. His eyes flicked down to the food then back up to Cricket over the top of Becka's head, but Cricket did not meet his gaze. He was busy talking with Anstice about something.

When Takayoshi looked across at his sister, she was watching them both with a knowing smile. As if she could see down into the very heart of Takayoshi, and know the warmth that spread through him like a woolen blanket. She likely could. She always had been able to.

"I heard you'll be starting meditation practice tomorrow," Atsuko said, putting a bean sprout on the edge of Anstice's plate who looked down at it with her nose wrinkled. "Just try it," Atsuko murmured softly.

Anstice let out a dramatic sigh, and took the bean sprout but she did not look happy about it. Cricket choked on a laugh, the sound quickly turning into a wheezing cough that had him pushing his chair back from the table. He stood, coughing into his elbow.

"Do you need some water?" Atsuko asked, already reaching for the pitcher, but Cricket shook his head, and fled the dining hall, still coughing wetly. Takayoshi turned to watch him go, a frown pressing his brows together.

"Is papa okay?" Becka asked, her little voice too loud in the suddenly silent room.

"I should check on him." Takayoshi took Cricket's glass from the table, and refilled it before he stood as well to follow after Cricket.

"I can do it." The sound of a chair scraping against the floor stopped him, and he looked back to see Anstice making her way around the table.

"No. There is no need. I will see to him. Please look after Becka, we will be back shortly." With a little wave, Takayoshi stepped out into the hall. The sound of Cricket's coughing led him down the corridor to a little alcove where Cricket braced himself against a window, his arms wrapped tight around his middle. There was something wet, and shiny on the sill, but when Cricket felt Takayoshi's presence, he whipped around and hid whatever it was behind his back.

Takayoshi held out the glass of water, keeping his face carefully neutral as he took in the burst blood vessel in Cricket's eye, the paleness of his cheeks, the way his lower lip looked a little puffy. "You are not all right."

"No. I'm not." Cricket grabbed the glass, and took a deep sip to smooth over his ruined voice, but he did not offer an explanation.

"Have you been to see the healer?" He could not imagine that Cricket would not have. Anstice would not have allowed for her brother to be this sick, and go untreated, unless he was hiding it from her just as he had been from Takayoshi.

"No." Cricket's fingers tightened around the glass, the water in it turning icy. His mouth opened as if he wanted to say more, to explain, but he stopped himself, took a breath and looked at something over Takayoshi's shoulder. "Anstice and I have it sorted out. She's been making me tea. I'll be fine in no time, I promise."

"Perhaps we should see them, just in—"

"No. Yoshi, I'll be all right." Cricket leaned forward patting Takayoshi's shoulder, then he stepped past him to head back toward the dining hall. "We should get back to dinner before your uncle thinks I've abducted you."

Takayoshi frowned, turning his head to follow Cricket's retreat to the dining hall. When he looked back to the ledge of the window, whatever Cricket had been trying to hide was gone. Pocketed or otherwise discarded, he was not sure. All that sat on the frame was a few petals, likely blown in from when the window had been cracked at some point.

"I know I've said this before," a voice drew Takayoshi's attention away, and he saw Anstice behind him, her fingers fiddling with the sash on her dress, "but if you love him, you need to tell him."

She *had* said it before. She had made her stance on Takayoshi's obvious attachment to her brother very clear. She thought they were both being fools in not talking about all of this. And perhaps she was right, perhaps if they got everything out into the open things would be easier, but they also might be a lot harder, and Takayoshi had never been a gambler.

"I have not hidden my regard for your brother. He must know."

"Must he?" Anstice tilted her head to one side, a little smile lighting her face. "I hate to be the one to tell you this, but as much as I love Cricky, he's terribly oblivious when it comes to certain things. Your regard *has* gone unnoticed. If you want him to know, you will have to say the words, explicitly."

"Now is not the time for bold declarations of love," Takayoshi countered, and although it was the truth, it felt like a lie. Because if now was not the time, then when *would* be? When Sunil came banging on the doors of Helio demanding Cricket's head?

"That sounds like a whole lot of excuses to me, Takayoshi." Anstice shrugged, turning on her heel to head back to the dining room, but not before murmuring, "I didn't take you for a coward, Your Highness."

The door to the dining hall closed behind her, and Takayoshi was left with the ringing of those words in his ears.

He was *not* a coward.

CHAPTER 20

The silence was getting under Cricket's skin, crawling like an itch, making him unsettled, and unmoored. He had never been one for silence, and it only grew worse, it seemed, the older he got. The quiet was heavy. The minutes ticked by in a slow drag. Cricket swore he could hear his hair growing!

"You are fidgeting," Takayoshi chided softly.

Cricket opened his eyes to look across the mat where Takayoshi was sitting, and frowned. His eyes were still closed, face impassive. "I am not."

"You are."

"How do you know I'm fidgeting? You're not even looking at me." He *wanted* Yoshi to look at him, but Cricket couldn't quite explain why. Cricket huffed, slumping forward against his knees. The urge was there, to poke at Yoshi, to stretch his lips into a true smile for perhaps the first time in his life with just Cricket's fingers. But he shook it off.

"Sit up straight."

"I'm trying." His back hit the mat with a soft *thud*,

blinking hard against the stars in front of his vision from moving too quickly.

"You are not. You are lying on the floor." Takayoshi let out a soft breath that could almost be misconstrued as a sigh.

"It's not working." The stone ceiling loomed dark, and cold above Cricket, judging him for his lack of ability to do something so simple. He never liked doing things he wasn't good at, it made him feel like a failure. Which was why he always opted out of ballroom dancing when Father offered to hire a tutor. He knew that to get better at something one had to practice, Father had told him that often enough, but Cricket didn't have the patience for things that he didn't have at least *some* aptitude for early on.

"That is because you are being impatient." Cricket heard Takayoshi shift, his clothes making soft *shush*ing sounds, but he didn't lift his head to look at him. "Would it be easier if I were not here?"

"No. You're not distracting me." Cricket sighed, pushing up onto his hands so he could meet Takayoshi's gaze. That wasn't quite the truth, Yoshi *was* distracting him, but Cricket didn't want him to leave. "I just have a hard time sitting still."

A frown-wrinkle appeared at the corner of Takayoshi's mouth, and he hummed thoughtfully. "You do not hear the dragon's call?"

"I don't hear anything, Yoshi. I never have. It always just sort of. . . happened." Cricket shrugged, resisting the urge to flop back against the mat again. Being dramatic wouldn't get either of them anywhere, and Yoshi was right, Cricket needed to get this thing under control so they could use it.

"Close your eyes."

"I've tried that, Yoshi." Cricket drew his knees to his chest, and slumped forward onto them. He didn't even know what he was supposed to be listening *for*. He assumed there would be a voice, or a growl, or something to indicate where the dragon resided in his mind. But without the stimuli of danger, all was silent. Or maybe not silent, rather, too loud. Cricket could not focus on anything but the racing of his thoughts, and the realization that this was a waste of time. He should be preparing for a war that would come to Yoshi's door to get him, and instead he was sitting in a room, closing his eyes, and trying to relax into something he'd just never be *good* at. "This is pointless."

"It is not pointless. Close your eyes." Yoshi scooted himself so that he was close enough Cricket could reach out and touch him if he wanted to. He *did* want to, Cricket realized. The thought sobered him a little, had Cricket clearing his throat and settling back into the careful lotus pose Yoshi insisted was proper form for meditation. Then Cricket closed his eyes, and let out a long breath through his mouth.

"Now what?"

Yoshi didn't answer, but a moment later Takayohi's his sword calloused hands took hold of Cricket's own, seeping warmth into his ever chilled skin, and threading their fingers together, palms pressed against each other. A soft hum filled the air, Yoshi's voice moving over some song that Cricket didn't recognize as Cricket felt their magic buzz between their palms like static.

"What're you doing?"

"Focus on the push and pull of our magic. Focus on the softness of my voice. Let those things drown out your mind."

"This isn't going to—"

"Just try it, My Prince," Yoshi insisted. He took up the humming again, the tune gentle, and leading.

Cricket sighed, and let his shoulders sink. There was no fighting Yoshi on this, it seemed. Cricket hadn't realized how stubborn Yoshi could be, nor how lovely his voice sounded when creating a tune all his own. He wondered what Yoshi would sound like playing an instrument. What it would feel like to get lost in the music that poured from him.

"Focus," Yoshi chided gently.

His magic pulled a little harder at Cricket's, and Cricket was lost to it. Lost to the softness of his voice. Lost to the feeling of their magic moving between them like the tides. There was nothing else. No thoughts. No voice. Not even the hint of the dragon lingering at the edges of Cricket's mind. Just the calming shift of the warm and cold currents between them.

What felt like both minutes, and hours later, Yoshi was pulling his magic back, the connection between them dissolving. Cricket opened his eyes, the lids heavy, and watched as Yoshi straightened his posture. Then he asked, "did you hear anything?"

And Cricket knew he'd have to let Yoshi down, again.

"No. I didn't. I just. . . it was just really calm. I'm sorry, Yoshi. I tried." The words left something raw behind in Cricket's throat that he tried not to think about lest it bring on another coughing fit. He didn't want Yoshi looking at him like he may break again.

A wrinkle formed between Yoshi's brows, as if he didn't understand what happened, but he shook himself before he could say whatever was troubling him. "It is all right. We will try again tomorrow."

Cricket nodded, although he was sure the following day would be no different. "If we don't get control over this thing, maybe it would be better if I didn't use it. Or I could use some iron to–"

"No. We will find a way," Yoshi said, his gaze hardening.

"Oh. All right." Cricket shifted a little, his knees starting to ache from where they were curled uncomfortably beneath him.

"How are you feeling? The cough–"

"It's fine. I told you last night, Annie and I have it covered. Don't worry about me, I'll be all right." Cricket forced on a smile. He wouldn't be all right. Not so long as he kept his feelings hidden, and tried to swallow around them. But he imagined rejection of them would be far worse—maybe instant death—than letting them slowly strangle him. At least this way there was some chance Anstice might find a cure.

"Hmm," Yoshi said thoughtfully, his fingers flexing where they were still linked with Cricket's. Threaded through, in fact. Yoshi's long brown fingers curving delicately around the backs of Cricket's lighter hands, rubbing callouses against Cricket's dry knuckles.

"Uhh. . ." Cricket laughed awkwardly, pulling his hands away, even though he wanted to do anything but. "I should umm. . ." He cleared his throat, his gaze flicking away from Yoshi's intense golden gaze to literally anywhere else in the room, which was unfortunately empty and not very interesting. "I should go and ummm. . . check on Becka!" Cricket leapt to his feet, and was already halfway to the door before he turned back to look at Yoshi over his shoulder.

Yoshi was still sitting there in the middle of the floor, his posture just as straight as it had been all morning, but his hands flexed against his knees.

Rubbing his palms on his trousers as if they too were tingling, Cricket rushed out into the hall. He allowed himself one breath to slow the strange rabbiting of his heart, and swallow around the tickle in his throat, then he was off again to find Becka, and distract himself.

But not before running into Atsuko, it would seem, who came around the corner just as Cricket was about to turn that direction and barrel straight into her.

"Oh, Cricket," Atsuko said, a little laugh escaping her as she brushed a strand of dark hair back from her face. "Where are you rushing off to? I thought you and Shishi were working on meditation?"

"We were! But uhh. . . we're finished now. And I need to go check on Becka. I know Annie's with her but–" Cricket rocked back on his feet, tucking his hands behind his back. He knew they didn't look any different. He knew that Yoshi left nothing behind. No mark. No sign. Just the faint tingling left over of skin on skin. But Cricket was sure that if Atsuko saw them, she'd know.

"Ah. I see." Atsuko smiled a little, and Cricket wasn't sure *what* she saw, but he was sure whatever it was was too much, and it was going to get him into trouble. "I'll walk with you to the library. I think that's where Anstice and Becka are holed up today. I was on my way there anyway."

"Sure?" Cricket squeaked, and fell into step beside the queen.

The only sound for an entire hallway was their footsteps echoing back to them. Cricket tried not to think about what Atsuko could be thinking. He tried to keep himself focused on the task at hand, reaching the library to see his daughter. But the longer they walked in silence, the more the nervousness crept under his skin. He wanted Atsuko to like him, he wasn't sure why, but he did.

"How did it go?" Atsuko asked, mercifully breaking the stalemate with perhaps the question Cricket wanted to answer the least. Something on his face must have given Atsuko the answer, because she frowned and said, "that poorly then?"

"He should just give up on me." Cricket stared down at the toes of his boots, watching them tap softly against the stone floors of Helio's castle. Stone. Cold, and hard like Cricket always thought Yoshi was. But he was beginning to wonder how much of that was true.

"He won't."

He stumbled, gaze widening when it jerked up to look at Atsuko. She wasn't looking at him, she'd kept her eyes carefully on where they were going as if having this discussion while facing him was as embarrassing for her as it was for him. Which was just silliness, but Cricket found himself relieved. The scales lingering on his neck may have hidden much of the warmth crawling up it, but that didn't mean Atsuko would miss it entirely.

"Why not?" Cricket wasn't sure he wanted the answer. But he knew he needed it. He needed to understand better who Yoshi was. To make sense of everything he had seen from the man since arriving in Helio. There was a softness that lay under all of Yoshi's actions, a protectiveness that hadn't been there in their first adventure together. Was that because of whatever Yoshi had gone through in the five years they were apart? Or was there another reason?

Atsuko turned her head to look at Cricket, her brows raised so high they disappeared into the dark fringe on her forehead. She looked at him as if he should know the answer to his own question, and when he didn't, she just let out a soft "huh" and shook her head. "It's not in his nature to give up on things he cares about."

Cricket's heart gave a traitorous lurch, a tickle forming at the back of his throat. He opened his mouth, whether it was to ask what Atsuko meant, or cough, he wasn't sure, but he never got the chance to do either.

"Here we are." Atsuko pulled the door open, and gestured for Cricket to head inside with a serene smile on her face, as if she hadn't just rocked his entire worldview in the span of a few minutes.

"Thank you." Cricket bowed his head, and entered.

"Papa!" Becka screeched, running headfirst into his stomach and dislodging the cough he'd been swallowing down for hours.

He hacked, retching against the feeling of flowers crawling up his throat.

"Papa?"

"It's okay, little sunflower." But it wasn't, he knew it wasn't. He heard how wrecked his voice was, a fresh cluster of stems clogging his airways. Somehow, he managed to choke them down, scrubbing away the tears that slid down his cheeks.

"Are you certain you shouldn't see a healer about that?" Atsuko frowned at him, her hands still outstretched in front of her as if she'd been about to reach for him to help.

"He'll be all right," Anstice said, moving so she was between Atsuko and Cricket to hide him as he regained control of his breathing. "He just needs some tea."

"Yeah, tea." Cricket winced around the sharp scrape of the words in his throat.

"All right. But if that cough doesn't get better soon—"

"Then I'll see a healer. You have my word." Cricket flapped his hand. "Go on about your business, Your Highness. Annie and I are going to go back to my rooms to have some of that tea."

Atsuko watched them for a moment longer, her brows creased, before she turned to head deeper into the library and Cricket let himself relax a little.

"It's gotten worse," Anstice said after Atsuko had turned a corner. Cricket took Anstice and Becka's hands and tugged them out into the hall, hoping they wouldn't be overheard.

"It's still manageable. I just need to be more careful." He dipped to pick up Becka and perch her on his hip where she promptly buried her face in his neck, clearly upset by his coughing. "Have you found any solutions?"

"None aside from the obvious. Why don't you just—"

"Annie. Think about it. What do you think will happen if I just pick any old person and they reject me?" That had been

Anstice's plan, find someone to love him, and hope it was true love. It was foolish, and not just because people lied, but also because it was a dangerous game of chance he didn't think he could afford to play.

Anstice stopped where she'd been walking beside him, tugging at his free arm, and frowned. "You don't think. . ."

"I do. So it's better if we find a solution outside of the normal cure." Cricket hitched Becka up further on his hip. "Why don't you tell me what Aunt Annie was teaching you today, huh little sunflower?"

Becka nodded, sniffling a little. "She taught me how to use a fan to smack someone in the *face*."

"She what?" He turned to glare at Anstice who still looked like she was deep in thought.

"Self-defense," Anstice said, flapping her hand to brush off his question. "But Cricky, what if it's Tak—"

"Do you want to take that chance, Annie? Because I don't." Heat crawled up the back of his neck again, although he wasn't sure why. Just the insinuation that the curse might think *Takayoshi* was his true love was ridiculous. Not only was it ridiculous, it was impossible. They were hardly even friends. And even if Cricket did care for him, there was no way Takayoshi felt the same. No way it was returned.

"I guess I'll just have to work harder." Anstice frowned, and muttered something under her breath that Cricket decided was likely better he not hear.

"Right. In the meantime, meditation was a bust this morning, so I'll have to work on something else to get my dragon under control. You didn't return those books I was reading, did you?"

"No."

"Papa, where are we going?" Becka asked, poking her head out from where she'd been hiding.

"Back to our rooms. Why?" Cricket's hand moved to steady her back so she wouldn't topple out of his arms.

"Shishi promised he'd teach me music. Can I go there instead? I don't want to sit and watch you and Aunt Annie read boring books."

Cricket stopped, looking down at his daughter with wide eyes. "*Shishi* said he'd teach you to play music huh?"

"Mhm."

"When did he say that?"

"After dinner last night." Becka shrugged, unconcerned, her little legs starting to wriggle in a request to be put down. "Can I go?"

"Can Aunt Annie walk you?" His gaze met Anstice's over the little girl's dark head, a question in his lifted brow. Anstice shrugged in return.

"I can go alone. I'm a big girl." Becka grumbled.

"I know you are, princess. But I'd feel much better if you let her take you."

"Oh fiiiiine. Just put me down." He lowered Becka to her feet, and she moved obediently to take Antice's outstretched hand.

"I'll meet you back at your quarters after we go see *Shishi*." Anstice winked, then she was gone, her and Becka whirling down the hall in all their finery, and laughter, and Cricket was left reeling at the idea of stiff, stoic Takayoshi allowing Cricket's daughter to call him *Shishi*.

CHAPTER 21

The door to Takayoshi and Anstice's war room was open just a handful of inches. The light from inside spilling out into the dark corridor beyond, and while Takayoshi knew, logically, that no one could reach them inside the walls of the castle, the knowledge that someone was in that space, *his* space, had him clenching the hilt of his sword. He stepped forward on silent feet, and pushed the door open further.

It moved with a faint creak, but the midnight-blue head did not look up from where Cricket sat looking over the papers sprawled messily over the table. He shuffled aside one of Anstice's blueprints to a list of possible ingredients for the potion they found to make someone look like Cricket and Becka.

"I didn't know," Cricket said, not looking up.

"Did not know what?" Takayoshi pulled out a chair, and settled in beside him.

Cricket set down the paper in his hands, and looked at Takayoshi, his blue eyes too wide in his face when he said, "That you did all of this for us."

Takayoshi was not sure who Cricket thought had done everything needed to help him and Becka escape, but clearly he had been living under some false assumptions. Maybe that was why Anstice said that Cricket did not know how Takayoshi felt. If Cricket did not know the lengths Takayoshi had gone to protect him and his daughter then of course he would not know.

"I had to ensure that you were both safe." It was not precisely what Takayoshi wanted to say. What he wanted to say was that he loved Cricket, desperately. That meeting Cricket had changed who he was on a base level, and made his life richer, and fuller for it. That if it were not for Cricket, Takayoshi would not have made friends, or have learned to disregard his uncle's rules, and be himself. "All I have ever wanted was to ensure you are safe, My Prince."

Cricket blinked at him, his mouth hanging open just a little, and color staining his cheeks as if he were looking at Takayoshi for the first time. That thing that had curled up warm and content in Takayoshi's veins flared to life, making him want to surge forward and steal the breath from those lips, and the color from his cheeks. But he did not. He stayed where he was, and waited for Cricket to say something else. Cricket remained silent, his flustered state seeming to take up every other thought.

"Was there something you wanted?" Takayoshi prompted. He both wanted to bask in Cricket's attention forever, and shrink from under Cricket's wide open gaze. It was very confusing.

"Oh. Uh. Yes." Cricket cleared his throat, snapping his mouth shut as he tore his eyes away from Takayoshi. "I wondered if you might have some way of communicating with my people back home. I thought Ignacia would reach out, but she hasn't. And I'm honestly a little worried about her and the others. I shouldn't have left them behind for

Uncle to—" He stopped himself, swallowing hard enough that his Adam's apple bobbed. "Anyway, have you heard anything from them?"

"I have not. My last communication with Claudia was shortly after you left the capital to let me know that you were on your way here." Takayoshi frowned. He had not thought much of it at the time, likely because he was so worried about Cricket making it up the mountain safely that everything else seemed trivial by comparison.

"Can we try? If you have a way of communicating with Claudia and Leo. Can we try?" Cricket's tone went pleading, his hands tightened to fists atop the piles of papers on the table. There was no denying him, not that Takayoshi wanted to. He wanted to give Cricket anything and everything he could ever need or want, and this seemed a small thing for Cricket to ask of him.

"Yes. We will try this evening, after supper. Until then, I have training." Takayoshi rose from his seat, his hand twitching at his side to reach out for Cricket's, but he forced it to stay where it was.

"Oh! Me too. Annie set up some time for me." Cricket scrambled out of his own chair, the legs making a loud squealing noise against the floor.

Takayoshi's brows lifted at the statement. He noticed that he had been running into Cricket a lot more lately. The castle was not that large, no, but it was also not small. It seemed conspicuous that they should run into one another multiple times a day. As if someone else were pulling the strings, and seeing to it they had constant contact. Takayoshi made a mental note to confront his sister about it later. If Anstice were up to something, Atsuko would be in on it, Takayoshi had little doubt, and he wanted them both to know that he saw what they were doing, and he did not approve.

SWEAT TRICKLED down the back of Takayoshi's neck, his tunic sticking to his back as he rounded on Cricket again, sweeping for his legs with his sword.

"Missed me," Cricket chuckled, springing out of the way, and winking as he landed softly. He was out of breath, his words near a wheeze, but he had not stopped yet, seeming incapable of giving up. "You'll have to try harder than that."

Takayoshi could not force down the smile that twitched at the corners of his lips, nor ignore the heat which coiled up the back of his neck making loose strands of hair stick to the damp skin. It was good to see Cricket like this, lively, playful. Good to know he was still capable of such things. Although Takayoshi could maybe have done without the flirtatious wink. "You have been practicing."

"Well of course I have." Cricket snorted. "I couldn't have you putting me on my ass the next time we met, could I? Not now that I'm king. How would that look?"

"You have gotten quite good."

Cricket squawked at the compliment, his feet getting caught up in one another, and stumbled.

Takayoshi pressed the advantage, and had Cricket backed against the wall, the point of his blade pressed to the soft underside of Cricket's chin in seconds. It was the third time he had pinned Cricket as such.

Cricket wheezed another breath, and Takayoshi began to worry. He thought the first time they dueled Cricket had been unable to keep up because he was exhausted, and malnourished, but that had been weeks ago. Since then, Cricket had plenty of rest, and food, and yet, he looked worse than he had when he arrived. Dark circles weighed heavily under his eyes, and there was a thinness to his cheeks that looked almost skeletal in the too-bright lights of the training room.

"You got me." Cricket laughed, the sound hollow, as he leaned his head back against the wall and coughed a little into his elbow. He was breathing hard, but the flush had not left his cheeks from his momentary embarrassment. If it were not for the rattling in his chest, Takayoshi might have done something unbearably stupid, like reach out and feel that warmth for himself.

"Your illness has gotten worse." Takayoshi frowned, lowering his blade. His weight shifted forward on the balls of his feet, the urge to press in closer twitching in his muscles like static. But if Cricket wanted him to help, he would ask for it, would he not? He would tell Takayoshi what was wrong.

"It's just a little cold, Yoshi. Nothing to worry your pretty little head about. Now, should we go again?" He fell into a fighting stance, his borrowed sword gripped tightly in one hand. But Takayoshi had seen enough for one day. "I think I almost got you that time."

"We need to try meditation again." Tucking his blade into the sheath, Takayoshi made his way across the room once more. "If you would like to continue training, we can do so afterward."

"Meditation? *Again?*" Cricket's shoulders slumped, his arms falling limp at his sides, the edge of a whine in his voice. "It's not working. I really think if I just—"

"Prince Takayoshi," someone said from the door to the room, and both men turned to see the bedraggled looking page. The girl was panting roughly, her hair falling into her face in long dark waves. In spite of that she managed to hold herself upright, her arms at her sides as she fell into a low bow. "Your sister asked to speak with you in her study. Both of you." The girl bowed a second time to Cricket.

"What has happened?" Takayoshi asked, already halfway to the door. He heard Cricket's soft tread behind him, the other man falling into step with him easily.

"I was just asked to retrieve you." The girl shook her head, but there was a paleness to her face that was too much even for a Helion winter. It looked more like dread than anything else.

"That doesn't mean you didn't hear something," Cricket piped up, a light note to his voice that Takayoshi recognized from the few times he watched Cricket interact with scared children while on their travels. His own special way of putting others at ease, and getting them to open up to him. Takayoshi did not think it would work on anyone in Helio.

The girl cleared her throat, looking at Cricket over her shoulder.

He gave her an encouraging smile, and a little nod. "You won't get in any trouble. Yoshi and I won't tell anyone you told us. Will we, Yoshi?"

"Stop antagonizing the messenger, My Prince. We will find out what this is about soon enough." Takayoshi cut Cricket a look which to many might have been considered irritated, but if anyone who truly knew Takayoshi had seen it —Atsuko or Claudia or Leo, perhaps—they would have seen the fondness in it. It was a struggle not to let the corners of his lips lift into a smile.

"Spoil sport." Cricket huffed, crossing his arms over his chest, but he let the subject lie, and the girl's shoulders relaxed a fraction. She still looked terrified, but at least she no longer seemed anxious about being the one to lead Takayoshi and Cricket to the queen.

The girl stopped in front of Atsuko's study, and gestured

for them to go inside. Takayoshi gave her a small bow, and headed in.

"Thanks for the escort Miss. . ." Cricket let the words trail off, a friendly smile in his voice. Takayoshi did not have to turn around to imagine the way he shifted his weight onto one foot, his shoulders hunching forward a little to make himself smaller, less threatening. A technique that was sadly wasted when one had antlers, and scales enough to make people nervous.

"It was my pleasure, Your Highness," the girl said, then she pulled the door shut behind them without giving her name.

"So it's not just you, Yoshi. All you Helions are stiff." Cricket chuckled, shaking his head.

Takayoshi turned to the big desk where his sister sat, Anstice at her side. "What has happened?"

"I think you both may want to sit down," Atsuko said in a tone that made it clear this was more of an order for their own good than a suggestion.

Takayoshi nodded, and took one of the chairs on the other side of the desk, sitting on the edge of the seat, his back so straight he was almost leaning forward. Cricket flopped down onto the one beside him, his hands moving to fidget with the ends of his tunic in his lap. Once they were settled, Takayoshi got a better look at his sister. The lines at the corners of her eyes were more pronounced, tension pressed into every angle of her face. Her lacquered nails were digging into the top of the armrests on her chair. And she was leaning, subtly, towards Anstice like a flower seeking sunshine.

"What has happened?" Takayoshi asked again, ignoring the way his shoulder blades pinched in the middle of his back. He could not show weakness, not now, not when everyone around him needed for him to be strong.

"There was an attack in Gisli." The words landed like a slap across Takayoshi's face, he reared back, blinking hard.

"That is at least a three days' ride from the border." Takayoshi struggled to keep himself from reaching for his blade. "There are at least two towns between Lunette and Gisli."

"Three," Anstice corrected. "Sunil and Craven took the others quickly, and quietly."

"How many survivors?" Cricket's own tone had gone quiet, real anger lining the edges of it. Takayoshi could feel the cold emanating from him like mist.

Anstice shook her head, and the temperature in the room dropped another five degrees.

"He's gone too far!" Cricket slammed his fists on the arms of his chair.

"There's more," Atsuko said, and if Takayoshi were not her brother, he would not hear the subtle tremor in her voice. The underlying current of fear. "A pack of rabid restless spirits led the charge."

Quiet blanketed the room, settling over them as heavy as wet snow. Takayoshi took a breath to force down the panic welling up inside of him. He knew, of course he knew, that this was coming. Anstice said as much. It was why they had been trying to teach Cricket control over his dragon. But he thought they had more time. That the winter cold of Helio would provide them at least some protection.

Foolish. I have been so foolish.

"How many?" he asked when no one else in the room seemed capable of voicing their thoughts any further.

"Our scouts said at least a hundred. Too many for the small contingent stationed at the bottom of the mountain to handle without help. He'll be pushing up the mountain before the season is through." Anstice's tone was calm, all business, and Takayoshi appreciated it. They did not have time to get emotional about this. Not when there were things to do.

"I am afraid we must step up your training. There is no other option." Takayoshi turned to look at Cricket whose face had gone ashen, the scales on his neck heaving with every labored breath.

"There isn't time, Yoshi." Cricket's words came out a rasp. "There isn't time for *any* of this. We have to go. We have to leave today."

Takayoshi shook his head. "We have at least a fortnight before he makes it to the bottom of the mountain with the snowfall." Takayoshi's hands itched to reach out to Cricket. To provide him with some small measure of comfort. But he knew the gesture would be unwanted, so he kept his hands folded carefully in his lap. "The summer palace is there, we can treat that as a stronghold. Till then, we should take all the time we have to find a solution for controlling your dragon without the pearl. It is our best hope of felling the restless spirits."

"He'll have made more by now," Cricket mumbled, as if he were speaking to himself. "He'll have used every person he killed in battle and turned them over to fuel his war machine."

"He will." Atsuko let out a breath, her shoulders slumping. "Our scouts are keeping an eye on the numbers, but my brother is right. Our best hope is to meet him at the bottom of the mountain. It will be the easiest to defend, and it will give you the time you need."

"What about all the towns and villages between Gisli and there!" Cricket's head jerked up, his eyes flashing as the pupils narrowed to slits. "Are we just supposed to let them *die*!"

"I already have people working on evacuating everyone that we can." Anstice frowned, her knuckles pale around the fan in her hand.

"What of my family? What of the people I left behind?" The words sounded broken, and hurried, desperation making them a heavy, leaden thing.

"We will contact Leo and Claudia for information on them." Takayoshi reached over, heedless of whether it was wanted or not because now it seemed necessary, to take Cricket's hand in his own, giving it a faint squeeze the way Claudia had done for him so many times. Cricket's head jerked to look at Takayoshi with wide, slitted, blue eyes. But something within his gaze seemed to settle at the continued contact, and he nodded. "Come, let us contact them, then we will return to your training. We are short on time. We cannot waste any of it panicking."

"Yeah." Cricket swallowed, his hand turning over so he could thread his fingers through Takayoshi's in a gesture that was so soft, so trusting, it made Takayoshi's heart stutter in his chest. Then he turned to fix Atsuko and Anstice with a wide, triumphant smile. "Let's get to work."

CHAPTER 22

Yoshi had not let go of his hand.

Cricket wondered if he noticed. He had to notice, didn't he? There was no way for a person *not* to notice when they were holding another person's hand. But Cricket wasn't going to call attention to it. Not when the feeling of Yoshi's warm, calloused fingers threaded through his own seemed to settle something within him, bringing a calm to Cricket he hadn't known since. . . Well, he wasn't really sure when the last time he felt so calm was. Maybe not since before all of this began, five years ago.

"Claudia and Leo," Cricket started, his tone thoughtful, "they went with you to find the archive."

"They did." Yoshi led Cricket down the hall back to the war room where Cricket found the plans to save himself and his daughter. He wasn't sure what all of it meant yet, but he knew it meant *something*. Just like the fact that Yoshi had taken his hand when he'd needed it the most meant something. Just like Cricket not asking him to let go, *meant* something. Cricket wished he knew what that something was.

"They are my friends. I would trust them with my life, just as I trusted them with yours and Becka's."

Cricket was sure he only meant the words as a reassurance, but there was so much more to them than that. So much that lay beyond them. A weight Cricket wished to understand better.

"So you learned to make friends?" Cricket asked, hoping to dispel some of the weight with a soft, but teasing tone. And then he said, "I'm proud of you" the words half strangled in his throat as they left him.

Yoshi ducked his head, long pale hair hiding whatever expression he wore on his face. "My Prince taught me. I took very diligent mental notes."

Cricket blinked at him a moment before barking out a laugh, his hand moving to cover his mouth when the sound echoed too loud off the stone walls of the surrounding corridor. "Stars, you're still so funny."

"Claudia has said the same thing." Yoshi's voice was warm with. . . something. Fondness, maybe? Or maybe it was a smile. His expression was still hidden behind his hair, and Cricket longed to get a better look at it. To know what sort of emotions would cross Yoshi's face in a moment like this one. "Here we are."

Yoshi released Cricket's hand, and opened the door for him. He stood like a doorstop, waiting for Cricket to pass in front of him, and followed Cricket in when he did. Flopping into a chair, Cricket drummed his fingers nervously on the table. Without Yoshi's hand in his, every second ticked by as their time slipped away from them like water. Uncle Sunil could be on their doorstep within a month, ready to cart Cricket back to Lunette where he would–

"My Prince," Yoshi said, his words cutting through the sudden spinning of Cricket's thoughts. "We will find a way to combat your uncle's attacks. My people, as well as yours, will be protected."

"We've already lost so many." Cricket hunched further in on himself, watching the ragged edges of his bitten fingernails snag against the grain on the table.

Yoshi sat beside him, and took one of Cricket's hands in his again, the warmth spreading like a blanket up Cricket's arm to his tensed shoulders. "We will not lose any more."

It was a promise they both knew Yoshi couldn't really keep. Still, it sounded like a vow. A pledge to do everything in his power to protect their people. Cricket would have to do the same. There was no other choice. He gave Yoshi's hand a squeeze, letting that warmth settle him further. His buzzing mind slowing, and quieting.

"Are you ready to contact Claudia and Leo?" There was a gentleness to the tone. Like Yoshi was afraid if he spoke too loudly he might scare Cricket, and they would get nowhere. He wouldn't, and where normally the kid gloves would have chafed, Cricket found he appreciated it. He was glad Yoshi saw the unease that settled into him, and made allowances for it.

"Yeah. Let's get this done." Their fingers untangled from each other, and Cricket sent up a silent prayer to Selene that there would not be more bad news. He didn't think he could handle more bad news. His heart already ached in his chest, making it hard to breathe around that and the flowers growing in his lungs. How much worse would it be if he found out Ignacia or Youta had suffered for their part in his escape?

Yoshi pulled a mirror from his pocket, and set it on the table between them. Pressing one finger into the glass, condensation fogged it, and he murmured the name, "Claudia."

The glass rippled, the condensation disappearing shortly after Yoshi removed his finger. When the ripples evened out,

Claudia's face filled the frame. She had aged since Cricket saw her last, or seemed to have anyway. Her cheeks were thinner, her eyes more haunted, but she fixed the image of Yoshi and Cricket in the mirror with a bright smile.

"To what do I owe the pleasure?" Claudia tilted her head, pushing her glasses further up her nose. Then she took a better look at them and her smile fell.

"Tell me my family is okay." Cricket pleaded, the words leaving him in a rush as his hands gripped the mirror and turned it so Claudia was looking at him. "I left so many behind. Tell me Uncle didn't take my escape out on them."

"They're all safe, Cricket." Claudia's tone was gentle, but firm. Meant to soothe as much as it was meant to head off any arguments. "Ignacia and Youta were imprisoned shortly after Sunil realized you escaped, but Leo and I got them out. Leo is with Youta and a few others now, escorting them to one of the towns housing refugees, and Ignacia is–"

"Here! On the battlefront. Or the battle backside, rather?" Ignacia shouldered Claudia out of the way. She, too, had aged, and there was a purpling bruise on her jawline, but a vicious smile stretched her lips wide, a sign of victory to come. "We took what soldiers we could and followed Sunil to the border of Helio. The knights who were working as relief aid are seeing to the refugees."

"Iggy," Cricket gasped. She was there, she was all right. He couldn't reach for her as he might have liked, but he could see her, and that would have to be enough. "I've missed you."

Ignacia scoffed, not one for sentimentality, especially not where others could see. "Not too much I hope."

"No. Not too much." Cricket laughed and slumped back in his chair, a breath leaving him. Seeing Ignacia's face, even if it looked a little thinner, a little paler than he remembered, it took the fight out of him. Her words settled in a moment later, and he sat up again. "Wait. You're *following* him?"

"Yes. We've been picking off the men he leaves behind as he goes." Ignacia was all business now, a general leading a ragtag army, her chin tilted back in pride. "We thought we'd be able to circle around in front of him, and cut him off, but so far there hasn't been an opportunity. Annie has been in touch."

"Of course, she has." Cricket didn't know if he ought to be aggravated or relieved that at least someone was looking after his people when he was too distracted to do it himself. He should have checked in sooner. He should have asked Yoshi about them. He should have been a better—

"Cricky. Hey," Ignacia called, ripping him from his thoughts. "We're okay here. We aren't taking Sunil and Craven head on, and we won't be until we can flesh out our numbers. You don't have anything to worry about with us."

"Will Leo be rejoining you?" Yoshi leaned over subtly in his chair, his shoulder pressing into Cricket's returning that sense of calm to him.

"Yes. He'll be meeting us once he has Youta situated. We expect him within the week." Ignacia looked at something over the top of the mirror, her nose wrinkling.

"We plan to meet Sunil at the base of the mountain, and use the summer palace as our home base." Yoshi reached for a map from the middle of the table. "It would take us at least two weeks to reach it. Can you tell me approximately where you are?"

"We're a town behind him, in Ravi. His attack on Gisli was last night," Claudia cut in, reappearing in the frame, her chin hooked over Ignacia's shoulder. There was a strange closeness to the action that Cricket decided they didn't have time for him to think about. Besides, interrogating Ignacia wasn't possible with so many eyes around them. "But the roads aren't good here. I'd estimate it'll take him about a little over a month to reach the base of the mountain. Maybe more if the people in the villages fight back well enough. We could maybe get in front and fortify-"

"No." Cricket cut her off, a subtle growl in his voice. He was not having his family risk their necks that way, it would be suicide. "Annie is evacuating everyone in his path. We don't need to add more bodies to his army."

"Bodies to his army?" Ignacia frowned, her eyes narrowing.

"Uncle is using hungry spirits to lead the charge." Cricket winced at the stricken look he saw on both Ignacia and Claudia's faces. Once shock filtered away, it was replaced with a rage so tangible Cricket could feel the heat of Ignacia's gaze through the mirror.

"He's desecrating his own people's remains to build an *army*?" Ignacia's jaw was so tense Cricket could hear her teeth squeak where they rubbed against one another.

"The hungry spirits in the forest manor-" Claudia gasped.

"Were likely a test run," Yoshi said, not looking up from the map he'd ducked his head over. His expression hidden behind his hair.

"The silkworms, and plants?" Claudia's face grew pale, her dark eyes too big in her brown face, wide enough that her glasses looked small by comparison.

"There have been no reports of him using those magics yet. But I will speak with Anstice, and ensure we are watching for them, and prepared for those eventualities. I do not suppose either would work well in the middle of winter." Yoshi grabbed another piece of paper to write down a reminder, all the while his shoulder remained pressed to Cricket's, a warm and comforting weight.

"No. They wouldn't." Claudia ran her hand through her short crop of tightly wound curls.

Ignacia and Cricket shared a look.

"Excuse me. Plants? Silkworms?" Ignacia asked.

"I'll explain that to you when we're done here." Claudia rubbed at the bridge of her nose, pushing her glasses up onto her head. "Two weeks you said, to reach the stronghold?"

"At least." Yoshi ran his finger along the route they would have to take down the mountain.

"When do you plan to leave?"

"I would like at least another two weeks to work with Cricket on his draconic abilities. We have not yet found a way for him to control the transition from man to dragon." Takayoshi's voice was calm, and relaxed, as if he were listing off things he would need to research in the library, not talking about a schedule that was far too tight for any of their liking, and a war that would be at their door in a matter of days.

"Or the ability for me to control the dragon once I've changed." Cricket muttered, feeling shame crawl down his spine. He should have worked harder. He had known this was coming. He had known Uncle Sunil would be after him, eventually. And instead he'd been complaining about how difficult meditation was, and letting the weakness of his body hold him back. He would have to redouble his efforts.

"Can you cut that down to a week?" Ignacia's gaze shifted from Cricket to Yoshi, her expression unsure.

"No," Yoshi said at the same time Cricket said, "Yes."

They turned to look at one another, Yoshi's golden eyes narrowing, searching. Cricket scrubbed at his nose with the back of his wrist, hoping to hide the truth of what he was thinking.

He knew Yoshi wouldn't agree with it. But what other options did they have? They needed to cut Uncle Sunil off before he made his way up the mountain, and Cricket and Yoshi were the only ones who could fight against the spirits. They did this, or more people died. Cricket was not selfish enough to let more lose their lives in his place. Not when he could end this himself.

"Right. Well. We'll let you two sort that out." Claudia laughed nervously. "In the meantime, Ignacia and I are going to sort out a route so we can go around Sunil's contingent and meet you at the summer palace."

"No." Yoshi shook his head, dragging his eyes away from Cricket. "Continue coming in behind. Close the distance as much as you can without being noticed."

"Ah. A pincer maneuver!" Ignacia crowed, excitement replacing the lined expression on her face. She always did love a good war tactic. "I like the way you think, Yoshi."

Yoshi bowed his head in acceptance of the compliment.

"Very well then, we'll leave you to it." Ignacia cut her gaze to Cricket once more, but although there was a question in her eyes, she didn't voice it. Instead, she waved her hand over the glass and the connection was lost.

When the glass stopped rippling once more, Yoshi turned to Cricket, his eyes narrowed the smallest bit, just enough for Cricket to know that he was angry. "What are you planning?"

Cricket took a breath, preparing for the inevitable argument that would come from this plan. Yoshi wouldn't like it. *Cricket* didn't like it. And he would lay money that if Anstice or Ignacia knew about it, they would do everything within their power to stop him. But he didn't have a choice. He didn't.

"I want you to have an iron cuff made for me. Something I can slip on and off as we need," Cricket said, and he watched as realization dawned on Yoshi the moment before rage sizzled under his skin, and lit the map he still had his hand resting on ablaze.

CHAPTER 23

Cricket's words froze Takayoshi to his seat in a way nothing else ever could. The image of Cricket standing in the rain flashed through Takayoshi's mind. His shoulders bowed, his body sagging under the very weight of his clothes, and the hollowness of his cheeks. There was no way to know if being cut off from his magic had contributed to how he became so sick so quickly, but Takayoshi had his suspicions. It would be easier to know if he were right if Cricket would submit to seeing a healer, but without that, Takayoshi was not willing to take that risk again. Not now. Not *ever*.

Fear raced through his veins like a wildfire, lighting them up hot and sharp. It was of very little surprise to Takayoshi when the smell of burning paper reached his nose, but he did not care. Let the entire table turn into a smoldering pile of ash for all he gave a damn.

"No." The word left his mouth before Cricket had finished exhaling.

"Yoshi, I know you don't like this. But it's really the only–"

"I said, *no*." Takayoshi snapped, and met his eyes, gaze hardened to steel. He drew the fire back into himself, pulling it away from the ruined papers. Anstice would be angry, but she would understand once he told her what Cricket had planned. She would see the danger in this just as well as he did.

"Well, why not?" Cricket sat up straighter, his own anger flaring out of him in cool curls of air. His pupils still had not returned from their slitted state. Takayoshi wondered how much longer they had before the transformation was permanent. Perhaps it would be better if Cricket did not fight in this war at all. Leave it in the capable hands of Takayoshi and his knights.

Takayoshi's face hardened further. He did not want to explain himself. He did not feel he needed to. Cricket had to know the dangers that this posed, he was not a fool. If anything he was the smartest man Takayoshi had ever met. But oh how often he chose to play the fool if it would benefit him. "When you arrived here you were ill."

"So?"

Teeth grinding together, Takayoshi fought against his annoyance to remain in control of his temper. He could not help but feel that Cricket was being intentionally dense. Anstice was right about the fact that Cricket could be painfully oblivious when it most benefited him. "Perhaps the reason you were so ill was because you had been cut off from your magic for so long. We cannot take the chance that cutting you off from it again would cause you to become more ill. Not now. Not when war is imminent. We will continue with your meditation prac—"

"War is imminent and you want me to *meditate*?" Cricket shouted, and stood, the chair legs screeching across the stone floor, the sound making Takayoshi want to cringe away from it. Too loud. Much too loud.

"We have time for you to—"

"We do *not* have time, *Takayoshi*." Takayoshi's name landed like a hard slap across his face. He found himself blinking at Cricket. "We have the exact opposite of *time*. If we do not get down that mountain and help those—"

"I will not take that risk. Not with you. Not with your health. This discussion is over. I will see you in the morning for meditation practice." Takayoshi rose from his own chair, and brushed past Cricket into the hall without another word. He expected Cricket to follow behind him, to continue the fight. But Cricket did not, and he was unclear on if that was better or worse. Takayoshi let out a breath past the horrible thing clenching his chest as he headed back down the corridor toward the library.

There was nothing more he could do for Cricket. Not today. Not with Cricket in that state. But Takayoshi would find a way to help him before the sun rose again. He swore it to himself.

"You're not going to give in to him, are you?" Anstice's voice drifted around the corner of one of the tall shelves in the library.

The place had gone dark, and silent around Takayoshi over the last couple of hours, even more so than was usual for the library. Exhaustion had begun to blur his vision, but still, he stayed. He would find an answer. There had to be something that could help Cricket somewhere in Helio's vast stores of literature. A society built on the premise of meditation, and balance, there had to be *something*.

"The iron. You won't do it, will you?" Anstice pressed,

coming into the small circle of light that Takayoshi's lanterns were giving off.

"I will not. Not so long as there is another option." Takayoshi's jaw ticked with the tension residing there since he had spoken with Cricket. The fact of the matter was, he had yet to *find* another option. Perhaps if he could contact the monks on the neighboring mountain, their literature on the balancing of magical elements far outweighed any other, and Brother Magan had always been willing to help Takayoshi when he had a problem.

Brother Magan was the only reason Takayoshi survived on the mountain, if he were honest with himself. He was the only one willing to treat the princeling like a person, and not like the future king of Helio. The only one who really made Takayoshi feel like he was more than the destiny birth order had laid out for him. Without Brother Magan, Takayoshi would have been crowned king, just as his uncle wanted, and would never have met Cricket.

"But you haven't found another option. Have you?" Anstice settled into the chair across from him, taking one of the books from his discard pile. He thought to tell her that he had already been through those, but maybe she would find something he missed. He was willing to hope.

"Just because I have not found it, does not mean it is not there." If only he had access to the archive. If only he could reach out to Hazel and Sashi, and get them to answer a few questions. But he knew better than that. The archive was locked away on that island for a reason, and Takayoshi had almost ruined it once, he was not willing to tempt fate a second time.

"I don't think the iron was what was making him sick."

Takayoshi looked up from where his head was ducked over a book about the cardinal directions and how they connected to the elements to blink at Anstice. Her head leaned casually against her fist as she flipped through the book laid open on the table in front of her. She did not seem to notice his obvious shock, or if she did, she was forcing nonchalance. She knew something more and she was not telling him. Takayoshi's jaw ticked again. Annoyance lingering in the muscle beneath his skin.

"What do you mean you do not think it was the iron that was making him ill?" Takayoshi forced his words to be calm, almost impassive, to hide the irritation that simmered beneath them. He did not like being kept in the dark, and if Anstice was keeping something about Cricket's illness to herself—something that could help him—Takayoshi would not be held responsible for his actions.

"It may have contributed to it." Anstice shrugged, still not looking up from the book. Her eyes were not moving though, he could see that. She was not reading, she was just staring at the words on the page as if they held the answer. "I told you once that Sunil would curse Cricket in an attempt to make his death look natural."

"You did, but you have not mentioned it since. I assumed that there had been no evidence of such a. . ." Takayoshi's words faded off, and he frowned. He assumed incorrectly, it seemed. Just because Anstice had not mentioned it again did not mean there was no evidence of Cricket's curse. It did not mean that Sunil had not already enacted whatever dark magics he would use to bring about his nephew's seemingly natural end. "His illness is not natural."

"No. It is not." Anstice looked up finally, her wide eyes full of something Takayoshi could never even begin to understand. It was not sadness, or the complete loss of hope, but there was dismay mixed in with whatever else lay there. "It is a part of the curse that Sunil cast."

"You know which curse it was." He leaned forward, his hands bracing on the table. It would not solve all of their problems, but knowing what curse it was, breaking the curse, could at least restore Cricket's health. Then perhaps meditation would work. Perhaps without whatever poison Sunil planted in him that continued to choke the life from him, Cricket's magic could work properly.

"Of course I do." Anstice's lips turned up in a smug smile, she leaned back in her chair, arms crossed over her chest.

"What curse is it?"

"I cannot tell you that." Hair fell into her face, and Takayoshi would swear he saw a glint of mischief in her eyes, which was so very contrary to the discussion they were having.

"Why not?" The worlds left him half on a growl, the fiery creature that lived inside of him lifting its head, and demanding answers for why their prince was ill.

That hint of mischief seemed to take on a life of its own, lighting up Anstice's face in something that made Takayoshi shift in his seat. He decided he did not like the turn of this conversation, not at all. Then a moment later that mischief slipped away into something more somber. Something that was distinctly sad. "Because, if we try to force it, it'll kill him. The break has to come naturally."

"What does he need to break it?"

"I can't tell you that either. You know better, Yoshi. Curses are tricky like that." Anstice shook her head, then she stood from her seat to lean over the table, her face pressed closer to Takayoshi's. "All I can tell you is that being cut off from his magic by iron? It'll only speed up the process. The only thing keeping Cricky upright now, is the dragon. Without it. . ."

"He could die." Takayoshi sank back into his chair, the very fight leaving his veins in a whoosh of air.

"Exactly. So. Find another way."

"I shall do my best."

Anstice nodded. "That's all I can ask of you. And in the meantime. . . cut my brother some slack. He's under a lot of pressure, all right?"

She turned and disappeared into the darkness of the library again before those words could catch up to Takayoshi.

"What do you mean cut him some *slack*?" But she was already gone.

THE FOLLOWING MORNING, after Takayoshi finished his routine, he went down to breakfast to find Becka seated at the table, her feet swinging to kick against the chair legs as she stuffed a bite of pancakes into her mouth. They did not usually eat such sweet things for breakfast, but Takayoshi noted that the kitchens had taken quite a fondness to Becka's charm, and were willing to give the child anything.

"Ah! Shishi," Atsuko said, her head lifting from her own breakfast to fix him with a smile that looked oddly strained. "Good morning."

"Good morning." Takayoshi nodded, taking his seat beside Becka, and filling his plate.

"Perhaps you can watch over Miss Becka this morning? I would do it myself, but I have some meetings, and Annie is busy with planning, and Uncle is. . . Well. Uncle." Atsuko laughed, her head tilted to the side so her long hair almost fell into her porridge. She was up to something. He could practically hear it in the forced brightness of her voice.

"And Papa is sleeping," Becka added helpfully.

"Yes, and Papa is sleeping." Astuko smiled broadly at Becka. "We know he needs his rest, don't we, Miss Becka?"

"Mhm."

"So would you mind? I know you've been giving her music lessons. Maybe you can move them up, and add in some extra training with Cricket later instead?"

Takayoshi narrowed his eyes on Atsuko as he looked her over, trying to find out what exactly it was she was up to. But there were no outward signs. No clues. Just the cheerful lilt to her mouth, and the soft happiness in her voice.

"Cricket will fetch her once he wakes in an hour or so. I'm sure you can keep her occupied that long," Atsuko said, seeming to take his silence for concern.

"You promised to teach me to play Selene's lullaby on the piano." Becka turned her head to peer up at him with wide eyes, her nose wrinkled in concentration. "This might be the only time we get once Papa is up for the day. I know you. . . you're going to be busy."

Takayoshi deflated. There was just no denying the child after that. "Of course. It is no trouble at all."

Becka gave a cheer, and even if it was a little bit of trouble, as he had been planning to devote his morning to more research, Takayoshi could not find it within himself to begrudge the fact that he would be spending that time instead with Becka.

CHAPTER 24

Anger and irritation burned through much of Cricket's calm, making it difficult to sleep that evening. He had always known that Yoshi was stubborn, but he never thought that Yoshi could dig his heels in so much when something like this was such common sense.

Iron would offer him control over the dragon. It would allow him to keep those around him safe. It didn't matter if it made his illness worse. Which Cricket didn't think it would. However foolish that thought might be. Even if it did, it didn't *matter*. *Nothing* mattered outside of stopping Uncle Sunil from waging war on everyone in his path to Cricket's doorstep.

None of that was the point. The point was that his lack of calm left him tossing and turning all night, and *that* more than anything else, Cricket was convinced, was why he felt like he had been run down by a carriage the following morning. His chest was tight, the scratchy feeling of leaves or roots or *something*, lingering at the back of his throat making every breath an exercise in control. Every muscle in his body ached.

And when Cricket lifted his hand to rub his face he found his nails had grown into talons.

"Stars, that isn't good," Cricket rasped, leaning back until his head thumped against the headboard.

None of it is.

His eyes narrowed to squint through the sheer curtains that hung over the windows in his room. It was hard to tell what time it was in Helio what with how dark their winters were up on the mountain, but he'd wager it was already past breakfast.

"Why didn't Becka wake me?" Cricket groaned. He tilted his head up to the ceiling for a moment to catch his breath before he rolled out of the big comfy four-poster that adorned his borrowed chambers. Helio wasn't home, but he found himself comfortable there in a way he decided it was better he not think overly much about.

"Yoshi is giving her music lessons," Anstice said from the other side of the cracked bedroom door. Cricket wondered how long she had been there, but wasn't going to ask. Anstice was a wily one, and she'd do as she pleased whether he questioned her motivations or not. He'd learned that long ago. He'd also learned to know when she was up to something. Her voice would go up just a tick, not even a whole octave. Maybe most people wouldn't have noticed. But Cricket had spent a lifetime learning Anstice and all her little idiosyncrasies, so he knew when her voice did That Thing, like *now,* it meant trouble. "They should be taking a break soon. Why don't you go meet with them for lunch?"

Cricket leaned against the doorframe, his gaze narrowing on her where she sat at the little desk near the window of his sitting room. "Don't you have a desk in your own rooms? I'm sure the queen didn't skimp on furnishings when it came to her. . . I'm sorry, what are you?"

A soft laugh left Anstice, but she didn't turn around to

rise to the bait, which may have been for the best, he wasn't really up for a verbal spar. Not that he'd win even if he were up for one. Anstice always bested him at such things, and Ignacia wasn't with them to break up the ensuing bickering match when he lost, sore loser that he was. "I like the view from your windows."

"It's just the courtyard." He moved across the room to peer out said windows, and snorted when he saw Queen Atsuko making a slow circuit of the empty space with some of her advisors and uncle in tow.

"She thinks best on her feet," Anstice said by way of explanation.

"Of course she does." Cricket shook his head, stepping back to stand beside Anstice again. "Is that all you're up to?"

"Maybe. Maybe not." Anstice shrugged, not even bothering to hide the way her mouth twitched up into that devious little smile that he'd known since childhood. Whoever the innocent act was for, it wasn't him, they both knew it wasn't working. "Get dressed. Go down to the music room and pull those two away from the piano for some lunch. You have training to do."

At the reminder, Cricket groaned, his shoulders sagging. "I thought I'd gotten away from all the responsibilities of being a king."

"No, you didn't." Anstice looked up finally, her brows raised high enough they disappeared into the curled bangs over her forehead.

"No, I didn't," Cricket agreed readily.

"Now, are you going to go so I can get back to work, or what?"

"I feel like I got hit by a runaway carriage," he muttered, heading back to his room to get changed. He left the door cracked so they could still speak. Dressing quickly, so as not to have to see all the new scales that had appeared on his skin, winded him, leaving him leaning against one of the posts on his bed as he tried to regain his breath and his sense of equilibrium.

"Scale of one to ten, how bad is it?"

"Does it really matter? The point is it's gotten worse. And so quickly, I feel like." Cricket slipped into his boots, not even bothering to tie them, before he headed back out to the sitting room. Anstice turned in her chair to peer at him over the back of it, her lips pressed into a hard line. "I'd give it about a seven. But yesterday I was at about a five."

"You jumped two ranks in one day?" Anstice's fingers gripped the back of the chair hard enough that it looked like it was the only thing keeping her from taking flight that very moment. Maybe it was.

"I got into a fight with Yoshi yesterday, so I didn't sleep well." He wrapped a scarf tight around his neck with the hope that it would ward off the chill. It had done little to help so far, but Cricket was an optimist.

"You need to take better care of yourself." Anstice tsked.

"I'll be fine." Cricket shouldered on his heavy cloak, ready to brave the slight chill of the Helio palace corridors.

"Will you?"

He stopped at the door to his quarters, his shoulders hunching inward. "It doesn't really matter if I'm not. We don't have time to worry about me, Uncle's on his way."

A breath like a wheeze left Anstice, whistling on the way out. "I'm going to find a way to fix this."

Cricket swallowed, lifting his chin, and forcing his mouth into a smile that he didn't really feel but knew would make his voice sound lighter. "Of course you will, Annie. We'll get this all sorted."

Then he left before she could say anything else, already tired of the discussion. It wouldn't do them any good to go back and forth about it. It didn't do them any good for Anstice to check in with him constantly about how he felt, or where he was on what they were calling the 'feeling awful' threshold, either. Not that he'd ever told her the truth about it, because the *truth* was, he was inching closer to an eight than a seven, and every new day made ten seem a little closer than he cared for.

Music drifted through the halls, accompanying Cricket to the music room. It seemed like such a novel thing, a music room. He was sure they'd had one in Lunette, but if they did, Cricket never visited it. Music had never been the thing he gravitated toward, that had always been art, and Father never pushed him to do something he didn't like.

Becka, it seemed, didn't take after her papa in that sense, Cricket realized as he stood in the shadow of the doorway, watching her chubby fingers pluck away at the keys on the piano. It didn't sound like a tune, not yet, but it might one day.

Perched beside her on the piano bench was Yoshi, his white-clad figure crouched down a little in a posture that was so wholly unlike him it took Cricket a moment to recognize him. They were murmuring softly to each other, their voices indistinguishable from the music. And whatever they were saying had them both smiling. Becka's eyes squinted to accommodate her too-wide grin. Yoshi's own lips tilted just so at the edges, in something that anyone else might have missed for the smile that it was. The very sight of it sent Cricket's heart skittering away in his chest.

The music stopped almost abruptly when Becka's eyes caught on him and she gasped loudly. "Papa! Papa! I can play the piano. Did you hear?"

"I did, little sunflower. It was beautiful." Cricket dipped his head, taking a step into the room so he didn't look like he was skulking in the shadows. He had *not* been skulking in the shadows. Kings didn't skulk. "Yoshi is a good teacher, isn't he?"

"He is!"

"Your papa is a good teacher as well," Yoshi murmured, his eyes warm as they drank in the delighted features of Becka. Then he lifted that gaze to fix it on Cricket, and Cricket would swear to Selene he felt his heart stop entirely. *Stars.*

"Oh? What did papa teach you?" Becka tugged on Yoshi's tunic, her little form wiggling as if she wanted to stand up on the bench but had likely been told numerous times not to.

Yoshi leaned over as if he were going to tell Becka some great secret, but his eyes remained on Cricket as he said, "He taught me how to make friends."

"Did it work?" Becka whispered back.

Yoshi merely nodded, his smile, if possible, growing even wider, and Cricket choked on his own spit. He coughed into his fist, hoping to hide his embarrassment, while scrubbing at his neck.

"Right then. It's lunchtime." The clap was a little too loud, Cricket realized with a wince, but it pulled Yoshi and Becka out of whatever, frankly adorable, moment they were having. "Who's hungry?"

"I am!" Becka jumped to her feet, almost toppling the piano bench, and Yoshi with it. Cricket bent to scoop her up and settled her onto his hip when she came running. "You're coming too, right Shishi?"

"I am," Yoshi said, closing the lid over the keys, and rising from the bench. "When we are finished eating, your papa and I will have to get back to our training. Do you think you can stay with your auntie then?"

"Of course." Becka nodded, face serious. She didn't fully understand what was going on around her, but she wasn't so young as to not realize that something bad was coming.

Something that her papa would need to be ready for. "You'll be nice to him, though, won't you?"

"I am always kind to your papa," Yoshi said, which was a blatant lie, but he seemed to know Cricket wouldn't call him on it. Not in front of his daughter. Not when Becka so clearly idolized Yoshi. No. He'd keep his opinions to himself. And ignore the way his stomach did a strange flip flop that left him feeling more sick than hungry when Yoshi's eyes met his over the top of Becka's head like he knew exactly what Cricket was thinking, and found it amusing. He probably did.

"Are you well, My Prince?" Yoshi's words pulled Cricket from his thoughts just as they made it to the dining room.

"I'm fine. Let's get some food, we have work to do. Anstice said we have time on the training field this afternoon." That was a lie too, and Cricket waited idly for Yoshi to call him on it, but he didn't.

Yoshi simply nodded, and began to layer food onto Becka's plate, making sure to cut anything too large for her, and they settled into their meal.

CHAPTER 25

He was not focused, Takayoshi could tell that the moment Cricket stepped out onto the training field. His mind was elsewhere, and the lack of sleep made his steps slow, and stumbling, his movements uncoordinated. It was dangerous to train in this state, and perhaps Takayoshi should have said as much. Perhaps he should have put a stop to all of this the moment he noticed Cricket's step stutter on the uneven ground, but he had not. Whether it was to save Cricket's pride, or his own, he had not.

Perhaps he thought, however foolishly, that the physical movement required to engage in hand-to-hand combat would focus the frenetic energy he could practically feel buzzing under Cricket's skin like bees. No. Takayoshi shook himself, loose feathers fluttering through the cold air like snowfall.

No, he had not put a stop to this because he had been afraid to. Because he had thought that if he did, Cricket would leave. Cricket had not said as much. He had not spoken a single word to indicate that he may be thinking of leaving Helio, and Takayoshi with it, to face his uncle alone.

But Takayoshi could feel a change on the air. A tipping point approaching, and they were on the knife's edge of it. Takayoshi would do anything in his power to keep them from falling off the wrong side.

Takayoshi swiped at the dragon with his talons, the pointed ends not even leaving a mark behind on Cricket's thick blue scales. The dragon roared, head thrown back in agitation, whiskers blowing in the rising wind.

"Yield," Cricket commanded, his voice a growl in Takayoshi's mind.

"I cannot." Takayoshi's wings flapped harder to brace against the rush of an angry breeze that seemed to heed the call of the dragon. Takayoshi was—not for the first time—in awe of the power that Cricket could wield. If only he could learn to control the beast that came with it.

The cold air made the flames on the tips of his wings fizzle, and pop. Takayoshi took a breath, feeding the fire that burned through his veins to keep them lit. He did not know what would happen if they went out, but he was sure he did not want to find out.

"Cannot or *will* not?" Cricket's lips peeled back to reveal jagged fangs that would no doubt tear a hole in Takayoshi's wing if they were to latch on. His long tail whipped out, smacking Takayoshi away from him, batting him like a cat might a mouse.

Takayoshi righted himself far easier than he had during some of their previous sessions. Something in the gesture made it seem that Cricket was holding back. That maybe he had found some level of control over the beast he had been lacking before.

"Cannot," Takayoshi repeated, beating his wings hard enough to send Cricket's long serpentine body reeling. "I yield when My Prince has finally conquered you on his own."

A scream left the beast, Cricket's slitted eyes lighting with a fury unlike Takayoshi had seen before. "*Conquered?*"

Takayoshi barely had a moment to register the anger before the creature lunged at him again, wrapping its entire body around him like a snake might prey. A distressed caw left his beak before all of the breath was squeezed from his lungs. There was a sound of snapping somewhere in his chest that echoed through the cavern of his body like a scream to his ears. A rib, he had little doubt. No. Maybe it had been two. He could not tell. All he could feel was the jolt of pain that flooded his veins, temporarily burning hotter than the fire.

His hold on the phoenix slipped, white feathers sloughing off his skin like drifts of snow until Cricket's serpentine body tightened further around a man instead of a giant bird. The movement jarred his ribs, and Takayoshi hissed a wince that left his lungs aching from the cold.

"Yield," the dragon snarled in his face, breath icy enough to chap Takayoshi's wind-burned cheeks.

"I cannot," Takayoshi repeated, he wriggled his fingers, prickling with pins and needles, down toward the dagger tucked into his belt. He did not want to hurt Cricket, but in the position he was in, it would do more damage to himself to use the phoenix to continue this fight. The only choice he had was to convince Cricket to let him go. A quick glance at the ground told Takayoshi the fall would likely hurt, but it would not be enough to cause any more damage than Cricket already had. It was a safer option.

"Foolish! Why not?" Spittle crystalized on Takayoshi's cheeks, making them grow numb.

Cricket's pupils were slits, narrowed to the point that they were nearly eaten up by the blue of his eyes, but Takayoshi would never be able to look into that gaze and see anything but the prince he had sworn to protect. The man he had fallen in love with. Takayoshi bit down on his tongue, hard enough to draw blood, if just to keep those words from tumbling from his lips. He could not tell Cricket. Not like this. It was not the time. Not now that they were on the brink of war with Sunil. Not now that Cricket's mind was already clouded with too many conflicting emotions. Takayoshi would not complicate things further for him.

"Why?" Cricket shouted again, shaking Takayoshi so his head bobbed hard enough to strain his neck. But it loosened the grip on his arm just enough for Takayoshi to get his hand around the very end of the dagger. With numb fingertips he tugged it up, little by little until the pommel pressed against his palm.

"I cannot." Sliding the dagger up further, and further, the blade bit into his fingers where he was not careful, but eventually he had it turned point up in his hand. Blood made his hold on it precarious, but Takayoshi was nothing if not determined.

"Yield!"

"I cannot. I *will* not." Takayoshi took a breath, and sent up a silent prayer to Selene that Cricket would forgive him for this, and the wound he was about to inflict would not simply enrage the dragon to the point of no return. "My Prince needs me."

"*Needs* you," Cricket snorted, his breath leaving him in a cold puff that made Takayoshi's nose burn when he inhaled. "He does not need–" then he was screaming as Takayoshi drove the point of his dagger into the soft flesh at the center of one taloned paw.

Cricket dropped Takayoshi, the cold air rushing past him, unbinding his hair, and making his tunic flutter uselessly. He was able to latch onto the feeling of fire under his skin for a flicker of a moment, just long enough to shift his arms to wings, and catch himself before he hit the ground too hard.

His feet settled onto the grass, and he let out a groan at the feeling of his ribs settling back into place.

The screaming had not stopped, the dragon thrashing about in the air above Takayoshi, but it had changed in pitch. Shifted from the deep guttural growl of a beast, into the pained cry of a man. Takayoshi looked up just in time to see the scales fall away, then Cricket was falling through the air, his face slack.

Takayoshi barely registered Cricket's descent before his feet were scuffing against the snow-covered ground to put himself beneath Cricket in enough time to catch him.

The weight of another man in his arms jarred his broken ribs again, but he managed to break Cricket's fall, and lowered him to the ground without further injury. Wet settled into his trousers where Takayoshi pressed his own knees to the ground, trying to regain his breath around the catch in his lungs.

"Stars," Cricket rasped, lifting his hand to examine where the dagger was still stabbed into the middle of it. "Did you have to put it all the way through?"

"Apologies, My Prince." Takayoshi fell back onto his heels, his head spinning a little with the pain. Black spots danced before his eyes, threatening to narrow his vision to a point. He struggled against them, sucking in breath after breath to force them back, but they remained persistent. He was going to lose consciousness, and soon, Takayoshi realized as he began to wobble on his heels.

"Yoshi." Cricket's voice swam in his ears, the sound high and worried. There was something else there, on the edge of the calming breeze, another noise. Takayoshi blinked his eyes open, and saw the blood dripping from Cricket's bent elbow to stain the ground. He had removed the dagger. That was likely not wise. "Yoshi. Just breathe. It'll be all right. Just breathe."

Cold seeped in through the back of Takayoshi's tunic, chilling his skin, where Cricket had lowered him onto the ground. It did make breathing easier. Put less pressure on the bones that he could feel already beginning to knit back together with magic. It hurt. Of course, it hurt. Even magical healing was not painless. A dull throbbing ache that made the nerves of his torso tingle.

"Oh, thank Selene, Annie, go and get the queen, and a couple of men," Cricket said to someone over his shoulder. Anstice, it must be. "And a litter."

"Oh, Cricky, what have you done?" Anstice's voice shook with a fear Takayoshi had never heard in it before.

"Just do as I say, Anstice!" Cricket barked, and Takayoshi almost swore he heard Anstice jump at the command, but then she was gone. "You're going to be all right. I don't think I punctured your lung."

"It is already healing." The words were hard to say around his shallow breath, but they seemed to bring a relief to Cricket's too-pale face that Takayoshi took comfort in. He hated the look of grief on Cricket's face. The way the pain lined his bright eyes. "It is not irreparable."

"It is!" Cricket cried, eyes filling with tears as he bent his head to press his forehead against Takayoshi's shoulder, hiding his face when all Takayoshi wanted was to watch the emotions filter across it. "It *is* irreparable. I should never have done that to you. I can't believe I did. I can't believe I lost control and—" he hiccuped around a sob. "It could have been worse, Yoshi. It could have been so much worse. And then what?"

"I would not have let it get that far." Takayoshi ignored the catch in his side to reach up and thread his fingers through Cricket's unevenly cut midnight blue hair, without thought to what the action might mean. The softness against his fingers had Takayoshi letting out a breath, something in his chest easing. It was nice to be this close to Cricket. Closer than they had been in years and years. He felt Cricket relax under the touch.

"What if you couldn't stop it?" Cricket asked, his voice strained against a throat that sounded like something was blocking it.

Inhaling, Takayoshi prepared to tell Cricket that it would never happen, that he would never *let* it happen, but the moment he did Anstice reappeared with Atsuko and four men carrying a litter. Cricket pulled away, his hair slipping through Takayoshi's fingers, and tucked himself into Anstice's side so she could examine his hand which was still dripping blood onto the snowy ground. Their voices became a soft buzz just on the edge of hearing when one of the men helped Takayoshi roll onto the litter, and the pain blotted out his sight again.

"Oh, Shishi," Atsuko murmured, her hand taking his in a grip so tight he could feel the bones grinding against one another.

"I will be all right, Koko. It is already healing." Takayoshi blinked the dark spots from his vision. The watery sunlight through the clouds burned at his sensitive eyes, but it was better than the darkness. Anything was better than the darkness.

"Shhh. Don't strain yourself." Atsuko patted his head like a child, and Takayoshi had a moment to catch Cricket's wide, worried gaze before the litter jolted, and the burst of pain sent him under again.

CHAPTER 26

Cricket felt the bite of talons in the meat of his palms. A sharp pain he deserved for hurting Yoshi. How could he have been so careless? How could he have let the dragon do that? Did he have absolutely no control over himself or the creature and its magic? He should have! He should have stopped it! And if he couldn't stop it then he should have gotten himself away from Yoshi. Put as much distance between them as possible.

There was no excuse for hurting Yoshi, none at all. As stubborn as the man was, as stoic, and almost unfeeling at times, he had never done anything to hurt Cricket. Yoshi had done everything in his power to help Cricket and his daughter escape Lunette and the fate that awaited them under Uncle Sunil's rule. He had been kind, and caring, and had even started giving Becka music lessons. There was no world in which Yoshi deserved Cricket's ire.

He paced in front of the door to the infirmary. The men carrying Yoshi had disappeared inside with him, Atsuko, and Anstice, then shut the door. Cricket knew they didn't mean to bar the way for him, but it seemed like that even still. And he hadn't the courage to push through and insert himself into whatever was going on on the other side of the threshold. Nor did he deserve to be there.

The door creaked open, showing Cricket just a glimpse of Yoshi laying on an infirmary cot before Atsuko was in the way, and stepping out into the hall. Anstice followed right behind, closing the door before Cricket could see him again.

A soft cough drew Cricket's attention to Atsuko. She nodded her head down the corridor toward her office, and he followed behind, silently. All the while feeling like he was about to get a scolding from one of his tutors. Maybe he was. He was just grateful it didn't look like their uncle had seen what happened yet. If he had, Cricket had little doubt that their uncle would be calling for Cricket's head. He'd have every right to.

Anstice closed the office door behind them, and it sounded like the slamming of a prison cell. Cricket turned to face Atsuko where she stood behind her desk, her hands clasped at the small of her back the way Yoshi often did when he was trying to keep himself under control. But unlike Yoshi, his sister wore her emotions in the lines of her face. Stress pursed her lips, turning them a lighter color than they typically were, and there were wrinkles at the corners of her eyes that spoke of displeasure. Not that Cricket could blame her. If someone hurt one of his siblings that way, he'd have been angry too.

"This cannot happen again," Cricket said. The wound on his palm gaped a little as he opened and closed his fists at his sides, but he ignored the strange ache of flesh knitting itself back together too quickly to be natural. There was so much else happening. So much else to worry about. What was one wound? What was one cut compared to Yoshi in a bed and looking far too pale?

"No. It cannot," Atsuko agreed, her voice tight as if she

were trying not to yell at him. Honestly, Cricket wished she would. He wished someone would be truly furious with him for what he'd done to Yoshi. He wished someone would punish him for it. "Have you made absolutely no progress with your meditation practice?"

The deep, exhausted inhale Cricket took caught in his throat, almost sending him into a coughing fit, but he managed to choke it down. He shook his head, unable to get the words past his lips. Unable to disappoint Atsuko verbally.

"How much longer will it take for the meditation to work?" Atsuko looked like she wanted to collapse into her chair, but she didn't. She kept her posture as straight as she could, and faced Cricket and their current problem head on.

"I don't know, Your Highness." The words left Cricket barely loud enough for him to hear with his own ears. Shame making every syllable hammer against his ears like a war dum. "It may never work," he admitted, although the confession felt strange on his tongue. Like it had grown wrong in his lungs on the way up. Even if he'd always known that was the case, hadn't he?

"Is there no other way?" Anstice's voice was a tightly controlled thing, showing none of the fear, or upset that Cricket could see playing behind her brown eyes. She was in Advisor Mode. Cricket had to respect her ability to compartmentalize her feelings that way, it was something he never quite mastered. Maybe that was why he was struggling so much with the dragon now where Yoshi seemed to have an easy enough time with his phoenix.

"There is. . ." Cricket swallowed around the feeling of leaves in his throat.

"Cricky–"

"No." Atsuko held up a hand to silence Anstice.

Anstice's jaw ticked with the urge to press on with whatever she'd been about to say, but ultimately, she stayed silent, and swallowed loudly around her words. Cricket wondered what she would have said. How she would have tried to protect him in this instance as she had protected him for so many years growing up. Just as Ignacia had. But none of them were there to protect him now, it was just Cricket up against the dragon.

"Your brother will not be pleased," Cricket warned. It was important that Atsuko know that when Yoshi was well enough to argue against this plan, he would. That this closed-door meeting that decided his fate would infuriate Yoshi like nothing else ever had. He wanted to protect Cricket from this inevitability. But that was just it, this *was* inevitable. There was no escaping it. This was always going to happen, whether Yoshi approved or not.

"I will take that under advisement, but as it is his safety I am concerned with, I'm sure you'll understand that his opinion holds little weight." Atsuko's lips curled down at the corners into tiny frown that Cricket knew very well. It was the look of a little sister doing something she knew would upset her big brother. Atsuko took no pleasure in this, it would seem, and Cricket could appreciate that. She was a queen, and she was doing what she had to, what she thought was best.

"When my uncle used me against the village in Lunette, he fitted me with an iron collar," Cricket explained, ignoring the itch around his throat at the reminder of the burning metal digging into his skin. "The iron muted the magic in my blood, keeping the dragon under control even if my emotions were high. We could utilize the same—"

"It'll make you sicker," Anstice said, cutting him off. Her eyes narrowed on Cricket in something that would have made anyone who hadn't been on the receiving end of her glares for most of his life cower. Cricket merely raised a brow at her.

"We have no proof of that." He ran a hand through his

short hair which was knotted and matted with something. Likely blood. Hopefully his own, and not Yoshi's. "My illness may have been made worse by the cold and the—"

"Cricky. You and I both know that the magic of the dragon is the only reason you're standing right now." Anstice fixed him with an unimpressed look. "Without it you'd be too weak to walk down the hall, much less go into battle."

"We *don't* know that." It was a struggle to keep his voice even, to breathe through the restricted passage of his throat, to keep the talons on the ends of his fingers from lengthening far enough to slice through his hands entirely. But Cricket managed somehow. He kept some small modicum of calm about himself. Maybe the meditation was doing some little bit of good. Not enough though. It would never be enough. Not in time.

"So you want to test it!" Anstice asked, her tone incredulous, and hurt. There were tears making her eyes shimmer, and Cricket had to rip his gaze away before he backed down.

"Your Highness, I do—"

"Please call me Atsuko." The queen's voice was soft, her eyes pleading as if she were asking him not to do this. Not to make her make this choice, and go against what her brother, and Anstice wanted. Cricket wished he could give her that. He wished he could give them all what they wanted. But it was not to be. It never would be.

Cricket opened his mouth to argue further, but was cut off by the smacking of the door against the wall hard enough to make every painting hanging upon it rattle.

"Your Highness, the—" the young person stopped, their eyes gone impossibly wide when they took in the group they'd interrupted. "Apologies, Your Highness. I didn't know you were in a meeting."

"No need, Captain Arya. Clearly it is important." Atsuko

waved them out of their deep bow, and the knight rose on wobbly legs. "What is it?"

Arya's dark eyes flicked about the room, seeming unsure of the company around them. But when Atsuko gave a soft nod, they took a deep breath and continued on. "It's the stronghold at the base of the mountain. We've just received word that Yue Sunil is almost at the gates."

Atsuko's hands fell from where they'd been tucked behind her so she could grip the edge of her desk tightly. Cricket wondered how long she'd be able to hold herself in place that way. Not long, it seemed, as a moment later she was stepping around the desk and heading toward the door with Cricket, Anstice, and Arya in her wake.

"How long do we have?" Atsuko asked, her quick strides taking them back to the door of the infirmary.

"At most a week before he breaches the walls and starts up the mountain." Arya was panting as they strode along beside Cricket, their hands stuffed deep into their pockets, likely a habit acquired while trying to break a nail biting one if Cricket were to guess by their ragged nail beds.

"If we fit me with an iron cuff, I can start the trek tonight, and get into place to hold them off," Cricket said, following the others into the infirmary where he looked everywhere but at Yoshi who was still laid across one of the beds.

"Healer Orion," Atsuko moved to an older looking gentleman who was scribbling something across a stack of papers at a cluttered desk in the corner, thoroughly ignoring Cricket.

"Your Highness!" Orion squeaked, leaping from his chair to bow deeply.

"How long will it take my brother to be back on his feet?"

"Hard to say." Orion scrubbed at the gray stubble along his chin. "He's healing at an astronomical rate thanks to his abilities. But even still, broken ribs are always a little. . . hazy."

"An estimate." Atsuko frowned, her eyes focused firmly on the old healer.

"I'd say at best a couple of days, at worst a week. If we can keep him asleep, and not moving around, it'll be more the former than the latter." Orion pushed his glasses up into his unkempt hair, his watery eyes flicking across the room to the bed that Cricket refused to look at. He couldn't. He couldn't see Yoshi like that. Not when he knew he'd been the one to put him there.

Atsuko nodded and turned back to the little group who had followed her from her office. "Captain Arya, I want you to tell Captain Declan that we will be sending reinforcements to the stronghold first thing in the morning. Five-hundred knights to start, another five-hundred in a couple of days should Takayoshi not be better by then."

"Yes, Your Highness." Arya dipped into a low bow, and scurried off.

Cricket bit the inside of his cheek, the sharpness of his fangs drawing blood. "Atsuko, I could—"

"No. I will not send you into battle without my brother there to control the dragon. I can't risk my people that way. I know you mean well, Cricket, but you have to understand." Honey-brown eyes met Cricket's with a knowing look. She understood, of course she did, she had been queen long before he'd ever become king, she knew the burden he carried. And likewise, he knew the one she'd been shouldered with. If only they'd had more time to become proper friends.

"I do." Cricket's shoulders hunched forward, his fingers tightening again at his sides. He was a liability.

"When Takayoshi is better, you will both head down the mountain to help, but until then—" Atsuko cut herself off, her teeth biting hard on her bottom lip as she looked at something over Cricket's shoulder. Likely Yoshi's still sleeping form. He had not made a sound since they joined him in the room. Not even a shift of the bed linens. Whatever they had given him would likely keep him under until morning. She let out a breath, her posture deflating, and suddenly she looked like a scared little girl, worried that she'd disappointed her brother. "I think an iron cuff would be our best bet."

Cricket nodded. There was no question. "Something with a catch that I could easily undo, or something with a bit of sizing magic woven into it, so that it can shift up or down depending on what I need."

"I'll have someone come by to take measurements soon. Until then, I'm afraid I have to leave you. I've got to arrange the soldiers."

"Of course." Cricket fell into a deep bow, and didn't stand again until the door shut behind Atsuko again, leaving him alone with the healer, Anstice, and the still sleeping Yoshi.

"I don't like this," Anstice said into the ensuing silence.

"You don't have to." Cricket moved to drop into a chair next to Yoshi's bed. Yoshi's chest moved up and down slowly, still a little shallow from the bandages, but most of the color had returned to his cheeks. Cricket's fingers itched to brush a strand of white-blond hair away from Yoshi's face, but he kept them firmly in his lap where they belonged.

"He's going to be all right, Cricky. You heard the healer." Anstice's voice drifted over his shoulder. He could feel her, standing just behind him, her eyes on him and not the man in the bed.

It didn't feel that way. Objectively, Cricket knew it to be true, but it didn't feel that way at all. It felt like what he'd done to Yoshi had ended something, maybe before it had even really begun. And that thought left a crack in his chest that made the flowers seem to grow that much faster.

Cricket cleared his throat. "I think I love him," he said in a voice so soft he was sure only Anstice would hear it.

Anstice clicked her tongue, a sound that was usually accompanied by an eye roll. "You've got to be the stupidest man I've ever had the pleasure to call family."

"What?" His neck ached from how quickly he whipped his head around to eye her.

"Of course, you love him, you absolute nitwit." Anstice met his bewildered gaze with a deadpan one of her own. "Why do you think I kept shoving you two together?"

"Oh," was all Cricket could find within himself to say as he turned to look at Yoshi with new eyes. That's what that feeling was, like warmth curling up in his chest. It all made so much sense now.

Anstice was still speaking, but Cricket was lost to it, his mind drawing up images of every conversation, every look, every time he'd made a complete ass of himself in front of Yoshi.

"*Oh.*"

CHAPTER 27

It was distracting—the shift of the dark iron as Cricket twirled it between his fingers like one might a lucky coin. Takayoshi could not take his eyes off of it, the conversation around him not more than a soft murmur in his ears that hardly made any sense. Because he was not—in spite of what everyone around him seemed to think—a fool.

Maybe they thought he would not notice the way Cricket looked more drawn, and tired than he had since coming to them, like he had gotten much sicker somehow overnight. Maybe they thought he would miss the darkness that lined his already dark eyes. Or the way his skin had gone just slightly sallow from whatever sickness was eating away at him. And maybe they would have been right. Maybe he would have missed it—he was exhausted, still, himself, despite having slept for almost two days—but he could not miss it. Not with Cricket fiddling with that damnable trinket like a child might with an uncomfortable bit of clothing.

Becka was nowhere to be seen, her absence palpable as soon as he woke. Not because she had not visited, she had if the sloppily folded paper bunny on his nightstand meant anything, but because someone had clearly decided this was an adult conversation, and she should not be included. They were likely correct in that assessment. He did not want to think of how much she would be crying if she were to know what her Papa and Prince Shishi were about to face.

"You'll leave in the morning. We've already gathered men who will go with you," Atsuko was saying, her tone stilted and rigged in a way Takayoshi had never heard it before.

He did not like that either. But it was far less concerning than the blasted iron cuff, which seemed to be leaving some kind of burn on Cricket's fingers. The scales along the backs of Cricket's hands should have upset him, he knew that well enough, they were a sign that Cricket was losing the battle with himself. But Takayoshi could bring him back from the brink of that. He could not bring him back from the brink of whatever this sickness was.

"Yoshi, are you listening?" Atsuko asked, her tone worried. "Maybe we should put this off if you're not up to traveling, I don't want to—"

"I am ready to travel." Takayoshi ripped his gaze away from the dark iron to meet his sister's assessing eyes. "Provided My Prince is feeling well enough."

Cricket did not say anything, he simply cleared his throat, the sound wet, and choking, then nodded. Like he was afraid to speak, afraid to put words to whatever was going through his head.

"Good. Then you'll leave in the morning," Atsuko continued, standing up a little straighter, and lifting her chin. "I've put Domani in charge of your retinue. You will of course be the one giving orders, but I thought this would allow you to focus on the spirits for—"

"How many men will be left behind to protect the castle?" Cricket asked suddenly, his face grew warm when every eye turned to him. He shifted in his seat, his weight leaning one way then the other as he scrubbed at his nose.

"I'm sorry?" Atsuko frowned a little. "I'm afraid I don't understand the question."

Cricket took a deep breath that sounded like it hurt, and lifted his chin. "I'm leaving my daughter, the future of my kingdom, in your care. I want to ensure she's well-protected."

It looked like he wanted to say more, but Takayoshi could not imagine what other words might need to be said. Unless— No. Takayoshi would not think such a thing. He would not acknowledge that maybe Cricket was planning for if he could not return. Because to put voice to such thoughts would make them solid, and real in a way none of them wanted.

Atsuko softened, her shoulders going a little lax, and a gentle smile flitted over her face. "I'll look after Becka as if she were my own family. You don't need to worry about that, Cricket."

She reached over to give Cricket's shoulder a squeeze that made him relax as well, relief flooding every line of his body, but Atsuko's eyes were fixed on Takayoshi. Meaning hidden there that only her big brother could read. They had not properly spoken of his feelings for Cricket, not since he returned from the archive, but she had to know that nothing had changed. She had to know that Takayoshi still loved Cricket as much as he did all those years ago.

With one dark brow raised, Atsuko tilted her head in question, her eyes smiling in a way that they had not since the pair of them had been children. Takayoshi gave a curt nod, and looked away, hoping to avoid any further questions about his feelings, even if they were unspoken.

"If that's all, I'll leave you two to discuss final preparations." A smug smile warmed Atsuko's voice, and she left before Takayoshi had a chance to call her on her meddling. She had no doubt been instructed by Anstice to butt in. Why younger sisters felt the need to have a say in their older siblings' love lives, he would never understand.

The door shut behind her, and Cricket shifted uncomfortably in the chair again, making it creak under his weight. His long fingers were fiddling with the cuff still, drawing attention to the puckered, pink scar along the back of his left hand, the one Takayoshi where had driven a dagger not even two days ago to stop Cricket's rampage.

Two days. It seemed a lifetime already, everything was moving so quickly. But then, Takayoshi supposed, that was how things were with war on the horizon. Their continent had known peace so long—

"I know you're angry with me," Cricket said, breaking Takayoshi from his thoughts.

"I am not upset that you injured me." Takayoshi lifted his gaze from Cricket's hands to look him in the eye. He needed Cricket to know that. That he did not hold any grudge for what happened. That it was an accident of a kind.

"No. I didn't—" Cricket shook his head, letting out a strangled laugh. "I didn't think it was that. I knew you'd forgive me for that. How you could, I don't know, but I knew you would."

"Then what, pray tell, am I angry with you for?" Takayoshi asked. He *was* angry with Cricket. He was furious with him. And with Atsuko. And with Anstice. And with anyone else who seemed willing to disregard the danger that bloody cuff posed Cricket all in the name of bringing a swift end to Yue Sunil.

"I don't have a choice. Don't you understand that?" Cricket said, instead of answering the question.

"I do not believe that is the case."

Cricket's fingers tightened around the cuff, fury bringing the temperature of the room down at least a handful of degrees. Takayoshi saw him slip the cuff on out of the corner of his eye, but he said nothing, simply waited for an explanation. "I'm not going to apologize for doing what I have to."

"Then I suppose I will just have to remain angry with you."

"Yes. I suppose you will." Cricket bit out the words, and rose from his chair. He did not look back at Takayoshi on his way to the door. Did not even hesitate for a moment to perhaps try to salvage the conversation, but Takayoshi could hear him clear his throat loudly just as he reached the door. "I will see you in the morning when it's time to leave."

"Sleep well, My Prince." Takayoshi bowed his head, not wanting to watch Cricket walk away from him for what might be the last time.

THE MORNING ROSE COLD, and early, the air sitting like a leaden thing in Takayoshi's chest. It did not feel right. *None* of this felt right. The timing. The fact that he had not heard from Ignacia and Claudia. The way the weather had cleared to make it easier for them to get down the mountain. It was not right.

"Why can't I go with you, Papa?" Becka asked, her fingers clinging to Cricket's thick cloak like if she just held on tight enough, long enough, her Papa would not leave her. Takayoshi knew that desperation. He had *known* that desperation often throughout his life. He knew how it could settle into a child's bones, and turn them into a person they never thought they would become. Had seen it happening to himself, even as he could not stop it. Had seen it happen to his sister.

"Because Aunt Annie wants you to stay here with her. She

and Atsuko have lots of activities planned for you. Shishi and I will be back before you know it. I promise." Cricket leaned in to press his forehead to the little girl's, his color bleeding over onto her as it always did when they were standing together like this. They were both so bright and vibrant it made Takayoshi's eyes water, and for the first time in his life he wished he enjoyed art. That he could capture their likeness so the next time Cricket was feeling sad or lonely, he could look at it, and see all the love that seemed to overflow from both of them.

"Aunt Koko said you might see Uncle Sunil. . . is that true?" she said the name with only lingering traces of apprehension.

"Aunt Koko?" Takayoshi asked, moving over to them in the hopes that his presence would distract the child from the gut-wrenching fear that crossed her father's face at Sunil's name uttered from his daughter's lips.

"Mm." Becka nodded. "That's what she told me to call her."

"Did she?" Takayoshi turned his eyes to where Anstice was standing, absent her usual companion. Anstice only smiled the smile of a younger sibling who was deeply pleased with themselves. The thought crossed his mind that maybe these two had been planning something to force Cricket and he together for the last five years, and Sunil got in the way of it. Takayoshi shook it off. It was likely true, but they did not have time to bother with it.

"Mhm." Becka leaned over to hold her arms out to Takayoshi for a hug from him as well, giving no further explanation for why she so readily accepted Atsuko as her aunt. But then, why would she? She seemed to accept everyone as family no matter what their tie to her really was. That was something Cricket taught her, Takayoshi supposed, the ability to love anyone.

Takayoshi took her from Cricket's arms which looked like they had begun to flag under the weight of the child, and hugged her close to his chest. "Well, you will behave for Aunt Koko and Aunt Annie then, will you not?"

"I will." Becka pulled back to fix him with her most serious face.

"Excellent. And I hope that you will keep a log of your adventures while we are gone. Your Papa and I would like to hear all about what you got up to." Takayoshi raised a brow at Cricket, who smiled back at him, small and tentative. A momentary truce between the quarreling men.

"A log? You mean like a journal?"

"Yes, like a journal." Takayoshi tilted his lips up at the corner to fix her with one of his rare smiles. "And be sure to give them plenty of trouble," he whispered to her, just loud enough for Cricket and her to hear, "so you have lots to write about. Yes?"

"Yes!" Becka's laugh was so loud it echoed off the walls of the gate.

"Good." He gave her another tight squeeze before setting her down on her booted feet. "Go on to Aunt Annie, your Papa and I need to head out."

"Okay." Her feet skidded across the stone ground.

Once she was beside Anstice she turned to watch them settle onto their horses, and waved at them until they disappeared through the gate.

"Thank you for that," Cricket said, scrubbing at his face with the lining of his cloak. Takayoshi could not see his face, but he was sure he was crying.

"I will get you home to her," Takayoshi promised, and nudged his horse on through the empty streets of the city surrounding the castle.

BOOK III
TRAP

CHAPTER 28

The iron made it hard to focus on much other than the feeling of roots growing into his lungs. Cricket hadn't noticed it before. Or if he had, he simply brushed it off. But with nothing other than the white-on-white landscape in front of him, and the silent Helion knights around him, the iron seemed to sizzle against his scales all the more. It muted, and blocked his magic. And the way the snowdrops grew like ivy in his body, threatened to choke off his very life. The sensations taking up, and swallowing whole anything else that might have been around him to pay attention to, even the passage of time itself.

So, while he knew it took them at least a handful of days to reach the base of the mountain, he had not noticed the travel. Then all at once the slow decline of their path leveled off, and they were riding on flat land.

But it was not that which truly drew Cricket from the place where he'd holed himself up in his head to escape the aching, suffocating squeeze of snowdrops blooming in his lungs.

No.

The thing that drew Cricket from his mind was the stench. The foul odor of decay that rose above the fresh cleansing smell of winter pine, pulling him to a stop hidden amongst the trees before he even properly understood what he was doing. Like some instinctual part of himself was afraid to go any further. To let whatever was attached to that smell see him.

Next came the shambling sounds. With their small retinue having stopped, and no other forest noises present, the faint *shush*ing of shuffling feet was near deafening in Cricket's ears. He did not have to lay eyes on the creatures to recognize the signs of hungry spirits, those were sounds no living thing could make.

He turned to slide from his saddle to find Yoshi already beside him, hands held out to help him dismount. Normally, Cricket might have brushed him off, too proud to admit he needed help, but the muscles in his legs had grown weak, and he knew his knees would not hold his weight. It would wound his pride far more to stumble in front of his soldiers. He gave Yoshi a nod of gratitude, and slid down into his waiting hands.

There was a beat, perhaps too long, where their chests were pressed together. Where Yoshi's fingers flexed on his waist. Where Cricket was oh so aware of the warmth that seemed to hover over Yoshi's skin like a blanket. It would have been easy to lean into it, and let Yoshi ward off the chill.

But then petals caught in the back of Cricket's throat, and he had to clear it to dislodge the tickle, and the moment was lost.

They moved on silent feet to the edge of the forest, still hidden among the pines, to where Cricket could hear the sounds more clearly. His eyes narrowed on the dark figures of what might have once been people, but was now not much more than desecrated corpses. Hungry spirits with no will of their own. Puppets animated by hate and blood and put on strings by the vindictiveness of one who had no respect for anyone but themselves. Acid and bile rose in his throat, and he had to duck back to the horses to be violently sick where the spirits wouldn't hear him.

A warm hand on his back had Cricket kicking snow over the pile of slick blossoms, and leaves, hoping Yoshi hadn't seen it before he turned back to look at him.

"I'm sorry. I just. . ." Cricket shrugged. He didn't know what he had just. Maybe he had *just* thought that Uncle Sunil wasn't capable of such a thing. Maybe he had *just* thought there wouldn't be so many. Maybe he had *just* thought that someone had been mistaken. It didn't matter. What mattered was there were at least fifty hungry spirits shambling around the outside wall of the stronghold, and it was hard to tell if it was because Uncle Sunil had taken the stronghold, or if it was because he was trying to flush the people out of it.

"I know," Yoshi said, asking for no further explanation. He never seemed to need it. He always seemed to understand. *Stars.* Cricket had been so blind to not see how he ached all over with his love of Yoshi before. What a fool he'd been.

"Do we know if they're guarding it, or trying to intimidate those inside?" Cricket ran the back of his hand across his mouth, wishing he'd thought to fill his waterskin on their last stop. But he'd been so out of it for days now, it was no surprise he'd forgotten.

Yoshi held out his own, and waited for Cricket to take a small sip before continuing, "We cannot tell. I have sent scouts to look for a camp nearby. If your uncle and his men have not breached the walls yet, there will be signs of them somewhere."

"Good. Good." Cricket handed him the waterskin and moved back to the edge of the wood. Not as close as before, but enough to watch the stilted movements of the hungry spirits. How long did they have before the creatures noticed them? Or were they too well-leashed to have even the desire to feed when not specifically instructed?

"Some of them are wearing Helion uniforms," one of the knights said, her hand in a tight fist at her side.

"He'll have been building up his forces as he goes. No sense in wasting bodies," another supplied, their tone carefully neutral, even as their face looked a little green.

"We will have to burn the corpses." Yoshi stepped up to stand beside Cricket, his warmth seeping into the one side of Cricket's body, where their shoulders nearly touched, making the other side that much colder by contrast. "It is the only way to truly lay them to rest now."

"But their families. . ." Cricket's shoulders hunched.

"It is what must be done."

"We found a camp, Your Highness." A young man came to bow on the other side of Yoshi, his long dark hair falling into his face. Cricket couldn't be sure, but he thought he saw a twitch of annoyance on Yoshi's face at the bow. "A mile due east. It has clear sight lines to the stronghold, but has been tucked amongst some of the rocky outcroppings at the base of the mountain."

"Friend or foe?" Cricket spun the iron cuff around his wrist, the burn of it against his fingertips a visceral reminder of the thing keeping the dragon at bay even as anger buzzed under his skin. Anger at his uncle, at Craven, at this situation. This world. His father. The gods. The whole blasted—

"We are unsure, Your Highness," the young man said, ripping Cricket from his spiral.

Cricket let out a breath, forcing the muscles in his shoulders to relax, then inhaled again, and tried to breathe into the space left behind as Yoshi taught him. Tried to feel the way the air expanded the parts of him that were clenched too tight. It didn't help much. But it did at least give him time to make his body relax. "I suppose we'll just have to find out for ourselves."

"Do you have a plan?" Yoshi was watching him with those golden eyes, his face a mask of impassivity, but Cricket had learned where to look. He saw the subtle twitch of Yoshi's eyebrows upward, a tiny shift that anyone else would have missed, but Cricket knew meant he was curious. And curiosity, Cricket could work with.

"We should have enough men to surround them," Cricket called over his shoulder as he headed back to his horse. "We just need to be quiet to keep them, and the spirits from noticing us. I'd rather not be torn into bite sized pieces today."

"Or any day," one of the men muttered, and Cricket nearly choked on a laugh. Perhaps Yoshi wasn't the only Helion with a sense of humor.

WHICH WAS how they found themselves hidden among the rocks that surrounded the encampment as the sun sank low in the sky. It was still early yet, maybe not any later than five or six in the evening, but the winter sun fell heavily and he tired easily. And with the clouds blotting out much of the light of the moon, it was easy work to set themselves up around the camp without being seen.

The plan, which Cricket thought was brilliant thank you very much, was to lay siege to the camp once everyone had gone to sleep. There would no doubt be a few scouts awake, but not enough to slow down Yoshi, Cricket, and their knights.

Cricket had positioned himself on one of the higher rock forms, thinking that if he had to he could take to the skies as a dragon and draw the fire of their enemies for long enough that Yoshi and the others could decimate their forces.

He had not realized that it also made him highly visible to anyone who might be looking from the surrounding trees. Or that indeed anyone was *in* the surrounding trees. A vast oversight, he realized when the cold bite of a blade pressed against his neck.

"Well. Well. Well. If it isn't a little princeling," a voice that was far too familiar sing-songed.

"King, actually." Cricket chuckled, not turning to meet the soft green gaze he'd known all his life. "Am I to assume that this is not, in fact, enemy territory?"

"No. It's not." Ignacia scoffed, tapping his cheek with the flat of her blade before she pulled it away. "You're an idiot, you know that? You could have been shot up here."

"That was, ironically, the plan." Cricket turned to fix her with a smile. She looked thinner than he remembered. Her long auburn hair cut so short it didn't even cover her ears anymore, and her cheeks had hollowed out likely from all the nights on the road. But, he was sure, he didn't look much better.

"Call off your goons, Cricky. And for Selene's sake, come get something to eat, you look awful."

"Gee. Thanks."

"Chop chop, Your Highness. You're wasting moonlight," Ignacia called over her shoulder as she cut a path through the rocks down to her camp.

It was the work of a half hour to round up Yoshi and the others, and explain to them they were not, in fact, surrounding an enemy encampment. But when that was done, Cricket was plunked in front of a roaring fire, loaded down with furs, and someone shoved a bowl of stew of some kind into his hands, likely Ignacia.

"We weren't able to hold the stronghold," the man who had re-introduced himself as Leo, for indeed Cricket had mostly forgotten what he looked like, said. He was leaning heavily on a cane where he stood on the other side of Yoshi. "We tried."

"There were too many of them." Claudia scuffed the toe of her boot into the snow. "And those spirits can't be cut down. We tried. Ignacia even started decapitating them. Nothing."

Cricket's stomach rolled again at that; he tightened his grip around the bowl in his hands. "Yoshi says we'll have to burn them."

Ignacia sighed, leaning back against Claudia's legs where she sat at her feet. "Then that's what we'll do."

"How many of the knights that my sister sent are left?" Yoshi asked.

"Twenty." Leo itched at his bearded cheek. "We did what we could to help them. But. . ."

"This is not your fault." Yoshi frowned, his hands tightening where they rested on his knees. "None of this is your fault."

"They've got Estia with them," Leo said like it explained everything, and the nod Yoshi gave him seemed to say that it did, but not to Cricket.

Yoshi swallowed the last of his soup and set his bowl aside. "Commander or prisoner?"

"Commander." Claudia's fingers moved to hold onto Ignacia's shoulders like Ignacia was the only thing grounding her.

"Well. That's what it looks like, anyway," Ignacia supplied, optimistic, seeming to sense the tension between the three friends. Cricket wasn't sure why. He knew Estia traveled with them to the archive. But he had never gotten the full story of it from Yoshi.

When the quiet between them stretched on for too long, Leo said, "They know we're here."

"Why haven't they attacked yet? Cleared you out?" Cricket set aside his now cold bowl of soup. He wasn't hungry. He wasn't sure he'd ever be hungry again.

"We think they're saving their forces so they can start pushing up the mountain once the weather clears." Claudia shifted again, her fingers so tight in Ignacia's cloak that Cricket could imagine he heard the seams creak.

"Well, we won't be giving them time for that." Cricket rose from his place at the fire. "Show me what you have, and let's form a plan. I want that stronghold back in the next forty-eight hours."

He felt the eyes on him, bewildered, unsure, surprised, from the others, but when he looked at Ignacia she was smirking. Her nose wrinkled just a little in pure delight and pride. "I'll show you to the war tent, Your Highness."

CHAPTER 29

The frigid wind bit at Takayoshi's bare neck, but he barely noticed it, too focused on the not-so-subtle shifting of Cricket at his side. The crunch of snow beneath Cricket's booted feet. The way the iron cuff at his wrist reflected the watery sunshine when it was spun just right. Cricket was *overall* a distraction, but even more so when he was anxious.

"Stop fidgeting," Takayoshi said, hoping his tone did not come off half as scolding as it felt. If Cricket was not careful, he would draw the attention of the spirits.

"I can't help it." Cricket mumbled, scrubbing at his nose with his knuckles. "How long does it take people to walk around a stronghold? I mean *really*. Everyone should be set up by now."

Takayoshi took a deep breath, and focused back on the shuffling, shambling corpses. From what the scouts said, the creatures never stopped moving. They continued their circuit around the front of the fortress all hours of the day and night, creating a barrier between any invading forces, and whoever had decided to hole up inside. They knew Estia was with them, but Takayoshi had not been able to get a straight answer on who else was amongst the commanding officers. It could very well be that Claudia and Ignacia did not know them. Sunil had decided to use so many outsiders, that was a very real possibility.

There was another rustle of clothing, Cricket resettling himself against the tree where they had hidden themselves. Takayoshi reached down and took the hand fiddling with the iron cuff, and threaded their fingers together as if by instinct. Maybe it was instinct. He did not have time to inspect it, nor the emotions that spread through him at the almost casual contact. They had not held hands, this was a very new thing, not even before when they had been adventuring around Lunette together. Not like this at least. It had always been Cricket grabbing his wrist, or his elbow, and tugging him along.

"There is no need to be anxious," Takayoshi said, and if his voice was a touch rougher than it normally would have been, he was glad that his friends were not there to hear it. "We will regain control of the stronghold."

Cricket let out a long, audible breath, his shoulders hunching forward as he curled against the tree. He did not say anything, he did not need to, but he soaked up the comfort Takayoshi was providing him like a sponge. Takayoshi was not sure how he could tell, he simply could. Cricket squeezed his hand back, a soft gesture of thanks, and they fell into silence, waiting for the signal to attack.

It came ten minutes later. The soft caw of what might have been a crow, or an eagle, or maybe a chicken, it was always hard to tell with Leo's horrible animal impressions—a hobby he picked up while on the island.

"That is the signal. Give me your cuff." Takayoshi held out his hand for the iron band.

"You'll stop me, when it's over?" Cricket looked up at him

with those midnight blue eyes, and Takayoshi nodded. He would promise Cricket anything if it meant he could bask just a bit longer in that gaze, stand just a little closer to that warmth, and thread his fingers through the ones that had lengthened to talons some days ago.

Perhaps Anstice was right, perhaps he should tell Cricket how he felt. Tomorrow, he vowed to himself. Tomorrow, after they regained control of the stronghold, and pushed Sunil back toward Lunette. Tomorrow, once this battle was won.

The iron made his skin itch in all the places that it touched as Cricket laid it in his open palm. And it would have been a relief, if he did not look down and see the red irritated scales that circled Cricket's wrist. The iron could not reverse what had already been done, it could only slow the process, and the more of a dragon Cricket became, the worse it would be.

Cricket seemed to breathe easier without it. He lifted his chin and started through the last small stretch of trees separating them from the shuffling sentinels. Takayoshi tucked the cuff into his pocket, knowing it would be there when he shifted back from being a phoenix. He hoped he would not need it to stop Cricket, but he would not chance that. Then he followed behind him.

The hungry spirits noticed them the moment they broke the tree line. They stopped, heads lifting like dogs to scent the air, then they were looking at Cricket and Takayoshi with the gaze of the truly ravenous.

A heavy silence fell over the clearing, as if everything for miles upon miles was holding its breath. Cricket took a sure, unwavering step in the direction of the spirits, and the creatures seemed to make up their mind as one that they were tired of being hungry.

They lunged forward. Waves upon waves of bodies, far more than it had looked like when they were simply circling the compound, hit Takayoshi and Cricket like a wall. He hardly had a moment to draw his sword before two of the creatures threw the full weight of their bodies at him, and he was knocked back into the snow, the wet seeping in through the back of his tunic.

The plan was simple, cause a distraction, and take out as many of the hungry spirits as they could on their own while the others infiltrated the compound. It was, in practice, anything but, Takayoshi realized as blunt teeth scraped at the muscle on his forearm.

He lost Cricket in the melee. For all he knew the young king had fallen under the weight of a wall of bodies. One of them knocked Takayoshi's sword from his hand, not that it was doing him much good. He had managed to behead one of the creatures before it could take him down, but just as Claudia said, the thing simply got back up and kept moving, guided by some innate instinct toward the heat of him.

And that was it, he realized, noticing Cricket on the edge of the hoard that surrounded him as he pushed himself up to a seat, drawing upon the flames flickering under his skin. The creatures were searching for heat. Not power the way those in the mansion had, just warmth.

Well. I can give them that. His lips twitched.

He did not relish what came next, he knew he would not, as his burning fingers touched the first creature, sending its dehydrated husk of a body up in flames that rivaled any bonfire. But it was what had to be done. It was what he would have to do many more times, Takayoshi realized, before this war was well and truly through. He tried not to think of how many bodies would not return to their loved ones as the first caught a second, a third, a fourth, the softly falling snow only able to put them out when they had been reduced to cinders.

Where those fell, ten more replaced them, their weight bearing down on Takayoshi, piling up like fallen trees. All grappling for a piece of him, tearing at his clothes, his bound hair, his skin. He could not light them fast enough, even as his hands and arms sparked to life.

There was blood on the snow, but he no longer knew if it were his own or one of the creatures', then he heard the scream. An anguished cry like someone's heart breaking.

"Yoshi!" He thought it might have said, he also thought the voice might have belonged to Cricket. But he hoped it was not, for he did not want to hear his prince in that kind of pain.

A moment later, the dragon burst into the sky, two hungry spirits hanging from his tail like limpets. Cricket shook them off, sending them reeling, before he dove at the creatures swarming Takayoshi, and took one of them between his great jaws. There was a crunching sound, followed by the squelch of blood, but Takayoshi did not have time to watch as Cricket tore the creature in half, he was too busy finding his feet again.

With a moment to breathe, and a bit of a circle cleared around him, he too took to the sky. The phoenix lighting every dried bit of skin and hair in its wake, leaving not more than charred bones behind. At least there would be something left for them to bury to put the souls to rest. Perhaps he could ask Selene for a special blessing for this. But that was something for them to deal with later.

Between phoenix and dragon, the army of hungry spirits was reduced to ashes and pieces, leaving the way clear for the knights to attack the stronghold. Black blood dripped from Cricket's whiskers, and beard, but he looked hungry for more. His dark gaze following the knights as they were met with resistance on the other side of the wall.

Takayoshi saw Cricket flinch, a moment of hesitation, like he was not sure if he wanted to join the fray or not. Then the hungry look returned, ravenous in the way those lifeless creatures had been, and Takayoshi knew he had to stop Cricket before things went too far.

"Enough," Takayoshi called, hoping his voice would break through to Cricket when it never had before. Foolish thing, hope, he realized perhaps too late as the dragon's paw reached for a knight wearing Helion armor. "Cricket! Enough!"

He did not make it in time to stop him. Maybe he should have known he would not. Takayoshi had always thought himself brilliant at battle tactics. But none of his lessons, or training, could have prepared him for war alongside a dragon, and fighting the dragon when he stepped out of line.

The knight's body hit the ground with a *thud* that Takayoshi heard above the sounds of battle, and Takayoshi dove before Cricket could reach for another, putting himself in between Cricket and the knights on the ground, not stopping to check if the man was still breathing or not. The knights were not celestials. They could not fight a dragon. He could.

"I said *enough*." Takayoshi slammed his winged shoulder into Cricket, knocking him back over the wall of the compound and into the gray snow on the other side. The cold made the flames on his wings and tail sputter, but he did not stop until he pinned Cricket's top half to the ground.

The impact knocked something loose in Cricket, and when Takayoshi met his gaze again, he saw his prince in those slitted eyes. Cricket shook himself, making his whiskers and beard flutter in the breeze, then with a ragged swallow that Takayoshi was sure would taste like blood, he let the scales slough away, leaving the fragile, tiny body of Cricket beneath the phoenix in the snow.

"I'm sorry. I'm so sorry." Cricket sobbed, his eyes already brimming with tears. Takayoshi was sure his weight was almost too much for Cricket, making it difficult to breathe past it, but he did not have the fortitude to change back. Not yet. Not when he watched the pain cross Cricket's face and settle into the very marrow of him. "I killed him. Oh gods. I killed him."

"You were not yourself." Takayoshi said, wrapping the warmth of his wings around them, acting as a shield for Cricket to hide away from the world, and the carnage that was still going on behind them.

"That doesn't matter. You know it does not." Cricket sobbed again, and the sound came out more choked. Then Cricket was coughing. Coughing. *Coughing.* Blood. And phlegm. And something that looked like leaves coming up and out before he turned to wretch into the snow beside them. All the while Takayoshi stayed, his wings a protective barrier, to keep out the world, to keep in the fragility of his prince. When Cricket was finished expelling what looked like plants into the snow, he covered it before Takayoshi could see, then lay on his back in the cold, and the wet, and just breathed. "I'm sorry."

"I know." Takayoshi finally let the feathers fall away, rolling onto his side to sit beside Cricket in the snow as he pulled the cuff from his pocket, and slipped it on. "And they will too. Whatever you might have done when you were not yourself, they will understand."

"How could they?"

"Things could have been much worse, if we had not been here to deal with the hungry spirits. Every knight who fought today would have died if not for you." Takayoshi took Cricket's hand, the one with the cuff on the wrist, and threaded their fingers again.

They sat there for a while, the snow falling lazily around them, and waited. The sounds of battle had died away, Takayoshi was not sure when, likely while he was still trying to regain control of Cricket, and soon enough Claudia emerged from the compound. She was limping, a trail of blood dripping down from her right arm into the snow, but she was whole, and that was more than Takayoshi could have hoped for.

"We have control of the stronghold," she said, but her face did not show this for the victory that he thought it was. "Sunil wasn't here."

CHAPTER 30

"What do you mean Sunil isn't here?" Cricket asked, his head lifting so quickly it jarred something in his neck. But that didn't matter. *Nothing* mattered. Because he came here to hunt down his uncle. Came to stop him. To put an end to this war before Uncle Sunil hurt someone else who didn't deserve it, who had nothing to do with this.

"We searched everywhere, he wasn't inside." Claudia shifted on her heels, her eyes darting from Cricket to look at Yoshi, regret lining her face.

"Estia?" Yoshi asked, pushing to his feet, and holding a hand out to help Cricket to his own. Cricket's legs were still unbearably shaky from everything that happened, although the memories were fuzzy around the edges, hard to decipher through the rage and the carnage. Was that because of his lingering curse, or because he'd lost more of himself to the dragon? He couldn't tell.

"We have zir." Claudia nodded, but she didn't seem pleased at all with the announcement. Cricket would have to ask more about that later, when all of this was over, when he was sure that Uncle Sunil wouldn't raze a path of destruction through Helio to get to him.

"Why wouldn't he be here?" Cricket frowned, following them into the compound on unsteady legs. It didn't make sense. None of it made sense. Uncle Sunil wanted Cricket, he'd been very clear about that. He wanted his hands on Cricket's power, and the ability to kill him at his leisure. But he couldn't get to Cricket if he ran away from the battle where Cricket *was*. Right?

"I'm more concerned with the how, than the why," Ignacia said, joining them a moment later. She had blood trailing down the side of her face from somewhere in her hairline. Cricket had to resist the urge to reach out for her, and make sure that she was all right. His family was slowly disappearing around him, he couldn't lose another one of them.

"The how?" Yoshi's tone gave away none of the inner turmoil that Cricket could see twisting behind his eyes, writhing like a beast waiting to be set free.

Cricket wondered how no one else could see it. How even *he* hadn't until recently. He'd missed so much over the years. Been so blind to so many things. . .

He shook himself, now was not the time to think about how he'd been foolishly in love with Yoshi since almost that first moment they'd met. There would hopefully be time for those thoughts later. Once Uncle was dealt with.

Ignacia grunted irritably, leading them into what looked to have been the dining hall at one point, but the tables and benches were pushed aside and stacked along the walls so the floor was clear. That was the first thing Cricket noticed, but the second was something that made his stomach churn enough to almost have him vomiting up flowers again.

Blood.

The scent of it. The sight of it. The slick of it beneath

their feet. It lodged in his nostrils making it hard to breathe. Too much for one person. Too much for one battle.

"All this from the fight?" Cricket asked, hoping, praying, that's what this was. That he wasn't about to learn of more of his Uncle's deplorable acts in the name of power. But even as he said the words, he saw the chalk lines on the floor. They swooped all the way around the center of the room in a big circle. Characters scrawled into the eight directions of a compass, four major, four minor, and more, covered up by the red of the blood, almost indecipherable for how large they were.

Claudia shook her head, her brown face had gone pale, her hands shook down at her sides. Cricket had to look away when he saw Ignacia reach to her, to provide what comfort she could. It was too intimate, too raw, and it made something sickening like jealousy turn in his gut. Why couldn't *he* have that?

"What kind of array is this?" Yoshi crouched to inspect the character closest to them, the lines an angry slash against the stone of the room.

"Best we can tell?" Claudia took a deep breath, her voice suddenly more solid than it had been since she'd first walked out to find them sitting in the snow, that was Ignacia's doing, Cricket realized. Whatever bond they'd formed in his absence it had been something. . . something he'd never seen Ignacia bother with before. Then the next words left her lips, and Cricket's world tilted. "It's a traveling array."

"No." Cricket gasped, his feet stumbling across the stone too quickly, a foolish, restless attempt to inspect all of the characters still visible through the blood and the scuff marks of other people's feet. The room was large, it took him at least ten paces to get from one end to the other.

"Where— Where did it take them to?" he asked when no

one said anything else, just left him to his frantic examination.

"There's no way to know." Claudia shifted a little, her shoulder tucked under Ignacia's arm.

"What?" Cricket spun around, his gaze narrowing on her. "What do you mean there's no way to know? There has to *be*." His voice broke on the last word, his throat impossibly tight.

"There isn't. Not that we can find." Ignacia frowned. She looked like she wanted to reach for Cricket, to hold him close to her chest, and bring him back to himself, but she wasn't sure if it was the right choice or not. It might not be.

"No discernible coordinates, or place names," Claudia continued Ignacia's unfinished thought. "I checked. If they *were* there they've been covered in blood, or scuffed away."

"We will find him," Yoshi said, his hands on Cricket's shoulders, stopping Cricket's shaking. He hadn't even realized he had started.

"We could interrogate Estia." Claudia's weight shifted from foot to foot.

"Will ze know anything?" Yoshi's voice rumbled up through his chest where it pressed against Cricket's back. The grip on Cricket's shoulders tightened, pulling Cricket in closer to Yoshi, letting the solidness of Yoshi settle whatever panic had started to make him feel like he was about to vibrate out of his skin.

"Only one way to find out." Ignacia's mouth twisted into something almost nauseated. She didn't relish the idea of whatever was about to happen, that much was clear.

"We cannot injure Estia," Yoshi said, seeming to read the situation just as Cricket had. "Ze is still the Prin of Cytherea. To do so would be to invite war with King Craven as well."

"He's already aligned himself with Sunil," Ignacia spat, her hand tight on the hilt of her sword at her side.

"We have no definitive proof of that. Nothing that would hold up in the court of nobles, at least." Yoshi's heart had begun to pound in his chest, Cricket could feel it against his back, but his voice was as calm and impassive as it ever was. Cricket wondered idly if that happened a lot, if Yoshi's heart skipped a beat, or pounded just as his own did, Yoshi was just able to hide it better.

"What do I care about the court of–"

"He's right," Cricket cut her off, putting a stop to the fight before it could begin. "It'd just make more of a mess of this situation than it already is. We can't take that chance. We have to try *bargaining*." The word was acid on his tongue, but Cricket knew it was the right way to go.

"*I'm* not bargaining with that filthy little traitor." Ignacia glared at him, her shoulders a tense line.

"I will speak to zir. We were friends once." Yoshi finally released Cricket, taking a step back from him, leaving Cricket cold with the lack of him. "Will you accompany me, My Prince? It might be beneficial to have someone who can offer Estia sanctuary."

Cricket merely nodded and followed Yoshi through the stronghold. He seemed to know his way to the dungeons, and Cricket was grateful to be away from the smell of blood, and the reminders of a massacre that could have as easily been caused by him.

"I can't." Cricket realized suddenly, his voice echoing off the solid stone of the narrow hall.

"Cannot what?" Yoshi's steps did not falter. Of course they didn't. Nothing about Yoshi ever faltered. He was steady, sturdy, a safe harbor in the storm of war that Cricket hadn't realized he relied on until that very moment.

"Offer Estia sanctuary. Or anything, really." He laughed, and he wasn't sure if it was the echo or if the noise really was that hollow. "What's a king without a kingdom?"

"That will not always be the case."

"It might be."

Yoshi shook his head, as if he saw what a lost cause it was in arguing with Cricket, a huff of exasperation leaving him. Then he reached between them, and took Cricket's hand, threading their fingers together as he'd done in the forest just hours before. Their palms pressed together, Yoshi's warm and dry, Cricket's clammy and slick with sweat. He turned back the way he'd been going, and continued on, his hand still holding firm to Cricket's, and Cricket was helpless but to follow.

"I see you found your prince," was the first thing Estia said when ze caught sight of them. Cricket expected Yoshi to drop his hand, to be almost embarrassed by the show of intimacy in front of someone who didn't seem all that friendly now they were face to face, but he didn't.

"I did." Yoshi gave Cricket's hand a little squeeze, as if in victory, but didn't say anything else about it.

Estia huffed, brushing teal strands of hair back from zir light brown eyes, so ze could meet Yoshi's gaze without it in the way. They stood there in silence for what felt like forever, the soft drip of snow melting somewhere among the cells the only sound.

"I suppose you want to know where he went, don't you?" Estia asked finally, after Cricket had begun to wonder if ze would speak to them at all.

"That would be most appreciated." Yoshi dipped his head in thanks.

"I'm sure it would be," Estia murmured mostly to zirself before ze shook zir head, "but I'm not going to."

Yoshi's jaw ticking was the only outward expression of his irritation, though Cricket would swear he could feel his skin grow warmer. "What *will* you tell us?"

"Nothing." Estia shrugged, flopping onto the bench along

the back wall, zir back hitting it with a dull thud. "I can't. You know I can't," ze said, zir voice so soft Cricket almost wasn't sure he'd heard it.

"I can offer you sanctuary," the words tumbled out of Cricket's mouth before he even thought about them. He wasn't sure if it was the heat of Yoshi's palm against his own, or the soft tremble of Yoshi's fingers, but he knew he had to do something. He had to pave the way, if he could. "I can protect you from him, and your brother, if that's what you wish."

Estia barked a laugh, zir face still turned up to the ceiling so the sound bounced off it, echoing, and ringing in Cricket's ears. "And who is going to protect you and yours, Your Highness?"

"Wh-what?" The room tilted under Cricket's feet. "What do you mean—" Cricket licked his suddenly dry lips, trying not to breathe too hard as it made the pressure in his chest that much more difficult to gasp through. "What do you mean, me and mine?"

Estia turned zir head to look at Cricket, something like pity shone in zir eyes. "You left her unprotected, didn't you?"

Becka.

Cricket didn't know when he'd started moving, but he'd dropped Yoshi's hand, then he was running, running, *running*, out to the courtyard, out into the snow. Slipping the cuff off his wrist and throwing it to the ground before taking to the skies, his slitted eyes turned toward Helio's capital.

CHAPTER 31

Takayoshi was going to be sick. His heart lurched up his throat, lodging somewhere behind his tongue, making it hard to breathe. Panic lingered at the edges of his awareness, threatening to swallow him and send him into a spiral. The only thing keeping him from completely losing himself to it was the image of Cricket's serpentine body blotting out the sun as he flew away.

Not for the first time, Takayoshi wished that he were the type of man to curse, to swear a blue streak, to spit venom at a situation, it might make things a little easier, he thought as he watched Cricket disappear into the graying clouds. He knew where Cricket was going, of course he did, but he also knew that he could not follow. Not yet. There were still matters to settle in the compound before he could abandon his people in favor of fighting another battle on another front.

In the privacy of the courtyard, where no one would see the strain and the stress, Takayoshi scrubbed at his face with his hand, and pinched the bridge of his nose where a headache was beginning to form. How many more times would he have to watch Cricket fly away like that? How many more times would they be separated? Would Takayoshi be able to reach him before the worst happened this time?

"I'd say I'm sorry," a voice jerked him from his thoughts, making Takayoshi whip around to fix an irritated gaze on Ignacia that she seemed wholly unbothered by.

"Sorry for what?" He crouched to pull the iron cuff from the snow, tucking it back into the pocket of his trousers where it would not burn him. Would Cricket even be able to come back to himself without it? If something happened to Becka, would he want to?

"For how he's acting." Ignacia's boots crunched in the snow as she came to stand beside him. She did not sound apologetic at all, not that there was really anything for her to apologize for. She could no more control Cricket's actions than Takayoshi could control Atsuko's. "But I think we all know that I'd be lying if I did."

"You heard what Estia said to us." It was a reasonable conclusion, just because Ignacia and Claudia had opted out of participating in the interrogation did not mean they would not listen in. In fact, it was likely better they had. Takayoshi would rather not have to tell everyone what happened, not when the words were still festering in his mouth like a wound.

"I'm surprised you didn't leave with him."

"There is too much still to do here. One of us must be sensible." Someone needed to stay behind and be sure that Sunil did not have a second force coming for the stronghold. Someone needed to ensure their people were safe, and settled, and protected before flying off on another dangerous mission.

Ignacia nodded, her brows pressed together in the middle. Something was bothering her, but she was unlikely to tell him what it was. They were not friends, after all, whatever time they traveled together it had been years ago, and they were not friends now. Although, he might like to think they could be again, in future, when she and Claudia had settled into whatever they were, and all of this was behind them. Takayoshi never thought of himself as one to daydream, but he found himself idly visualizing what that might be like as the snow started to fall around them again, soft and silent. A little family all his own. . .

"Claudia is attempting to contact your sister," Ignacia said, ripping him from his thoughts again. He wondered if she knew he was drifting off somewhere into his mind, if she were used to pulling Cricket back from the same flights of fancy, but he did not want to ask. Instead, he turned to look at her, one brow just twitching upward in question. "If he went to the capital, we need to warn them that he's coming."

Unless he has already laid siege to your castle, went unsaid, and for once Takayoshi was grateful for the things someone did not say. He only wished he had not heard them in the space between her words. It would have been so much easier if he could simply pretend Sunil had not used the stronghold as a distraction to draw Cricket and Takayoshi away from the people who most needed their protection. What fools they had been to think they could head the man off.

"I know you're worried about him." Ignacia shifted closer as if she wanted to reach out and provide Takayoshi with some measure of comfort but recognized that she should not touch him. He was grateful for that as well, for the intention without the act. "But we'll figure out what's going on with him. Just as soon as we get rid of Sunil."

Takayoshi bit the inside of his cheek until he tasted something metallic and thick on his tongue to keep from telling Ignacia all he learned in the archive. He told Cricket of the pearl, but the truth of his lineage had never come up. Or if it had come up, it never seemed the right time. There was too much else going on, and Sunil was knocking on their door before Takayoshi had even a moment to consider what being the son of the moon goddess Selene might mean for Cricket.

"Your uncle is irate," Claudia called across the courtyard, her tone irritable. "Come tell him to be quiet before Leo does it and causes a diplomatic incident."

Takayoshi tilted his head back, his eyes drifting to where the moon would shine through the clouds when night finally fell. He prayed to Selene for strength, and patience, and the wherewithal to get through the remainder of this war without losing another person he loved.

"Well?" Claudia asked, an insistence in her tone that bordered on disrespectful when speaking to the heir to a kingdom, but Takayoshi was used to that. It was hard to keep the distance of cordiality between oneself and another when spending several years traveling together.

"I am on my way." Takayoshi dropped his head and turned to follow behind her, Ignacia at his back. He could hear his uncle shouting from down the hall.

The room where Leo and some of the men had set up a home base of sorts was the only one that seemed untouched by Sunil and Estia's carnage. Likely because it had been emptied of inhabitants and acted as a storage closet until that moment. The hall outside was stacked high with furniture, but Leo and the others had dragged one of the long narrow tables from the dining hall inside so they could go over their next steps somewhere that did not smell of blood and decay.

"Where is my nephew! You get him here right this instant! I will not say another word to you, you hooligan. Do you hear me? Not another word!" Takayoshi's uncle's voice had hit that shrill note that it always hit when he was deeply offended by something. The one that made Takayoshi's ears prickle.

"Honestly, I wish you would," Leo grumbled back, and

Takayoshi bit down on his tongue to hold back a huff of laughter at the bored tone in his friend's voice.

"What was that? Are you sassing me? Was that sarcasm? Do you have no respect for your betters–"

"Uncle," Takayoshi said, stepping up to the mirror beside Leo, and cutting the man off before he could say anything to infuriate Leo further. Already he could see where Leo's hand had moved behind his back to reach for the dagger tucked into his belt, no doubt considering how upset Claudia would be if he put a blade through the mirror, she worked very hard to turn into a communication array. She would be irate, they both knew from experience, likely worse than Takayoshi's uncle. So, it was best to get Leo away from the device before he could lash out at it. "Leo, we need a tally of our assets. Particularly the horses, if we are to ride back up the mountain with our current forces."

Leo's face twitched as if he wanted to argue, the words heavy on his tongue, but his dark eyes flicked back to the mirror and he sneered, bowing deeply at his waist, and saying with not a single trace of sincerity, "Yes, Your Highness," before he left the room.

"That disrespectful, pompous rogue! Do you let all of the men under your command speak to you like that, Takayoshi?" Uncle Reiji's face was screwed up with rage at the indignity.

"Leo is not under my command. He is my friend"—Uncle mouthed the word *friend* as if it were an expletive—"and it would behoove you to treat he, and Claudia with the respect they deserve as friends of the crown."

Uncle Reiji's eyes narrowed for a moment, as if he were trying to decide how serious Takayoshi was about the under-lying threat in his words, and how far he could continue to push his nephew. Whatever he saw on Takayoshi's face must have made him uncomfortable, because he cleared his throat. "Yes, of course. Do send along my apologies to this. . . *Leo.*"

If Cricket were there he might have snorted at the words, as it was, Takayoshi struggled to keep his own reaction in check. Another time, another place, perhaps he would have huffed a laugh at Uncle Reiji's clear pettiness. But there was no room for it now. "What is it you wanted, Uncle? I am very busy at present, as you heard, making sure the stronghold is secure."

"Oh," Uncle Reiji said, seeming to remember there had been a reason for his demanding to speak to Takayoshi that had nothing at all to do with his irritation at Leo. "Right." Uncle straightened himself up, his chin lifting. "I demand you turn that– That– *Beast* over to Sunil at once."

Takayoshi breathed through the rage that threatened to set his hands, and every piece of wood furniture within arm's reach, up in flames. He thought they had gotten over this. That they were past it. It would seem he had been wrong. "If you are referring to His Majesty, King Cricket," Takayoshi said, the title awkward on his tongue, but he knew he needed to use it to get his point across. "That will not be happening."

"Excuse me?"

"You are excused."

"Takayoshi! This has gone on long enough. Whatever– Whatever *attachment* you have with that boy–"

"Man," Takayoshi murmured, taking great joy in watching his uncle's face pinch in frustration at being not only ignored, but also cut off and corrected by another person.

"*Beast*," Uncle retorted, spitting the word like a slur.

Takayoshi's eyes narrowed on the face of his uncle in the glass. "Choose your next words *carefully*, Uncle."

"He should turn himself over to Sunil and put a stop to all of this. Sunil is at our gates as we speak, Takayoshi! He has set the city ablaze! You need to–"

"It's not ablaze," Atsuko's voice broke him off, her face appearing over his shoulder. "But he has set up camp outside of our walls." She shouldered her way into the mirror, pushing Uncle Reiji out of the way, which Takayoshi had never been more grateful for in his life as he realized his fingertips had begun to singe the table. "You need to get back."

Takayoshi nodded, standing up straight again, his hands fisted behind his back. "I will be there as soon as I can. Leo is checking to see how many horses we have now. I will leave a contingent of our forces here, and come with Leo, Claudia, and Ignacia to aid in the effort to drive Sunil out of our city."

"Thank you, brother." Atsuko's shoulders relaxed.

"Cricket is on his way. He should reach you within the next couple of days."

Atsuko's shoulder tensed again. "What?"

"I will be there when he does. I just need to ensure the others are on their way before I leave here. It should not be more than a couple of hours."

Atsuko nodded, and before anymore could be said, she closed the connection between the mirrors. Then he turned to face Claudia who was standing in the doorway.

"Ignacia has already gone to prepare our horses," she said, her face set into a serious expression. "You'll be flying ahead, I assume."

Takayoshi nodded. "I cannot leave Cricket without someone strong enough to bring him to heel for long, you saw what happened to Hollis."

"Hollis will be all right." Claudia shrugged. "It's Cricket I'm worried about. We'll be behind you as soon as we can. Maybe we can cut him off before he can escape again."

"Selene willing." Takayoshi headed from the room, already mentally preparing himself for the long flight back to the capital.

"Selene willing," Claudia repeated.

CHAPTER 32

There was darkness, and rage, so *much* rage that it colored the world red like blood. Between those two things there was nothing left of what the dragon had been, whatever that may have been, whether it be man, king, father, or brother. Nothing left of the soft gentleness that might have made its claws less dangerous and deadly. And the man that it had been gave himself wholly over to it.

What other choice was there? None. Not really.

So, he was swallowed by the dark, and murderous fury, drowning in it until he forgot his own name. The cold against his scaled cheeks, ice forming in his beard, none of it was enough to bring him back to himself. None of it enough to pull him out of the single-minded urge to find, destroy, protect.

The dragon didn't even know where it was going, not really, just letting the heading the man had set guide it forward. The man would tell it when it was time to stop, and the dragon would level whatever was in front of it. Whatever had brought that heartache, and fear that clouded the man's mind with nothing but screaming. Screaming. *Screaming.*

"My prince," a voice whispered in the dragon's mind, quieting the screaming if just for a moment. "My Prince, you must stop."

The dragon didn't answer. What was there to say? It couldn't stop. Not until it got to where it was going. Not until it destroyed anything in its path in the name of protecting the thing the man loved. That's what it was made for. That's all it was *good* for. Destruction. Protection. Doing the things the man couldn't. The things he'd never been able to do. Weak. The man was too weak to do what needed to be done. Too weak to put an end to the things that threatened the people he loved. The dragon wasn't weak. Made of scales, and steel, and power. Not like the man all flesh, and bone, and a soft, soft heart.

"My Prince. Please," the voice all but begged, the tone pleading enough to make the dragon slow down at least.

It turned to face the white bird, lips pulled back from sharp teeth. "Don't get in my way again!"

"We need to wait for the others."

"No!" The dragon roared, lashing out at the bird, its tail whipping to knock the creature from the sky. The bird swooped out of the way, flames catching on the dragon's own long tail, flaring warmth against its scales. A warmth that spread under the dragon's skin like an ache, right to the heart of it, wherever that might be. Lighting it up and chasing away the cold. "Don't *touch* me!"

"I apologize. I did not mean to." The phoenix shifted in the air, creating space between them, and the dragon longed for his warmth. Longed to lean into those flames and let them burn away the cold that had seeped so deep into its bones and made itself a home there.

The dragon grumbled, continuing on its way in the direction the man had sent it. If the bird wanted to follow, that was his business. It wasn't even sure what it was protecting, but it knew it was something important to the man. Something that the fear of losing it sent the man into a blind panic. Let the icy winter wind seep down into his bones, hardening his heart, making him vicious with it.

"My Prince, we must wait for the others," the bird tried again, tone reasonable. And that was more annoying than anything else, the ability for him to be *reasonable* and *level-headed* when nothing about this situation was reasonable or levelheaded. All of it was a swirling cyclone of anger and fear and the possibility of loss.

"I will not *wait*!" The dragon snarled, snapping its jaws at the bird, nearly clipping his wing with sharply pointed teeth. A promise of violence it had no qualms fulfilling if the blasted bird continued to get in its way. It didn't have time to wait for whatever pitiful reinforcements the phoenix thought it needed. It didn't *need* reinforcements. Not when it could level whatever came for it with one fierce swipe of its tail, and the wind that answered to its call.

Let them come! Let them try to stop it! Let them stand in its way! It would demolish them. It would leave the snow painted red in blood. It would leave nothing behind in its righteous fury. It would–

"They have not breached the walls yet, My Prince," the bird's words were soft, gentle, meant to be a comfort, the dragon was sure, but it found no comfort. It did not understand what walls he was speaking of, or what that meant. Nor did it care. "She is safe."

"She? She who?" The dragon's pace slowed, the wind it was riding on dying down just a fraction from the screaming force it had been. Is that where it had been headed? To save someone specific? To save this she of whom the phoenix spoke? What was she to the man?

"Becka."

The name echoed, silencing the screaming, and the rage, and the panic entirely.

Becka. Becka. Becka. Becka.

"Your daughter," the phoenix said as if the dragon needed the reminder. It *knew* Becka. It knew what she was. It knew—

Cricket sucked in a breath of relief, then he was falling.

Falling.

Falling.

The wind rushed past him, icy and painful as he plummeted toward the ground. Something swooped out of the corner of his eye, white, and bright, and beautiful. Yoshi. Selene bless him, Yoshi.

Talons pricked at the backs of Cricket's shoulders, ripping his tunic, but Yoshi's wings beat hard enough to slow his descent. Yoshi didn't release him until Cricket's boots sunk down into the snow beneath them, the uneven ground making him stumble.

"Becka's safe?" Cricket asked, his hands shaking where they reached out to grip Yoshi's tunic in tight fists once he let the feathers float away.

"She is safe." Yoshi's hands fell to Cricket's waist, holding him up when his knees threatened to give out beneath him. "Sunil and his men have not breached the walls yet. We still have time to reach them."

"How much time?"

Yoshi's grip tightened on Cricket's waist. "Not as much time as I would like. Come, I saw a stable and a small house a little way back, we can barter for a horse and be on our way again."

"Flying would be faster." Cricket huffed, annoyed. He wanted to be there already, in the heat of the battle. He wanted to be where he could reach for Becka, and *know* that she was safe, where he could see it for himself. But the bland look Yoshi gave him told him he wasn't going to get his way.

"When we have found your pearl, and you can control the dragon better, you may fly wherever you like," Yoshi said, dropping his hands from Cricket's waist only press his warm palm to Cricket's, threading their fingers. "Until then, we will ride horses."

Cricket grumbled, but let Yoshi lead him through the storm that he had kicked up, back the way they had come. It left something unsettled in his stomach to be going the wrong direction, but when Yoshi said it wasn't far, he'd meant it. Not but a mile back from where they landed there was a small cottage, lights burning in the windows to ward off the rising dark, and beside it, a stable not much bigger than the cottage itself. It couldn't house more than a couple of horses, if that.

"How far is it to the capital?" Cricket asked, his arms tight around Yoshi's waist. They'd only been able to find one horse, and Yoshi insisted that he be in control of where they were going. It was likely for the best, the cold wind bit at Cricket's lungs making every breath catch on the inhale. He didn't know how long he could hold out before another coughing fit started, but he'd endeavor to make it the entire ride, however long that might be. Because Yoshi couldn't know. He couldn't.

How embarrassing would it be if he found out? If Yoshi knew that Cricket was getting sicker and sicker because he was in *love* with him? Cricket almost winced at the very thought.

"A day and a half ride. You should rest. You will need your

strength." Yoshi reached down to give the arm Cricket had wrapped around his middle a soft squeeze. And when Cricket pulled one of his hands away, Yoshi took that too, threading their fingers together till their palms pressed against each other, the dry warmth of Yoshi's hand fighting off the clammy chill of Cricket's own. "Please, My Prince, rest."

When he said it like that, Cricket supposed, there was no fighting it. Between the warmth of Yoshi body pressed to his front, and the soft shift of the horse beneath him, it was easy to let himself drift off. To let the weariness of his body drag him down into sleep as the night turned dark around them.

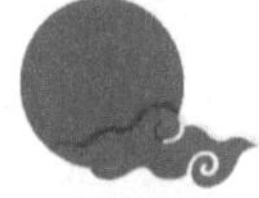

THE CAPITAL WASN'T EVEN in view yet, but Cricket could smell it burning. He could smell the charred wood on the wind, and the soft hush of a place holding its breath in terror. Yoshi tied their horse to a tree and slipped from its back before holding his hands out to help Cricket down.

"We are not too late," Yoshi said, seeming to read Cricket's thoughts.

Cricket nodded almost numb with the fear that Yoshi was wrong. His hands trembled with it, threatening to shake the iron cuff from his wrist where he'd lose it in the underbrush and shin-deep snow. Yoshi took his hand, tightening his fingers around it, and brushing his thumb over Cricket's knuckles in a soothing gesture.

"We should get a closer look." Cricket hoped his voice didn't shake as much as the rest of him did, but if it did, Yoshi wouldn't point it out. He was good like that. So kind. And sweet. And strong. And—

Okay, Cricket get it together. Now is not the time.

"If we head a half mile to the east, we will be far enough up the mountain to see over the walls." Yoshi didn't wait for Cricket to agree, he was already headed in that direction, tugging Cricket along by his hand.

When they crested the hill to look down at the city, what Cricket saw made his knees buckle, only Yoshi's quick thinking, and strong arms keeping him from falling into the wet snow.

It was on fire.

Smoke billowing out from almost every building, or at least the ones that remained standing. And someone was screaming, their voice so loud it echoed off the mountain, threatening to cause an avalanche.

Yoshi sank beside him in the snow, holding him by his waist, murmuring something soft and soothing into Cricket's hair, but Cricket couldn't hear it for the screaming.

The screams were cut off by coughing, retching, gasping as Cricket hacked up another full plant. His vision blurred, the skin on his hands stinging as he hurriedly covered it up, hoping Yoshi wouldn't see. If he did, he didn't say anything.

"When will the others be here?" Cricket asked through his ruined throat.

"Three days."

Cricket sucked in a breath, forcing himself to straighten his spine. Three days was too long. Uncle Sunil may breach the palace walls by then. "You and I will move down into the city when night falls. We'll protect the palace until reinforcements can get here."

"Yes, My Prince." Yoshi held him closer, and there they kneeled on the hill, watching the sun slowly sink, and the fires smolder out by the softly falling snow.

CHAPTER 33

It was almost eerily quiet when night had well and truly settled around them. Cricket had been silent for what seemed hours, his throat raw from screaming, and being sick. And Takayoshi decided it was better not to ask about the plant that sprouted from his tongue and fell into the snow with a wet slap.

A part of the curse, something in his mind whispered viciously to him, *a sign of what is killing the man you love*.

That same voice would not let him rest, although he needed it, having spent the whole night prior guiding the horse back toward Helio. It forced him to sit up, watching the slow rise and fall of Cricket's chest as he slept on the cold wet ground. It asked him how much longer he thought Cricket could survive like this. It reminded him that had he simply found the pearl before returning, perhaps all would have been well. It nagged at him, incessant, and brutal every second of the hours that followed as the fires in the city beyond turned to embers.

When the night was finally at its darkest, with not but a

sliver of moonlight slipping between the clouds, Takayoshi shook Cricket awake.

He had half a mind not to. Half a mind to wait until the others joined them. It would be safer for all of them if the numbers were larger, especially Cricket. Maybe then he would not need the dragon at all. But the sound of something hard knocking against metal, and the sight of a group of men using a battering ram to try to break through the front gate of Helio's palace, made the decision for him in the end.

It took a moment of groggy, nonsense muttering for Cricket to regain his bearings, then his eyes fell to the same scene that captivated all of Takayoshi's attention, and he hissed.

"This ends now," he said, his voice still raw. He ripped the iron cuff from his wrist and took to the skies so quickly Takayoshi had no time to stop him, no time to hesitate. Takayoshi scooped up the cuff, tucking it away in his pocket, before he shifted into the phoenix and followed behind his dragon.

"Do you have a plan, My Prince?" Takayoshi asked, his wings flapping hard against the breeze Cricket's rage kicked up in his effort to stay astride him.

"Plan? Who needs a plan!" Cricket barked a laugh, throwing his head back with it. It was the first time Takayoshi thought he had heard Cricket's voice in weeks where it did not sound wet, or aching, and it made something in Takayoshi's stomach unknot. He was himself, for the moment, until the dragon got the better of him again.

When this was done, they would find answers. When this was done, Takayoshi would be able to save his prince. He just had to wait but a few hours more. Because as Cricket said, this ended now. Enough was enough. Sunil would not walk away from this battlefield. Not if Takayoshi had any say in the matter.

"The plan," Cricket said, his lips peeling back from his teeth in a snarl, "is to leave none of them standing." Then he dove for the city.

That was not a plan, and they both knew it. But Cricket was too lost to fear and rage to be reasoned with, and Takayoshi would not leave him to the mercy of Yue Sunil's men alone. He would just have to form a strategy of his own.

Cricket's taloned claws scooped up first two, then another four of the hungry spirits Sunil had directed to tear down the gates into the palace, throwing them away to land somewhere among the debris of the city, before Takayoshi could even reach them. Cricket snarled and snapped when one latched onto the fur lining his back, clinging to him like an errant child.

Takayoshi swooped down, flames licking at the dried-up shells of men and women as his tail flicked over them. They screamed, sounding oh so mortal, and alive, as they tried to put themselves out. But they were not, Takayoshi reminded himself, they had not been alive for some time. The battering ram dropped to the ground with a thud that shook the walls around it but seemed quiet compared to the heavy landing of Takayoshi's talons on the ground. He flexed them against the paving stones, uprooting the stones, and burrowing himself neat little holes to make it impossible for anyone to unseat him.

Someone needed to help Cricket, he knew that, but there were not enough of them. Had they waited, had the others come in time, they could have protected the palace entrance, but they had not. And thus it was left to Takayoshi. His wings flapped, spewing flames at anyone who tried to come close.

Over the sound of approaching soldiers and spirits, Takayoshi could just hear the roar of the dragon. The unsettling noise of bones crunching, and bodies smacking against stone walls. All of it loud enough to sound like a victory, and for a moment—just a moment—Takayoshi let himself believe that was it. That the tide had turned, and in spite of not having the forces he knew they needed, in spite of the lack of tactical support, the battle had been won.

Then he heard a roar unlike any Cricket had ever released before, the sound pained, and his eyes caught on the blue-black scales of Cricket rising into the sky, a sword thrust deep into his under belly where the scales were the softest. He should have gone down. But he did not. He just screamed his anger at the moon, and thrashed violently trying to unseat the sword, only digging it deeper with every movement.

A quick glance around revealed the men left standing had turned their attention to Cricket, their weapons drawn, ready to bring down the dragon in any way they could. Takayoshi would not allow that. Flapping his wings, he darted into the sky after Cricket, putting himself in between as many of the drawn bows and Cricket as he could.

He reached for the sword, focused solely on saving Cricket from putting it through his own heart on accident, and ripped it free. It fell to the ground with a clatter, Cricket's midnight eyes looking up at him in surprise, and perhaps gratitude, before his gaze must have caught something over Takayoshi's shoulder, and he was shoving Takayoshi out of the way.

Takayoshi went down hard, his wing bending and snapping at an odd angle along one of the buildings. He squawked, trying to slow his descent with one wing, but it was no good, he realized a moment before his head smacked against the paving stones.

He must have lost consciousness for a moment, everything going black, because when he was awake again it was to his arm bent at a strange angle, and his white hair, not feathers, mottled in blood.

"Is this what you want, *nephew*!" Someone was shouting,

Takayoshi realized, pushing himself to unsteady feet. He had to get back to Cricket. He had to help him. He focused on that burning need in his veins, but the fire wouldn't catch through the pain, and he was left to stumble down the alleys towards the voice on unsteady feet, every movement jarring the already-knitting bone in his arm. "I will burn any city or person who chooses to stand in my way, boy! Any city or person who chooses to stand with *you*! Make your *choice*!"

"Never." Cricket snarled, breath ice cold, freezing the buildings that remained standing, and making the streets slick enough to send any nearby forces to their knees. Takayoshi had eyes on him now, just a little further, if he could just get to him.

"Then you leave me no choice." Sunil snorted, and suddenly there was a scream. A child. Takayoshi's vision wavered when Becka came into view, her neck bowed backward where Sunil had a hold of her long dark hair, his fingers fisting viciously in it.

Cricket lunged for him, jaws snapping, but the man's visage rippled like a mirage or a reflection on water. Then Sunil was laughing. His head thrown back in sickening delight at the fury and terror that lit in Cricket's eyes. Takayoshi was not close enough. He would never be close enough, he realized perhaps too late, to reach Cricket in time to stop that particular hurt. The damage was already done.

"End this now. You've been the cause of so much misery, end it now. Come to me, and they won't have to suffer anymore. Turn yourself over to me, no one will mourn you. Stop this nonsense, and I will return this child to the halls of Helio where she will grow up safe, and happy in all of the ways that you could never give her." Sunil's image flickered, blinking out for a moment, before reappearing. "You know where to find me, don't you boy?"

Then he was gone.

Cricket let out a sob, a broken, horrible thing that made the walls of the shattered city quake and collapsed onto the ground. Takayoshi ran to him, skidding across the stones. He wanted to–

No. He *needed* to tell Cricket that it was not true. It was not true. Not a word of it! Takayoshi would scream it to the skies if it would make Cricket believe him.

Boots scrabbling against the ice, and the slick, Takayoshi reached for Cricket, and fell to his knees hard beside where the dragon was bleeding in the street. There was so much to say. So much to tell Cricket. That Becka would not be better off without her father. That the land would mourn him if he made this choice. That Cricket had not sullied the world and the people he loved. That he had not brought misery and pain to them. But Cricket did not give him the chance.

Cricket reared back, set alive by Takayoshi's warm touch, and bared his teeth at him, threatening and terrifying if Takayoshi actually believed that he would attack.

"You cannot do this. You cannot turn yourself over to him," Takayoshi pleaded, instead of saying all of the things he wanted to say, all of the things Cricket may have actually needed to hear. "I will not allow it."

"Who are *you* to stop me?" Cricket asked, snapping his jaws at Takayoshi, rising to his paws, and Takayoshi realized there was not time.

Not time to tell Cricket what lived within Takayoshi's heart. Not time to murmur words of affection and devotion. Not time to recount how he loved Cricket from the very first. That they were two halves of a whole, two parts of one soul. Takayoshi choked on the words, trying to get any of them, even just one, even just the simplest ones, the 'I love you' ones, past his mangled tongue. But they would not come. And a moment later Cricket launched himself into the sky.

He disappeared in seconds, naught more than a shadow

puppet against the moon, and Takayoshi, broken wing and all, realized he would never catch him. Cricket was going to turn himself over to Sunil's mercy, and there was nothing Takayoshi could do to stop him, because a bird could not fly with a broken wing.

Takayoshi's knees were already bruised from hitting the ground, but he sank back down onto them, ignoring the ache and the cold, and wondered how long it would be before Becka appeared? Before he knew for certain that the exchange had been made, and Cricket had signed his own death warrant?

The tears started a moment later. Burning tracks down his cheeks, leaving behind the salty stickiness of sadness. Takayoshi's fists tightened in the legs of his trousers, and he threw his head back, stared at the watery moon through the clouds, and screamed, a long unintelligible cry to wake Selene. To make sure she was watching. To let her know he was furious with her for letting this happen.

"You should come inside, Your Highness," a rasping voice said from just in front of him. His eyes traced from their well-polished boots up their Helion uniform to their face, one of the royal guard. "You should come inside."

Takayoshi nodded weakly, only half in control of his body, and his mind, as the knight led him through the gate, to the infirmary.

CHAPTER 34

The cold had settled into his very bones, slowing his heart, making every breath ache. And as these realizations dawned, so too did the realization that these were *Cricket's* thoughts, not the dragons. And that's when he realized that he and the dragon had finally become one. Fused together into a singular, aching creature.

Yoshi's screams were a knife to Cricket's steadily slowing heart. It wouldn't be long now, he realized perhaps too little too late. In the midst of a battle he had no hope of winning, it had dawned on him, just as his consciousness finally broke through the dragon's he realized he wasn't going to live to see the winter turn to spring, or the month change. Maybe not even to see the sun rise, if the wound on his belly had anything to say about it.

So what did he have to lose? What was left for him to hold onto? Yoshi wouldn't have him like this. His people wouldn't have a dragon for a king. The only role left to him was father, and the least he could do for Becka was to give himself up so that she could live.

My little girl.

Cricket's heart gave a sick lurch—as if trying to restart itself at a normal elven rhythm—at the thought, before it lulled back to its lazy cadence. He wished he could say goodbye to her. Fill her ears with empty promises, and platitudes. Tell her that everything would be all right. Lie to her, if only to keep her from worrying for a little bit longer. But he didn't want her to see him like this—hollowed out and empty and dying. The others would have to do that for him. Yoshi, and Anstice and Atsuko, Ignacia. They would have to take care of her now. They would have to dry her tears, and teach her to be strong, just as his father had done with him.

She'd be a good queen, when the day came for it, he was sure of that, and that knowledge brought a little smile to his bearded face.

Dragons can smile, the thought startled and delighted him. *Shame I was never able to show Yoshi that, I bet he'd have liked it.* And that brought another foolish jolt to his heart. If he wasn't careful, he'd give himself a heart attack before he was even able to reach home.

"Home," the word lingered on his tongue. It didn't mean the same thing it used to mean, he realized as the mountain stopped sloping downward beneath him and he sailed over the stronghold at the base. The one not more than a couple of days prior he'd helped Yoshi and their friends secure. He shook himself, and looked out ahead again, toward Lunette, and the capital, and the end of his journey.

It would be good to rest, he decided. He didn't want to die. No one ever did. But it would be good to rest. To lay down his sword and his claws and surrender.

Yue Cricket was not made for war, he'd known that since he was a boy. He was raised by a king who had been raised by a king who had been raised by a king during a time of peace. It had been so many generations since Lunette knew war that her kings didn't know how to fight anymore. Not really. They didn't know how to sacrifice the lives of others in the name of whatever it was they were fighting for—land, or money, or power, etcetera, etcetera, etcetera.

Cricket had hoped he'd never have to know what that was. But then there was Uncle Sunil, and this blasted civil war. Stars, so many lives had been lost. He should have just turned himself over in the beginning. He should have just let Uncle have the title, and the crown, and whatever else he'd wanted. It would have saved so many.

Another jerk in his chest nearly sent him tumbling through the air, but he managed to stay aloft. He couldn't die. Not yet. Not yet. Not yet. Not until he reached Lunette, and saw Becka safely away. Not until he'd ended this thing the right and proper way. But it was becoming increasingly hard to focus on the blurry shapes of a city in the distance. Was that the capital or some other Lunette city? He couldn't even tell anymore. Maybe he'd gotten turned around and wound up back in Helio. It was so hard to tell in the winter when the snow filled landscape all blurred together.

How long had he been flying? Hours? Days? He hadn't noticed the sky changing, but the sun was high before he realized it. Cricket shook his bearded head, he had to be getting close.

But he was so. . . *tired*. Why was he so tired? When had he last slept? *Really* slept? He couldn't remember. Even after he'd cried himself out in Yoshi's arms, he'd lain there with his eyes closed, listening to the steady rhythm of Yoshi's heart for what he hadn't known would be the last time. Enjoying the moment as they prepared for war.

War.

It would be over now. All of it would be over now.

Rest.

He'd be able to rest soon. Sleep until the end of time. Uncle Sunil would probably cart his carcass through the streets of the capital, bragging about how he'd slain the dragon. That would be fine, Cricket thought. Let Uncle have that glory, for when Becka was old enough she would have all of Helio behind her, and she would have her throne. Uncle Sunil's reign would only last at most another decade, if that. Then Cricket's daughter, his bright little girl, his sunflower would take her rightful place.

It was that thought that finally lulled Cricket to sleep. His body drifted back down to the ground before it landed in a hard thump just at the edge of a forest.

He awoke sometime later, when the sun was low in the sky, to the press of a blade at the scales just below his eye. It was strange waking as the dragon, was Cricket's first thought. He'd never woken as the creature before. And his next thought was one that would have sent his elven heart into a tripping rhythm but hardly had any effect on his lumbering dragon heart. . .

I truly will not be able to turn back. Likely not ever. Stars.

"Don't. Move. You've kept him waiting long enough," a rasping voice said close to the pointed ear just below his right antler.

Cricket blinked his eyes open again to take in the soldiers that surrounded him. There were men, all dressed in Lunette armor, circling him, their bows raised, and arrows pointed. He might have been able to escape some of them. Maybe even avoid a lethal injury. But why bother? This was what he was there for, wasn't it?

"Him who?" Cricket asked, not lifting his head. He still felt far too heavy, and oh so tired, and there was a tickle in the back of his throat that he knew well, although he'd never experienced it in his form before. He'd been truly foolish to think that losing himself to the dragon would save him from the curse.

"King Sunil," the man growled as if that were not

perfectly obvious. Cricket supposed that it was, given the circumstances.

"Ah. Well, my apologies." He resisted the urge to snort, and experiment to see if dragons could roll their eyes. "Let's not keep him waiting any longer, shall we?" Cricket shifted to rise to his feet, and every man jerked back, fear in their eyes.

"I told you not to move." The man's blade pressed into the place whereas a man there was a scar left behind by his last adventure with Yoshi. Selene, but he'd been so young then. Young, and foolish. He'd thought himself invincible, using himself as a tracking talisman. He'd been drowning then too, his lungs eaten up by something he couldn't see and couldn't fight off. Strange how history repeated itself. "Well?"

"Sorry. Sorry." Cricket swallowed down a laugh when he realized he'd completely missed whatever else the man said. Maybe this is what people meant when they said that one's life flashed before their eyes before they died? "You were saying?"

The man huffed, the blade pushing closer. He wouldn't be able to cut Cricket there, unless the blade slipped and it went into his eye, but Cricket didn't think the man was aiming for that. If he were, he'd be holding the blade a little higher. Maybe he thought he could pierce dragon scales with that little thing. *Foolish, really.*

"You need to turn back into a man," the man ordered, his tone brokering no argument. Which was delightful coming from a creature that wasn't even half Cricket's size, but Cricket didn't think he'd take kindly to him pointing that out.

Cricket did roll his eyes—miracles upon miracles, dragons *could* do that—and inhaled deeply before focusing on the magic flowing through his veins. He'd been able to do this before, when it had been early days. But it had gotten harder and harder every time he shifted. And now, when he went searching for that thread that he'd used to tug himself back to himself, it wasn't there. It was like it had just vanished. He should have been panicked by this realization, but he wasn't. He'd known anyway, hadn't he? And what did it matter really, dragon or man, he was going to die soon.

"I said turn back!"

"I'd be delighted to, but that seems impossible at present," he grumbled, shifting his weight where he lay on the ground. The deep wound along his belly had mostly healed, but it still ached from lying on it for however long he'd been there before these men found him.

"No lies." The blade pushed into his scales, pressure, but not piercing. A threat, or at least the man thought it was one anyway.

"I would if I could, but I can't. You'll just have to take me as I am to Uncle." Cricket shrugged, ignoring the way the motion made the men with their bows twitch in alarm. Uncle Sunil really found himself some desperately brave men, hadn't he? And put the fear of the goddess into them when it came to Cricket.

"What's going on?" Another voice broke through the man's grumbling at his side. *Uncle.* Cricket couldn't get a good look at him from where he lay, but he'd recognize that voice anywhere.

Ah, so the king has come out to inspect his war prize, has he?

"He says he can't shift back."

"Nonsense. I've seen him do it a dozen times. Cricket, shift back so we can be on our way," Uncle Sunil said the way he used to say things to Cricket when they were still a family. Like he was bored of Cricket and his foolishness. Had he always been so condescending? Were his words always so laced with derision and hate? Why hadn't Cricket ever noticed before? Maybe if he had, he'd have been able to save all of them. Father. Anstice. Becka's village. The people of– "I said now!"

"I can't." Cricket lifted his head to find Uncle Sunil sitting on a horse behind the circle of bowmen.

"You're being obstinate."

"I wish I were." A frigid huff left his nostrils and the men right in front of him whimpered at the cold, taking a half step back.

"Get me the iron!" Uncle Sunil ordered, and several shouts went up through the men around him. Then there was much grunting, and groaning, before a large iron collar was brought to rest in front of Cricket's muzzle. "I had it made specially for you. It will follow your shape," Uncle Sunil informed him, a sick twist of his mouth that might have been a smile at another time in his life. As if that were some great triumph when Cricket had already thought of such a thing, and been employing it himself. *Just like Uncle not to have a single original idea in his head.*

"So generous."

Cricket stayed still, letting the men fit the collar around his neck. He knew what his uncle expected to happen, the same thing that happened with the cuff, and the man-sized collar before that. The iron would stem the flow of his magic, and force him into a shift. But when it latched around his neck, nothing happened.

Well. Nothing aside from the itching burn of the iron on his scales. Other than that, nothing.

"Isn't this better, anyway?" Cricket asked, hoping to finally get this over with. He was tired of laying on his belly on the hard ground, and the sooner they got to wherever Uncle Sunil decided to hold him, the sooner this could all be over, the sooner he could make sure that Becka had been sent back to Yoshi. "Now you can drag me through the streets, and show everyone what a monster I am. Isn't that what you wanted?"

Uncle Sunil stared at him for a long moment, eyes narrowed and hard, before he nodded. "Bring me the lead. And Cricket, if you fight me on this, I'll have my men start firing on the citizens of the capital."

"I'll behave," Cricket promised, even as it burned like fire in his throat.

"Good." Uncle Sunil's smile twisted sharp, and grotesque up his cheeks, as he took the lead in his hands. "Move out."

BOOK IV
DUNGEON

CHAPTER 35

Becka appeared two days later. Shaking and scared and crying for a father who had flown away to protect all of them from a man with no respect for life or love.

Takayoshi wished he could say that her presence brought him comfort. That the weight of her head on his shoulder when they sat together looking over the storybook she chose for that evening's reading helped to make him ache a little less. It did not.

It had been three days since she returned to them, and the ache in Takayoshi's chest was no less present than it was the very moment he lost sight of Cricket on the battlefield. The weight of the words he was unable to say to Cricket before he lost him, sat no less heavy on his tongue. He could not focus, he could not think, and he knew while the others may understand, his uncle, at least, was growing sick of his "theatrics".

"This has gone on long enough," his uncle said one evening during supper. Why he decided they all should have supper together, Takayoshi did not know. He was given to understand he was not very good company, and yet his uncle insisted he, Atsuko, and Takayoshi take a meal together when it was really very obvious that Atsuko would rather be with Anstice, and Takayoshi would rather be with Becka.

"What has?" Atsuko asked, setting down her teacup with a soft clatter. The table had been silent up until that very moment. Takayoshi preferred it that way, it gave him time to escape into his own head, and contemplate what came next. For Becka. For Helio. For Lunette. For Takayoshi. What *was* he without Cricket?

"This sulking," his uncle went on, breaking through Takayoshi's thoughts again. "You cannot continue to mope about simply because Sunil has decided to put that monster to death."

Takayoshi's stomach plummeted, then it lurched back up in such quick succession it was a small miracle he did not vomit up what little food he had been enticed to eat all over the table. "What?"

"You heard me. Sunil has decreed that he will kill the beast lest it cause any more harm to all of us. And really, I can't say I disagree. I mean what with all the damage it did to the city. We'll be rebuilding for—"

Takayoshi stood abruptly, throwing his napkin onto the table, his chair scraping loudly behind him.

"Where are you going?"

"To gather my forces." He had not known that was what he meant to do until he said it. All he had known was he could not sit at the table and listen to his uncle's misguided, truly heinous, slights against the man he loved.

"And what do you mean to do with your *forces* once you've gathered them?" Goatee quivering in vague irritation, Uncle Reiji leaned back in his chair to fix his gaze on Takayoshi as if he was a particularly errant child. As if he would come to his senses eventually. As if this was all some vague folly that did not mean anything. *Foolish.*

"I mean to ride out and put a stop to this farce." Takayoshi's hands were strangely steady at his sides, far more than they had ever been when he faced down his uncle's disapproval in the past.

He had gone against the man time and again for Cricket over the years, but this felt final in a way he did not wish to consider. Like the burning of a bridge. Maybe not on his uncle's end, maybe Uncle Reiji could still repair the damage if he decided he wanted to, but on Takayoshi's end at least. He would not continue to seek a man's approval who chose to willfully misunderstand himself and the man he loved.

"Farce?" his uncle spat.

Atsuko's eyes drifted between them, she opened her mouth as if to placate them both, to dissolve the tension and make them all friends again. Takayoshi cut her a narrow-eyed look, and her mouth snapped shut.

"Yes. *Farce*." Takayoshi repeated. "Sunil will not kill Cricket so long as he is useful to him, and what is more useful than a monster everyone is afraid of? He will use Cricket to keep the people of Lunette in line. And I dare say, should he have call for it, he will use Cricket to strike out against any neighboring kingdoms he decides he would like a cut of."

"He would not do such a thing. He is a man of—"

"There is not a trace of honor left to be found in a man who would take a *child* hostage to be used against her father," Takayoshi spat the words like poison on his tongue. "Whatever you knew of Yue Sunil from when you were children is gone, Uncle. And you continuing to hold onto this image of him is doing not more than harm yourself and this kingdom. He will come for us. When he has settled himself in Lunette, he will come for our borders, and our people, and our mountain. He has no respect for the lives of anyone besides himself, and you would do well to finally come to terms with that. I understand that you may have loved him once, but he is not that man anymore."

"You will not go after that *beast*. I forbid it." Uncle Reiji's words were low, and ominous, as if he could do anything to truly stop Takayoshi once he had gotten it into his head to do something. He could not. That had been proven time and again.

"You, Uncle, are in no position to forbid anything."

His uncle sputtered, eyes comically wide in his face looking more like a frog that had been trampled by a horse than anything else. Cricket would find it amusing, Takayoshi decided, but he himself could find no joy in the look of sheer shock on the old man's face.

"And when you are through acting as judge, jury, and executioner for a man you hardly spoke five words to while he was here, I suggest you go down to the infirmary and meet some of the people whose lives that man saved." Takayoshi did not wait for a response, he spun on his heel and headed out into the hall. He could not believe he had missed time with Becka for that– That– That absolute *travesty* of a family dinner!

"He's right though," Atsuko said, the door shutting softly behind her.

Takayoshi's hands tightened into fists at his sides. He did not want to discuss this any further. He knew what he needed to do, and that was to go to Cricket, to save him from himself and from Yue Sunil. And if it looked like Helio had invaded Lunette, damn the consequences. Takayoshi was sick of waiting around and hoping problems like Yue Sunil would resolve themselves.

"You can't go after him. You know, that don't you?" Atsuko pressed, her voice soft, like she was afraid he would snap at her too. Which was fair, and he very well might if she did not explain herself well enough.

"And why can I not?"

"It's not what Cricket would want." Atsuko sighed, leaning her back against the wall of the corridor. She looked so tired, he had not realized it until that exact moment. She may not have been a part of the battles, but she had been fighting in her own way, to keep their people safe, to help Cricket as best she could. Still, what was she doing now? "He'd want you to look after Becka. That's why she was sent here."

That was the exact wrong thing to say, Takayoshi realized as the rage welled up inside of him, making flames dance along his fingers. "And who will look after *him*? Who will take care of Cricket while he sacrifices himself for his daughter's life, and for our safety? Should I just sit back and let him die? Or worse, be used as a weapon against his own people?"

"No." Atsuko's shoulders sagged, curling in on themselves. "No. Certainly not. But send Ignacia, and Leo to do this for you. Let them take the Lunette soldiers they brought with them. Then it won't look like Helio is waging a war on Lunette. We can't be seen to—"

"You are more afraid of the image that the prince of Helio marching on Lunette with an army at his back would portray than you are of what might happen to Cricket and his people?" He was so furious he could scream. May even still, once he was out of present company, and free to shout without half of the palace hearing him. Not that it would matter. They would all know come morning anyway, because he was not staying.

"It's not—," she took a breath—seeming to try to regain some of the control that had slipped—lifting her chin, and straightening her shoulders, "it's not about that Shishi. It's about protecting our own people. As you said, Sunil has already shown he'll use any excuse he can find to attack a neighboring kingdom. I don't want to invite more of his scorn, especially after he found Cricket hiding here."

"Cricket was not *hiding*," Takayoshi hissed, leveling his sister with a look so seething she shrunk back under the force of it. "He was a guest of the royal family."

"Well, yes, but–"

"Enough." Takayoshi held up his hand to silence her. "Denounce me if you must, I have already given up my rights to the crown, my title as a prince means little to me, but I will not sit back and watch this happen to him. I will understand whatever choice you feel you need to make to keep our people safe, Your Highness." Takayoshi dipped into a low bow, then he turned and made his way down the corridor without looking back. If he did, he knew he would change his mind. He knew he would feel bad for what he had just done. Because Atsuko did not deserved to be abandoned that way. But she would understand, he knew she would, if anyone might.

He did not slow his pace until he reached the closed off quarters of his father. It had been many years since the doors were sealed, the rooms left to rot, and he was not sure why his feet carried him there. Perhaps because he knew above all other places, it would be abandoned, and for the moment Takayoshi just needed to be alone. Or maybe it was because out of all of the family he had, his father would have been the one to most understand the choice he was making. The man who took his life to be with his beloved, he would have understood Takayoshi's need to save Cricket at any cost. Even himself.

The door creaked loudly on hinges gone squeaky from disuse, and the smell of stale air and dust left to sit too long filled his nose, but Takayoshi pushed in anyway. His footsteps dulled by the plush carpet. One corner of it still rolled up from where he and Atsuko had hurriedly covered the array all those years ago. Takayoshi moved to kick it back into place just before his eye caught on the light chalk of the array.

"All these years, and it is still here," he marveled, bending down to uncover it. The characters were a little smudged, the circle a little lopsided, but it was still in good working order. And in the end, what did he have to lose by contacting the goddess of the moon again? Nothing. It was a struggle to roll his sleeve up past his feathers, but when he did, he cut a line across his arm with his dagger and dripped the blood on the chalk to activate it.

The array came to life with a blinding flash, and Selene's voice echoed off the walls of his father's still chamber, "Takayoshi, I fear this is becoming a habit."

He should likely apologize for calling upon her so frequently, but he did not have that in him, instead what he said was, "Your son is sick, and his uncle means to execute him."

"Oh Cricket," she said on a deep exhale. "I should not have sent you alone." She fell silent, a somberness to the tone that suggested Takayoshi should give her time to sit with the news. Even for all the time he did not have, he did not feel he could rush her with this. So, he waited. But then a moment later she made a noise like an epiphany, almost a laugh, and said, "but you're not alone, are you?"

Takayoshi wanted to say something else, to volunteer that he meant to go after Cricket, and save him. He opened his mouth to do so, but Selene just continued on, like Cricket did when he was working something out in his head, needing to talk himself through it, ignorant of anyone around them.

"There are others like you. The phoenix, of course, of course. And the kitsune. And the qilin." She laughed, the sound bright, and sharp, then she seemed to realize Takayoshi was listening for she cleared her throat. "You mean to return to my kingdom and save my son, do you not?"

"I do."

"You'll need help to go up against Sunil's armies of the damned. You'll take with you Anstice and Ignacia."

"Anstice is not a warrior." Takayoshi frowned. He did not think he wanted to take Anstice into battle, however much she may want to save Cricket. It would not be right.

"No. But she is a celestial. And you'll need all the magic you can get," Selene said the words through what sounded like a smile.

"She is?"

"Of course, she is. Ignacia too. Everyone in Cricket's family— Hasn't he told you?" Selene made a sound like a disappointed hum, and Takayoshi could imagine her scrubbing at her nose the way Cricket sometimes did when he was frustrated by a problem. "You were supposed to speak to him about this when you met again."

"There has not been time." Takayoshi let out a sigh, his knees beginning to ache on the stone floor. He knew he should have *made* time for such a discussion, but there had been so much else to deal with.

"Of course not." She did not sound like she believed him, an edge of annoyance to her tone. "Either way, celestial magic runs in families, and Anstice and Ignacia are Cricket's family. They just need to learn to tap into it. I'm sure you can help them figure it out, you were able to control yours so quickly. Anyway, yes, take them with you." He imagined she nodded at that, pleased with herself. "And Your Highness?"

"Yes?" Takayoshi asked.

"This time, be sure to tell him *everything*. Including how you feel about him. I've seen enough of you two dancing around each other to last even me a lifetime. It's really quite painful."

The array flared to life again, and Takayoshi was left kneeling in the dark in his dead father's quarters, running the conversation over and over in his head. Celestial magic ran in families. Ignacia and Anstice were Cricket's family, thus they had celestial magic. But if that were the case. . . then what was *he* to Cricket the reason he had celestial magic?

He shook himself. One thing at a time.

First, he needed to gather his forces.

CHAPTER 36

Someone was shouting Cricket's name and it sounded like a curse. The word all ragged, and sharp, like a wound from a serrated blade. His head swiveled, heedless of the tightening of the iron collar around his neck, looking, searching, trying to understand who would say his name that way. Then the first bit of rotted vegetation hit him in the head with a dull *thunk*, bouncing off and joining the muck that coated the streets of the capital.

It was thick, like wading through sludge. Cricket had never seen the capital this way before. Dirty, and dark, and Selene's people—*his* people—looking hungrier than they'd ever looked in all the years he lived among them.

"How dare you!" someone shouted, a rotten head of cabbage smacking against his cheek, the pulp and mush splattering into his eye, and temporarily blinding him.

How dare I what, he wanted to ask, but the iron collar tightened further, choking off the air he needed to get the words past his lips.

"How dare you come back here," she said, not seeming to need his prompting. "After you left us behind! After you ran away to safety! How dare you come back here and expect us to forgive you, to feel sorry for you. You are no king of mine!"

I had to, he tried to tell them, sucked in a breath and tried to force words past his vocal cords, but nothing happened. None of them came out. Not the explanation of how he had to save Becka. Not the story of how Uncle Sunil followed him to Helio intent on tearing Helio apart to find him. Not that they would have believed him anyway, he knew what it looked like to his people. He knew it would take a lifetime and then some for him to regain their trust.

"*Your* daughter?" the woman asked, her haggard face finally coming into view. She was wrinkled, and disheveled, and looked like she hadn't bathed in the entire time Cricket had been away. "What about *my* daughter?!"

She held up a dingy blanket in her arms, whatever was inside moved limply like a rag doll, and that's when Cricket got a better look at it. It was a body. The child's head flopped about as the woman shook her, holding her high up in the air for Cricket to see even from several feet away where he stood.

"You left us," she accused, pointing a shaking finger at Cricket. "You left us to his mercy! You ran away to be with that *boy*!"

It wasn't true. None of it was true. Cricket would never leave them just to chase a crush, or even to chase the man he loved. He was a king first, and foremost. He would lay down almost anything for his people.

Almost. Anything.

But not Becka. Never Becka.

His breaths came hard, and fast, panic settling into his lungs and growing like a weed, planting roots, and blocking his airways with petals.

"Cricket," a new voice said. This one calm, and familiar, and it took Cricket a moment to see past the blur in his vision to realize he was no longer standing in the soiled streets of his capital, but in the gardens of the castle, Yoshi before him, looking resplendent in white as usual. "My Prince, you need to calm down."

"I can't!" The words sprung from him this time, and when Cricket looked down, he realized it was because he was looking at hands, and fingers, not paws and claws. A man. He was a man. But that didn't quell the anxiety, and the truth that sunk into his very marrow. "She's right! She's right! I left them behind, and they're starving, and hurting, and people died, Yoshi. People *died*! It's all my fault. I did this to them."

"You did not." Yoshi was suddenly in front of him, his hands warm on Cricket's shoulders like the sun, and the flame that he hailed from.

"I did!" Cricket ripped himself away, unworthy of the comfort Yoshi provided. "I did this to them! It's like. . . I may as well have. . . I *killed* them, *myself* Yoshi! The day I walked away, I killed them."

Yoshi and his sunshine eyes. Yoshi and his never-ending patience. Yoshi and that slight downturn of his lips that was more a wrinkle than a frown. He took a hold of Cricket's shoulders again, and pulled Cricket into his chest, not letting him go as he wrapped him in a tight hug.

"You're not real," Cricket realized, and the ache worsened. "You're a dream. This is a dream."

"Yes. It is." But Yoshi did not let him go, he held Cricket close until Cricket's breaths evened out again, and his eyes dried. Held him close until all Cricket could smell, and sense was the sunshine and sandalwood warmth radiating from Yoshi's clothes.

"Is this like when I visited you?" Cricket asked into the thick fabric at Yoshi's shoulder.

"I do not think so. I do not think I am a part of myself. I think I am simply a part of you. A part that does not think you deserve this. A part that is not blinded by self-hatred, and sorrow, not yet."

"Will you stay with me? Until the end?" Cricket wished he could stay there forever. Let Yoshi hold him close, and soothe away his fears and aches, even if it was a dream. Even if it would never be real. Cricket hadn't felt so light in ages.

"I do not think I can." Yoshi pulled Cricket back by his shoulders to meet his eyes. He was already fading, the vision of him going washed out and indistinct. "You need to wake up now."

"I don't– I don't want to." Cricket swallowed around fresh tears. But before he could latch onto Yoshi again, he was gone, and Cricket was in the dark.

The shouts of his people echoed off the walls that surrounded him. Fresh, and awful, and so loud, that Cricket jerked awake with a start, his large muzzle banging against the iron bars of his cell. He drew in a short, sharp breath, shallow enough to not dig the iron collar deeper into his neck, but deep enough to calm his racing heart.

Becka. Yoshi.

With the nightmare fresh in the back of his mind, Cricket realized he needed to reach out to them. He'd done it before, or so they'd told him. Let his magic take on a life of its own so it could reach for Yoshi and protect him when danger loomed. Maybe he could do it again. Just to– Just to see. To make sure they were safe. Maybe not talk to them, but to check in. To make sure Becka was getting on all right, and Helio was rebuilding. It couldn't hurt to check. Right?

It was too much to ask for, it would seem. For the harder he focused on that single bright star in the landscape of magic surrounding him that was Yoshi, the more firmly Cricket felt rooted. His consciousness chained and tethered to the body just as the body itself was chained and tethered to a ring attached to the stone floor of his cell. No way out. No escape.

Cricket took a breath and tried again. Pushing through the pounding at his temples, and the sweat building under his scales.

Nothing.

Nothing still.

Stuck.

He wouldn't stop. He couldn't. Not yet. Not if there was still hope of seeing them one last time before—

Well. One last time.

It was through the ringing of his ears that Cricket heard the door to his cell creak open loudly. He didn't have to open his eyes to see who it was, for a moment later Uncle Sunil announced himself with a smug, "Do you like your new home? I had them make it specially for you."

Cricket kept his eyes closed, forcing his breathing to remain slow and calm, matching the sluggish beat of his dragon-sized heart. Maybe if he pretended to be asleep Uncle would go away.

"I know you're awake in there. The guards outside heard you muttering to yourself." Uncle Sunil's sneer was obvious in his voice, getting louder until Cricket heard him brace himself against the bars of the big iron cage.

They'd placed it in the middle of the dungeon—everything else had been cleared out to make room for it—and boarded up all of the windows. So all Cricket had for company was stone, and bars, and the soft *drip-drip-drip* of water from a leaking pipe in the kitchens he had been meaning to get looked at.

"You were saying his name. Over and over again." Uncle made his voice go up a few octaves, mocking and hateful when he said, "Yoshi. Yoshi."

Cricket opened his eyes to peer at the almost gleeful look

on Uncle Sunil's face. How he hadn't seen the horribleness before, he didn't know. Marwa had. Anstice had. But Cricket missed it. He hadn't seen Uncle for what he was, even though the man hadn't hidden it well. Love made people blind, Cricket supposed.

"He won't come for you," Uncle Sunil said, tone almost conversational, "because he doesn't love you."

That, at least was probably true. Yoshi didn't love him, not in the way Cricket wanted him to. Yes, Yoshi cared for him, had shown it over and over again. Had willingly put himself at risk to protect Cricket, to help him. But what was there was friendship, camaraderie. Born from their journey together all those years ago. It wasn't the same as the warm weight in Cricket's chest that beat only for Yoshi. Cricket knew that better than anyone. He had the flowers growing in his lungs to prove it.

As if hearing the confirmation in Cricket's silence, Uncle Sunil smiled wider, the expression going vicious and jagged. "And in the end, his not loving you will kill you far more painfully than I ever could. That's why I chose Hanahaki, after all," his uncle said, tone gone almost idle in his boredom. As if he were predicting the weather by merely looking at the sky, stating the obvious that anyone could see. "Because you're unlovable. And yet. . ." Uncle chuckled, plucking lint from his clothing. "You give your heart away freely."

"Is this what you came for?" Cricket asked, his voice drifting through the air like magic, without him even having to move his giant jaws. "To gloat about how you cursed me? About how you defeated your only remaining family? How you're killing your *nephew*?"

"You are not my nephew! My nephew *died* years before you were even thought of! He died and he took his mother with him, and nothing was ever the *same*." Uncle Sunil spat the words at Cricket's feet.

Cricket jerked back, stricken. He'd known what happened to Father's wife and child before Father prayed to Selene for another chance at a family, but they didn't talk about it. Not out loud. Not where others could hear. And he never once heard Uncle speak of it before. Not even in passing. Cricket thought maybe he understood the man a little better for those words, but they didn't change the fact that, "I had nothing to do with their deaths."

Uncle Sunil glared at him, sucking in a deep breath to calm whatever anger was racing through him, threatening to boil his blood from his veins. "That is not what this is about."

It sounds like it is. Cricket swallowed the words down. Now wasn't the time to delve into all of that. "Then what *is* this about?"

"I want to know how you became a dragon." Uncle leaned in closer, the grief that flashed across his eyes a moment ago replaced by something far more dangerous, hunger and greed so raw it threatened to swallow the dragon before it.

"I can't tell you that." That much at least was true.

"You will before you die. Even if I have to chop you into itty bitty bite-sized dragon pieces to–"

"I cannot tell you what I do not know!" Cricket growled, jerking away from where Uncle Sunil leaned against his cell, wishing for the first time that the dungeons had more shadows he could disappear into, to hide away from the look in Uncle's eyes.

"You're lying," Uncle hissed. "You passed that power on to the prince of Helio."

"I'm not. I promise you I'm not." He wasn't begging yet, but he knew he would be soon enough. Uncle Sunil would stop at nothing to get his answers, and Cricket wasn't sure how long he could hold out against whatever cruel torture he had planned.

"Before you die, you *will* tell me," his uncle promised, then he spun on his heel and headed for the door.

"I can't!" Cricket shouted after him, hoping to make him see the truth of it. Hoping to make him understand. But the door to the dungeons slammed a moment later, and Cricket was left with nothing but the *drip-drip-drip* of the leaky pipe from the kitchens.

CHAPTER 37

The first slice of the knife hurt worse than Cricket was expecting it to. It burned, slow and hot, chasing sensation after sensation up the length of his arm as the good "doctor" cut away a section of scales. Cricket had been cut with a sword plenty of times during sparring practice, but that was a different kind of pain. Hard won and hidden under layers of adrenaline. There was none of that here, in this cell, chained to the floor like an experiment waiting for dissection.

No. Not *like*. That's what he *was* to Uncle Sunil and his men. Just another specimen they could use in the name of furthering their power. Another body to desecrate to feed Uncle's war machine. How long before his uncle took all that he learned and turned it on the other kingdoms? How long before the hunger in his gaze turned toward the mountains of Helio again?

"If you'd just tell me how you did it," Uncle Sunil said, his tone light, carefree in a way ill-suited to the current situation, "then we could stop all this nonsense and I could put you out of your misery."

"I don't *know* how I did it!" Cricket roared, yanking on the restraints they'd used to chain him to the ground. He was too weak, much too weak, for that. He realized, sometime over the last week, that he hadn't changed back when Uncle caught him. That even with the iron around his neck, he couldn't seem to slip back into the man he'd been. And he tried, thinking idly that it would be a means of escape, but it didn't work. For all of his effort, he remained a dragon.

A *dying* dragon, the wheeze that accompanied the roar reminded him.

"You must know. You cast a spell of some kind. Or drank a potion. That prince of yours gave you some secret magic from the monks. Something!" Spittle splattered against Cricket's cheek, Uncle's knuckles turning white where he gripped the bars to Cricket's cell.

Cricket snapped at him, teeth knife-sharp getting close enough to Uncle Sunil's hands that he jerked back, afraid of the beast in its cage. He couldn't reach anyone, even if he tried. The iron around his neck made sure of that, tight as it was, and attached firmly to the stones below. But it was good to see the fear flicker across his uncle's face. Good to know that he still had some power here.

A chuckle started low in his throat, the sound raspy and ruined by the snowdrops crawling up it. "Scared, Uncle? Afraid of what I'd do if I got free?" Cricket's tone went soft, and idle, condescension lacing every word. "You walked into Helios's kingdom, and waged war on his people, and now you're afraid of your nephew? Where did all that arrogance go?"

It was perhaps ill-advised to goad Uncle Sunil at the current time, but Cricket had never been one for thinking things through. And the longer he held Uncle's attention, the longer Yoshi and the others had to recover before he fixed his sights on the next available celestial. Cricket just had to hold on, and hope that by the time this was all over they would be ready for the fight his uncle brought to their door.

"You've grown insolent without a staying hand to make you hold your tongue, nephew." Uncle's eyes glinted in the dim lighting, his smile a vicious slash across his face. "Perhaps it's time I remind you who you're dealing with."

"Please do." Cricket tightened, and pulled back his lips in an arrogant snarl of teeth. More rictus than smile.

"Scales might not be enough for us to tell what magic he's using," Uncle Sunil said, his attention never straying from where he'd fixed his gaze on Cricket's. It was a struggle against his instincts to not look at what the doctor was doing, but Cricket managed it. He would not back down. He would not show fear, or pain in the face of this man. The one who he could hardly even call family anymore. "Take some skin samples too."

The doctor's hand slipped, the knife digging deeper into Cricket's arm, shaving away the top most layers of skin and drawing a hiss from Cricket's lips. Iron bit into Cricket's neck as he reared back to snap his jaws at the man, unable to do anything to protect himself other than wriggle as the man skinned a large section of his arm, leaving behind a jagged patch of oozing red.

"Keep it up, boy, I told you once already. I have no qualms about taking you apart bit by bit until I get my answers." Uncle cooed, amusement slippery like grease around the words.

"I'm not afraid of you!" It wasn't quite the truth. He was *terrified*. The fear sat low in his stomach, a flopping fish, threatening at every turn to make him sick with it. But he swallowed it down and focused on the strain of breathing past the tangle of flowers in his lungs.

"And besides," Uncle Sunil continued, smug, "like I said before, I don't have to kill you, do I? Your own love is already suffocating you." Uncle leaned in, his arm stretching through the bars, and patted a patronizing hand to Cricket's muzzle. "Don't you worry, nephew. Once I'm done with you, I'll move on to your Yoshi. Perhaps he'll give me the answers I want."

Cricket reared back again, snapping his jaws at Uncle's retreating fingers, but his uncle was faster, unhindered by sickness and blood loss as Cricket was. His laugh, a low, throaty rumble, echoed off the walls of the cell. Then Uncle turned on his heel, stuffed his hands into his pocket, started up a jovial whistle and practically skipped from the dungeons.

The doctor's hands shook where he held the blade, his eyes flicking about the room, to the guards, and the closing door of the dungeons as if he were unsure what to do now that his master had gone.

"Just finish what you came for," Cricket snarled, making the man yelp, eyes wide and stricken. Cricket almost felt guilty about that. It wasn't this man's fault all of this was happening. For all Cricket knew this man was a prisoner, just like him. Held hostage, and used for what he could offer Uncle, and nothing more.

"Do you want," the man started, his voice so low only Cricket's keen ears could hear it above the *drip-drip-drip* of the leaky pipe, "something for the pain?"

"No. Just leave me alone." Cricket hissed through his teeth, hoping the whisper of his voice in the other's minds would travel the same way an actual voice might. It was all very confusing, and tricky, but he didn't have the capacity to think on it, not now.

IN THE LIMITED peace of being left alone, Cricket realized that he was fading, faster than he'd thought he would.

When he left Helio behind, there had been the vague thought that he might last at least a month, giving his friends the time they needed to bounce back from Uncle Sunil's prior attacks. Surely once Uncle had what he wanted from Cricket, he wouldn't turn his sights on the other kingdoms for at least a couple of months. He would need to experiment, recoup his own forces, build back up his stores. He may even be content with the power and land he had for a year or better. Cricket wasn't fool enough to think that would be the end of it entirely, that Yue Sunil would settle for just Lunette. But he hoped that his turning himself in would buy them time.

What he hadn't realized was how bad off he was before he left. He knew he was sick, there had been no hiding it. But something about the distance between himself and Yoshi—the string that tied them together pulled so taut it was near breaking—made it that much worse. Made the plants grow that much faster. Their roots dug into his lungs, making him fully aware of organs he didn't usually even notice when they were functioning well enough. And with the tight iron collar around his neck, he could hardly cough up the blossoms.

Still, he managed, retching a long stem with the soft bells of a snowdrop onto the dark floor. Their white petals stood out harshly against the gloom, just as Yoshi always did. His clothes so clean, and well-pressed it was hard to believe they weren't brand new.

How hadn't he seen it before? How hadn't he noticed? Snowdrops, the perfect flower to represent Yoshi. Stars, he'd been such a fool for so long. Wasted so much time. And now there was none of it left to waste.

"Don't tell me you're missing your prince," Uncle Sunil crooned, his face twisted up with malice. Cricket was so focused on the blossom he hadn't heard the door or the footsteps until Uncle was upon him, pressing his face to the bars. Arrogant, and mean.

"Come for another pound of flesh, Uncle?" Cricket asked, putting one massive paw over the tiny flowers to protect them, and hide them away from the prying eyes of his uncle. "Or were you just bored?"

"My people are still going over the samples," the words slid from Uncle Sunil's tongue like a lie. His eyes were a little too tight for the snarl or the smirk of victory on his lips to be real. Whatever he'd found, he wasn't happy about it. And Cricket relished the fact that for all Uncle didn't seem to know Cricket, Cricket still knew Uncle. Could still read him like a book.

"Not finding the answers you want then?" Perhaps it was unwise to infuriate his uncle further, but what else did Cricket have to lose? He'd lost his kingdom, his family, the man he loved. All he had left was his life, and if the ringing in his ears was anything to go by, he wouldn't have that much longer. Let Uncle take that too, put them both out of their misery. Then at least no one would get it into their heads to foolishly stage a rescue. Which was a very real concern, he was just now realizing.

"I want you to write a letter," Uncle said, clearly deciding to pretend not to hear the taunt in his nephew's voice. Which was a pity, because Cricket thought he might enjoy riling him up.

Cricket rolled his eyes, and slumped forward more on his paws, careful of the pressure he put on the blossom he'd hidden away. "To whom?"

"To the prince of Helio." Uncle Sunil came to lean against the bars of Cricket's cell, clearly, he hadn't learned his lesson the last time Cricket nearly took his fingers off.

"Well, that's not happening." Cricket snorted, closing his eyes to dismiss his uncle without even bothering to lift his head. "I don't know what you think that'll accomplish, but I'm not doing it."

"You will. You'll write him a letter, and you'll tell him to come to your aid!" Uncle Sunil snarled, his thin patience already snapping like the string of a bow. How easy he was to trigger. Had it always been that way? Or was it just these new circumstances? Cricket couldn't tell, and honestly, he was getting to the point where he didn't care. Let Uncle be furious. Cricket would be dead soon anyway.

"And if I don't? You'll what? Torture me some more?" A wide yawn cracked his jaw and irritated his throat making Cricket have to clear it to deal with the tickling feeling again. "I hate to break it to you, Uncle, but I'm not really afraid of you anymore."

"Yes, well. We'll see about that. Won't we?" Uncle leaned in closer, so the dim lights of the dungeon reflected off his teeth.

"Guess we will. For now, go away. I'm napping." Cricket laid his head onto his paws, heedless of the danger Uncle may pose him, and waited. Uncle Sunil was gone again, before he lifted his head, and his paw to turn his attention back to the blossoms.

A little bit longer.

He just had to hold out a little bit longer to protect Yoshi and the others. He could do that.

CHAPTER 38

"As if you even had to ask," Ignacia snorted from the middle of the training field. She and Claudia had been sparring, their cheeks darkened with a color Takayoshi could not name, eyes bright with an emotion he had only felt a handful of times.

Soon. Soon he would have that emotion within reach again. Then he and Cricket could perhaps spar like this. Takayoshi had not realized how much he missed it until that very moment. The subtle push and pull of two people who spent enough time together to know one another well. Could predict one another's movements so much so it became a dance, almost. The wanting for it sat as an ache in his lungs, making him want to cough to perhaps dislodge it. He would not be able to, he knew that, but no one could fault him for trying, surely.

"I've just been waiting around for you to say the word." Ignacia's grunted words drew Takayoshi from his thoughts, and back into the situation at hand. Which was a missing Cricket, and a war on the horizon, with no time for idle daydreams.

Claudia snickered—whether because she noted Takayoshi's distraction or for some other reason, he could not tell—her sword sweeping out for Ignacia's seemingly unprotected middle. Ignacia stepped quickly out of swiping range, not bothering to spare Claudia a glance, which just seemed to make Claudia all the more eager to impress.

With a brush of the back of her wrist across her glistening forehead, Claudia turned her attention to Takayoshi. "When do we leave?"

"As soon as possible." Takayoshi's arms folded behind him, the nervous clenching of his fists hidden away where no one could see them. Claudia might recognize the posture for the tell that it was, but Ignacia would not. Not that it mattered. Ignacia would know soon enough what a fool he was for Cricket, if she did not already, he was utterly incapable of hiding it. "However, I had a," he stepped forward, his voice lowering as his gaze swept the rest of the training ground, before finishing, "conversation with the lady Selene."

There were no doubt spies for Sunil and his cohorts amongst the ranks of Helio, and Takayoshi did not want to expose Ignacia and Anstice if he could help it. That particular secret would give them the element of surprise where they might otherwise be lacking it.

His attempts to keep things quiet didn't go as planned, however, because at the mention of the goddess' name Ignacia released a strangled, "You *what?*" that had everyone looking their way.

Takayoshi let out a long, slow breath, and clenched his fists tighter behind his back when the urge to pinch the bridge of his nose against an impending headache crawled along his muscles like an itch. Then he shifted his attention from Ignacia to Claudia, their gazes meeting across the frigid air of the training field, a whole conversation spoken with just one look.

Claudia lifted her chin in question, one brow curved high on her dark face.

Huffing a breath, Takayoshi moved his eyes toward the entrance into the castle proper, a subtle tilt of his head that for anyone else might have been a jerk. When his gaze returned to Claudia she ducked her chin into her chest, a little smile tilting up one corner of her mouth. There was hardly a breath between the agreement and the pair turned to head for the door, steps in tandem.

"Wait. *What?*" Ignacia grumbled in confusion, hair falling loose from the haphazard tail she had tied it into as her head bobbed on her neck trying to follow the silent conversation.

"Just come on." Claudia reached back, her thin fingers latching onto Ignacia's wrist in a movement that was an all too familiar sight to Takayoshi, and half-dragged her toward the entrance behind them.

Takayoshi's hand moved subconsciously to circle his own wrist, the skin of his palm too hot and dry against it where Cricket's had always run cooler, and clammier. A bump from Claudia jostled him from his thoughts, and when he focused on her again, she had her brows raised high in question, a worried purse to her lips. Goddess, when had he become so utterly transparent?

Releasing the hold, Takayoshi turned his attention back to the hallway, and the trek to the war room where Anstice and Leo would be waiting. Out of the corner of his eye he saw Claudia's lips purse further, her jaw clenching around words she wisely chose to keep to herself, at least for the time being. He was not fool enough to think that would last. If she could get him alone, she would force a confession from him, as she had done so in the past. Sometimes, he wondered why he bothered to make friends at all.

But then he rounded the corner into the war room, and came face to face with Leo's firm expression, the table already littered with plans and maps, everything they would need to save his prince, and he remembered. He bothered because going at it alone never really served him as he thought it did. And sometimes, one needed someone on their side, whether they wanted them there or not.

Leo lifted his head from where he was sharpening a blade, his gaze flicking to the hold Claudia had on Ignacia, and a little smile lifted one side of his scarred face. Fondness lining his eyes. It was nice to see it, both the smile on Leo's face, and the happiness in Claudia's bouncing steps, after so many years of misery. After the betrayal, and the struggle, Takayoshi's two friends were finally finding contentment again. He just wished it could stay that way.

"So what is all this about?" Ignacia hissed, dropping into a chair next to Claudia like a petulant child. The group at large ignored her, busy settling in.

Anstice shut the door behind them, then pulled a bit of talisman paper from one of her sleeves and stuck it to the door. When Leo lifted a brow at her, she merely lifted one shoulder and said, "One can never be too careful."

"Now can someone *please* tell me what this is all about?" Ignacia asked again. Her expression pinched, and irritated, gaze carefully avoiding Anstice where she sat at the table between Leo and Takayoshi.

Takayoshi frowned, unable to fully understand how Cricket was so willing to forgive and forget what Anstice had done, but Ignacia clung to it like a nettle. He shook himself, that was a problem for another time. After he had Cricket back, and Sunil was taken care of.

Someone cleared their throat, drawing Takayoshi from his thoughts again, and when Takayoshi lifted his head from where he had been examining a map on the table, he saw Leo leaning in closer, arm lifted as if he were about to nudge Takayoshi. Leo's nose wrinkled, his lips going tight under the thick stubble of his beard when he asked, "What's going on?"

"I have spoken with Selene," Takayoshi said, not answering the unspoken question in Leo's eyes.

Leo dropped his arm, returning to an almost casual lean, one foot braced on the table, the other dangling to the floor as he sharpened his blade. But that too, Takayoshi knew, was forced. A farce for Anstice and Ignacia to see, put in place so Takayoshi's friends could help him keep his secrets lest he not wish to expose himself in front of strangers. He appreciated it, for all that it was unnecessary.

"And what does the moon goddess have to say?" Ignacia asked, her tone disbelieving. Takayoshi resisted the urge to roll his eyes at her. She had not been there, he reminded himself, when all of this was explained to Anstice and Atsuko. She knew nothing of what he found on his journey. She was just trying to be realistic.

Takayoshi took a breath, held it for a moment, letting the burn of lungs begging for release ground him, then he dove into the entire thing. He told Ignacia all about the curse by the Lady Venus, and the spell he cast. He told her about Selene, and her antics, and how she was Cricket's mother. And when that was done, he told them all about how Selene said magic ran in families, and so of course Cricket's sisters would be celestials just as he was.

"They aren't blood," Leo tried to argue. He had long since stopped sharpening his blade and tucked it away somewhere on his person.

"Magic has never cared one whit about blood," Anstice said. She had taken a fan from her billowing sleeves and was tapping it against the edge of the table in a steady beat, like a metronome. "Further reason why this whole thing with Sunil is completely ridiculous. So long as Jaxith had a child, blood or not, that child would always be ruler of Lunette."

"Are we just going to ignore the assertion that Cricket is Selene's son?" Ignacia asked, her voice a little strangled.

"You've just been told you're a Celestial beast, and that's the part you have a problem with?" Leo fixed Ignacia with a bored look. Some of his shaggy hair fell into his face, hiding the jagged scar that ran down the side of it. If Estia were there, ze might have reached out to brush it away, but Estia was imprisoned in the dungeons. Left to rot when the information ze provided proved useless.

Takayoshi meant to go down and check on zir, but they were rapidly running out of time, the hours ticking away like seconds in a countdown that not even Takayoshi was sure what the ending would be. For all he knew, they were all headed toward complete destruction.

"He's my brother," was Ignacia's only explanation, and that, honestly, was enough, even for Takayoshi. No one argued, and it seemed to please her, because she leaned forward, her elbows bracing on the table and asked, "So how long before we march on Lunette?"

He had thought about this. Taken some time to consider how long it might take him to train Anstice and Ignacia to do what he failed to teach Cricket. It would be a tight schedule, but Ignacia, Takayoshi knew at least, had the head for it. "We should take a few months to—"

"We don't *have* a few months." Anstice closed her fan and sat up straighter. Takayoshi did not know much about Cricket's younger sister as she did not join them on their first journey together, but he did not think he had ever seen her so serious. The softness slipped away from her full face, with her jaw clenched, and her eyes which were usually round and smiling, had gone hard. This was not the queen's consort, or the king's fashion-loving baby sister, this was a woman who knew how to win a war.

"What am I not accounting for?" Tension ripped through

Takayoshi's body, making every muscle tense, every hair and feather stand on end. Something was wrong.

"With the curse—"

"What curse?" Leo asked.

It was a struggle not to reach over, grab Anstice by her shoulders, and shake her until she gave them every bit of knowledge she had been hiding for Cricket. So much so that Takayoshi could feel the bite of his nails into his palms.

Anstice seemed to notice, for she slouched in on herself, shifting away from him lest he try to grab her. "Sunil cursed Cricket before he left Lunette, just like I told you he would. We've been trying to find a way around it the entire time he's been here, but so far all I've been able to do is slow it down."

"What kind of curse?" Ignacia was on her feet, her body tilted like she too wanted to grab Anstice and not let go until Anstice spilled everything.

Lifting her fan, Anstice ducked behind it, her eyes flicking from Takayoshi to Ignacia and back nervously. "I really can't—"

"I don't care if that idiot swore you to secrecy, Annie. You will tell us, and you will tell us now!" A soft grating sound accompanied Ignacia's words, the threat of a blade being drawn, and Takayoshi stood as well to put himself in between the two sisters lest things come to blows. Ignacia pushed against him, snarling, "*Now*. Anstice."

"Hanahaki." Anstice winced at the word, as if saying it was a wound in and of itself.

"A *love* curse? A stupid love curse is going to take my brother from me?" Ignacia stepped back, her tone bewildered, uncomprehending, then all at once her face shuttered, turned hard, she understood, and she rounded on Takayoshi. "This is your fault."

Takayoshi stumbled under the force of her shove and

ducked his head. He wasn't sure what she meant by it being his fault, but it sounded like the truth.

"I will fix this," he vowed, even if he did not know how at this time. A love curse. Did mean that his love for Cricket could save him? Or did it have to be someone who Cricket loved in return? And what if that person was not— No. Takayoshi gripped his sword more tightly, the hilt biting into his palms, a cutting pain that brought him back to his senses. "How long do we have?"

"With how it's been progressing?" Anstice frowned, rubbing her cheek with the end of her fan. "A month. Maybe two. It depends on how badly injured he is."

"Then our work begins now." Takayoshi turned to brace his hands against the table so he could look to them all in turn. His own little army. "Anstice, I will need you to secure a training room for us."

Anstice nodded, already pulling talisman paper from her sleeve and starting to scratch characters onto them that she no doubt learned from Cricket. "The room you and Cricket were using before should be private enough once it's warded."

"Leo and Claudia, you are in charge of gathering our forces. Be discreet, I do not want to tip off Sunil if we can help it."

"Anything else?" Claudia pulled a bit of loose parchment to herself and started scribbling on it, writing a list of names of people she thought they could trust.

"We will need weapons. I do not want to go to my sister for them, she has made her position on this very clear." He frowned, hating the words even as he said them. Atsuko would no doubt be upset by the betrayal that lingered in his tone, but he could not seem to help it.

"We have some arms from when we came up the mountain," Ignacia volunteered. "Many of the soldiers will also have their personal weapons they can use if they join us."

"Good. Until we have acquired a small force, you, Anstice, and I will train behind closed doors. Hopefully, you will have control of your beasts before the end of the week, leaving us another handful of days to train with the soldiers should we need it, and descend the mountain." Takayoshi stood up, his hands going behind his back to clench into fists again. He took one look around the room, meeting each of their eyes in turn.

His friends. Cricket's family. *Their* team. They would do this. There was no other choice.

"I said one month, *maybe two*," Anstice repeated, stress lining the words "maybe two".

"My Prince will hang on until we reach him. He is strong." He would have to, Takayoshi realized, what other option was there? "We begin tonight."

CHAPTER 39

Cricket didn't know who sat the piece of parchment in front of him, whether it was Uncle Sunil or one of the many mercenaries he brought with him to keep Cricket in line. Not that it mattered much, Cricket was in no shape to fight them, he was hardly conscious.

He was sure, by this point, Uncle's plan was merely to let him die. To let the roots and stems choke him, leave him gasping for breath. It would be a terrible way to go, Cricket was certain, but at least it would not be bloody. He would leave behind a corpse that was mostly intact for his loved ones to bury, if Uncle Sunil bothered to release it to them and didn't just destroy it out of spite.

A morbid thought to ponder over later, when he was alone.

Either way, Cricket didn't know who sat the parchment there, the edges going dark and rust-colored with moisture and blood. He also wasn't sure how Uncle Sunil thought this would work. He could not shift back to a man—he tried numerous times to no avail, growing weaker with every attempt—and he could not possibly hold a pen with his large dragon paws. So how was he supposed to pen a letter to Yoshi convincing him to come to Lunette? This was ridiculous, even in the abstract.

"I realize you can't sign it," Uncle Sunil said, and Cricket's blurry vision focused enough, finally, for him to realize it was not just a blank piece of paper. No. There were words on the page in a hand that was not his own, not even close. Anyone who knew him at all would not be fooled by the handwriting. This would not convince Yoshi to come. Relief flooded Cricket at that thought, his loved ones were safe, at least for a little while longer. Provided they didn't do something recklessly, honorably, foolish like try to save him.

"What does it say?" Not that it mattered, he wasn't going to do whatever Uncle Sunil wanted him to to verify the letter was from him. The longer he could waylay Yoshi and the others coming for him, the better. Who cared if by the time they came it was too late? Because it *would* be too late, he could feel that now. However long it took them, whether it be a week, a fortnight, a month, it would be too late. Darkness swam at the edge of his vision, making that clearer than it had ever been before.

"It's just a letter asking for your Helion prince to come to your aid." His uncle shrugged, tone disinterested, even as his hungry gaze remained fixed on Cricket. "It has enough sentiment to get him–"

"Did you tell him I love him?" His throat clenched around the words, threatening to send him into a coughing fit at the mere thought that Uncle Sunil might have said as much just to get Yoshi to return to Lunette, not realizing just how true it would have been.

"What?"

"Did you tell him that I. Love. Him?" For all the miscommunication that happened between them, all of the words gone unspoken, Cricket wanted to be the one to tell Yoshi the truth. He wanted to be facing Yoshi when he said it, even if it would kill him to be rejected. Ultimately, he may never get the chance, but still, he didn't want Uncle Sunil to be the one to do it.

"Should I have?" Uncle's voice went up an octave in a way that meant he was intrigued by something, seeing it from a different angle. He was going to use this, whatever Cricket said next, he was going to use this.

Blast. I should have held my tongue.

"No. You shouldn't have." Cricket tried to force his vision to focus on the words, to make sure his uncle wasn't lying, but he couldn't. And the more he tried, the more the words swam, a pressure building behind his eyes that felt as if it might push them from his head at any given moment. He wondered, idly, if Uncle would make use of his eyes too. There must be potions or magic that required dragon eyes. Something high level enough to intrigue the power-hungry man. Maybe something that he wouldn't quite be able to handle.

Wouldn't it be amusing if ultimately, that's what ended Uncle's reign of terror? A spell—using dragons eyes—gone wrong. At least I'd have my revenge.

Cricket shook himself. Now was not the time. "Either way, I'm not signing it."

"I know you aren't." Uncle huffed, a sulk in his voice more childish than Cricket thought he had been in many years.

"Are you pouting, Uncle? How unbecoming." Cricket lowered himself to the floor again, his head cushioned on his paws. "Whatever it is you want me to do with this paper, I refuse."

"You cannot refuse!"

"I can. And I did." The press of a blade was cold against the length of his tail, a threatening bite that Cricket didn't even raise his head to acknowledge.

"I told you I'd carve you up into tiny bite-sized dragon pieces," Uncle murmured with a nod, and the blade cut into Cricket, finding a place where the scales had been removed days ago, soft and unprotected. Cricket hissed against the burn of it, the slow digging in of sharpened steel. Blood *drip-drip-drip*ped from the cut, louder than the leaking pipe he had yet to find the source of. "Don't make me make good on my threat, Nephew. You don't want your daughter to only have pieces to bury, do you?"

"What does it matter?" Cricket asked, tiredly, the pain making his vision darken further. If he was not careful, he would pass out very soon. "After what you've told my people," he swallowed around the threat of tears, and bile, "I won't be allowed to be buried with my ancestors."

"They aren't *your* ancestors!" Uncle Sunil spat, the spray from his lips splattering on the parchment, darkening it further, and making the ink bleed. He'd have to rewrite it now. Good. "You're an orphan!"

Cricket peeked open one eye so that he could see the vermillion of his uncle's face. It had been quite some time since he had seen him that red, pity, considering how often Cricket used to delight in naming each new shade he could make his Uncle's face turn. Puce, had always been a particular favorite. There was little enjoyment to be found in it now, Cricket sighed. "Do what you will, Uncle. I won't legitimize this farce."

"Do it," was the only warning Cricket received before the man behind him cut into Cricket's tail, severing the very end of it, and drawing a scream from his lips.

Tears, and pain darkened his vision further, and he was coughing, hacking, retching, ripping a bouquet of snowdrops out by their roots to splatter against the parchment in front of him. Silence followed, the only sound the dripping of blood, and Cricket's wheezing breaths.

"Think about what I've said, nephew," Uncle said, patting the bars with a soft *tap-tap* of his rings that made the ringing in Cricket's ears increase. "I'll be back soon with a fresh letter."

"It won't *change* anything!" Cricket screamed, throat raw from retching, and tears. "I won't bring him here. I won't let you hurt him, or use him as some– Some– *Experiment*! If it's the last thing I do, I'll keep him from *you*!"

Tilting his head in thought, long dark hair falling across his eyes, Uncle Sunil smiled, twisted and cruel. "It very well might be."

"So be it!"

"You'll change your mind. I'm sure of it." Uncle turned to the man standing behind Cricket again, the one who's blade had sliced through him like butter. "Deliver that to the good doctor. Waste not. Want not."

Cricket watched Uncle Sunil and his men leave from under lowered lashes, breathing deeply through his nostrils to remain conscious. Just a little bit longer then he could give into the spinning of the floor and the tunnel of his vision.

Just a little bit longer.

SOMEONE WAS WHIMPERING.

The sound high-pitched and echoing off the bare walls of Cricket's cell. At first, he thought it was a dream, something his mind had conjured up to punish him further for all that he'd done. Then he thought perhaps it was himself, the end of his tail was still bleeding, the pain a dull throb by that point which probably indicated infection. Good thing he wasn't going to live long enough to know what damage such an injury would translate into on his elven body.

"Wake up!" Uncle Sunil snarled, a loud bang on the cage bars ripping Cricket from his thoughts.

His eyes jerked open, and he was faced with two women kneeling in front of the bars, their chins tilted back where Uncle's mercenaries held blades to their throats. Cricket didn't recognize them. They were likely from the city, or maybe the new maids his uncle hired. It didn't matter. They were innocents in all of this. They hadn't asked for this. They shouldn't have been brought here. They shouldn't have to suffer.

"What're you doing, Uncle?" He was suddenly wide awake, all traces of dizziness, and fatigue pushed to the back of Cricket's mind as he tried to think of a way around this. A way to save the women. A way out of the cage. All without giving in to Uncle's demands and endangering Yoshi or Becka.

"I've come to tell you I don't need that letter anymore." Uncle Sunil's lips curled back from his teeth, less smile, more sneer. It was cold, and sharp, a knifepoint ready to slice into Cricket's soft underbelly.

Fear crept along Cricket's spine, raising gooseflesh in its wake. Cricket's tongue clicked dry against his teeth, floundering around the words, "What do you mean to do with those women?"

"These women?" Uncle asked, moving up behind one of them, his fingers grasping her chin to force her to look at him. The blade cut into her skin from the odd angle, drawing a trickle of blood that ran down the length of her throat. She whimpered again, the sound louder still in the quiet of the room, the threat imminent. "They're for protection."

"Protection?" Maybe he was more sleep-addled than he thought. That didn't make sense. *None* of this made sense. Why would his uncle need protection? Cricket was well and truly bound to the floor of his cell. Strapped down with iron manacles and locked away behind bars. There was no way Cricket could reach his uncle, even if he wanted to. Which he did not. He did not think he could kill Uncle, even now. Even with all that Uncle had done to—

"Your prince is on his way," Uncle Sunil said, tone disinterested, and soft, but a blow all the same. Cricket reeled.

"What?"

"My spies spotted him when he crossed the border. He will be here within the week, nephew. And then—" Uncle chuckled, looking down at the woman again, his eyes almost softening.

For a moment Cricket considered that he'd let her go, show mercy. But then he looked up to meet Cricket's eyes and his gaze narrowed, communication enough for someone who had grown up with him to understand.

He said, without words, "I will do this to your prince" before he reached down to grab the back of her head, and in one swift motion there came the *crack* of her neck, and the *thud* of a lifeless body against the floor.

Cricket roared, throwing himself against the chains. They gave under his weight, and the ferocity of his rage, allowing him to slam against the bars, denting them outward. It hurt. It all hurt. His body was on fire with pain, and sorrow, but none of it stopped him. Because he was going to put an end to this finally, before anyone else could—

"Ah. Ah. Ah." Uncle clicked his tongue, the mercenary holding the now sobbing other hostage pressed his blade in closer, drawing a choking gasp from her.

Cricket stopped his thrashing. Talons dug deep into the stone beneath his paws, but the fight left him, leaving his muscles weak and aching.

"Keep it up and I'll kill her too. How much blood on your hands before they're so stained, you'll never get them clean?"

He tsked softly as he stepped away from the bars, the darkness of the outer edges of Cricket's cell engulfing him. The soft tapping of boots accompanied Uncle's retreat, but the mercenary stayed, the girl on her knees sobbing.

"It's your hands that will never be clean again, *Uncle*." The words rumbled up from Cricket as a growl more than a voice.

"Perhaps. But when I'm done with your prince. . ." Uncle let the words hang for a moment, another soft, grating chuckle escaping his lips. "Well, I suppose you'll see. Won't you?"

The door to the dungeons slammed behind him with a finality and Uncle–

No. Not *Uncle*.

Sunil.

Yue Sunil.

Because anyone who took such perverse pleasure in holding the thing their family loved in their hands and crushing it to dust, did not deserve the title of family. And Cricket was through pretending there had ever been any love between them.

It was time to put all this childishness behind him. It was time to stop clinging to a man who would never love him. A man who had never truly seen him as family.

It was time for Yue Sunil to face the consequences of his actions.

It was time for Yue Sunil to die.

BOOK I
BATTLE

CHAPTER 40

They had been spotted.

Takayoshi knew perhaps long before the others. He saw a flicker of something on the ridge just past their camp. The reflection of moonlight on a sword maybe, or the fluttering of a cloak in the darkness. He was not sure, and it did not matter, because the point was, they had been spotted.

A smile twitched at the corner of Takayoshi's lips.

In spite of what Sunil and his men might think, Takayoshi was not trying to hide their movements. The approach of his forces was not meant to catch Sunil by surprise—the surprise would be Ignacia and Anstice who latched onto their dual natures like a fish might to water.

Takayoshi wanted Sunil to *see* them coming. He wanted Sunil to know long before the final blow that it had been Takayoshi who delivered it. And he wanted Sunil to know—based on the limited forces he brought with him—that this attack was personal. It was not because Sunil had attacked Helio and tried to burn the capital to the ground. It was because Sunil had taken something from Takayoshi that Takayoshi treasured.

"You're smiling," Leo said, voice soft, and gruff. He moved up beside Takayoshi, pressing his shoulder into Takayoshi's in something that felt both companionable and soothing. It was good to have friends, Takayoshi reminded himself. Good to know that when he decided to take the fight to Sunil, he did not have to do it alone.

"Sunil knows we are coming." Takayoshi stopped trying to smother the vicious quirk of his lips, letting it curl a little further up his face. Maybe still not as much emotion as someone else might show, but certainly more than he usually allowed himself.

A soft chuckle rumbled up from Leo's chest, his own face splitting into a wide grin beneath his scraggly beard. "He'll be ready for us?"

"It would seem we are in for quite the fight." Takayoshi turned away from the edge of their encampment, back toward the safety of the fire that Ignacia and Claudia built. The pair of them were curled up together on one of the logs Takayoshi dragged from the surrounding forest, their heads leaning closer as they murmured softly to one another. The sight of them together made longing—a feeling he was intimately acquainted with these days—pang in his chest, tight, and sharp. He lifted a hand to rub at the ache, not bothering to worry if anyone would notice. These were his friends, his family. What point was there in hiding his pain from them?

Warmth, and a soft squeeze to his shoulder, drew Takayoshi's attention back to the man at his side. The one who knew how this felt, perhaps better than Takayoshi himself did. Takayoshi wanted to apologize for what happened, for how they had to lock Estia up. He had not done so yet, and perhaps he should have. Would it be too late now? Would the words be empty? There was no way to know until he said them, he supposed.

Leo did not give him a chance. "We're going to get to him before it's too late."

The tightness in his chest eased, and Takayoshi exhaled deeply, his shoulders sagging just the slightest in relief at the reminder that they were a *we*. He was not alone in this, and he did not have to fight this battle as if he were. With Leo and Ignacia's steel, Claudia's cleverness, and Anstice's cunning, Takayoshi would save Cricket, and bring him home. What home would look like, he was not sure at this time. But he knew it involved Cricket safe, and in one piece.

"And then you'll confess, and you'll both live happily ever after." And the tightness was back, clenching at his heart, squeezing his lungs and threatening to send Takayoshi into a coughing fit.

Takayoshi huffed a laugh, bumping Leo's shoulder hard enough to jostle him off balance, where he had been leaning heavily on his cane. "Stop it."

"Stop what?" Leo asked, his hand flying to his chest as if the physical blow hit him there instead of his shoulder. "Isn't that what you want? To have your prince all to you–"

"You are teasing me." Takayoshi's lids fluttered around an involuntary eye roll. Uncle Reiji would throw a fit if he were to see it. More reason to be thankful he was not with them.

"Am I?" Leo's voice went up an octave, his smile crinkling his eyes into crescents. "Honestly, you're no fun anymore. Ever since we got off that island–"

"We are at war, Leo," Takayoshi reminded, hating himself even as he did it. He missed the lightness of Leo, Claudia, Estia, and he adventuring together. They lost that when Estia betrayed them, showing zirself for who ze really was. Takayoshi knew that knowledge sat like a weight across Leo's shoulders. A mantel he wore with more pride than Takayoshi ever thought he would be able to.

"We are," Leo agreed, voice gone low, and serious once more. "But I wasn't lying when I said that we would get him back. You deserve to be happy, and I want to help you have that."

"You deserve to be happy too, Leo." A quiet truth, was still a truth. And even if Leo did not seem to feel it himself, seemed to think he deserved the bad things that befell him, but did not deserve the good, Takayoshi did not see how that could possibly be true. He did not know the entirety of Leo and Estia's story, but he thought he knew enough to make a sound judgment on it. They both deserved to be happy. They both deserved to be free from the tyranny of Craven. And once they settled this business with Sunil, Takayoshi would ensure that happened. He would ensure the people who were most important to him—to Cricket—could have the happiness they had all strived so hard for.

"Yeah, well, who's to say?" Leo said with a soft snort, his gaze gone far off and hazy remembering something Takayoshi could not hope to understand as he never shared it with them. "But, one thing at a time, right?" He did not wait for Takayoshi to agree, instead, Leo straightened up, and started back to the fire, his cane making soft taps against the hard ground, before calling over his shoulder, "I'm taking first watch. You should get some rest."

"Rest," Takayoshi murmured to himself, the word feeling foreign on his tongue. As if he could possibly rest with Cricket so close. They were a mere two days' ride from the capital of Lunette. Not much longer and they would be at Sunil's door.

"Please, my lady," Takayoshi said, tilting his head back to look up at the moon hanging heavy over their encampment. He had not spoken to Selene since she told him about

Anstice and Ignacia's abilities, but he knew she was watching them. He knew she was doing everything she could within her limited power to ensure he made it to her son in time to save him, and her kingdom. "Please tell me he is still safe. Tell me that I will not find him—" He stopped himself there, swallowing around a sharpness in his throat, the threat of tears. "Let him know I am coming for him."

The breeze whispered through the empty trees, fluttering the flakes from where snow rested on their branches until it fell down like fresh snowfall. Takayoshi looked back to the fire, noting the small whirlwind surrounded just him, leaving the fire and his companions untouched. A tiny blizzard of his own making.

"Tell him yourself," an all too familiar voice whispered on the wind. Not for the first time, Takayoshi imagined a woman with Cricket's brows, and lips, rolling her eyes at the audacity of the mortal contacting her. Before he could ask her what she meant, the breeze died away, leaving the flakes clinging to his eyelashes the only proof it had been at all.

"Yoshi," Claudia called from the fire, drawing his attention away from the moon. She stood up, her expression tight, a clear sign she had been watching him, and noted the short exchange he had with seemingly thin air. He could not see her eyes, but he imagined her gaze flicking to the soldiers who sat on the other logs surrounding the fire, nervousness setting her lips into a hard line. "You should come make up your bedroll."

With another sweeping gaze up to the moon, his brows raised in question to the goddess, Takayoshi said, "I am coming."

Then he turned away from Selene and followed Claudia to the place where she and Leo set up their bedrolls a little ways from the rest of their squadron. Some may look at it oddly, but Takayoshi understood. The three of them had grown used to sleeping within arm's reach while they were hunting the archive. So much so they found it hard to sleep without knowing the others were close at hand. Even in Helio, he struggled, although there were other things to worry about then.

Claudia was waiting for him, her legs straightened out in front of her where she sat up beneath the blanket of her bedroll. Ignacia had not followed her, which likely meant Claudia had decided this conversation ought to be private, and Takayoshi appreciated the way his friends took his feelings into account, even here, on the battlefront.

"What did Selene say?" Claudia's voice was soft, almost under her breath as she turned away from the fire and the others in the guise of fluffing her pillow. "Judging by your expression, it was something annoyingly mysterious."

"I asked her to tell Cricket that we were coming." Takayoshi settled beside her, laying onto his back to stare up at the field of stars that rested above them.

It would likely be better that the rest of the soldiers not know Takayoshi had a direct line to the moon goddess. Who knew what they would think of that. Would they think him insane? Or would it be worse? Would they think they could use his connection somehow to their benefit. He instructed Ignacia and Claudia to only bring along soldiers they could trust, but he was not fool enough to think such knowledge would not tempt them into. . . He was not sure what one would do with the knowledge, but he was sure greed was a strong motivating factor, and he did not want to find out.

"And?" Claudia prompted when he let the silence stretch between them for too long. Lost in his own head as he tended to get, or so he was told by Claudia on multiple occasions.

"And she said I ought to tell him myself." Takayoshi folded his hands over his stomach, the blanket pulled up to rest under his arms, warding off most of the nighttime chill.

He closed his eyes, his brows pinching together against an oncoming headache, because he knew what Claudia's next question would be, it was the same one he had.

"What does that even *mean*?" she hissed, the blankets rustling under her as she got settled. Turning his head to the side, Takayoshi opened his eyes again, and found Claudia laying on her side facing him, her head propped up by her elbow.

"I do not know. As you so aptly pointed out, it was annoyingly mysterious." A laugh tickled at the back of his throat, and he released it with a soft exhale, his lips turning up at the corners into a little smile. It was nice to laugh about these things, he had come to realize in their time on the island that housed the archive. Nice to let humor alleviate some of the strain.

"Helpful as always, I see," Ignacia said as she flopped down beside Claudia. When Takayoshi's gaze flicked to her, she rolled her eyes, scooting herself closer to Claudia's back. "Don't give me that annoyed look, I'm not the one giving you vague hints without any real instructions."

Looking back to Claudia, Takayoshi raised his brows in question, and she let out a soft snicker. "You did have that look of having just eaten a lemon. Just a little bit. Though, I'm impressed Iggy even noticed. She's usually less–"

"Watch it," Ignacia warned.

"Maybe you should try sleeping on it?" Claudia suggested, skillfully changing the subject.

The corner of his mouth ticked up with a tiny, knowing grin, and Claudia winked at him where Ignacia could not see.

"Maybe try thinking about him, and your connection as you go to sleep. His subconscious was able to visit you before, I don't see why it wouldn't work the other way too. Especially now that you're also," she waved her free hand in front of his face, gesturing to the all that was Takayoshi, "you know."

"That is a decent hypothesis. I will try it." Takayoshi turned his head back to look up at the sky once more, and shut his eyes, effectively ending the conversation.

Claudia—who was used to this sort of thing—merely let out a soft snort, and Takayoshi heard her shift some more in her bedroll until she was comfortable.

Taking a deep breath, Takayoshi blocked out the sounds of the others in the encampment and focused instead on the last conversation he had with Cricket. The blue of his eyes. The tightness of his smile. The pallor of his skin. Cricket had been *so* sick—cursed—even then, how had he missed it?

No. Now was not time to chastise himself for what he missed. Now was time to focus on the connection between them. On the subtle pull that sat in the center of his chest. He imagined giving it a tug, pulling it taut, following it.

Then sleep took him.

CHAPTER 41

Yue Sunil had to die.

The question was, how?

Cricket, for all the rage that simmered low in his gut, was still locked in the dungeons of his own castle. He had broken the chains that bound him to the floor, but that didn't change all of the other issues. Primarily, the bars, the guards, and *finding* Sunil. Because Sunil would not be returning to the dungeons, not even to gloat, if Cricket knew anything about the man. He had gotten what he wanted from Cricket, there was no reason to return.

So whatever he did, would have to be thought through carefully—usually not his forte. Ignacia and Anstice were the planners. The strategic thinkers. The tacticians. The ones who one wanted to take into a war because they would know how to win it. Cricket had always been more the type to jump in feet first, and hope he learned how to swim before he drowned.

Perhaps that's where this whole thing had gone awry. Perhaps if he hadn't left the capital unprotected while he chased down those curses all those years ago, things would be different. Sunil wouldn't have been able to build such a foothold with the villages he was unable to help, the ones Anstice decided would be best left to work themselves out.

Discontent settled into the kingdom while Cricket was trying to prove himself. And although he spent the last few years fighting for his people, protecting as many of them as he could from Sunil and his attacks, personally, it was not enough. It would likely never be enough for some people. That was the hardest blow of all of this. *Cricket* would never be enough for some people. There would always be a place for someone like Sunil who was deeply rooted in their culture to find unhappiness and sow his seeds.

He'd just have to work harder in the future. Even if he'd already been spreading himself thin. There was always room to—

A glimmer caught in the corner of his eyes, bringing his thoughts to an abrupt halt. Turning his head, careful of the bars which felt too tight, and close to his body, Cricket watched as the glittering, shimmering air resolved first into a blurry whisp, then into something he recognized. A shape he had come to consider beloved.

"Yoshi?" Cricket asked, disbelieving. How could— It didn't matter. Because it was too dangerous.

If Sunil saw him. . .

His next words left him in a hurried whisper, "You can't be here. You have to go."

His gaze flicked to the door of the dungeons, his breath lodged in his throat as he waited for the guards outside to hear the commotion in the cell, and come to check. If they saw Yoshi, it would all be over. That would be the end. Cricket couldn't have that. He wouldn't. He needed to get Yoshi out of there before someone noticed him. It was the only way to protect him.

"I am not here," Yoshi said, his voice soft, and tranquil, as it always was. Infuriatingly calm even in the face of so much danger, so much death. Cricket didn't know how he did that, kept himself so level.

It wasn't because Yoshi didn't feel, Cricket was sure. He had seen the emotions flicker across Yoshi's face too often to think him unfeeling. No, if anything Cricket thought perhaps Yoshi felt things too deeply. His emotions—empathy and hurt—ran bone deep. Perhaps that was the key, he was able to hide it because it *was* so deep.

"What do you mean you're not here?" Cricket's eyes flew from the unmoving door back to Yoshi's shimmering form. Now that Cricket really looked, Yoshi didn't look solid. He could see the bricks of the wall through his semi-transparent form. And there was a washed-outness to his golden eyes that made Cricket's chest ache.

"I am. . ." Yoshi paused, his lips pursing just the slightest as he chose his next words carefully, perhaps worried what reaction Cricket would have to them.

Cricket held his breath, terrified to hear that maybe Yoshi had died already. Maybe he was too late. Maybe there was nothing he could do to stop Sunil. If Yoshi was dead, what would be left for Cricket? Becka, yes, but she'd be better off in Helio anyway. Maybe that would be better, then he could go in peace, and be with Yoshi wherever it was their people ended up—that particular part of their belief system had never been very clear. Yoshi left him suspended long enough that his lungs began to burn.

"I am asleep. . . somewhere else."

"*Asleep?*" The word came out strangled, like he was trying to force it out past something choking him. He supposed he was, but he didn't think the snowdrops should affect the dragon's voice that way. Especially since it wasn't coming from his lips.

"Yes." Takayoshi nodded to himself, seeming pleased with his explanation before continuing. "This is an extension of my subconscious. I believe you did much the same when I was away on my search for the archive."

"I don't— I don't remember that." He did, though. In a hazy sort of way. There had been dreams in those years while Yoshi was away. They hadn't made a whole lot of sense, and Cricket had always just brushed them off as nonsense, especially as he was only able to remember them vaguely. Just the need to find Yoshi. Just the feeling that he was in danger. Just a forest, a town, an old manor, a jungle. The places more an impression of what they were than any actual details. Cricket wouldn't even have been able to tell you what the buildings looked like, or what types of trees surrounded him.

"Perhaps not." Yoshi hummed, but he didn't seem altogether bothered by it. "But you visited me."

Ah. That he did remember, at least from what Leo said to him. His eyes must have lit in recognition because the purse of Yoshi's lips smoothed out, the corners ticking up in a barely-there smile. "Leo said something about it."

"Of course, he did." A soft snort left Yoshi, his tone affectionately annoyed, and Cricket found himself aching anew.

He spent some small amount of time with Yoshi since his return from wherever he had gone, but he hadn't seen Yoshi interact with his friends yet. Pride swelled in his chest, threatening to crawl up his throat, and make him say something that they likely didn't have time for.

Yoshi made a sound in the back of his throat, just loud enough for Cricket to hear it above the *drip-drip-drip* of the pipe in the back corner of the room. Or maybe it wasn't really just loud enough, because Cricket wasn't hearing it with his ears. Maybe it was—

"Focus, My Prince."

"Yes, of course. I apologize." Cricket tried to laugh, but it came out a little choked.

My Prince. Even after all that happened. Even after almost destroying everything Yoshi loved, he still called Cricket *My Prince*. There was something behind that, something he hadn't heard before. Possessiveness, yes, but not in the constricting sense. Like Yoshi considered himself to be Cricket's, and vice versa. There would hopefully be time to examine that later.

"Well, why is your subconscious visiting me then?"

"To let you know that we are coming." Yoshi smiled a little more, the expression crawling up his face enough to wrinkle the corners of his eyes. Cricket suddenly wished to live long enough to see that in person. To maybe know what that smile felt like pressed against his own.

He shook himself. "You can't come here. Sunil plans to capture you and use you. He's going to—" Cricket choked on the words, coughing around them. He turned his head, hoping to hide the wateriness of his eyes, and the blooms crawling up his throat.

"Breathe, My Prince," Yoshi said from somewhere much closer now, his voice quiet and soothing. "Just breathe through it. I will reach you, and all will be well."

"He's—" Cricket swallowed thickly, forcing the blooms back lest Yoshi see them. "He's been experimenting on me. He wants to know how I became a dragon. And he knows about you. He knows you're the phoenix."

Yoshi tilted his head to one side, a strand of long white-blond hair falling across his eyes as he thought about Cricket's words. "I am not concerned by this."

"Well, *I* am!" Lurching forward, Cricket smacked his muzzle on the bars. A wince tickled his throat, then he was coughing again. This time, unable to keep the blooms down.

There were so many more of them now. And they just kept coming. Littering the floor in white petals, like freshly fallen snow, so many that Cricket couldn't hide them from Yoshi.

When he finally finished retching, his breath coming in hard pants as his shoulders heaved, eyes burning so much he could hardly make out the shimmering form of Yoshi anymore, Yoshi said, "I cannot leave you here to die like this."

"You can!" He was angry, all of the sudden, so angry that Yoshi didn't see the ridiculousness of this plan. That he didn't see the impossibility of it.

Of course he knew the battle between Sunil and Helio would have to happen at some point, but if Yoshi would just go home, just leave Cricket to his fate. Then maybe Cricket would have time to get rid of Sunil before it came to that.

The next words came out on a growl, frost puffing up on a cloud from his nostrils, "You will."

"I will not." Yoshi's chin tilted back, that stubborn frown wrinkling the corner of his mouth, an old friend Cricket couldn't say he'd actually missed. All right, he *had* missed it. He had missed everything about Yoshi, he would be lying if he said he hadn't.

"I'm sick, Yoshi," Cricket said, almost a whine, pathetic and weak. He'd have thought it was obvious that he was sick from the coughing, and the blossoms that were sticking to the stone of his cell, turning translucent with the gathered moisture there. "Even if you could save me–"

"I am aware of your curse." The ticking of his jaw was the only sign he was irritated. Whether it was about the curse itself, or Sunil having cast it, or the problems it would present them, Cricket couldn't tell. But he let himself languish in the fact that perhaps it was irritation about the fact that something was threatening to part them permanently.

In his final hours, Cricket thought he was allowed some

delusions, some idle daydreams about Yoshi perhaps loving him back. That underlying fury making Yoshi's teeth grind because he didn't want to lose Cricket. Foolishness, he knew, but no one could fault a dying man his folly.

"I have spoken to Anstice about it in depth."

"Of course you have. Meddling little sister," Cricket muttered with a huff of annoyance.

"I will not let this thing take you." A vow, solemn, true, and it sounded so much like *I will not lose you* that Cricket itched to reach out to Yoshi. To pull him close, and tell him how much Yoshi meant to him in return. How much losing Yoshi all those years ago ripped him up inside. But there wasn't time for that, there never would be, it seemed. "I must go."

"Go? Go where?"

"It is my turn to take up watch of the encampment." Yoshi tilted his head to one side, listening, his brows drawn together. "I will see you again soon."

"I told you, you can't come here!"

Yoshi smiled, a real smile this time, the corners of his mouth ticking up enough that even someone who didn't know him would know it for the cocky grin that it was. So sure, and beautiful, it nearly stopped Cricket's breath. His brows rising in challenge, Yoshi murmured, "Try to stop me."

Then he was gone. And Cricket was left reeling.

He had to stop this. He had to– He had to regain his strength so he could protect Yoshi, if nothing else. Even if it killed him. He had to keep Sunil from hurting Yoshi.

"Rest," a voice whispered, the words barely there in the silence of the cell. So quiet he almost thought he had imagined them until it continued. "When you need it, you will have the strength to fight."

It was likely a hallucination, something to make him feel

better in the face of certain destruction, but Cricket sucked in a breath and asked, "Who are you?"

The voice hummed for a moment, thinking, then they laughed. "A friend. Don't question it, just close your eyes, and rest. You will need your strength."

"The snowdrops—"

"Forget about the snowdrops. Focus your magic on rebuilding your center, your core of strength. The Helion prince has taught you to meditate, do that." Cricket wasn't sure how the voice knew, but he thought it might be rude to ask.

"The meditation never helped before."

"You were focusing on the wrong thing before." The voice scoffed. "Honestly, it's like I have to tell that boy everything. You were focusing on the dragon, what you need to focus on instead is the magic. The dragon is not separate, stop treating it as if it is. Close your eyes and listen to your inner magic."

"My inner magic," Cricket repeated the words slowly, uncomprehending.

"Yes, you're always spouting off about listening to the magic of the world, and like calling to like. Listen to what's inside you for once." The voice sounded like it wanted to add *idiot* to the end of that sentence, and it was a herculean effort not to. But Cricket didn't see the harm in trying.

He closed his eyes, taking a deep inhale that itched a little at his throat, and focused on the gentle hum of his internal magic. Another deep breath, and he followed the flow of it through his body.

It stopped at a spot somewhere in his sternum, tucked away behind his ribs, where it swirled around something. A tiny glowing orb.

"There you are," he murmured to himself in delight, and poured what residual magic he could find lingering in his body into it.

When that was spent, leaving Cricket panting, he reached into the stones below him, and pulled from them, drawing magic straight from the source—the earth—and feeding it to the orb as well.

He would be ready.

When an opportunity arose, he would be ready.

CHAPTER 42

The capital of Lunette lay sprawled out before them —a buzzing hive of life, the center of Cricket's heart —but Takayoshi only had eyes for a single tree. It was the one he had helped Cricket climb all of those years ago. The first time he had seen the color green. The leaves of the tree still clinging to their hue even as autumn rolled around. It was beautiful, and he remembered thinking idly that if he could paint, he might like to try his hand at capturing the image of the young prince in his midnight blue tunic, hidden amongst the branches.

Strange, how the memories were coming for him now. He spent the last five years rushing, racing, fighting to find answers and get back to Cricket, and now that his prince was within reach, all Takayoshi could do was remember how things had been once upon a time. How they had gone from resentful teammates to friends in a few short weeks.

It brought a smile to his face to think about the first time they met, that day in the inn. How Cricket looked then, all gangly limbs, and eyes so dark Takayoshi would swear he could see stars in their depths, sparkling to life. He remembered thinking how ridiculous it was that he could be destined for someone so hapless, annoying, silly. But even then, it had taken all of a few moments for Cricket to capture him entirely. As soon as that dimpled smile crossed his lips, and his eyes twinkled. . .

Well, Takayoshi did not stand a chance, even with the knowledge of his own curse hanging over his head. Even when Cricket nearly tipped from his chair and made an absolute fool of himself in the next breath.

The tree was just gray now. Gray, and dull, and lifeless. Devoid of any of its green leaves because of the season, but also devoid of any of its color because of its lack of a prince hanging from the branches. Takayoshi's palms itched, fingers twitching, the desire to carve his name into the trunk, to leave some lasting proof that he had been there with Cricket, an ache under his skin.

Selene, he was losing his mind with the waiting.

They decided to approach the capital at dusk, when the curfew would chase all of the innocent civilians into their homes, and leave the streets empty enough for them to march right up to the castle. He did not particularly care for the idea of taking the fight to Sunil in that way, of giving the unruly tyrant the unfair advantage of home territory. But it would give them the advantage of surprise, and Anstice assured him that was the better hand to have. Besides, if it meant they could back Sunil into a corner, and prevent him from escaping, Takayoshi would do it. He wanted to ensure that when this was over, it was *really* over.

"Someone's coming," Ignacia growled, her voice dragging him from his revery. He did not know when she had joined him where he stood looking at the tree.

"One of ours?" Takayoshi asked, his gaze flicking from the gray bark to the path up the hill that cut through the scraggly undergrowth still clinging to the frozen ground. They had chosen this hill not just because there was history there, memories clinging to the trees, but because it was a good vantage point. No one could sneak up on them.

"Sunil's." Anstice moved up to his other side, her keen eyes narrowed on the approaching figure. It was hard to tell if they were man or woman, soldier or civilian, armed or not. But Takayoshi did not suppose any of those things mattered. The person would be wholly outnumbered up there on the hill, so whatever Sunil's plan, it would not work. "I believe they're just bringing a message."

"How can you tell?" Ignacia leaned forward, trying to see what Anstice saw.

Takayoshi was not sure how Anstice knew that either, but he would take her word for it. He learned over the last few days that it was better to not question the information Anstice provided. Whatever innate magic or skill she had to find these things out, she was not about to share it with anyone. She would make a formidable queen's consort, and something about that thought settled Takayoshi, knowing that his sister would be safe in Anstice's hands.

Anstice tilted her head to one side, her lips pursed a little as she flipped a fan between her fingers. It seemed a frivolous motion, idle and silly, but Takayoshi knew better now. Had seen how Anstice could use that fan to cut a man down many times over during their training. Anstice was not a woman to be trifled with.

After a moment of thought, Anstice said, "There's just one of them. Not much of a force if this is meant to be an attack. No?"

Ignacia huffed, seeming annoyed that she had not thought of that. "No. I suppose not. Should we go down and meet them?"

Takayoshi pursed his lips, considering, then lifted his

chin. "Yes. I think so. We do not want Sunil to know exactly what our forces look like."

"You should go, Yoshi. Take Claudia for back up." Anstice hummed her agreement. "It would be better if Sunil not know that Iggy and I have joined your small army. He'd begin to wonder why."

"We don't want that." Ignacia sneered, and Takayoshi was not sure if it was because Anstice had out-maneuvered her strategically, again, or if it was because of how much Sunil disgusted her. He should likely do something to try to bridge the rift between the sisters. It was what Cricket would have done. But he was not really capable of such a thing.

"No. We don't." A chill ran up Takayoshi's spine at Anstice's icy tone. He was glad to not be on the receiving end of their ire, Cricket's sisters were terrifying. No wonder he had been allowed to be frivolous and silly growing up, with family like Ignacia and Anstice.

"Claudia." Takayoshi turned back toward the small army at their back. Claudia was ready, and waiting, her sword strapped to her hip. "Where is Leo?"

Claudia tilted her head back, and when Takayoshi followed her gaze, he found Leo perched in another of the trees, bow at the ready. When he lowered his head to raise his brows at her, she said, "Just in case."

"Clever girl," Ignacia murmured with a fondness that bordered on embarrassing, causing Claudia to duck her head, effectively hiding her face.

"You two should get a move on, if you're going to cut them off before they crest the hill." Anstice was still looking at the approaching messenger, but Takayoshi could hear something in her voice he could not identify. Something soft, and kind. Like she hated to break up whatever was happening between Ignacia and Claudia, but ultimately felt she had no other choice.

When Claudia lifted her head again, her eyes had narrowed behind her spectacles, her jaw set. She was ready for a fight. Takayoshi hoped there would not be one, but he supposed it was best to be prepared for the possibility. With a tilt of his head, he beckoned Claudia forward and they started down the hill to meet the messenger.

"You need not go any further," Takayoshi said, his voice only loud enough for the messenger to hear where they stopped a few feet away.

"I'm unarmed." The messenger swept their cloak back to reveal the lack of weapons belted to their waist. Not that it meant anything, Takayoshi had learned that the magic humming in a person's veins could be weapon enough.

Although, as he allowed his own magic to reach out through the air, to gain a sense of the messenger's capabilities, he felt nothing in return. This person did not possess the magic required to so much as rustle the hairs on Takayoshi's head, much less cause any real damage.

With his chin tilted back a little—a challenge—Takayoshi asked, "what have you come for?"

He felt more than heard Claudia move at his side, as attuned to her movements and the magic humming through her as he was. She did not trust this situation, and that was likely for the best. One of them needed to be on high alert, and it could not be him. If he were to move the wrong way, the messenger might think they meant to attack them, and Takayoshi may never get whatever message it was Sunil meant to send.

"I come bringing a deal," the messenger cleared their throat, awkwardly shifting from foot to foot as if this whole situation made them very uncomfortable, or they expected a horrible reaction to whatever news they came bearing. It was *that*, that made the hair on the back of Takayoshi's neck stand on end, the fire rise in his veins in defense.

"What sort of deal?" Claudia shouted over his shoulder when Takayoshi had obviously been silent too long, making the messenger more nervous than before.

"The phoenix for the dragon," they said, and flinched back at whatever expression they must have seen flicker across Claudia's face. It was likely murderous, if Takayoshi knew anything of his friend. Not that he could blame her, the idea that Sunil thought Takayoshi would simply hand himself over to save Cricket was– Well. It perhaps was not as completely ludicrous as it should have been. After all, Takayoshi's love was going to kill him one day, was it not? Why not make that day today? Why not make it before the curse could take Cricket from him?

"That's insanity! We won't be–"

Takayoshi waved his hand at Claudia, silencing her before she could finish her refusal. "When will this exchange take place?"

"Dusk," the messenger said, swallowing around some other words they looked as if they wanted to say. Perhaps a warning. Perhaps they meant to tell Takayoshi that Sunil had chosen this time because Sunil was under the assumption that Takayoshi would be at his weakest then. The pale light of the sun, and what little power it might be able to give him, tucked away for the evening as the moon rose high in the sky. It was a false assumption. A fool-hardy thing to do. But then, Sunil did not know that Takayoshi had learned long ago how to channel his power from the moon as well. He did not know that over the last handful of years Takayoshi had been honing his skill, and the new power he was gifted with thanks to his love of Cricket.

"Very well." Takayoshi dipped his head, hoping that this messenger, like so many others, would not notice the subtle uptick of his lips at the corners.

Claudia's boots made a faint creaking sound beside him, and he could just see her posture relaxing out of the corner of his eye.

With a silent prayer to Selene that the messenger would misread her shifting for upset, Takayoshi returned his attention to the person before them. "Where?"

"His Highness"—Takayoshi tried not to snarl at the calling of Sunil by Cricket's title, but it was a near thing —"will meet you outside the gate to the capital. You are to come alone."

"And what will he do if I do not?" Lifting one brow, Takayoshi tilted his head just the slightest in further challenge. He could not imagine what leverage Sunil thought he had to keep Takayoshi from bringing his army.

The messenger lifted their gaze from where it had fallen to their boots, their face grim as they met Takayoshi's eyes. "Then His Highness will kill the dragon."

Clenching his jaw against the swooping of his stomach, Takayoshi took a deep inhale from his nose. "I will be there."

With a stumbling bow, the messenger turned on their heel and started the return trip to the capital.

Claudia waited until they were out of earshot before stepping in front of Takayoshi to round on him, metaphorically and physically. "You're not doing this alone."

"There is not a choice." He swallowed around a still squirming stomach, hating himself for letting this happen. Cricket should never have been allowed to leave Helio, and turn himself over to Sunil's mercy.

Claudia opened her mouth as if to argue further, but Takayoshi held up a hand to silence her.

"But you will not be far behind."

She tilted her head, a smile flickering over her lips. "No, we will not."

"Come. Let us tell the others what we have heard." Turning on his heel, Takayoshi led her back up the hill toward where the rest of his army waited, pleased with himself.

Sunil had signed his own death warrant.

CHAPTER 43

What started as a tiny ball of light no bigger than his thumbnail, grew exponentially in the time it took for Sunil to come for him again, determined to prove him wrong even in the end.

It was now about the size of a small apple, sitting lodged behind his sternum. Cricket hadn't thought he would feel it there. It wasn't a physical thing, right? But he did. It sat heavy beneath his ribs, threatening to weigh his torso down to the cold stone floors. A heavy core, humming with the magic he collected from every cell of his being, and packed together like a snowball. It was cold too. A lump of ice, that seemed to make him neither chilled nor shivery. Strange.

It spun, and pulsed, and beat like a second heart. Shooting magic through him to soothe the ache at the back of his throat. To nullify the stiffness from being crouched in the middle of a cell for so long. And with all of that comfort, came the memories.

Giggling, and freezing, making snow angels with Anstice and Ignacia.

Father's laughter, rumbling low and content, when Cricket came in trailing mud from the rabbit pin.

Yoshi's expression when they first met. At the time he thought Yoshi was annoyed with him, stoic, and put off by Cricket's too-loud Cricketness. But after learning more about Yoshi, after spending months together, Cricket saw the interaction in a new light. Yoshi wasn't annoyed, he was stunned. Cricket still didn't know exactly what that meant, but he thought perhaps it was a good sign. And even if it wasn't, he was going to tell himself it was, because he was likely going to die soon anyway. What would a lie told to only himself matter?

Perhaps the globe of magic was trying to remind him of why he was fighting, what he had to hold on for. Or maybe this is just what happened before a person died. Their life flashing before their eyes, as it were. Cricket didn't know. What he did know was that finally, they reached his most recent memories.

Many of the last few years had been unhappy ones. A struggle, almost every day. With Father's failing health. With the borders of Lunette, and Sunil's invasion. Even, with himself. His mind slipping down a slope that there seemed no way back up from. But there had been one bright spot. One kernel of joy that made things easier.

Becka.

His little girl. The only thing that mattered, in the end.

He remembered finding her, cowering, and shivering under a white cloak. He remembered thinking that he had been destined to find her, just as his own father had been destined to find him in the woods. He remembered thinking it strange that the white cloak had the smell of sandalwood— a scent he'd come to associate with Yoshi—clinging to it, even with all the smoke in the air. And he remembered thinking. . .

Yoshi would approve of this. He would want me to save this little girl. So he had. And it brought him so much comfort and joy in the years to come. Even as he floundered with the idea of being a father.

It was Becka's smile he was thinking of when the creak of the dungeon door told him he was no longer alone. The apple-sized globe sitting behind his sternum gave a little pulse.

"Wake up," Sunil growled, kicking the cage bars hard enough to send the vibrations through Cricket's already aching head. His body had grown weaker. He hadn't realized it was happening as he pushed every bit of magic he possessed into a single place, but it had. The ringing of his ears, and swimming of his head was proof of that.

With a groan, Cricket said, "I wouldn't do that if I were you."

A warning that Sunil did not heed as he kicked the bars again, and said "Do what? This?" The ringing of the hard soles of his boots added to the noise in Cricket's ears.

Not yet, a voice whispered in the back of Cricket's mind that did not sound like his own. *It's not time yet. You'll know when it is.*

Under normal circumstances, he may not have listened to a disembodied voice. He would have shrugged it off as yet another sign that he was losing his mind with all of this. But these were not normal circumstances. And the voice made some small measure of sense. He was still trapped, surrounded. He hadn't opened his eyes yet, but when he reached out with his magic, he sensed the other men that joined him and Sunil in the dungeons. No doubt all of them had their weapons trained on the dragon, lest it decide to go on a rampage.

Foolish mortals, the voice scoffed, and Cricket couldn't help but agree.

Sunil clicked his tongue, the sound a blade of disapproval

that once upon a time would have cut Cricket to the quick and left him bleeding on the stones. But Cricket wasn't that boy anymore, desperate and aching for his uncle's approval. Sunil wasn't his *uncle* anymore. And Yue Sunil, had to die.

"I don't have time for this." Sunil sounded annoyed, exasperated. "Get him out of there. We have a meeting to get to."

"With whom?" He was sure Sunil wouldn't answer. Because it didn't matter to Sunil if Cricket knew what was going on. He was a prisoner, a hostage, an *experiment*, the throb at the end of his tail reminded him.

"Stop standing around looking terrified, get him up!" The bark made Cricket wince, Sunil's voice too loud and high for his sensitive ears.

A loud squeal accompanied the opening of the cell door that made Cricket's head pound so hard he wanted to raise his paws and cover his ears. He couldn't. He didn't have the energy to even lift them.

"What's wrong with it?" one of the men asked, his voice a low, disgusted rumble. Someone poked Cricket in the hip with the point of their sword, the sharpness of it not breaking through his scales to the skin underneath.

At least some of my defenses are still working.

"Who cares? Let's just get this over with," another replied, and Cricket could see the shape of a person coming around his head through the thin membrane of his first eyelid. They were moving slowly, as if afraid of the beast before them snapping its great jaws and swallowing them whole. A legitimate fear, Cricket supposed. But he was much too tired to bother with any such thing. Maybe if he just—

Don't go back to sleep. He needs you, the voice hissed in his ear, uncaring of the men that surrounded them.

He who? he responded, not really expecting the voice to answer, because why would it? It was just a manifestation of his own fractured psyche. He was going insane, and this was just more proof—talking back to a voice in his head. Maybe he'd die before he could completely lose himself to whatever this was clawing at the inside of his mind, threatening to make a home for itself there.

Takayoshi, was all the voice said, and that was enough to snap Cricket to attention.

A new iron cuff was clamped around his neck, replacing the one that kept him chained to the floor before his outburst, but he only felt the weight of it. Where the iron burned before, cutting into his scales, and the thin skin underneath them, this did nothing. It sat on his neck like a bangle. Cool, and innocuous. Strange.

The little globe at his core gave another pulse. Comforting in the face of what Cricket was sure would be his death.

"Come along, *nephew*," Dripped like venom from Sunil's tongue.

It was interesting how things shifted. How being pushed too far severed the relationship between himself and a man he had long considered family. Maybe one day, he would regret what was to come. Would look back on this moment and wish he made a different choice, and let Sunil live. But as things stood, Cricket couldn't see any other way out of it.

"Did you hear me? Move!"

Something thwacked his flank, sending a dull, stinging pain up through Cricket's body. Cricket grunted.

"I'd like to, Sunil. Believe me I would. But I seem to be rather . . . tied up." Cricket snorted at his own joke, then winced when he felt one of Sunil's men hit the infected end of his tail. "All right. All right. I'll get up."

Rolling his eyes, Cricket rose to his paws. He swallowed around the rise of bile, and itch of petals in the back of his throat. Was the room spinning or was that just him? Probably just him considering none of the guards that surrounded him were stumbling across the tilting floor like he wanted to.

"Well. I'm up. Now what?" He swung his head to narrow his gaze on Sunil who didn't look at all impressed by what he was seeing. Cricket wasn't sure what he expected. Torture, and a lack of food, water, and sunshine would do that to a person, even a dragon-shaped person.

"Now, we head off to meet your Helion prince." There was a smugness to Sunil's voice that Cricket could not wait to smack off his face.

Not long now, the voice said in the back of his head, soothing and soft. A promise—a vow—that settled his churning stomach.

"How did you get Yoshi to agree to meet with you?" Cricket asked, tone forcibly casual. No one seemed to notice that he was acting. Or that the dizziness and weakness that made him so malleable when they first entered his cell, was slowly fading. He was letting them drag him through the double doors at the top of the stairs, and the castle. Purposefully dragging his feet to make them think he was still weak, even as another pulse of power emanated from the softly glowing ball at his core, gathering magic as they walked the halls of *his* castle.

Sunil turned to look at Cricket, a tense blur in Cricket's peripheral vision. Good. Tense people made mistakes.

"He hates you, you know." Cricket snickered, his eyes flicking to Sunil then back to the corridor in front of them. The castle looked so different from how he'd left it. Colder. Emptier. Lonelier. Is this the kind of king Sunil wanted to be? One who ruled by force instead of loyalty? Disgusting.

"I hardly care what a foolish—"

"He's not *foolish*." A soft growl rumbled at the back of Cricket's throat. Yoshi was anything but foolish. Impulsive, maybe. A little brash at times, sure. But never foolish.

"Anyone who would willingly give up their crown is a–"

"Is wise." A cutting glare narrowed Cricket's eyes, puffs of cold air leaving his nostrils, threatening to turn the corridor into an ice rink.

Sunil scoffed, pressing forward to get away from Cricket and the chill that had run up his arms, lifting hairs in its wake. "You two deserve each other."

Cricket was sure that was meant as an insult, but all Cricket felt at those words was a fuzzy kind of warmth low in his gut, threatening to either send the snowdrops into full bloom, or burn them away. He wasn't sure.

That warmth escaped him as he was dragged through the vacant streets of the capital. It was silent. An emptiness lingering in the air. How many of his people were even still there? How many still believed in him? He wouldn't blame them if they had abandoned all hope that their king would save them. If they left Lunette in favor of a kingdom more able to protect them.

Those thoughts, too, were stolen away from him, along with his breath when the gates to the capital opened onto the wide, frozen field beyond, and Cricket saw the singular white figure in the distance.

Yoshi.

Alone.

CHAPTER 44

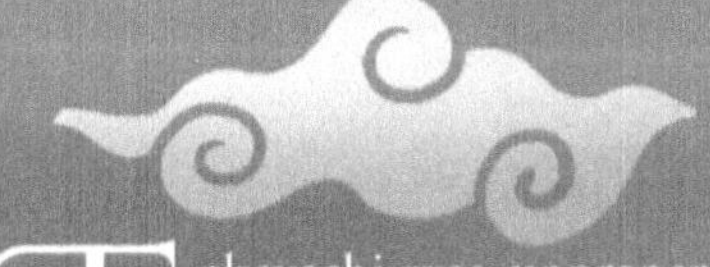

Takayoshi was unprepared for the sight of Cricket held by sword point before him. Not because he had not expected Cricket to be in danger—that seemed a given—but because he was beginning to wonder how he had missed Cricket's curse for so long. Especially when it was so clearly evident to him now.

Cricket's midnight scales had grown pale, and lost their luster, looking more a dusty gray—a color Takayoshi did not think he would ever associate with the vibrant young man he had grown to love—than the deep blue of a night sky. And his eyes, though open, were heavily lidded, and seemed to be moving listlessly as he took in the scene before him.

Then there was his head, which he had not yet lifted to meet Takayoshi's gaze, and Takayoshi could not tell if it was because he did not have the energy to do so, because it would hurt to do so, or if there was another reason. He sent up a silent prayer to Selene that there was another reason—that perhaps Cricket had a plan—that was cut short by a cold, cutting laugh.

Sunil smiled cruelly, his lips turned up at the corners, and practically splitting his face in two. "Well. Well. Well. It looks like you're as foolish as I thought."

With one raised brow, Takayoshi narrowed his gaze on Sunil. Did he think that Takyoshi had walked into a trap without a backup plan? Sunil must think very highly of himself for him to believe that he, Takayoshi, and all of the others, were fooled. It almost made Takayoshi want to laugh, if the situation were not so heavy perhaps, he would have, because he learned long ago that the person who thought themselves the smartest in the room was often the least intelligent. And Sunil had shown all of his cards.

Continued to show them as some of his men broke off from the main contingent to circle around Takayoshi. It would not be long before they blocked him in, cut him off from his own people. That was fine, they planned for that. Ignacia said it was what Sunil would do.

If Sunil had been half as clever as he thought he was, he would not have brought Cricket along at all. He would have disguised something or someone else as the dragon. But that was not the case, as when Takayoshi looked at the dragon, he could see the blue of his scales and the fur that clung to him. It may be duller than it had ever been, but the colors were there. And they bled over into the men holding him at sword point.

"Foolish," Takayoshi murmured to himself, resisting the urge to scoff.

"Excuse me?" Sunil lifted his chin, his face darkening with color—red, probably, but he was standing far enough away from Cricket that Takayoshi could not tell. Not that it mattered much to Takayoshi. He would be happy enough never knowing what color Sunill's eyes were.

With a deep inhale to hide the tremor of annoyance in his voice, Takayoshi said, "You agreed to a trade—"

"What?" Cricket's head flew up, his eyes suddenly wide

open, their color swirling and twisting in a way Takayoshi had never noticed before. Speckled with gold, as if stars were blinking to life inside of them. There was a sharp jolt in Takayoshi's sternum, the fire in his veins threatening to set him alight at the sight.

"So, you must release Cricket," Takayoshi continued, ignoring the way his heart pounded behind his rib cage.

Cricket was looking at him with the kind of wide-eyed incredulity that Takayoshi had grown to find so charming. That same expression accompanied any decision Takayoshi made that Cricket did not agree with. Any decision he planned to argue against. Funny how Takayoshi had grown to love that as well. He enjoyed that they did not agree on everything, saw the benefit in differing opinions. Cricket seemed the type to feel the same.

"That was our agreement, my life for his."

"*No.*" The word left Cricket like a sad, broken thing. Like it scraped his throat raw to get it out.

Takayoshi wished he could provide some comfort in that moment. Tell Cricket about his friends hiding behind the rocks at the base of the hill. That may not bring Cricket much comfort, now that he thought of it, because the distance they would have to travel to save him was quite far, and Sunil would see them coming. It was not ideal. But they did what they could without entering the city and drawing attention to themselves.

"And you thought you would just come out here, and what? *Make me?*" Sunil tilted his head. He had not taken his gaze off of Takayoshi, the greed lining it making the hair and feathers on Takayoshi's arms stand on end. He was not fool enough to think Sunil wanted him exclusively as a bargaining chip with Helio. Although, that would be an added side benefit.

"The phoenix for the dragon. That is what your

messenger said." Takayoshi's hand went to the sword at his hip but brushed only air.

Leo had been right; he should not have left his sword behind. Takayoshi would not tell Leo that, no one liked a smug Leo.

"Are you saying you wish to go back on your word, Sunil?"

"I never promised—"

"So, you *are* going back on your word," Takayoshi tilted his chin up to look down his nose at Sunil. "What kind of king cannot be trusted to keep their word?"

"You insolent child." Sunil's face changed color again, going a little darker. How long would it be before even Takayoshi could tell what shade of red it was?

With a quick flick of his gaze, Takayoshi saw Cricket watching the conversation with rapt attention, his mouth hanging agape.

"Seize him."

The men who circled Takayoshi, boxed him in, lunged forward, grabbing his arms. Takayoshi's eyes flicked to Cricket's again, and he tried to say without words for Cricket to remain still. For him to wait for his chance. But Cricket was breathing heavily, his shoulders heaving with it, and the light in his eyes had begun to spin at a dizzying rate. He was still held by too many men. Still trapped. They needed a distraction.

Whatever Cricket saw on Takayoshi's face, he dipped his head in a nod as if he understood. Takayoshi only hoped what he understood was what Takayoshi meant for him to read, otherwise this would all go to pot.

Cold seeped through the knees of his trousers where the men pushed him to the ground, making them ache. But Takayoshi did not lower his gaze, he kept his chin high as Sunil approached, spinning a dagger between his fingers threateningly.

Takayoshi scoffed, rolling his eyes. "Is that meant to frighten me?"

"It ought to!" Sunil's lips curled away from his teeth in a snarl that was not anywhere near as impressive as Cricket's tended to be—even when he was in his elven form.

Perhaps because Takayoshi knew Cricket had the power, and the will to back up such a threat. Yue Sunil was a child, the younger brother of the ruler, playing at the crown where Cricket had never had to pretend at the role, he was a king. Born of the goddess Selene and sent to their world to protect and care for her people. It was in his blood. Oh, how Takayoshi ached to tell him so. To dismiss all of Cricket's doubts, and insecurities. There would be time for that when all of this was over, Takayoshi was sure of it.

"Are you listening to me *boy*?" Rage simmered too loudly in Sunil's voice. The fury in his tone so much less terrifying than the coldness that Cricket exuded when he was truly angry.

"No. I am not." Takyoshi's lips twitched into a sly grin the likes of which he was sure had never graced his face before. He could practically feel the magic humming in the earth beneath him as Ignacia and Anstice prepared an attack. Sunil took another step forward, readying the blade. Just another step or two and Sunil would be within reach, leaving him defenseless to Takayoshi's fire. Ignacia and Anstice would wait for his signal, they agreed to that in spite of themselves, because Takayoshi wanted to look in Sunil's eyes as he realized his mistake.

"You- You- You insolent, fool-hardy," Sunil pressed the blade to Takayoshi's throat, drawing a soft hiss when he felt blood well up around it, "*child*! You two really do deserve each other, don't you?"

"I like to think so." The sly grin crawled further up his face, crinkling his eyes. He could not seem to help it, faced with Sunil's ire, and the ragged stink of his breath on his cheek, Takayoshi found himself amused. Perhaps this is why Cricket enjoyed pestering people so much, it was deeply satisfying.

"I should bleed you dry and make him watch." Sunil spat, spittle splashing against Takayoshi's cheek.

He lifted a hand to wipe it away, paying no heed to the startled guards around him who suddenly found themselves unable to restrain him. Oh, how foolish these men were, thinking they could stop a phoenix in its tracks.

Did they not know that he was a force of nature?

That he was a wildfire?

Would stop at nothing to see his prince safe?

Let them all burn.

The fire sang through his veins, licking at his fingertips in a threat that made the men holding him nervous. They would have taken a step back, very likely, if they were not afraid of Sunil as well.

Such a tough choice, who is more threatening?

I am.

"I, for one," Takayoshi said, tone conversational as he leaned into the bite of the blade at his throat. What was a little blood on the ground when he and his people were soon to soak the earth in red? "would like to see you try."

After that, three things happened all at once.

Sunil snarled, the dagger cutting deeper, too close to the artery.

Something moved out of the corner of Takayoshi's eyes.

And the air was rent with a roar so loud that it made Takayoshi's ears ring.

CHAPTER 45

Blood dripped from the point of Sunil's dagger down the blade of it and onto the ground beneath, soaking the frosted grass with red, the sound so loud it seemed to echo in Cricket's head.

That was all it took, a single, soft *drip*. And Cricket lost what little control he had gained over himself and his dragon.

The world was awash of crimson as he jerked from the hold of the men Sunil used to trap him. Knocking them to the ground hard enough that he swore he heard bones break.

A roar ripped from his lungs, clawing at his already battered throat, and threatening to bring up more of those beautiful blossoms. Then he lunged forward, paying no heed to the men who stood in his way as he ripped into Yue Sunil. Talons slicing through Sunil's tunic and into his back.

Sunil screamed, tearing the dagger away from Yoshi, but not before spilling more blood. It dribbled onto the ground, washing the frost away with its warmth, and making Yoshi crumple forward. Slamming his body into Sunil, Cricket knocked him out of the way and reached for Yoshi instead. Let Sunil come for him. Let him drive his tiny dagger into the hide of the dragon. Cricket had more important things to worry about.

"Yoshi. Yoshi, are you all right?" Cricket pressed his muzzle into Yoshi's torso, supporting his weight as Yoshi's hand flew to his neck, seeming to try to hold his wound closed.

The air was thick with the metallic scent of blood. So much of it. *Too* much of it. There was no reason Yoshi hadn't fully collapsed yet. A normal elf would be dead by now.

A hand Cricket hardly recognized anymore moved to try to staunch the bleeding.

But Yoshi just lifted his head with a wince at where the motion strained against his wound, fire blazing in his eyes. His next words left him in a hoarse rasp, but there was a smile twitching at the corners of his lips. "My Prince, you are no longer a dragon."

"I– What?" Cricket frowned, then looked down at himself. His body was clad in the remains of a soiled, ripped tunic, stained red with blood where Sunil had his men torture him, but Yoshi was right. He was a man, not a dragon. The core of power behind his sternum gave a hard thud, as if pleased with his sudden control. "Never mind that, let me see the wound. Let me see it."

Yoshi merely smiled wider, the expression crinkling his eyes in a way Cricket had never seen before, and Cricket's heart gave a traitorous lurch. Stars, how had he not noticed until the curse just how beautiful Yoshi was? He had always known, in an abstract kind of way, of course. But had never realized before how it could affect him personally. He'd been a fool.

"I am all right." Yoshi lifted his free hand to brush hair back from Cricket's face, his fingers gentle, reverent. Cricket leaned into the warmth of Yoshi's palm, soaking it up like he was drowning.

"You are not all right," Cricket mumbled, his voice all gravel.

The bleeding had slowed, he didn't know how, but when Yoshi let his fingers relax around the wound, no blood dribbled from between them as it had. Maybe this too was the magic of the phoenix, of a Celestial. Handy.

"No. I am not. But I will be." The soft brush of Yoshi's fingers lingered on Cricket's cheek, brushing down over the stubble that remained there from days, perhaps weeks, without shaving. "Now that you are here."

Cricket's eyes flew open, gaze flicking from where he had been watching the wound on Yoshi's neck close entirely, glowing softly as it did, to meet Yoshi's golden gaze. Yoshi's eyes were soft, warm, in a way Cricket never noticed before. Like he was trying to tell Cricket something with just his eyes alone, and Cricket thought he understood.

A thud in his chest the only reply he could give for a moment as his heart slammed against his ribs, almost as if it were trying to escape to be with Yoshi. To settle itself inside Yoshi where it would be safe, and warm.

His lips parted, to tell Yoshi something. Maybe that he loved him. That he had *always* loved him. Maybe that they should get married. Maybe that he was grateful that Yoshi had come for him. Or maybe it was to ask Yoshi if he could finally, *finally*, kiss him. But he never got to say any of those things because a moment later searing pain ripped through his shoulder, burning hot and fast through the nerves of his left arm.

Spinning, Cricket roared, the anger taking hold again, the golden ball of magic buried deep inside of him giving a furious jolt, and the dragon swooped down on the man standing between himself and Sunil. Knocking him aside with one giant paw. He landed a few feet from Sunil, ducking his head to meet the man's eyes, frost licking at the ground from his breath.

Sunil blinked, once, then turned to flee.

Cricket watched him go, a smirk quirking up the corners of his lips at the mere thought that Sunil would run from him. He could run, but he could not hide. Cricket would find him. And when he did . . .

There was a loud slam as Sunil ordered the gates to the capital shut, perhaps thinking they would slow Cricket down.

Chuckling, Cricket focused on that kernel of energy at his core, calling on the magic that surrounded them, in spite of the collar still heavy around his neck. The air turned colder, its currents lifting him up, leaving the frozen earth behind, preparing to push forward after Sunil. To break down the gates and chase Sunil though the streets, consequences be damned.

"My Prince!" Yoshi's voice broke Cricket's focus, making him spin to see what could bring on such a distressed tone from the stoic white knight. When he turned, he found the field, previously barren, ripped open anew as corpses climbed from the ground.

"The old goat really thought of everything," Cricket chuckled to himself, rolling his eyes heavenward in silent prayer. He hoped Selene would watch over them, keep them safe. But he didn't have time for a proper request as a moment later Yoshi was surrounded by corpses, not even his fire able to rip through them all.

With one last look to the closed capital gates Sunil hid behind, Cricket let out a huff, and reeled around to throw himself into the battle ahead.

He lost track of himself, and Yoshi after that as more bodies joined the fray. He thought he saw Claudia, Leo, and maybe the red hair of Ignacia at one point, but he couldn't be certain. All he could know for sure was that the forces Yoshi brought with him were struggling against the spirits, unable to cut them down properly.

Darkness lingered at the edges of his vision, his blocked airway becoming increasingly a problem. He was going to die out there, whether from suffocation or from an angry spirit was yet to be seen.

Every spirit they felled two more took its place, ripping from the ground, and joining the fray. How many of his own people had Sunil killed to make his army? How long had it taken him to bury them so he could launch this attack? Cricket didn't know, and he didn't think he really wanted to find out. It made him sick just thinking of it.

Tearing into another of the spirits that surrounded Yoshi, he finally made it to the knight's side.

With a huff of a laugh, Yoshi tilted his head at him, a little smile curling up the corners of his lips, hardly there if Cricket weren't looking for it, but enough to send Cricket's heart skittering in his chest. "Have you come to save me?"

"Something like that." Cricket smirked back, touching down beside him on his booted feet, and scooping up a fallen sword from one of Sunil's men. It may not be as effective as his talons, but he wanted a moment, just one moment, to talk to Yoshi before this was all through. Before the breathless suffocating feeling of his love for Yoshi made him lose consciousness.

"I think I should tell you something, before–" He broke off, swallowing thickly around the creepy crawling of roots and stems up his throat.

"I think we ought to get married," Yoshi said, not waiting for Cricket to finish.

"I'm sorry. What?" Cricket choked and spun to stop the swipe of a dirt covered hand as one of the spirits lunged for him. Backing into Yoshi, he tried not to notice how the warmth of Yoshi's back against his settled something inside of him, making the ache of the flowers blooming in his lungs and esophagus ease.

"I said, I think we ought to get married," Yoshi repeated, his tone calm, and steady.

Cricket wished he could see his face, to know what he was feeling, because he couldn't tell by his tone. But there were too many of the spirits surrounding them, there was no time for that.

"And why's that?" Cricket forced out a little chuckle, hoping Yoshi wouldn't hear it for the nervous tick that it was. Yoshi was hitting too close to home, and if he didn't mean what he said—if he didn't want it because he *loved* Cricket— Cricket didn't know what he would do. *Die, probably.* If the way his breath was turning into a harsh rasp was anything to go by.

Yoshi made a noise that sounded like a scoff, but it couldn't be a scoff because he was much too upright, and proper to scoff, wasn't he? Cricket was sure that he was. But when he turned his head to see Yoshi out of the corner of his eye, Yoshi was looking back at him, his lips pursed into an annoyed line. "Because I have been in love with you since the moment you knocked over my tea in Totchli."

"You *what*?!" Another cough ripped itself from Cricket's throat. Tears burned at the corners of his eyes as he bent over, retching up another set of blossoms. The petals fluttered away before they could hit the ground and be crushed under the spirit Cricket only just barely held back with his sword.

"Is that a no?" Yoshi frowned, turning back to swipe his sword straight through a spirit's torso, splattering the frozen ground in black, congealed blood.

"A no to what?" Cricket gasped for breath. The spots at the edge of his vision closing in. Stars. He was going to pass out.

"To my proposal. Do you– Do you not love me?" Confusion twisted Yoshi's tone into something that almost sounded hurt, and that was worse. That was *so* much worse. "I apologize I thought–"

"I do!" Cricket winced at the volume of his own voice echoing even above the sounds of battle around them. "Of course, I do. Of course, I love you. But. . ." And this was the bigger question, Cricket realized. "*You* love *me*?"

Something twinged in his chest, hopeful, and raw, as Cricket turned to look at Yoshi over his shoulder. Yoshi was beautifully disheveled, white-blond hair falling loose around his face, the cut on his neck a thin pink line that would likely leave a scar. *We would match.* But when Cricket's eyes finally drifted up to meet the golden gaze of Yoshi he was struck breathless again. Warmth spread through him, burning away the snowdrops, and letting Cricket take his first full breath in months.

"Are you truly asking me that?"

Cricket chuckled, nervous. "I suppose I am."

Yoshi rolled his eyes—actually, rolled his eyes!—and turned back to the battle at hand. "You have not answered yet."

"This is what you want?" Cricket had to ask, he had to. Because even if Yoshi did love him—a miracle amongst miracles—that did not mean they would marry. That did not mean they would be together. "To tie yourself to the demon king of Lunette?"

"You are not a demon." Yoshi grunted, felling another spirit, before holding up a hand to send a blast of flame through the group that surrounded them. It did little good, as a moment later more filled their place, like digging a hole in sand only for the tide to come through and sweep it away. "And yes, it is what I want."

"Are you sure?" Cricket cleared his throat, frowning when

he didn't feel the scrape of petals and roots. That would take some getting used to. "You better be really, *really* sure. Because–" he swallowed again, cutting down another spirit, his back pressing more firmly into Yoshi's as he practically shouted over the groans, and moans of the dead. "Because we may win this battle, and get my crown back, but this won't be the last."

An annoyed scoff accompanied Yoshi's next strike. He crouched behind Cricket, pressing his fingers into the ground, and lit the grass that surrounded them on fire. The flames licking at the toes of Cricket's boots, but not burning them, as if Yoshi were controlling it, telling it what to burn, and what to protect.

Then he spun, grabbed Cricket by the torn collars of his tunic, and crushed his lips to Cricket's, stealing his breath in a whole new way. Cricket swayed on his toes, pressing up into Yoshi's slightly taller frame, lips parting on a sigh as the sword fell from his fingers.

"Have I made myself clear enough?" Yoshi asked, his lips tilted up at one corner in a sly smile that made Cricket's skin tingle.

Cricket nodded dumbly, a breath leaving him, then there was a wrenching in his chest. A horrible tearing feeling that had him doubling over. Coughing. Choking. Retching. Worse than the blossoms, and the stems. Worse than anything he had ever felt.

He fell to his knees, the fire blazing hotter around him as Yoshi worked to protect them both while Cricket's eyes burned with tears, and something worked its way up his throat, almost lodging there and cutting off his airway if not for a harsh smack to his back from Yoshi.

A moment later, bile splattered the ground, along with a small, glowing, golden orb, not much bigger than a marble.

The core he had pushed his magic into for the last few days. The thing that kept him alive this long. The–

"Your pearl," Yoshi murmured, awe lining his tone. "That is your pearl. It is beautiful."

Cricket opened his mouth to say something snarky, probably tell Yoshi that it was strange how it was behind his ribs all along. But another wave of spirits broke through the flames, and he realized they didn't have time.

"We'll talk about this later," he said, scooping up the little glowing orb. It fit neatly into the palm of his hand and burned with the heat of a miniature sun. He tucked it into his pocket for safe keeping, grabbing the sword again. Before saying over his shoulder, "The answer is *yes* by the way" as he turned back to the battle, slicing through another spirit, a smile crawling up the corners of his lips that he couldn't control even if he wanted to. He didn't want to. Happiness sat a warmth in his bones, and he didn't think it'd ever leave him now that he had Yoshi.

"Yes?" Yoshi asked, almost disbelieving.

"Yes." Cricket laughed, and spun to press another kiss to Yoshi's lips, a quick brush but enough to send tingles all the way to his toes. "For luck," he murmured, then he leapt into the air, shifting into the dragon again so he could clear a path for them toward the gate of the capital.

CHAPTER 46

The world was a wash of color. Of reds, and browns, and the icy blue of a winter sky. Takayoshi had not thought color would be so. . . *overwhelming* after all these years. But as Cricket pulled back from the brief peck to his lips, Takayoshi found himself dizzy with the vibrancy of the world that surrounded him.

A world that would remain in color forevermore.

The browns. And the dusty greens. And the reds. So many new reds the likes of which he had not imagined when he had been a child, giving up his ability to see color for an impossible love. The glaring splash of crimson that was the fresh blood on the front of his tunic. The muddy brown burgundy that exposed all of the places Cricket had been injured during his time in captivity. The almost black puce color of the congealed substance coating his sword from the desecrated dead. It was all too much. Made bile rise in his throat. His stomach heaved to dispel its contents onto the frozen ground.

Standing up straight, Takayoshi wiped the sick from his mouth with the sleeve of his tunic, inhaling deeply to settle his stomach. It did little good as the smell of decay permeated the air so thickly it was practically a mist.

"You all right?" Leo grunted, throwing himself in front of a spirit that took a wild swing at Takayoshi's head, nearly knocking him to the ground.

Takayoshi sucked in another deep inhale, focused his gaze on the midnight blue dragon across the pale, and frozen battlefield, and nodded. Cricket was doing everything he could to tear through Sunil's army, to clear a path for them to the gate. Takayoshi should be with him. Helping. Fighting. But he was frozen. His feet anchored as he tried to take in all that surrounded him. For a moment, he almost wished he had not regained his ability to see color. The angry spirits that surrounded him had been grotesque enough in gray, but color made them doubly terrifying.

"Yoshi?" Leo asked again, his steps bringing him to Takayoshi's side. He bumped his shoulder against Takayoshi's, his deep brown hair—his hair was brown, not black how Takayoshi had always assumed—falling into his eyes. There was a growing stain of crimson on his right side where it looked like one of the undead army had gotten a good swipe at him. They would have to treat that, lest whatever cursed magic Sunil used to raise them infect Leo as well.

"I am all right," Takayoshi said after a moment that was probably too long, the torn and stained fabric enough to bring Takayoshi back to himself.

They were at war. And the enemy was winning. The hordes not stopping, not slowing. It seemed like Sunil had an unending source to fuel his war machine, and Takayoshi had to wonder how many of these creatures had once upon a time been Lunette citizens. The capital seemed strangely empty.

"We need your fire." Leo pressed in closer, his voice a shout above the groans and moans of the angry spirits.

"Ignacia and Anstice are doing what they can, but you and Cricket have the most experience with this."

Ignacia. Anstice. Takayoshi's gaze flew about the battle-field in search of them and found the pair sticking close to Claudia. Anstice's nine tails flicking out razor sharp like a fan whenever one of the spirits came close enough. While Ignacia had resorted to the use of her teeth, her qinlin head so much like Cricket's dragon muzzle.

"Fire would be faster." Another grunt left Leo as an angry spirit slammed into him with its shoulder, clearly trying to knock him to the ground where he would be more easy for them to attack. "Any day now!"

Takayoshi huffed a laugh at the exasperated tone, and dropped his sword before leaping into the air after Cricket. His wings spread wide, flames sizzling in the cold. It felt good to soar again. To let the wind lift him as it so rarely did in the days since they left Helio. Trying to keep a low profile had been a hindrance in more ways than one.

A caw left his throat, and Cricket turned in the air to look at him, his midnight eyes going wide in his scaled face.

"Come to join the fun?" Cricket asked, his voice light, and happy in a way Takayoshi had almost been certain he would never hear again. He ached to hear it from Cricket's own throat, not from the mental link that seemed to connect a Celestial to every other living thing. But this would have to do. Just for now. Just until they could defeat Sunil and finally settle things between them.

No. Not settle things. Things were settled, were they not? They were going to get married! Takayoshi's stomach swooped with joy, and his flames seemed to burn all the brighter for his happiness.

"I suppose I have," he murmured back, his veins burning with emotions that he could not even put names to yet. One day, he might be able to. One day in the distant future—for there would be a future, even Venus's curse could not part them now—when he had spent years with Cricket. When he had learned the shape of all that he felt for him. Maybe then Takayoshi would be able to name each individual feeling that passed through his body when Cricket stared back at him, his muzzle slightly agape in awe. But today was not that day, and he did not have time to try, as a moment later there was a loud roar from below and another sea of corpses flooded from the gates of the capital.

"There's our chance." Cricket's lips peeled back into a victorious grin, his beard fluttering in the breeze.

"The others—"

"We can't do much for them." With a shake of his head, Cricket turned back to look at Takayoshi, his eyes wide and pleading. "The only way to stop them from coming is to stop Sunil, he's the one controlling them."

"What if he is not?" Takayoshi did not think it would actually matter who was controlling them, Cricket was correct, if the leader was stopped then his men would flee, taking their undead army with them. They would not want to keep fighting for a cause that Sunil was the head of. Even if they still believed in it, they would want to leave, and regroup. It was their best course of action.

Takayoshi took a look over his shoulder at the field littered in bodies cut down by the magic of Ignacia and Anstice, and swallowed roughly. His friends were down there. Leo and Claudia were not able to defend themselves the way the Celestials were. And then there were all the other soldiers. He did not feel right leaving them behind.

"They'll be all right, Yoshi." Cricket murmured, his muzzle brushing at the side of Takayoshi's feathered neck, nudging him gently. "But the sooner we end this, the better for everyone. You trust me, don't you?"

"With my life," Takayoshi rasped, his fire burning

brighter, sizzling where it met the coldness of Cricket's ice. Then although it did not need saying, he said, "I love you."

"I love you too." Cricket's response was breathless, disbelieving.

Takayoshi could understand, he still was not sure it was real. If it were not for the world washed in red blood beneath them, he may not have believed it himself. Cricket loved him. Cricket wanted to *marry* him. They were going to—

"Come on. We need to finish this thing."

Right. They needed to get rid of Sunil before any of that could happen. When his gaze returned to Cricket, Cricket smiled, his beard quivering a little more in the breeze. He did not seem to need an answer from Takayoshi. He dipped his head, a knowing look in his eyes, and spun, expecting Takayoshi to follow.

And Takayoshi did.

The wind carried them through the gates of the capital, Takayoshi's fire blooming from his tail like flowers, catching on every dried husk that Sunil raised to protect him.

"Where is he? Where is he?" Cricket mumbled to himself, his head jerking this way and that as he searched for Sunil.

One would think that there would be a magical signature to follow, but the capital was steeped in the stagnant staleness of death magic. It was like the manor house all over again, and even when Takayoshi closed his eyes and reached out with his magic to feel for the source, there was nothing to find. It left his skin crawling, his feathers standing on end.

The streets of the capital were silent, barren, but for the shambling hungry spirits. Their shoes and feet shuffling against the cobbles of the capital streets. So unlike how the city was the last time he traveled through. It left something aching in Takayoshi's marrow, and he pressed closer to Cricket hoping to provide comfort for what he was sure would be that same ache at least doubled in the king of this land.

There would be so much to repair, so much to do, once this was all over. Where would they start? It left Takayoshi reeling, the color sapped from the streets, leaving it gray, and dull apart from the blood. So much life driven out, so much more lost.

It would take decades to rebuild all that was destroyed in the wake of Sunil's greed. All he could pray was that the people of Lunette would be willing to work with himself and Cricket until it was done. Until it was—

A *whoosh*, like a bug net through the air whizzed past Takayoshi's ears, and he jerked just in time to see the tightly woven web of magic close around him. Cricket had gotten ahead of him in his distraction, leaving them both unprotected, singled out. Foolish! He had been so *foolish*.

Electricity zinged from the fibers of the net, dragging him back down to the cobbles. Takayoshi wriggled, thrashed, his flames hissing and licking at the cold air. But nothing he did could stop his descent.

He hit the cobbles with a *thud*, the impact jolting his insides, and snapping something in his wing. Pain lanced up from the broken bone into the rest of his body, making him yelp, but it did not stop him from fighting. Nothing would.

The more Takayoshi struggled, the weaker he became. Darkness closed in around his vision until he let out a single, thready caw, before being dragged under entirely by whatever dark magic Sunil used.

CHAPTER 47

The pained caw was the only thing that pulled Cricket from his frantic searching. But as he turned to see the source of it, to find Yoshi, and make sure he was all right, he came up empty. The air where Yoshi had been drifting along behind Cricket was barren of the warmth, and fire of the phoenix.

Cricket's head jerked this way and that, searching, hoping, praying, he would find Yoshi before Sunil could do anything to him. But there was no sign of him. The streets of the capital empty but for Sunil's hordes. Cricket tried not to look too closely at any of them. He did not want to think about how many of his own people were lost to Sunil's greed. How many of them he would never see again. Were some the aunties who fussed over him in the market? Were some the grocers? Was one of them the man who sold him strawberries back before all of this began so long ago?

His world, his kingdom, would never be the same now that Sunil destroyed it.

"Looking for someone, nephew?" Sunil's voice echoed

through the empty streets, bouncing off walls, and cobbles barren of life. So much so Cricket could not tell where the voice was coming from.

He narrowed his gaze, hoping to catch some glimpse of Sunil's torn and bloodied tunic. It was purple, Cricket had noted prior to the beginning of all of this. And not just a normal shade of purple, it was a ridiculously ostentatious hue that one might see on a peacock. Silly when he had been planning to go into battle. Or maybe he hadn't been planning it. Maybe he thought Yoshi and Cricket would simply bow down to his will. He had really overestimated his power.

"You will live to regret the day you set foot back on Lunette soil, *Sunil*," Cricket called back, tone almost conversational. Maybe if he could keep Sunil talking, he could find him. Or maybe he could get him angry enough to expose himself.

"Will I?" Sunil asked, and Cricket was sure his voice was coming off to his right now. Likely closer to the castle. Maybe he thought if he got behind the castle walls, he would be safe. A solid theory, if the castle and the land beneath it had not already accepted Cricket as her king.

Cricket hummed softly, closed his eyes, and listened to the gentle buzz of the magic in the land surrounding him. His family's magic. His kingdom's magic. *His* magic.

Even if Sunil had been able to take the crown, he would never be Lunette's true king, and Cricket was willing to wager that if he hadn't returned to reclaim it, it would have revolted against Sunil at some point in the near future.

The pearl in his pocket pulsed gently, sending out a call, and the land answered, creating a trail for Cricket to follow to Sunil. A subtle tug at his chest, likely the call of Yoshi and his bond.

"Yes," Cricket said after what might have been too long. But if the snort of derision from Sunil was anything to go by, he was still listening. A snarl peeled Cricket's lips back from his teeth, vicious, and rabid. "But only just barely."

"Do you think you're funny?" Sunil's tone went high, and nasally, the same as it always did when he was looking down on someone. The same as it always did whenever he thought his nephew was being a fool. So many things had changed, but clearly, Sunil's attitude toward his only kin remained the same.

"I don't think I'm *not* funny." Cricket chuckled to himself, following the subtle tug in his chest. It grew stronger the closer he got to the castle. *Foolish, Sunil, very foolish.*

"Do not provoke me, child!" Sunil roared, and Cricket could imagine his face turning a vivid vermilion color, skipping several shades of red to reach it in seconds. His anger would be what undid him, Cricket knew. And Cricket would relish the victory. Relish knowing that after all of these years, after so much abuse, it had been Sunil's own greed and folly that brought him to ruin.

"Why not?" Tilting his head, Cricket approached the walls of the castle. Flying as low as he was, to hide his approach, he could not see over the walls, but he could feel the pulse of the magic emanating from it. The warmth of Yoshi's fire burning low, simmering.

Sunil had done something to him. Drained him of some of his power. But that was temporary, Cricket knew. Because the land would take care of them both. When all of this was through, Lunette would look after them, and they would look after Lunette in return. That was what good kings did.

"What does it matter?" Cricket continued, spite making his words biting, and hateful. "You're *nothing* to me," he spat. "Not even a man. You'll never be *half* the king Father was. I am. You'll always be this. A vapid, self-centered, waste of space. Do not waste my time, *uncle!*"

The wind pushed him upward, above the wall, so Cricket

could look down into the grounds of the castle. Sunil stood before a bird rendered flightless. Yoshi's left wing was twisted at an odd angle beneath the net, and his fire had been diminished to naught more than an ember. When Cricket searched his face, he found only slack, unconscious features, and rage soared through Cricket turning his own veins to ice.

Sunil lifted his head to meet Cricket's gaze, his lips peeled back in a sneer. "Or *what?*" he asked, reaching down to tangle his fingers in the net, and give it a hard yank. "Do you like this? Something I learned on my travels from a very good. . . friend."

Something jolted through it, and into Yoshi's lax form, making him shudder, and groan. His golden eyes opened, their depths murky, and unfocused as they fell upon Cricket.

"What will you do?"

"You shouldn't have done that," Cricket rasped, voice raked over frozen stones, grating, biting, a threat. His eyes narrowed on Sunil, trying to decide the best method to handle this without hurting Yoshi further.

"Done what?" Sunil laughed. There was a bright, viciousness to his gaze. Cutting. As if he thought he could stop Cricket with just one hard glance.

Cricket touched down on the lawn of the castle, his boots thudding gently. The widening of Sunil's eyes was enough to tell him that he had not been paying attention to the battle outside of his walls. That he holed himself up in the capital and hoped to hide away.

Cricket wondered, idly, if he had an escape plan, or if he simply thought his army of corpses would be enough to keep Cricket and his people away. He'd been wrong. Very *very* wrong. And now, he was about to find out just *how* wrong.

"Threatened my family." A smile crept across Cricket's face, not touching his eyes, showing off teeth still too-sharp to be elven. He raised one dark brow, and waited a beat, to see what Sunil would do. To see if he would cower and apologize.

But Sunil just lifted his chin, and reached for the net again, murmuring a spell under his breath that Cricket was sure would do irreparable harm to Yoshi, the choice made. Cricket had given him a chance to back down, to acknowledge the true king.

Sunil had chosen death.

Snarling, Cricket dropped to the ground—his hands smacked the frozen earth so hard it sent pins and needles up his wrists and arms—and pushed magic from his fingertips. The already cold ground turned frigid, freezing over with a thick sheet of glassy ice that spread from his hands toward Sunil at such a speed the man couldn't step out of the way even if he wanted to. It froze him to the spot, his feet stuck to the ground, crawled up his legs at such speeds it was amazing his heart was still beating. And only stopped when it reached his chest.

Sunil had but a moment to realize his mistake. A single breath for it to sink in how royally he had messed up, then Cricket shifted into the dragon again and hurled himself at Sunil. He slammed into the other man, throwing him into the castle wall opposite, making the entire structure shutter, and pebbles and dust fell around him.

Another roar left Cricket, before he flew across the dead grass toward Sunil as he struggled to stand.

Sunil produced a dagger from somewhere on his person, hissing a spell in a tongue Cricket recognized as Cytherean before thrusting the blade into Cricket's shoulder. But it did not stop him. Nothing would at that exact moment.

Snapping his jaws, Cricket pulled his paw back and swiped jagged talons at Sunil's middle, ripping through his clothes and his skin in one swoop.

Sunil let out a ragged gasp, half surprise, half pain, and

thrust the dagger into Cricket again. A bee sting compared to what Cricket was going to do to him.

"I'm not done with you yet!" Cricket's mouth opened wide, revealing sharpened teeth.

He watched the color drain from Sunil's face. Realization dawning that he was going to die, and there was nothing he could do to stop it. Then Cricket ripped into him again, his talons cutting through Sunil like a warm knife would butter, staining the ground in so much blood the dark red of it almost matched the crimson color that started all of this all those years ago.

Sunil slumped forward, he did not look like he was breathing anymore, but Cricket couldn't stop once he'd started. Not as images of his ruined kingdom ran through his head. Not as he remembered the stifled cry of Yoshi's pain. Not as the lowering of two coffins into the ground filtered through his head. He'd lost so many people. He'd seen so many hurt. And all because of this man. All because of this. . . this. . . this *bastard*! This *beast* who never loved him, and now never would.

"I'm not done with you," Cricket rasped, the sound more broken than anything he had said thus far.

"My Prince," a voice said from behind him, and Cricket only distantly recognized it as Yoshi. "That is enough," he murmured, soft and soothing as he reached to stop the next swipe of Cricket's talons that he only just realized were attached to hands instead of paws. "That is enough."

A sob ripped itself free of Cricket's throat, and he crumpled into Yoshi's arms, letting the other man hold him up, warm him from the inside. Pressing his face into Yoshi's soiled tunic he let himself cry, the first time since all of this began. For the young man he'd been five years ago. For the love his uncle had never shown him. For all of the people he lost along the way. For the kingdom that would need to be rebuilt, but would never be the same. For the daughter who would never know her grandfather.

For. . . *everything.*

CHAPTER 48

What should have been a loud, jovial celebration was anything but, and it left Takayoshi aching. Cricket deserved that kind of ending to the war between himself and Sunil. He deserved a hero's homecoming. But there was not much of a home to come back to, Takayoshi realized.

He looked around the dining room where some of the soldiers had managed to scrounge up enough food for a passable supper and realized that this was it. This was all that was left of the kingdom of Lunette's capital, because Sunil killed everyone else, turned them into hungry spirits to feed his war effort.

All that was left were the few soldiers Ignacia brought to Helio that returned with them, and fifty or so civilians they found hiding in one of the temples to Selene at the heart of the city. Takayoshi was unclear how they had gotten away from Sunil, and why he had not thought to search there, perhaps even Sunil was afraid of angering the goddess to that degree. Amusing, considering by that point Sunil had already done enough to invoke her wrath by hurting her son. But there was no accounting for sense in a man who was willing to kill his own people in an attempt to keep a stranglehold on his kingdom.

"Have you seen His Highness?" one of the survivors asked, her voice a soft tremor. Takayoshi thought she said her name was Charlotte, but he had so many introductions over the last few hours he could no longer be sure.

Cricket should have been there to help, but Anstice took one look at his still trembling, bloody hands, and sent him to his quarters to get cleaned up.

He had yet to return. Likely for the best.

"He is resting," Takayoshi said, bowing his head.

"Oh." She deflated, and Takayoshi got the sinking feeling that she had been hoping to meet the king to gossip monger about him. That would not do.

That would not do *at all*. He would have to speak to Claudia and Ignacia about handling that. None of them wanted the rumors Sunil started to continue to spread like a virus through Lunette. No. If Cricket was going to regain control of his kingdom, he would need for his people to stop thinking of him as some kind of demon.

"You should go and check on him, Yoshi." Ignacia moved to stand beside him, her gaze flicking to his out of the corner of her eye. She must have been thinking the same thing. "Take him a plate of food. I'm sure that final battle with the invader has worn on him."

*The invade*r. A term Anstice chose for Sunil, to illustrate what Sunil really was, a tyrant who had needed to be snuffed out. It would be a preferable narrative to the one Sunil and his people spread about Cricket being some kind of unholy monster seeking to bring Lunette to ruins.

"Yes. I am sure that it has." Takayoshi bowed his head to the woman again, then turned to bow to Ignacia as well, relieved for the excuse to escape the room of people. This was not where he excelled. It likely would not have been so bad if there were someone else he could cling to who would be willing to handle the socialization part for him. Atsuko perhaps. Or Cricket. He would prefer it to be Cricket.

When he turned to the table to grab a plate, Anstice already had one ready for him. Her chipped purple painted nails tapping lightly against the ceramic. Strange to know what color they were now. He wondered if Atsuko's matched. Or if perhaps she had chosen a color that was similar in tone, but different in hue. A deep blue, perhaps.

He shook himself and let Anstice press the plate into his hands with a murmured, "thank you."

Anstice stopped him, her hand on his wrist. She squeezed once, to draw his attention, and when he lifted his head to meet her brown eyes, she narrowed her gaze in an expression that could only be considered threatening. He had yet to sit down and speak to either of Cricket's sisters about their battlefield proposal.

"You will take care of my brother," Anstice said, more command than question.

"I will." A vow that sat heavy on his tongue, but once it left it Takayoshi felt his shoulders relax. It was the truth. He would take care of Cricket. And Cricket would take care of him in turn. It was what they promised each other, although not in so many words.

With a terse nod, Anstice released him, and Takayoshi strode from the hall out into the echoing corridors. Blood lingered in the air there, stale, and rancid from all the killing Sunil had done. They would have to air the place out, and even then, it would take months, perhaps longer, to return the castle to how it was when Cricket was a child, when Takayoshi first came there. Still, they were on their way, he reminded himself. One step at a time. And the first, the hardest, was done.

His knuckles rapping on the door sounded strangely hollow, and lonely in the empty hall. It would be so much better once Becka joined them in a few weeks. Her chirping voice would fill all of the empty spaces, Takayoshi was sure of it.

When no answer came, Takayoshi pushed in. "My Prince, I have brought–"

"Don't come in here!" Cricket shrieked, throwing himself behind the nearest piece of furniture that looked like it might hide him. It was a low four-shelf bookcase, and it did hide him for the most part. All except the antlers atop his head, which poked out. "You can't– I don't want anyone to see me like this."

"Like what?" Takayoshi asked, slipping in further so he could nudge the door closed behind him, and move to set the plate of food on the desk in the corner. It was a mess. The entire *room* was a mess. There were papers, and books strewn everywhere. Like in the last couple of hours since they took back the castle, Cricket had thrown himself into study instead of resting as he was specifically instructed to do.

"They haven't– I mean I lost– I mean–" Cricket's voice trembled, but slowly he came out from behind the edge of the bookshelf and Takayoshi got a better look at him.

The scales and antlers that had gone the moment he formed his pearl were back, leaving traces of his draconic nature on his skin like a rash. Takayoshi sucked in a breath, forcing himself not to show any emotion on his face lest Cricket see something that upset him. Not that Takayoshi had any bad feelings toward these markers of Cricket's Celestial origins, he did not, it was simply a surprise.

"You lost. . ." Takayoshi prompted, and when Cricket's shoulders hunched in more he continued, "what? You lost what?"

"I seem to have misplaced my pearl." Scuffing his socked

foot against the floor, Cricket looked up at Takayoshi through his lashes as if he expected Takayoshi to yell at him. He probably did. From what Takayoshi heard of Cricket's childhood within these walls, much of it had been spent with him being yelled at.

"Then we will find it. But first, you must eat." Takayoshi reached for Cricket's hands, taking them gently, and guiding him to sit at the desk. "There is much cleaning up to do. Very likely, you just dropped it somewhere. I will let Ignacia and Claudia know to keep an eye out for it. It is nothing to worry too much about."

Cricket took his fork, his fingers stiff, and unwieldy where he spent so long as a dragon. "What if we don't?" he asked, staring dismally down at his plate.

"Then we will think of something else." Brushing Cricket's hair back from his cheek, Takayoshi bent to press a kiss to it. "But you do not have to do this alone any longer. I am here."

A smile twitched at the corners of Cricket's lips, and he turned his head to look up at Takayoshi, his free hand lifting to take Takayoshi's pressing the backs of his fingers to his stubbled cheek. "I suppose that's true. Isn't it?"

"It is." Takaoyshi could not help the smile that overtook his face, crinkling his eyes, and stealing his breath at the soft look Cricket gave him. This was all he had ever wanted in his life. This was all he had ever desired. Was to be loved like this. But. . . "I should warn you, My Prince"—Cricket sat up straighter, preparing to receive bad news—"I am still very much cursed, as all of my family always has been. Until the sun and the moon become one."

"Oh well that's an easy fix," Cricket said, his smile growing mischievous.

Takayoshi blinked, confusion puckering his brow. "It is?"

"We just need to elope." Cricket grabbed a piece of paper

from underneath his plate to show it to Takayoshi. "Claudia said something about it to me before I left, and I got to thinking, what if the Lady Venus meant it metaphorically? Not the actual sun and moon. But the kingdom of the sun and moon. So all we need to do is elope, and your curse will be broken."

"It cannot be that simple."

"Only one way to find out." Cricket winked, stuffing the piece of paper into Takayoshi's hand for him to look over while Cricket applied himself to cleaning his plate.

"I suppose so," Takayoshi murmured. "We will have to get your mother's approval of course."

"My mother?" Cricket mumbled through a cheek full of food.

"The Lady Selene. We shall have to get her approval."

Cricket coughed, choking on a bite that he clearly had not chewed enough, and Takayoshi patted him on the back to dislodge it.

"Did you not know?"

"No, I didn't know!" Cricket huffed, voice strained. "Still, I suppose it makes sense." He hummed thoughtfully.

"It does. But for now, rest. We will deal with all of that when you are better."

"All right." Cricket let out a breath, leaning into Takayoshi's warmth like a flower seeking the sun. And a smile overtook Takayoshi's face again as his fingers ran through Cricket's knotted hair, a gentle reminder that they were both there.

Alive. Whole. Happy.

And soon Becka would join them, and Lunette could finally begin to heal.

ACKNOWLEDGMENTS

First off, thank you—the reader—for joining Takayoshi and Cricket on their journey . The Heir to Moondust was something I started during the pandemic, and one of the projects that made being stuck inside a little easier. I hope it has brought you the same wry amusement, and smiles it brought me to write.

Although this book is over, Cricket and Takayoshi's story is far from finished. Their world has so many more stories to tell. So rest assured, this is not the last you've seen of Yoshi and his new friends.

Next, I'd like the thank my small hoard of beta-readers. You guys gave some excellent insight, and I really appreciate all of your hard work!

And last but certainly not least, thank you to my small writing support group at MTP. Tiss, Elle, and Jasmine— without you there would be no Lou.

ABOUT THE AUTHOR

Born and raised in a small town near the Chesapeake Bay, Lou Wilham grew up on a steady diet of fiction, arts and crafts, and Old Bay. After years of absorbing everything, there was to absorb of fiction, fantasy, and sci-fi she's left with a serious writing/drawing habit that just won't quit. These days, she spends much of her time writing, drawing, and chasing a very short Basset Hound named Sherlock.

When not, daydreaming up new characters to write and draw she can be found crocheting, making cute bookmarks, and binge-watching whatever happens to catch her eye.

Learn more about Lou and her future projects on her website: http://louinprogress.com/ or join her mailing list at: http://subscribepage.com/mailermailer

facebook.com/LouWilham

instagram.com/lou.wilham

Also By Lou Wilham

The Curse Collection
    The Curse of The Black Cat
    The Curse of Ash and Blood
    The Curse of Flour and Feeling

The Clockwork Chronicles
    The Girl in the Clockwork Tower
    The Unicorn and the Clockwork Quest
    The Rose in the Clockwork Library
    The Marionette in the Clockwork Circus

The Heir To Moondust
    The Prince of Starlight
    The Prince of Daybreak
    The Crown of Night
    The Kings of Dusk & Dawn

The Witches of Moondale
    The Hex Next Door
    The Ghost of Hexes Past

Sanctuary of the Lost
    Of Loyalties & Wreckage
    Of Love & Ruin

Completed Series
The Tales of the Sea Trilogy
Villainous Heroics

MORE BOOKS YOU'LL LOVE

If you enjoyed this story, please consider leaving a review.

Then check out more books from Midnight Tide Publishing!

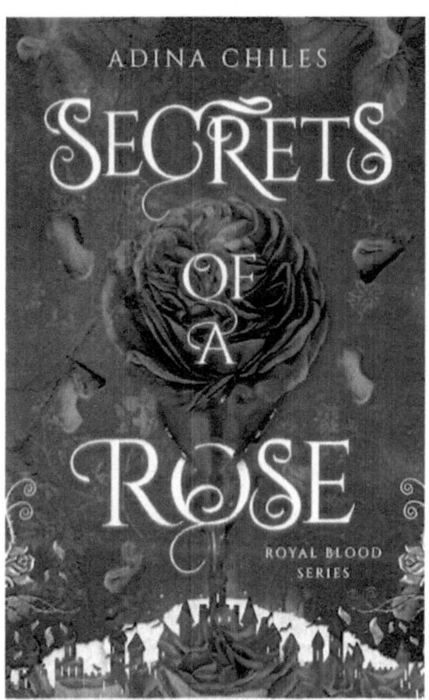

Secrets of a Rose by Adina Chiles

A kingdom built with secrets is bound to unravel.

During the month of Amira, the silver moon emerges, and the kingdom of Zyra comes alive with anticipation for its annual ball. Mellana Goodwick, finally at the rightful age of sixteen, receives her first invitation, but when unexpected events take place, immediate regret sets in. Mellana finds herself caught in a strange storm—casting down green lightning and filling the sky with ear-splitting thunder. To make matters worse, the kingdom comes under attack by Prince Lorian, a man removed from the line of succession for murdering his sister, the future queen, and her newborn child.

After escaping the attack with her best friends, Mellana stumbles upon a box left by a woman named Rose. With the power to see glimpses of the future, Rose warns Mellana of hidden powers the kingdom has covered up and Lorian's desire to unleash them all. Rose instructs Mellana to gather the sacred article from each of the seven kingdoms before Lorian and his deadly group can gain access to them. Together, the items unlock a barrier that is meant to stay shut.

In Secrets of a Rose, Mellana will discover remarkable abilities that stir around her and some that even rise within. In order to keep what she loves, she must embark on a race against the person who dares to threaten it all.

Available Now

The Rose and the Claw by Nancy O'Toole

A woman on a mission...

Rose Gardner never thought she'd leave the small town of West Ridge. But when her husband dies at war, she must return his arms to his place of birth to set his spirit to rest. After traveling into enemy territory, Rose falls into a trap. Held captive in an enchanted manor, she finds herself face to face with a beast who is equally horrifying and kind. Will she manage to complete her quest or be pulled in by the secrets of the manor?

A man haunted by his past...

Trapped within his own home and in the body of a hideous beast, Kris never wanted to share his prison with another. As much as Rose may draw him in with her beauty and stubborn strength, he knows she must escape before the next full moon. After all, he remembers all too well what happened to the previous caretaker.

The dead won't let him forget the blood on his hands.

Available Now

Fires of the Forsaken by *Stephanie E. Donohue*

Addie wanted a gosh-darn pizza.

Lass wanted to avoid being cooked over a spit.

Neither figured they'd end up with a one-way ticket to the end of days.

Addie did not have "getting plucked from the 21st century and thrown into a rudimentary fantasy world" on her "fun things to do at 30" checklist. Yet here she is, struggling to survive in the hellscape known as Sakar, a place where Wraiths flame-broil humans and Celestial armies wage war with each other over a centuries-old spat. Thankfully, Cheriour, the hunky commander of the human army, takes her under his wing—although he's allergic to giving straight answers. And talking.

As Addie reluctantly starts to care for him, and the rest of the Sakarians, she also learns why she was sent to this world. And it's a doozy...

The violent society of Sakar is the only home Lass has ever known, and it's been a wretched one. She has spent her life being tormented and twisted into an inhuman hybrid by the Celestials and hunted by the humans who fear her. But she finds solace with a cocky, blue-eyed boy who comforts her, even after she accidentally slaughters innocents.

As Lass struggles to control her volatile powers, she slowly transforms into the monster the humans believe her to be. And even the boy she loves is in peril...

At the end of time, there is only fire. And neither Addie nor Lass will escape unscathed.

Available Now